THE SOLITUDE OF DESTINY

A

NOVEL

OF

PLEASURE, PAIN AND DREAMS

by
Agustín Eliab Juárez

Flower Press Publishing
Montreal, Canada

ISBN:978-1-927914-08-3

Published by Flower Press
Montreal, Canada

I wish to thank those who helped, encouraged and believed in me when I thought this book would never come to be. Among the greats is my mother Josefa who inspired me to be a writer, my former teacher Dr. Enriqueta Ramos of San Benito, Texas who saw the light in me as a young man, Teresa Pulling who has always been there for me, my brother Saúl under whose tutelage I apprenticed manhood, Professor Michael Wilcox of Stanford University, my friend and Professor Dr. Servando Ortoll of Guadalajara, and Keeper of the Energy for the Orden Tezcatlipoca, Ehekatéotl of Mexico City.

THE SOLITUDE OF DESTINY
CONTENTS

THE SOLITUDE OF DESTINY

by

Agustín Eliab Juárez

CHAPTER ONE

My name is Jaguar. I was named after the beautiful, ferocious animal that roams the jungle looking for victims and seeking silence. My mother was pregnant with me, bathing at the waterfall one afternoon, scrubbing her body in the undulating ways that women do, when she looked up and saw the most ravishing creature staring at her. It was a jaguar, salivating at the mouth like some sailor too long at sea or so she thought; the cat seemed human, she felt his presence so. His member was hard and his eyes would not leave hers. She was a beautiful woman after all, and any man would have acted the same.

Mother smiled and spoke to her belly: *"I will name you Jaguar, be you boy or girl."*

*   *   *

This book is about many people, not just me, and it isn't really about me, to tell you the truth. It's about the man who shaped my life, gave me life, created me and damn well near destroyed me. It is about my father, Izquierdo.

See, Izquierdo is a little man who walks with a limp, a man who has never conquered his noticeable stutter, yet a man among men. He is the man we would all like to be, a man who was borne out of pure innocence and kept it for the best part of his life.

How is that possible, you might ask, to keep one's innocence into old age? Well, to begin with, he lived in a different world than you and me; he lived a life our ancestors knew: silence, power, simplicity. Izquierdo's world was not encumbered by our modern ways, you see, for he lived in a place so remote they knew not man existed but in a fantasy. The desperate milers knew there were men just like themselves living somewhere far, far away; human beings who lived for life itself, for love, for giving, for sharing. But they did not meet the strange ones until centuries later.

The simple people from Izquierdo's family lived in a place called the desperate mile.

***

Izquierdo was the best looking boy in the village. Deep in the jungle, hidden from view and the smog of modern man, the desperate mile was a pueblo like no other. Here there were only the sounds of the macaws and howler monkeys, the *perros salvajes* and donkeys, the roaming jaguar and so many more. Here the winds made music on the palm fronds; the hot sun dried the freshly poured torrential rain in a matter of minutes. Izquierdo picked mangoes.

There was a girl in the village who also loved mangoes and her name was Puta Madre. Puta Madre got her name from Father Serra, a Spanish priest who during a time unknown landed at the desperate mile by mistake, became a missionary and stayed forever. He ran around the village screaming *"Puta Madre!"* when he stubbed his toe, when disappointed, or when upset at one of his numerous personal inadequacies. My grandmother Luna heard him shout that name one quiet afternoon as he fell and scraped his knee: *"Puta Madre!"* he exclaimed, as he straightened his robes after standing on his feet. Grandma couldn't help but laugh at the sight of this ridiculous man. *"Puta Madre!"* she repeated after him, running off to tell the others, she, never knowing what the words meant. In her village no one spoke, for they were the mute ones. Spanish was a language of the mighty ones, and at the desperate mile only the Indian dialect was known.

At the desperate mile we lived in innocence back in those days, in peace, in light, instead of in the darkness of the today's cities; joy, happiness and contentment ruled our day. There were no complaints then because we knew that to complain was of no use. To complain about things meant you hadn't erased your past, and we knew that our pasts only kept us imprisoned. Imprisoned in a memory, unable to move into the future where everything is possible.

So when Father Serra came to town and found that he could not communicate with us, or 'get' to us as he later explained it to me, he started cursing like a sailor, using words we'd never heard. We weren't confused, no, no. We were intrigued by his speaking.

And so my granny Luna loved those words and in this way named her newborn baby girl, Puta Madre.

*   *   *

Izquierdo was at an early age exceptional, later becoming a phenomenon in his own right. How?

His childhood in those days consisted of running down to the river to catch fish. They were plenty in those days and of many varieties, most are not found today, not even in the Amazon, even less in the zoo or in museums. Izquierdo would take the basket his mother gave him, stand on the edge of the water and wait for the fish to offer themselves in sacrifice. In a matter of minutes, numerous *Pisces* would fill the basket and weigh my father down. He, poor boy, would limp back into town distributing his catch to the villagers along the way until he came home with the biggest fish for dinner. Grandma Luna would kiss his forehead and throw the catch into the fire. They would laugh and sing until the howler monkeys cried it's time for bed.

Izquierdo dreamed nightly, sharing his dreams with his mom and dad.

"*I have a story in my head, mother.*"

"*How does it go?*" she would ask.

"*I see things. Things I don't understand.*"

And he would explain the "*Obsidian knives and shiny armor; big, strong horses.*" They took him one day to a healer. The old man looked at him and asked:

"*Tell me, Izquierdito, what do you see?*"

My father was then six years old.

"They come and cut people with swords and I see blood spilled; women and children are hurt and weeping..."

The healer didn't understand. The villagers did not know about the Spaniard then. They only knew the jungle.

"Who does this, my son?" asked the sage.

"Men, with hair on their faces, they glisten in the sun. They have eyes like the water."

It was in those days that Father Serra arrived.

Izquierdo felt alone. It would take a stranger to interpret his dreams.

He sneaked to catch a glimpse of Father Serra and found the Spaniard mixing mud – but why mud? The Spaniard made blocks of adobe drying them in the hot sun as he'd decided to build a church for what he thought would be his new congregation of Indians, and so within days he took action. He first built an enormous wooden cross fastening it with ropes, digging a hole six feet deep to fasten it to the ground. As Izquierdo watched from afar, Father Serra turned. The two stared at each other as the holy man took a step forward. Izquierdo, being only a boy, got scared and took off running, the smell of this man's skin stuck to his nose. At the river he rinsed to get the stench off his body.

"That man smells of dogs,' he said to himself. *"Doesn't he wash?"*

His attempt to contact Father Serra, the stranger, failed, and the priest himself failed to get the young boy's attention.

"I wonder if all his people smell the same."

The village accepted the poor bearded priest who'd ridden into town atop a donkey like Jesus on his way to crucifixion, mostly because he was quiet, kept out of people's way and did curious things the village had never seen before. His stubble of beard spoke of youth instead of wisdom but that was good with the villagers. His energetic smile rubbed off on everyone quickly. Leaping off the beast, he showered the pueblo with love: *"Accept thy sins and pray for your salvation!"* he shouted. He knelt, only to be stunned at the reception: everyone in the crowd knelt too.

It occurred to him they were Christian like him, and he wept. Soon, and much to his surprise, all were weeping together, following his every move and action.

He thanked the Heavens for such a conversion, the easiest of his life! He'd walked in Jesus' shoes---barefoot, that is---and had done His work. His own entry into heaven was now assured as the Church believes if you bring one soul to Jesus you attain eternal salvation. Yes, he assured his ticket, said Father Serra of Barcelona, Spain, the Old World. He had the followers, now all he had to do was build the church.

All the villagers were laughing at him now. The *poblanos* loved to laugh, and at this junction in their lives they laughed at nearly everything, their delight in life was such. The laughter sounded like a choir of joy.

Father Serra was overjoyed at discovering the very people he sought to convert. He'd heard in the city there was a tribe of Indians deep in the jungle, so well-hidden by the jungle that nobody knew their true location. As Indians were unwanted and despised in that part of the world, they were like lepers, and so the civilized world ignored them. It was only Father Serra who took the task of finding them, and evangelizing them no matter the cost. To him they were no lepers. To him they meant salvation.

Now Father Serra found himself in a world he'd only dreamed of. A place so isolated no civilized being would ever find him. This village was so remote it nearly kissed the clouds. *El aire es transparente,* he said without realizing that one day Carlos Fuentes would use that as the title to one of his books. This was indeed a paradise! The Indians now knelt in prayer only minutes after Father Serra's arrival. *Miracles do happen,* he muttered through his already decaying teeth.

"*They must know my Christ!*" he said to himself. He'd traveled for months alone looking for this lost tribe, eating raw roots he'd learned to dig from the ground, catching iguanas and peeling bananas so plump they looked like pumpkins. Why once he even roasted a tiny bird that landed on his shoulder. Snap, went the fragile neck, and then the feathers. "*That was a dinner I will never forget,*" he said to no one. He had, over the years, developed a habit of speaking to himself, though he no longer noticed. Criticized by others for this, he cared not to listen. As far as he was concerned, he was directing his every word to God Almighty. At this moment, though, the priest became suddenly afraid. The laughing villagers looked irritated for some unknown reason, perhaps because he thought they were laughing at him for talking to himself.

"Stop it in the name of the Almighty!" he cried, like a helpless woman, shaking with fright. He meant to stop those gathered from laughing.

The poblanos repeated his cries: *"Stop it in the name of the Almighty!"*

Father Serra shook all the more now, believing this a supernatural experience. The villagers shook like him, imitating his every move. The shake turned into something resembling a ritualistic dance.

"What have I done?!" he asked himself only seconds after getting off his mule.

"What has happened? These people were smiling just a moment ago, and on their knees, praying. Now they look like cannibals about to eat me!!!"

"Why do they dance so?"

But what he didn't know is that in my pueblo, imitation was a form of flattery. And laughter ruled the day. You see, laughter filled our lungs because it was our tonic. We didn't know any better. We only knew that laughter healed the sick.

No one but Father Serra had penetrated those high mountains to reach us. We'd never seen a man like him. We'd never smelled such a stench either. These people with beards, did they wash their bodies down at the river?

Father Serra, he didn't know any better. He came with his donkey, on a mission, his intentions pure, his heart full of love, but with little understanding of others. He came to conquer the souls of sinners, to save their souls forever.

"To live in such a jungle, running naked, smiling stupidly and laughing, is such a sin! These heathens must learn the way of the Lord!"

It never occurred to him this might be his undoing.

*   *   *

The nights at the desperate mile were calm and quiet. The poblanos tucked into bed early, almost as the sun went down, almost as if living for the sun itself. A testament to this is the sun god emblem painted on the plaza wall. That painting has been there for a thousand years, and to this day you can see its faded colors stare at you as if alive and well and shining.

Father Serra grunted when he first saw our plaza, *"these Indians must see a real plaza one day, like in my beloved Barcelona!"* That day, the young Padre started one of his many projects in the pueblo.

He went about his business, doing as he pleased. Certainly the mutes would not object.

He took to meeting the Indians on the dirt paths to give them *la bendición* – a blessing by making the sign of the cross. The poblanos, in turn, would bow their heads and nod as the foolish bearded-one walked away pleased. On one occasion, Father Serra gave a sermon in Latin, with the villagers following his every move.

But still they did not speak.

I have still not heard them speak on their own, he thought. *I'll be patient*, he said, *and wait until they are ready*. They are so quiet and shy by nature, so beautiful their dark skin glistens as if oiled. I'll start cutting their hair one of these days when they get more familiar with *my ways*. The priest took to making the church his instead of the house of the Lord, a costly mistake on Judgment Day.

As the crowd dispersed Father Serra went on about his business gathering old, dried grass to mix into the adobe. At the river he found sand, white and quite refined. He placed some into his robe like an old woman carrying mangoes and soon found curious village kids doing the same, following him back to his hut. When he unloaded the sand onto the wet mud, the children did the same. Father Serra smiled. He would try it again to see if he had a willing work crew.

"*One day I'll understand these people,*" he muttered under his breath as he poured the mix into little molds he'd created out of palm thatches. The molds would hold the adobe together and in the hot sun would dry into blocks which he would later use to start the foundation of the church he was ready to build.

Without a church these people will never know Jesus!

He was thrilled to find these lovely people, as quiet as they were, helping him at every turn. They were smart, these ones, what with the silent observations and quick reproductions. They watched and learned from him. He was not a good teacher, this priest, but they were good students. They imitated his every move, copied and executed, creating blocks so perfectly squared they fit right on top of one another without need of filler.

These Indians, he noticed, made the foundation strong, strong enough to support his twenty-two foot ceiling. Father Serra sketched a simple design for his *dream church* now being built by the local villagers, an army of worker bees creating a beauty to last through the ages. What he did not know is that it would be of no use to anyone.

The priest scratched his head in wonder. He smiled and saw the Indians grin.

"What are these people made of?" he asked the heavens.

The poblanos were there every morning, noon and night, working without complaint, never asking questions, nor to be fed, following his every gesture without so much as a gripe.

In a matter of days they finished a Greco pillar entrance.

The priest was so impressed he moved about frantically looking to create an even more ornate church. *"I wonder... if I drew a garden?'* he muttered. *'Perhaps my rectory, and a school, and a..."*

The next day the villagers gathered river rocks by the hundreds, placing them behind the church in a square designed by this architect. Rakes came out of nowhere, the land was tilled and suddenly, a garden was ready to be planted.

"*My Jesus!*' he cried to the skies, '*I will build you a village of followers!*"

Life was so easy with these villagers the church was finished within a week.

Father Serra used his limited carpentry skills to make a door. As if by magic, the next day he found four ornately carved wooden doors ready to be installed, they leaned against the back entry, one was built to specifications for his rectory.

"*My, my, my, these people shall be blessed!*"

But something was not right. As Father Serra wanted to change their lives, their way of life, their nakedness that aroused him, he built a number of adobe homes to *civilize them. Surely these people would prefer to live in the comfort I know, instead of living in straw huts,* he muttered again to no one, believing as conquerors do that to change the savage is to civilize him. When the early anthropologists named the *noble savage* they did not consider the native did not seek change, nor did the anthropologist consider the savage was fine as he was. Now, the casitas built by Father Serra went unused as the poblanos returned to their thatched huts, preferring the comfort of their ways. The young priest would have to find another way to change their ways.

He had to figure out a way to convert them.

And that would prove a long time: an eternity indeed.

*

The young priest found himself in need of documentation. If and when he returned to Barcelona, he would have written work, ethnography, an anthropologists' dream to justify his disappearance from civilization, he would need a way to prove to the church he'd been doing his work all along.

"The public will soon learn of the mutes who live in the mountains undiscovered, uncovered, and living in sin," he muttered, a smile on his face as he lifted his arms in praise.

* * *

His journal:

Monday: three days after arrival.

These people are not like us. They prefer to live in their little palapas with dirt floors and no windows. Instead of bathing in privacy they bathe naked, together like one, big family. I have many times gone to the river to talk to them, but they do not understand! I often get pulled into the water by the children who hold their nose as if I smell. They are the ones who stink! I smell flowers and game, fruits and herbs they burn in a ritualistic fashion.

I cannot get them to church.

I pray for their salvation, hoping the Lord will forgive their ways. Often the women go off to the fields with a man other than their own. I do not think they are working, for the men are hunters and the women caretakers. That is their society. They drink a strange potion; the alcohol makes me hallucinate!

A beautiful woman has given birth to a little girl they call Puta Madre. What blasphemy! Where on earth would they think up such a thing?

These are the only two words I have heard from them.

Day 365

Today I am celebrating my first year here. The weather is hot and humid. Moments ago the rain fell hard on the trees and the wind blew.

I have been attempting to communicate with the villagers but they all seem to be mute! Perhaps they are also deaf! I know they hear what I say, in fact, I have heard them repeat a word of mine, "Burro" but aside from that, nothing. They do not look dumb and stupid like most deaf/mutes! These people can build a house in two days! They finished the church in no time!

I want to get close to them but they won't let me. I have to try something else, some other way to get them to hear me and His teachings. They are prime meat for conversion.

If only I could reach them!

Aghhhhh!

Jaguar found these barely legible, rumpled pages of Father Serra's diary years ago. The priest wrote volumes daily, hiding them in an ornate wooden box a villager made for him. Since no one in the village could read or even knew what writing was, the papers went untouched until his good friend and accomplice Jaguar found them. They tell the story of the desperate mile from Serra's point of view, the sad stories of his painful loneliness read like the crucifixion; others tell of his self-absorbed, bloody mutilations and flagellations, of times when he nearly fainted in his own blood. Father Serra lived his life for the church; his every breath was for God and His *word*. Father Serra's life was one continuous search to convert these Indians into Saints, these *perverted, naked men and women must be turned into God-fearing beings with a purpose in life*, he wrote in a different page. He lived only for conversion. But the sad part of this was that the villagers only learned of his life mission years after his death because Jaguar – by then an adult returning home from his travels around the world - revealed the stories in an all-night reading around the fire. Many of the villagers cried that night at the memory of the old man who so unsuccessfully tried for years to *reach them*.

CROCE DELIZIA

They say you can't go home, but I had to. My father was dying after a long life; my mother had been dead for forty five years. Izquierdo had been alone for countless years, and I didn't want to see him leave this earth alone. I had to be at his deathbed.

I was returning to see him again and for the last time before sending him back to the gods he loved, to the gods of nature, the very gods he honored throughout his life. There was no turning back for me.

I took an early plane to Mexico City connecting to a six-passenger Cessna waiting for me. I would be home soon. Home: a village so remote in Mexico it was only accessible by mule. I would disembark at a tiny airport near the border with Guatemala and pray the guerrillas did not shoot us on landing. There were heavy border skirmishes day and night as frightened Maya Indians from Guatemala crossed the border into Mexico seeking asylum, looking for protection from the killer elites of that tiny country who thirsted for all its land, oil, and water rights. The plundering of archeological sites was helping the greedy gringo steal our past.

The mule trip through the dense jungle would take three whole days and three nights. I looked about for Guillermo and Agustin Eliab, my two old friends who promised to wait for me at the tiny airport but they were nowhere to be found. They were out on a field trip with Americanos, someone said, out by the ruins, and only God Himself knew when they would be back.

I would wait an hour and if they did not return by then, I would contract two other Indians who stood nearby waiting for the signal to go. They knew the way to my village that was sure, for their clothes gave them away. *Campesinos* and trekkers dress for the jungle: boots, machetes, hats and raincoats.

I didn't have the time to wait for my two old friends, but I did have an hour. I was tired from the plane ride, the anxiety of my father's health enveloping me like a banana leaf, the waiting, the anticipation, the constant haggling with Mexican officials. One hour in this peaceful village would do me good. I sat and took notice of my surroundings. There were traces and memories of my father everywhere, for he looked like these people: the man in huaraches smoking a cigarette, the woman selling pastries walked with a limp; an *arriero* pulling a bull and cart, a dark-skinned gap-toothed child jumping rope. Tears swelled in my eyes as I missed him yet again for the millionth time; I thought of how I loved him, of how he'd been my best friend, of who he was and what he'd done in life. All through life people asked me what my father did for a living and I always smiled. I smiled because he'd given me a happy childhood, because he'd been good to me, a good teacher, a mentor, a disciplinarian. I smiled because I knew that if I told them the truth they would not believe me. They would say I was making up stories, that it was impossible for a man to be such a phenomenon. You see, I told them my father was a campesino, a fieldworker but they would confuse him with César Chávez. Surely no campesino had a son as educated as me!

I thought of the way my father walked and talked, of how he told endless stories of the past, a past that included a previous life in Aztec times. I told them how Izquierdo read people's minds. My father had only to look into someone's eyes to read his life story. Many a man had looked into his eyes, and probably lived to regret it, for no one in life wishes to be known so nakedly.

Few people believed me. I did not need another endless discussion on the history of Mexico, nor the Catholic Church, even less on Indian fatalism. You see, that Izquierdo lived in the Aztec times, was indeed a reincarnation and could prove it with stories never written in the *Códices*, was unbelievable to all, including my learned colleagues at the University.

Izquierdo told me things while I was still in the womb, he said, speaking to me endless hours as his wife Puta Madre lay sleeping. He had to empty his mind, he said, had to share the stories that filled his head at the age of thirteen. His wife would not believe that he had experiences in his head, so he spoke to me, but an embryo at the time.

As I grew older he repeated the stories to instill them in me, almost as if I were responsible for deciphering them. When he repeated a story it was always word for word, he never made a mistake. His was a photographic memory.

Later when I studied with Father Serra, the priest told me these stories came from ancient times; you see, he'd prepared for this trip by studying the history written by the conquering Spaniards. *Someone in your family lived in the Aztec times*, said the priest. He would have been burned at the stake for saying this in public.

The priest was excited to have me as his pupil for I was the first of the pueblo to talk to him and to take his teachings. He often said that the idea of reincarnation came from the Bible, why, Jesus Himself was resurrected! At first Father Serra believed it was me who was a reincarnation of an Aztec man, because I told him all the stories Izquierdo taught me through the years. I said, these are not my stories, they were told to me by my father.

And so, with thoughts of my childhood circling in my head, I waited for my two old friends, Guillermo and Agustín Eliab.

Through the years I had made a habit of taking the train home. Today was special, an emergency, so I took the first flight. In the past I would climb the train in Chihuahua, ride to Los Mochis through the Copper Canyon. I did not fly in those days because I thought I had all the time in the world and because I wanted to see the beautiful Mexican countryside that always brought me to my senses. This was a trip reintroducing me to Mexico. The vendors offered fresh tacos and *tesquino*--- a beer made of corn---tortas, tamales and fresh, steaming corn on the cob; candies and fruits followed by cigarettes and offers for handouts. I wanted to be on the train and see the Indians approach as we stopped at a station, they with their smiles, and we, with ours. The women ran wobbling toward us with big baskets balanced on their heads, a child following behind. The men carried water coolers full of beer and soft drinks, the young boys sold *Chiclets*. Seeing them reminded me of my youth. I had been that child long ago. These people looked like the people from my village. Although my life was different now, I was still that little kid with the snot on his nose, working the fields, my huaraches fastened to my feet, my clothes dirty from the day's work.

I wear a suit and tie now, much to the dismay of my father, who though old and dying, holds fast to the Indian way. He sleeps on his *petate* and not on a bed. He wears the traditional muslin shirt and pants but opts for bare feet like in the old days. *It makes you walk with attention*, he says. That is his way and I admire him for staying so Indian, but there came a time in my life when I could no longer live like that. Sometimes I regret leaving the desperate mile, other times I am glad I went to the city, to University and traveled the world, educating others on our way of life.

Ignorance abounds in this world, it is not just in the ghetto, or in the barrio, or in that remote third world country that lives in your mind. No. Ignorance is everywhere, it must be killed.

I left my wife and son in New York and headed for my place of origin, to a father who I betrayed so long ago it was not even a memory anymore.

On those trains I saw many people, Mexicans, gringos, Indians, Europeans, all of us headed somewhere, like during our lifetime, to a place we'd never seen before. I avoided reading their minds, and although I was able to do so, I simply gave people their privacy, and respect. Instead, we talked for hours and played cards, drank beer and sang songs. The trains are a wonderful place for a long trip. You have your cabin, your privacy and a dining room with Scotch, Gin and Vodka to keep you company.

When nostalgia hits, we have no choice but to deal with it. It is the past rushing at you, and all our past catches up with us. At this juncture in my life I needed all the strength I could conjure, because, soon I would be alone, I would be one of the last desperate milers on earth with only my son carrying this precious blood. The memories were ripping me apart.

I sat alone in the village smoking a cigarette, missing my wife. A sexual longing for her overcame me, and I got sad. It was a purging of the soul, I thought, a need to rid myself of loneliness, a hurt inside ready to cripple me.

I'd lived a full life, had many women, affairs and loves. Today when I ached, I needed a hug, I needed closeness, relatedness. I wanted to be inside of her, my wife, perhaps to escape this pain, this coming hurt signaled by my father's future passing. There were many things I had given up in life, but there were many things to face with this visit too.

I wanted to cry out, groan and yell at the top of my lungs.

I waited on the curb for my friends Guillermo and Agustin Eliab and thought of the things that come to mind on these trips: my father, the desperate mile, the sacred *cenotes*, Puta Madre, Indians, the Usumacinta River, Aztecs, Father Serra, Addison Stonefreund.

The sun was still hot, probably warming my father's bones; in my mind I pictured him breathing slowly, struggling at this point to fill his lungs. I could do nothing but wait, keep from turning to desperation, and remember the stories, the love, and the desperate mile.

*

THE OLD MAN

The old man sits in his chair, nodding his head, bringing everything back, the experiences, his life, the loves, the wars. It is all there at the tip of the tongue, and he will take his time. Presently it rains outside, he looks at the water splish-and-splash onto the earth; two boys soaked to the bone and covered in mud chase each other outside laughing and pushing in an attempt to see the other fall. The birds hide deep in the trees taking cover, occasionally flapping their tiny wings to keep dry. The sunshine cracks through the clouds as it continues to rain, disappearing just as quickly as it appeared. The clouds move away fast as if rushing to work, the wind up there is howling. Time is moving on and Izquierdo knows it.

I sit there waiting to hear more, like I did as a child, me waiting to absorb his every word, he, divulging his every story as it comes back to his withering memory.

People would say, *Well, how do you know he gets it right if his mind is weak from old age?* Let me tell you that ever since I can remember Izquierdo, he spoke word for word when repeating stories. Nothing was ever out of place because he had the sharpest memory, an impressive memory.

I wondered if he would continue with the Governor and Addison Stonefreund, or if he would go on to a new story. He gave no hint whatsoever.

I hadn't seen my father in some time and we were happy to be sitting together, me drinking my *pulque,* he smoking his tobacco. The smoke filled the dense air and did not move in this rain. No mosquitos bothered us today.

We'd had a disagreement I guess you could call it, years ago. Twenty eight years ago, in fact. Now he knew there was no more time to waste, that we needed to resolve the matter and drop the grudges that kept us apart for so long. He stared out into the jungle he loved so much, where he made his mark as a boy, as a man; he knew that jungle as well as anyone. He knew places none of us had ever been or ever would see. There was always something to see in the jungle and today was no different.

How does one describe the desperate mile? It is so many things to so many people. It was where we lived; it was a village, a place where we gathered, we the poblanos, the villagers. Someone named this place, but we don't know who because when I asked, no one could remember where the name came from. I did research this one summer while studying with Father Serra, going door-to-door interviewing the elders, looking for hints, investigating the matter to no avail. Nobody recalled anyone ever speaking of this, not even my father Izquierdo. Therefore, we surmised - Father Serra and me - that it was an outsider who must have dropped the name out of the blue. Whoever it was, it stuck.

The desperate mile was the river that gave fish, the sky providing birds, a jungle so full of wildlife we simply looked at the animals and they surrendered as kill. It was our town, our lifeblood; it was a thin veil of innocence protecting us from the outside world. We did not know humans exited out there until I was a very young boy. No stranger except Father Serra had been around until a man on a red Jeep crashed into a hill.

You see, the desperate mile was like a sore that needed a lot of attention and care, for it was a reminder of our long existence, of a thousand years of isolation, of joy, happiness, calm, harmony.

It was our hearts and souls, and Izquierdo knew this: it was our last gasp of breath before we went to the gods, a cry to wake the dead.

How else does one explain home? Is it the light and dark that envelop you day after day? Is it the neighbors who support you when sad? Is it the many ways in which we developed farming to feed our poblanos? It is the morning mist, the watermelon in the air, violets, roses, the children playing?

Yes. Home is all those things. In many ways, I remember a happy childhood. A youth full of yellow ants, red anteaters, blue armadillos.

I was the best looking boy in the village, he said, after launching a puff of smoke into the air, breaking the silence. *This would always get me into trouble; the others were jealous the girls loved me, the fathers and mothers afraid I would pick their girl.* He smiled at the memory. *I was no angel, else I would be a Saint by now,* he joked. He knew all the stories of Father Serra, knew the Bible indeed, the religion but did not practice it for his religion was nature. *Or else a Juan Diego, the old Indian man who saw the Virgin of Guadalupe appear and lived to tell it. He is a Saint now, you know? An*

Indian Saint, no less! he said to the wall, in an attempt to avoid me.

No, Izquierdo, you were more of a Don Juan, if I know you, I said and we both laughed, for, as a womanizer he had no equal. Until I grew up, that is.

I grew up in this pueblo of twelve families. Each was large, there were a minimum of twelve children in each, and that was so we could reproduce the stars in the sky, become a village. There was the Sanchez family, the Hinojosas, Cortez and Marquez, Neruda, Fuentes, Paz and Rivera, Juárez too – oh, those boys were wild; the Lorcas, Travin and finally my own family that did not have a last name. We did not know why this was, but it didn't matter. Some said we were descendants of original man.

He took another puff, this time tilting his head to the side. He always did that when he didn't quite understand something and I suspect that at this point in life he would have liked to know why his family had no last name.

Luna, his mother, named him Izquierdo because one night when she was pregnant she had a dream that the boy would be a warrior.

We lived here peacefully until the other men came, the whites, the Spaniard, the freaks looking for magic mushrooms. Those who found us stayed, others, legend has it, searched for years to find us, discover our people, our village, our peaceful way of life. They lived to regret that, son. Finding us in this terrain was frightening for anyone, the jungle is so. To this day, I believe the gods protected us. People were swallowed up at the cenotes, the big, pools of water where we practiced our sacrificial ceremonies. Others were eaten alive by the roaming animals of the jungle. It was meant to be this way, son, don't you see? We, living here forever undetected.

For the longest time he thought he had another name. It wasn't until later when I grew up and studied with Father Serra that my father discovered he did have another name, one given him by his Aztec father. You see, we discovered he'd been reincarnated from those times, and the stories he saw in his head were authentic and eventually documented and authenticated by the University. His unexplainable drive to search for a name he felt connected to was in the end justified.

Every man has a right to die in peace, he told me years and years ago. Back then, he was looking for answers to life. I remember thinking of him as an orphan looking for his blood parents.

What he didn't know then was that not many a man dies in peace. Most leave this world full of regrets, with mouthfuls of words never shared with loved ones.

Now as he stared at the falling rain - is there such a thing as *rising* rain? - the ancient one lit another cigarette and spoke elegantly, clearly, with purpose. All his life, his every word was important, he said because that was the way our ancestors spoke. With the Aztecs, he who spoke best, he who expressed himself best was anointed priest. This cultural hierarchy was based on clarity of mind.

I have been a fool many times, he said. He was comfortable now, gaining confidence as we shared time and got to know each other again. He always sat in his favorite chair, an old, handmade wood chair that he never painted. This day, a woven blanket hung over his slight shoulders to warm his old, cold bones. The rain stopped. It is so hot around here the earth will be dry in hours.

There were times when we could find no place to hide, after they found us. There were men I killed in battle, women I wept for, women I loved time and again, people I stopped speaking to when the going got tough. The single most foolish thing I did, I think, was marrying your mother. He chuckled.

This was news to me. I had never heard this before.

I have never told you this, Jaguar but it is true. I have lived to regret the day.

Naturally I yearned to know the story, but kept silent.

I was but a boy of thirteen, and she a Puta. I needed a mother to take care of me, instead of becoming a father myself at such a young age. Her breasts were milky and soft, and the comfort of a lifetime. We were not good for each other, and we both knew it. When the violence came, she took to it. She liked the seriousness of it and detested Violent Violet.

This, I did not know. I knew of Violent Violet and the story of their love triangle but he had never told me a droplet of Puta Madre's violent streak. I never suspected such a thing of my mother.

You have learned, my son, through time that women are not easy to be with. Your mother was no different: After a short time together, I could not please her enough. There wasn't a thing I would not do for her. When Violent Violet came to the door and told her of our love, your mother did something no desperate miler had ever done before: she got angry and hit me, pounded me with her fists until I bled. Women in our village were not like that. Somehow the violence took over our life and we became — just like the others, like the conquerors.

Until this day with Izquierdo I'd only heard part of the story of our conquest. As strange as that might sound, this is true. That day was not spoken about at the desperate mile, because many people died, women were raped, children thrown into the river, all in an attempt to rid the jungle of our kind.

He put out his cigarette on the dirt floor of the hut; the tire treads on his *guaraches* leaving a print for all to see. I suddenly thought of my Jeep driving deep into the snowy roads of the Jemez Mountains of New Mexico where I often went to meditate. The old man pulled out his handkerchief and wiped his brow. I saw his big, bright, shiny knife in its sheath by his side, *In its rightful place,* as he always said, *As all things in life have a rightful place.* He saw me look at it, and in a moment, handed it to me. *"I will not need this where I'm going,"* he said, and smiled that smile of his that rocked women's heart for decades. I took notice and smiled in return; it may be the last smile we share.

The time was ripe to tell me of things he'd kept inside forever. We would spend the next few days talking and eating, he smoking his last cigarettes, me, drinking mezcal to drown the sorrow. He would jump from story to story, sneaking in a revelation here and there, surprising me in the process.

That is the way he told me his life and that is the way I've written it down.

What a mistake that was to call me handsome, he muttered, recalling his wedding day. He'd been spending time in the jungle with Puta Madre, providing her every wish, when he returned to the village to the sounds of laughter. Several older men stood by the cantina slouched against the wall.

So you take her to the jungle, huh, boy?

Izquierdo - all of thirteen but big for his age, stood his ground. He needed not respond.

A big, handsome boy like you will have all the girls, but not Puta Madre.

Now, what you must know about Izquierdo is that you don't challenge him, because if you do, he will take you on. He was all of thirteen back then, and, young to boot, but he wanted to be a man and so he walked up to the men and whispered: *She is mine and no one else will ever have her unless she says so.   I will let her decide.*

I looked at him now and could see traces of the anger that was his strength for many years. It was his shield against hatred and war, he said, against people who encroached our ways, the desperate mile. More than anything, the anger drove him into leadership, a role he cherished like no one else.

He hadn't shaved for days and I could see the grey stubble on his face brought on discomfort as he was no longer young or handsome. He did want to live another hundred years, that's for sure mostly to see what would become of our homeland.

I saw he felt tired so I led him to his *petate*.

Take a little rest, old man, I said, and helped him to the floor. He lay down and closed his eyes. I covered him with a blanket and in a moment he was fast asleep.

*   *   *

And so off they went to the secret place hand in hand, Izquierdo gazing at the shining stars and Puta Madre adjusting her shawl in the late night breeze. They could hear the far-off music from the Cantina, the laughter of the poblanos celebrating and a drum beating out of rhythm as if by a boy learning to walk. Puta Madre carried a handful of flowers given her by the girl with the pigtails and a squeaky voice. Izquierdo had his hat in place, a *zarape* over his shoulder, his bare feet dragging on the ground. Poblanos dragged their feet back then, though nobody knows why. The women pitter-pattered and the men shuffled. To this day we do not know how this habit developed but one thing we can tell you is that after the bearded ones came, we stopped the practice because we did not want to be heard walking the earth. Being heard meant death.

Izquierdo dreamt of his wedding night. This afternoon's dream made him feel like he was living life all over again. He woke up refreshed and we continued talking. He did not run out of stories to tell.

*   *   *

Father Serra was writing his memoir the night the lovers went off to their secret place; he sat in the darkness of his room, candlelight in one hand, taking notes and writing with the other. Had he seen the newlyweds' joy he would have wept, for he too would like to love, experience love, have a partner to hold and kiss and caress. *Life has not provided for me,* he wrote that evening. And it hadn't. He'd lived at the desperate mile, teaching, giving, guiding, all to no results as the villagers continued to stay away. Why God Himself had not once come down to speak to him.

Forsaken, that is what I am, he added in black ink. The priest felt ex-communicated, forsaken, for he had no one, not even the Church to talk to; he couldn't help thinking the very God he lived for had abandoned him altogether.

Perhaps this is my penance, he mumbled.

As soon as he spoke these words, a booming voice came from the Heavens: *Follow the way of the Lord!!!*

He returned to the memoir, burying his face in the work, suppressing a scream that would have waked the dead.

*   *   *

After three days of celebration the village was quiet once again. The people hid in their huts, made love all day and all night, while the children played outside or slept in a corner. The elders sat outside soaking up the sun. The fields that went unattended retained their vigor as if inspired by the lovemaking. The fields grew green and thick. They would sprout the biggest corn in the history of the village.

Puta got fat in the stomach and Izquierdo grew taller by the day. The poblanos smiled as the newlyweds walked hand in hand through the village. The gods assured the marriage would last. They were gifted pigs and cows, burros and horses, one woman even brought Puta Madre a goat. The figs turned purple one day and the sun got hotter. A mystery muralist painted storks on a wall. The village was ready for the child to arrive.

One night Izquierdo woke unexpectedly.

That's when he heard the first sounds of footsteps.

*   *   *

Of all the people who came to the desperate mile, none was more of a legend than Addison Stonefreund. Izquierdo said he died in a car wreck, others said they'd seen him walking like a drunk. Whatever the truth, he was a young man who came to the desperate mile and lived to tell of it.

This is how the story went, according to my father.

This is not the way it should be, thought the Governor as the phone rang over and again. His hands were busy at the moment and the world wanted his attention. He did not like to be bothered, and even less so by his happy wife, Happy. He would not answer the phone because he knew it was his assistant telling of the latest controversy, Attica, and he sure didn't want to face that issue. His blonde bombshell hovered over him, her breasts bouncing up and down like volleyballs across the net. The Gov' did not want to disappoint her because she was a movie star, a starlet every man in Hollywood had already tasted. She was gesturing this way and that, bucking like a cowgirl. How he'd conquered her no one knew, perhaps it was his money, for he was a Stonefreund and a pillar of society; she, in turn, grew up in a trailer outside of Sacramento with cockroaches crawling in the sink. He reminded her of Daddy for the Gov' was a mean son of a bitch and took no crap from anyone. The little starlet's Daddy was, according to mommy, "dead as Croesus, poor as white trash and one hell of a womanizer." The Gov', at least, had money, and came from a good family.

Gov'nr, said the voice in a drunken voice, *have you got a minute?*

What, he replied, frustrated and hating himself for answering the phone.

Was it New Brunswick, or New Hampshire, she asked, drunk as a skunk at ten thirty in the morning.

Just what on earth are you talking about woman, he shouted. The blonde was riding him hard just now and beginning to moan. Her moans meant she was close to orgasm.

Happy sipped her third martini of the day, getting ready for lunch at Le Cirque.

You said, New Foundland, didn't you?

The vodka melted in her mouth, on the ruined palate that no longer tasted delicacies like *foie gras* or, white truffles or, even beluga caviar straight from the Balkan Islands.

Addison went somewhere. Newsomethingland, you said, Governor.

Is that why you called? The lovemaking was getting too loud and so the Gov grabbed the starlet's hair, forcing her mouth down there. Soon, she was suckling like a pig.

Newsomethingland, Happy. That's where he went, OK? Just...put your favorite word after the word "New" and you've got it. Now, I gotta go, this Attica business is getting outta hand!

He hung up the phone just as he spurted steam into her mouth. The blonde screamed in delight and ran to the bathroom. The Gov' heard the sound of vomiting.

That was perfectly good sperm, he laughed. Many a bank would cherish that!

The Gov' met this blonde bombshell at his friend Dick's birthday party. All the world's politicians were present, including the Prime Minister of Israel and the President of Toga. Old Dick was known to be perverted; he loved pornography and naked women dressed like whores. The press never got wind of his antics because they were busy with the War of the times: Viet Nam.

The party took on the air of an Ivy League frat house: women were excluded, cigars filled the air, drinking got out of hand. A huge, life-size birthday cake stood at the center of the room and when the band played Happy Birthday, Blondie herself popped-out; naked as the day she was born, a diamond necklace circling her throat, a pair of high heels standing her up.

Well, she said, *doesn't anyone want some cake?*

You can imagine the applause and excitement. Blond Baby smeared her breasts with frosting and it was up to old Dick himself to lick her dry. When he timidly took a whiff of her luscious pussy, she screamed bloody murder and laughed. The crowd loved it. Next, it was the Gov' who ate her breasts, exposing her nipples for all to see; the crowd cheered. Legend has it Blondie came that night and moved to New York just to be near him, she loved the experience so much. He rushed to secure a secret apartment on Lexington Avenue for future romps.

Happy missed her adventurer son, Addison Stonefreund. He'd always been a good boy, did as he was told, studied hard and received top grades. No mom could ask for more.

Old Happy knew her Gov' and put up with his antics and affairs. They'd been married for so long she'd forgotten the wedding day. She had her drinks, her luncheons and society to keep her busy; he, in turn, had his numerous blondes and earth-shattering politics to drive his ego. She would not make a fuss to smudge the good name of Stonefreund by going to the press to reveal the affairs.

Right now, though, finding her son Addison was what mattered most. She never thought her drinking was a problem.

*　　　*　　　*

Addison Stonefreund had long ago, while completing his studies at Harvard, discovered a rare bird that lived among the cannibals who would surely accept him with open arms. They would not reject him like his parents did. They, the naked black men from New

Guinea with the painted faces, would touch his white skin and run fingers through his hair. *Mom and Dad never did that.*

Addison Stonefreund lived with thoughts of rejection that dug deep into his psyche, his shattered soul and his daily life. He was sad all day long, others said depressed; and although he could muster enough motivation to go on with his life, there were few things that moved him. He dreamed of living a life of adventure among cultures different from his.

It all started when he was thirteen. He wanted to run off and live in the jungle, somewhere mysterious, but he lacked the fortitude of conviction. He settled at Haverford Prep, and waited for the day his studies were over so he could travel the world and meet people.

Now he was out to find the cassowary bird of the New Guinea myth; a bird that was said to possess special powers, powers that would make this weak man strong, powers he needed in life to accomplish something, anything, considering the pressures of his bloodline. His father the Gov' was back in New York killing inmates, ordering the destruction of a prison, backed by the administration in D.C.

Addison would not enter politics or the stock market. He was made of thinner stuff. He would not follow the footsteps of his ancestors, make money hand-over-fist, mow-down those who disagreed with him, socialize with the Mellons and Astors; no. He would be a man of the people if it cost him his dear life.

In this respect, he was a democrat, much to the chagrin of his daddy the Gov', a staunch republican who took every opportunity imaginable to ridicule the opposing party. It was either his way or the highway. More often than not he got his way.

The bird that interested Addison posed several problems, for it was the bones he was after. A live cassowary was known to be vicious, strong and unstoppable. Legend had it this feathered friend had on various occasions pecked a lion to death. What defense did a weak-willed rich boy who spent his summers in Greenwich have against such a creature? A boy from Harlem would have a better chance at it than this Ivy League malcontent.

This was not a bird to mess with.

First, you had to find this precious bird out in the jungle, chase it - they run fast, very much like the ostrich

- and wrestle it to the ground. To further complicate the question, one must not break a single bone in the bird's body in order to preserve the power within; which leaves you with few alternatives, maybe needing to choke, or rather, strangle the poor feathered-one, and that without breaking its long neck. After accomplishing this feat, one had the law to contend with because the bird is protected as an endangered species. In the end, though, the local cannibals who would somehow detect the intruder, take him captive, and have him later for dinner. These jungle people would welcome Addison's capture, at this point including the prized bird. In the end it would be the pigmies who received the bird's strength and not he.

Addison Stonefreund needed to befriend the natives as this would facilitate the chase and capture, and perhaps even help him enter the tribal circle. A little chatting would do, maybe a swig of whiskey would get them talking. Addison Stonefreund knew his anthropology background would now be of use in contacting the native, and that he had to get the bird one way or another. He needed the power within for himself as he was growing weak by the minute; the burdensome human weakness that weighed him down had to go.

The bone of the Cassowary bird is said to be an aphrodisiac when converted to powder, but what value was this for a loner like Addison Stonefreund? Would he hide it in a pouch for later use? Then, the bird's bones were to be worn as a necklace, as protection from evil spirits. Sadly, Addison Stonefreund thought he needed protection from such things, that he could not find this powder on the streets of New York City. What he didn't know is that it's easily found on the streets of Harlem, no part of the world for a man like him.

Addison would do his best.

There was one other simple problem. The jungle dwarfs of New Guinea did not believe in the same things that Addison did. These people did not know God or Jesus Christ; what they knew was to protect themselves from the conquering white people, from the clothed ones who ventured in there looking to change their way of life, people who wanted their land, their territory, people who took what they wanted in the form of entitlement. What these white people did not know is the pigmies would have them for dinner. If you spoke to the natives of civilization they would answer: *You want us to believe in what? But, we can see our gods! Look: up there in the sky is Father Sun; at night, mother Moon appears to show us the way. The Rain god feeds our people. The wind cleanses our souls. Do you understand? What is this 'anthropology', anyway?*

Addison Stonefreund had it coming.

*   *   *

Now my father looks at me through eyes full of rage, through the smoke filling the room, through the desire to see the world, his world, return to what it was in the old days. Ha, you might say, *Why on earth would you want to return to the old days?* And Izquierdo would look at you and say, *Because what you people call progress is not what you think. Because, you people do not know a different world: a world of silence, a world of kindness, unimpeded by violence and greed, destruction, death, atomic bombs and fear. Who we were at the desperate mile was original man; we lived like original man, in harmony.   And I know your anthropologists and archaeologists believe original man was a monkey – that he was savage by nature, but let me tell you that the white man, modern man is the savage, destroying people and cultures, religions and beliefs that are not in harmony with their version of civilization: money. That is their god, money.*

Izquierdo had a way with words. And it was not his intention to be right, or to argue a point, even less to sermonize. His intention was in telling history as he experienced it in a previous life, to tell the version that is hidden in the books with lies and pretense. Aztec documentation was destroyed by the Spaniard, only to be replaced with inflated, false stories by Spanish writings to please the Queen. Self-aggrandizement was the rule of the day for the Spanish in Tenochtitlán. Deceit was an honored badge worn on one's breast. Izquierdo was there, and Izquierdo knew the truth.

"And the truth shall set you free," he muttered.

*   *   *

The Spanish priests thought they destroyed our gods, our idols, our powerful calendar. But how can you destroy the sun, the moon, and the stars? Though, believe me, I think that if you left it up to the white man, he would find a way to do it.

Addison's myths were of his bloodline. His Grandpa handed out dimes during the depression and this made him a great American. But what was not told of this old man was how by murder he acquired this oil-rich land. That was the myth Addison kept in his heart. He considered his family a part of the founding fathers of the United States though they were mere immigrants in the 19th century. He lived in a world of lies: for politicians are the greatest liars of all, including the devil.

How on earth could such a young man like Addison Stonefreund, at the age of twenty-five consider himself 'a man of the people'? What does one know at that age? You know how to fight; you know how to continue on, how to get back up when you're down. But Addison was not worldly, and though he would momentarily benefit from his youth, his youth would eventually be his downfall.

He named his boat *Heart of Mine*. He'd taken up sailing long ago at the bequest of his friend Bobby, and now he considered himself a master.

Now, while presently out to sea in the tepid waters of the great Pacific Ocean, Addison made plans for suicide. As he rolled a cigarette with his free hand, the other steered Heart of Mine.

First, find the bird. Track it. Chase it until tired. I still have the stamina to run for days on end, after all. I will get it good and tired and force it to give up! Then, kill it gently. Watch the bones. I must eat the flesh, for that will empower me for life; perhaps creating a myth of myself! Clean the bones, let them dry, make the necklace, befriend the pygmies, and continue on my way. There is so much of the world I want to see.

He might have to shoot the animal through the head. He'd learned to shoot a gun at the range back in Cambridge. His Republican friends insisted he learn *in the event the Blacks take over. We'll have to defend our country. It was us white people who founded America after all. We have protection under the law, and we might as well use it,* they preached. The ammo and shotgun were by his side.

At the tender age of twenty-one, Addison Stonefreund received a trust he was responsible to manage for the rest of his life. Presently he received approximately $20,000 a month. With that he had no trouble doing anything he wanted in life. And so, he bought the sailboat for a mere $40,000. With its large, king-size bed, kitchen, and comfortable bathroom with plenty of toilet space, you didn't feel 'squeezed-in'; the bar was stocked with his favorite drink: *Glen Fiddich* Scotch, 25 years old. A variety of beers filled the custom-ordered refrigerator (cost: $1, 230 dollars) for the hottest days of the year. The closet was empty of t-shirts, for that was not his style. He wore safari shirts and matching shorts, sturdy boots and heavy socks. A Navajo blanket from 1950, in case he met with freezing weather, sat with numerous cameras, umbrellas and hats. His thin, translucent, white skin needed protection from the sun and so the hats. For a Stonefreund, a suit and tie were absolute necessities, and so, more out of habit than necessity indeed, his beautiful beige, Brooks Brothers suit hung quietly unused in the closet, a blue tie and black shiny shoes accompanying it. In those days few people wore colored shirts, as most business people dressed in starched white shirts. But, Addison Stonefreund, anthropologist extraordinaire, chose a baby-blue button down Oxford shirt that complimented his handsome, deep blue eyes.

Who knows, it might come in handy one of these days, he'd muttered to no one the day he sailed to sea. Having finished his Master's thesis on *The Evolution of Savage Men* and anxious to get going on his tour around the world, he went home to pick up the few things he needed for the trip. Mom was passed-out on the couch, the TV blaring some stupid game show, a bottle of Vodka by her side. The cleaning lady Rosario looked at poor Addison with kindness. *She'll be up in a minute*, she said, knowing full well Happy would sleep the afternoon away in a haze of depression, drunkenness and nostalgia. The room smells of alcohol and disillusion, he thought. He knelt beside Momma and whispered in her ear: *Je vais a connâitre le monde, ma Mère.* I am off to see the world, mother.

They spoke French from childhood. It was a game between the two: he pretending to be happy, he with a toothy grin while in truth he detested her because she was never around; when she was her breath stank of poison. He sensed she played with him in French to appease him, to rid herself of a guilt that ate at her teeth because she was a bad mom. *I bet she doesn't even know my favorite movie,* he told Rosario one day. The maid could only shake her head.

Poor Addison had been left to play by himself in the huge, empty house while mother and father played in their big, important world, controlling others, deceiving themselves and celebrating victories to be read in the papers.

On the rare occasions when family was together, he remembered now, as he collected his belongings, Mommy chatted in the French learned at the Sorbonne; Daddy tossed young Addison into the air, and people took photos. There were cars and trips and dinners and lunches, summers and skiing, hockey and horses. But what was never there, like the ever-present Vodka bottles on the floor, were the hugs and kisses he yearned for but never received. *That is the world I am running from,* he mumbled as he walked out the door.

His brother was living in a Berkeley halfway house, strung-out on heroin after leaving the Law School Daddy insisted he attend.

You will be a lawyer, his father commanded. *A great politician needs to know the law, so when he breaks it, he is prepared to defend himself.*

Now Addison looked at the ocean's water and it reminded him of Sarah's eyes. She was a girl from his past - at the moment everything about his life was his past – a girl who wore pearls in bed at his request, a young woman who fondled him under the table at private dinners, and who even once, crawled underneath as his colleagues smirked pretending the dinner was lovely. She was adventurous for an Ivy League girl but in the end, he lost interest in her because all she wanted was to get married and have kids. She wanted *little Addison Stonefreunds running about*, he'd joked with friends. Marrying a Stonefreund meant never working, it meant going to endless parties, and being part of society. Was she a mirror-image of his mother? Yes, she gave good head, but Addison was neither prepared for marriage nor willing to give up his freedom. Sarah disappeared from his life after he told her he would go to New Guinea. *How can you live with the savages,* she'd asked.

The sea calmed his nervous body. He'd been pushed to succeed since he could remember and now that he'd completed the basic requirements for Mom and Dad, and now that he'd mailed his diploma to the Gov's office, now with a living trust in hand, he took-off like lightning to experience what he'd dreamed of for so very, very long.

And what a time he had.

The supernatural world Addison Stonefreund yearned to encounter would shield him from evil, from the very forces his country imposed on others today, from the killings of war, from the napalm bombs destroying villages and taking lives by fire. Yes, the cassowary bird would bring him health and power, restore his vigorous youth and guide him to his destiny, a place that would bring him the calm a man needs in life. The bird was believed to be the mother of man.

Once in New Guinea, Addison belonged. *Being accepted by the natives means everything to an anthropologist*, he said, *I might even find a native woman, a cannibal girl who would eat me alive*, he joked. Wouldn't that be fun! Wouldn't that be a pleasure! She could love him to death and they would never part! He would exist in her innards, his fleshy taste a memory for the ages. Yes, he thought, he would civilize these people; get them to live the proper life. No more nakedness! No more superstition! Theirs would be a life of clothes, work, organization, money! They would learn to read and write, do arithmetic! Wasn't this destiny after all? The anthropologist enters a community longing to enmesh himself in the newfound culture, is no longer "the other." It is the *cannibal* who is the other, not the anthropologist!

Addison wanted to belong so badly he could taste it in his mouth. He did not know what these cannibals looked like, but, with video camera on hand, he would capture their essence. Later, back in New York, he would have showings for his friends and family. He could be famous in his own right, make a name for himself outside of politics, and perhaps be a great chronicler of participant history! He wanted to be remembered for something, and although he did not know it then, he would someday get his wish; but for now, he was off in search of the powerful bird that would change his life forever.

Izquierdo stood to stretch his legs. Every time he did that, he got silent as if thinking of the people he knew, remembering them like friends, because I think he came to know them after reading their past. When you have a person's life in your head they become as friend. *Few people believe me when I tell them what I know, what I have lived and seen in this life*, he once said to me.

The wind blew a light breeze and he sat down again. I offered him a Marlboro and he declined. He looked as I sipped the tequila I picked up in Oaxaca City.

If I told you that I heard his thoughts would you believe me? That is how connected we were. I waited for him to continue.

Addison Stonefreund disappeared the way Jim Morrison would have loved to, he muttered. Celebrity is an invention of hype, pretense, and ink. The anthropologist, the papers said, was believed to have been eaten alive by pygmies, cannibals in New Guinea, where he was headed on his sailboat. Happy Mommy was not so happy when she heard the news in Greenwich; in fact she fainted when Rosario showed her the morning paper, her son's picture on the front page: he, a big grin on his face, in proper coat-and-tie, his blond hair longish, a sparkle of joy in his eyes. It was widely believed, although no one investigated the murder, that his arms were chewed-off and his head was stuck on a spear for all outsiders to see. These cannibals loved white meat, it was said, and the 6 O'clock News warned 'Americans' (assuming all 'Americans' are white) to *'cease travel to New Guinea, or any points where cannibalism is found, most notably, in Africa.'* The television network, it turns out, received violent threats from the Black Panther Party for implying Africa was cannibalistic; the Klu Klux Klan flooded the network's lines with congratulatory calls asking for more of the same. No apology was given by the network and soon, white America was back in rhythm celebrating Europe and all things white.

Addison Stonefreund was no dummy. After entering the jungle of New Guinea and finding himself nearly eaten alive by the cannibals, he gave up on the bird and jumped back onto *Heart of Mine* for safer seas. The destination did not matter. He was quite alive, though naked to the bone as the New Guineans had managed to rip his clothes in an attempt to snatch him. Addison had defended himself well. His mother would have been proud.

About two months later, a private investigator sent by mom and dad to find his bones located only his khakis and initialed shorts 'A. S. S.' (Addison Scott Stonefreund.) meaning the body was missing. The investigator never found his decapitated head, nor any trace of bones, neither was there blood spilled to be used as evidence. Thus, Addison Stonefreund became a legend.

And so it happened that Addison Stonefreund figured out his life. *Hell, nobody loves me, nobody cares - I have no loved ones back home. I can simply disappear now and the world will think the pygmies ate me! I couldn't have planned it better. I can have a life now! Why, I have enough money for a lifetime. I can live the life I've wanted, go to South America without a worry. Wow!!! This is what Jim Morrison should have done to get away from the spotlight, not gone to Paris and to his eventual death! And Janis Joplin, Jimmy Hendrix, they coulda done the same. Here in the ocean I am me, Addison, alone, unknown; I can recreate myself at no cost!*

He would go to Mexico to the sacred *cenotes* he knew of, the enormous caves where young virgins were sacrificed in the ancient days. He could search for the desperate mile where it is said the people are mutes. *Someone told me they have an Indian dialect or something. That's good with me; I would dig learning a new way to communicate.* The world was his oyster - so long as he stayed away from the press.

And so he sailed through the rough seas; on his way to South America he heard on the radio that the son of a famous politician and financier had been brutally murdered and eaten by cannibals somewhere in the interior of New Guinea. America was losing the war in Viet Nam.

Addison Stonefreund had a good laugh. At long last, he was free. I will fight forever no more, he shouted at the top of his voice! He would reinvent himself, enjoy life, adventure, and become anyone he wanted to be.

He found his way to South America, arriving happy but tired, the feeling of accomplishment gushing through his blue veins. He was now the lost son of an American icon, murdered, dead and buried. He could live up to the family name without pressure from anyone, make his own decisions, and fail if he had to in order to discover himself. He could do as he wished for the very first time ever.

He sailed from Cape Capricorn where he opened a bank account under an assumed name, continuing on to Brisbane where he bought a pair of whores for a dollar a day. When he got his fill, he went to Cape Howe where he met a con man who sold him his wife. The woman was pretty and petite, loved to dance naked in the stars and please her man. Addison never had so much pleasure in life until then. He noticed he easily grew tired of people, and so moved on as if nothing ever happened. He liked that. On Flinders Island he drank for five days straight, for they love their Scotch too; he ate tortoise, crabs and fried jellyfish.

Tasmania was a hoot what with the fishermen who looked for the devil. He stayed in New Zealand for months, seeing the mountains and the beach, the skiing and snow, the deserts and pines, and the many ranches of a thousand acres. He befriended women by the dozens, for they loved his melancholic Irish songs and generous pockets. He nearly adopted an ugly bulldog, but left him on shore before leaving.

Life was good, but there was something that bothered him. He discovered he couldn't connect with people to keep a friendship, he found it difficult to be intimate when the opportunity presented itself. Something ate at him and he didn't know what. When asked his name he would grunt, and so the friendly beachcombers and surfers called him 'Grunt,' and it stuck. He couldn't make up his mind if he wanted to be Joe or Dante, Carlos or Jeremiah. It was all the same to him. He didn't care about that part of his life at the moment and suddenly realized that it felt good. *A loner pays a price*, he said one afternoon to a barmaid, thinking she was listening when in fact she wasn't.

After traipsing through New Zealand, he zipped to the Loyalty Islands where he had a nice dinner of crabs Cantonese, snails in garlic sauce---NOT escargot!!--- a middle course of local raised goose liver in an authentic Portuguese *porto* that was followed by a local red tuna filet with mashed potatoes and then dessert. The mango pie went down but not the vanilla ice cream as it reminded him too much of his childhood. The wine was good and Australian.

Fiji proved to be much more pleasant, for there was not a Frenchman in sight. He ate raw fruit and vegetables, drank bottled water and chewed on Macadamia nuts imported from Hawaii. The rippling waves of Suva soothed his mortal soul as he dined at Manu's house on the beach. He was said to be an actor of ill repute, chased from Hollywood for his British accent and exiled back home to care for his sickly lover, Jaime. *If there is anywhere he should die, it is in heaven,* said the actor, meaning Fiji was paradise. Manu cooked his delicious Tandoori Chicken with pineapple and cracked rice. After dinner, when the thespian suggested they go for a walk, Addison objected. Sex with a man was not his preference, and so he waved goodbye. To this day, when you visit Fiji, people still speak of the frothing Manu who lusted after Addison's blond locks.

The next morning a man fishing told Addison of Vanua Levu and pointed in the direction. The anthropologist sailed off without haste. He slept under a palm tree that was said had powers and he dreamed all night of orgies, and tossing, and fig leaves.

It took Addison time to understand that he was living life and not running away. He vowed to never return to his roots because if he did he would be seen as a fraud, a ghost perhaps coming back from the dead and that would not do, for people had made up their minds he was dead, and so, it was best to act so. He had to learn to enjoy life and leave the stress to others. And so, he thought, *South America might give me perspective.*

The boat was loaded with water and bananas, mangos and pears. He would have no more French food, he decided, *until I am good and ready.* He sailed for days and nights until he reached Punta Arenas in Chile. An officer by the name of Raúl Séndic asked for his passport and immediately recognized him as the murdered financier's son. He took the sailor aside and whispered: *Aren't you supposed to be dead?* And the dead man responded: *But I am dead.*

Raúl Séndic, communist rebel posing as immigration officer, who was overseeing the delivery of Soviet weapons to support his cause against the Pinochet dictatorship, asked they meet at the local cantina. Moments after Addison was stamped with a visa, he was pressured to contribute a large sum of money to the rebel cause in exchange for keeping his identity a secret. He withdrew one hundred thousand dollars from a local bank, a sum that brought joy to his eyes, for he detested the Head of the CIA, George Bush, the man who ordered the assassination of Salvador Allende. *If you can chase the Americans out of Chile, the money served its purpose* he told Raúl Séndic. He did not need to explain himself to Señor Séndic, for the latter was a learned man, a man who studied at the university and was up-to-date on the latest news from around the world. He knew the Stonefreund's and their money; even so, he knew the head of the CIA.

Raúl Séndic was something of a legend himself. It was a known fact that he'd been the *de facto* leader of the famous Montoneros in Uruguay, and was said to have been killed in action during a suburban firefight. The dead, masked man resembled him so well that the real Raúl was taken for dead. What the Uruguayos did not know, is that Mr. Séndic had outsmarted them and taken refuge in Chile where the political climate was more to his liking. The two men chatting in the cantina now had several things in common: each was believed to be dead, both were alive as the bird that sings outside your window, and both were rebels in their own way.

Addison had the *filet mignon* at the bequest of the rebel, for the Bistro was the best in town; it did not occur to Addison that he broke his promise not to eat French food until ready. He was in good company, and that was all that mattered.

The next few days he spent with Raúl, smoking Cuban cigars, listening to Tango and drinking wine.

There was something pleasant in helping topple America, he thought, that imperialistic; dominating country whose history was littered with massacres, killings and destruction. If Raúl Séndic blew-up the American embassy, so be it. It was high time the U.S. got off its horse and started helping its own people, the Blacks, the Indians, the Mexicans, the hungry.

One hundred thousand dollars can do a lot of damage, thought Addison.

He took off again on his boat and docked at Isla Grande, a small, remote island off the coast of Chile. His Spanish was not so good, and since most people had never seen an American, he went ignored for two days. After a quick espresso he skipped to Talcahuano, on to San Antonio, then Coquimbo, Antofagasta near the Tropic of Capricorn where he set anchor in the practically unheard of village of Iquique. You pretty much had to be either South American, or know geography to know these places, if you know what I mean. On his way to Peru, Ecuador and Colombia, he avoided large ports of entry not so much for fear of running into another Raúl but because he did not need to be recognized so soon after his disappearance. His face was in many newspapers and he wanted time to pass before visiting the big cities that he now detested. In Costa Rica he looked up old family friends: tax-dodgers, criminals and ex-patriots. There he felt safe in the big hotels, for even the Pope himself needed a good night's sleep. He drank Rum & Cokes and read crime novels until he got bored. He thought that falling in love again might do him good, but he didn't know what he was in for.

The anthropologist decided to lay anchor at Puerto Angel, a tiny village on Mexican land. Making his way up the coast by jeep, he stopped at Puerto Juárez where after asking around, he was given directions to the 'lost tribe' at the desperate mile. *But you want to stay away from those people,* a one-legged man said, *because they say they are cannibals!* Addison wanted to laugh, but instead continued on his search.

As it turned out, he could not have had better luck. In the village of Puerto Escondido he spotted a woman with decaying teeth who for some reason he thought would give him directions. Asking in his limited Spanish he described *a place with mute Indians and large holes in the ground, called cenotes,* and she said, '*Yes, the desperate mile!*'

Go into that store in the corner and ask for Agustín Eliab and his brother Guillermo, they will take you there. She put out her hand for a *limosna* being a beggar. Addison understood the gesture and in a flash popped a single dollar bill smack on her right hand. This would not be the first time a Mexican asked for a handout. He walked into the store where the man behind the counter sent him to the *mercado*. A few blocks away he asked again for the *two Indian brothers* and was led to an apartment building surrounded with bougainvilleas and hibiscus. This time it was the hand of a young boy selling *Chiclets* that got greased.

Agustín Eliab was scratching his head and brother Guillermo was smoking a cigarette as the door opened.

Pase usted, come in, they said without looking at him. You must understand that in Mexico things are this way. The brothers were businessmen and so people did not go to them to visit. Addison walked right in and made himself at home. The house was filled with clay pottery, every one original, Indian idols of mothers suckling their young, several phallic symbols from Zapotec times; fat, pregnant dogs staring at him, jade masks and even old *molcajetes* covered with a yellow powder resembling corn pollen. Addison the anthropologist knew these two men were not fakes.

Interestingly, the brothers tried to talk him out of going there.

I will pay you good for your worries, he said. They responded that they had no worries but that he should be concerned. It was a treacherous path, sometimes even the best guides got lost. Why even a Swiss climber with all the modern day gear of the times turned back complaining of the terrain, the rain, the foliage, the spiders, the howler monkeys and the many *culebras*. The snakes.

Es impenetrable, amigo, said Guillermo, now on his third Benson and Hedges.

Yo entiendo, said Addison, but I want to go.

Bueno, said the other brother, we'll take you to the base of the mountain where you can go on in your Jeep. But we are not doing it for the money. It is because something tells me you have what it takes to get there. It is a rare thing to see in a man, no, Guillermo?

The older brother nodded his head and smiled. He showed teeth of gold that glimmered straight into the eyes of the anthropologist.

We will charge you through the teeth, Agustín Eliab said in Spanish, knowing well Addison Stonefreund did not understand. Gringos come and go; they knew a rich one when they saw one.

They did not need the money. The building they lived in was theirs. Tenants paid rent, brought them food and drinks, respected them. Gringos and Europeans by the carloads stopped by for help, each paid handsomely. The brothers were rich and did not have to work another day in their lives if they did not wish to.

What the anthropologist /apologist rich boy did not know, is that the two brothers grew up at the desperate mile, and could lead him there blindfolded.

They would head-out early the next morning.

Addison Stonefreund gathered his things and headed into town. It was there that he met a lovely Norwegian girl who took his breath away.

Her name was Norwegian Helga.

He slept in her arms that night and dreamt of fireflies, armadillos and cactus.

*   *   *

Izquierdo shifted in his chair and I knew another story was coming.

Puta Madre wanted a vanity mirror. Izquierdo laughed and thought: *Que puta tan más vanidosa!* His wife made him laugh. She had all these curious ways about her, ways of speaking, saying things he'd never heard a woman say. They got along well despite the age difference. If the mirror made her happy, so be it.

I'll build you one with my own hands, he said, *one you can pass on to our children.*

There were acres of black Mexican walnut about and it was beautiful. He would cut down a young tree and fashion it to her liking. First though, he would ask its permission, the tree, to cut it down, this way clearing his own soul of wrong, respecting the gods of nature who provided everything. Puta Madre would own the most beautiful mirror in the village.

Once the wood dried, Izquierdo glued it with *chicle,* a raw form of gum that once dry, you cannot pry open with a nuclear bomb. Next came the varnish made of pink orchids, and finally, the artists' stamp. Izquierdo carved tiny butterflies on the frame, for they were his wife's favorite insect. This became his signature in life and that is why today in Mexico you find many antiques stamped with a butterfly motif. These were made by Izquierdo; it just happens that someone bought them long ago and took them to the city.

Puta Madre would be happy with his gift; she would squeal like a girl, throw herself on the mat and let the birds sing.

Young Izquiedo moved heaven and earth to please his wife, nothing made him happier. Life at the desperate mile was simple back then and now, to the delight of everyone, a son was on the way.

Izquierdo's wife sat for hours fixing her hair in front of the vanity mirror, putting on earrings and taking them off; changing a dress for one that looked better. The turquoise necklace and the *chongo* on her hair complemented her ravaging eyes. Izquierdo sat by her side many a day, watching her ready herself, curious at the way women do things. He laughed when she put on rouge and outlined her eyes, for that was the style of the day.

I will surprise her one day with a tiger tooth necklace, he said to no one, filing away the thought. Such a promise was hard to keep, it meant going to the jungle and capturing a tiger. At such a young age, anything was possible.

Puta Madre splashed her naked body with violet water and lay down.

*   *   *

The desperate mile went through a succession of Putas after Izquierdo married the only one in town. The first girl grew tired of the job quickly, the second was impatient, and the third didn't like to drink. Each was quickly forgotten and never spoken of again.

Until the day that Violent Violet showed up.

How she got her name was really a mispronunciation. You see, the men in town thought her name was 'violent' because "Violet" sounds so similar. When the village discovered her new trade, the name stuck. Peace was still the order of the day, but whispers of violence reached our ears. Thus, Violent Violet was born.

At the beginning, Violent Violet never got upset at anything or anyone. She was the "quiet type" who had the habit of smiling even at those who frown. She loved to kiss since the age of thirteen and did so freely with anyone within distance, sometimes attacking a man walking down the street. But this was not a bad thing as people thought she had that need to do so and she was left alone to carry on as she pleased – so long as nothing more happened in public. Others say she was like Izquierdo, who saw the violence coming and did something about it. Her kissing mania might have been her way of confronting the inevitable, who knows? It may have been her way of fighting the future, you know? Whatever the case may be, she was a sweet thing every man enjoyed having as a puta.

One day her name became a burden as unprovoked for some she started living, acting, and being violent. No one could understand how this happened, because at the desperate mile we didn't know such a thing as violence. Maybe she should have been named Sweet Violet to keep the village safe.

Fate and destiny have a way of their own, however, and now, it was too late to change what one stranger set in motion by mispronouncing her name.

Her temper got so out of hand that at one point the men could not kiss her anymore because she would fight back with the strength of an ox; instead of tenderness, you got slapped in the face, kicked in the groin, or punched on the nose.

With that energy she invaded my father's life.

*   *   *

Addison woke up in the morning and tossed the girl aside. She slept like a log, *God, almost like a dead person,* he thought. The night before there were too many drinks and spilled beans; he'd said too much about his identity. She called him 'Grunt', loved it and thought it a funny name. *I don't have to know your real name, Mister, it's all the same to me,* she'd said between drinks like a latter-day Viking princess. One little problem, though: he promised to take her with. He got stung by the bee, the love bird - or lust bird in this case - for he'd never known love like this before. She was suddenly there, this girl, and they hit it off. He recalled wanting to fall in love a few months back while on *Heart of Mine,* but he wasn't ready. Oh, poor Addison Stonefreund did not yet know that love surprises whether you are ready or not. Your life changes from one day to the next because your heart is racing and you can't stop thinking about her. As the young Harvard graduate knew little of intimacy he confused love with lust. He thought that sex was love and that a girl smothering him with kisses was just love. His head now buzzing with mezcal and tequila from the night before, he decided she was his great love, the girl he'd been waiting for, the one he'd always been looking for. As they chatted on the veranda the night before, her luminous skin called out to him like in a foreign language: *"Grunt,* it said, come get me.... *Touch me, feel me...*They both got carried away with the drinks, the tobacco, the fresh air, the newness of the situation, the excitement, the expectation of things to come.

His adventure quickly became *their* adventure. *I'll take you with me wherever I go,* and *I won't be able to live without you,* things like that a young romantic declares when fresh in love.

Now, though - this morning - he looked for a place to hide.

He suddenly felt sick to his stomach and wanting to vomit, he jumped into the shower with its freezing, cold water. The drinks were catching up; last night it seemed he could drink forever, now, though, he felt a bang in his head that nearly put him on the floor. He thought he could handle it, that he could have another, a last one for the road, but the truth was the last one did it, for it was *Hornitos* tequila green label: a potent and deadly potion known to paralyze even the best drinkers on earth when mixed with lesser beverages. Well, last night was a night like that for Addison. He wondered if Helga felt the same and was the wiser of the two for sleeping it off. After the shit, shower and shave, he walked out the door leaving the girl asleep and naked, her bra hanging out the French windows for all to see. Her angelic face made him wince and it occurred to him the affair was over. *This isn't love,* he chortled, embarrassed, indignant for having deceived himself while drunk. He knew he had to leave her behind. He didn't want to, in fact, and it hurt to think about it. A feeling surged in him to be with her forever, she by his side, he the father of her children. He would give up the Gruntman and be...somebody; he would be somebody for her, but not Addison Stonefreund. They would run-off to Timor or Tibet, Timbuktu or Thailand. He felt love, but did not want to admit it. Confusion was for him the order of the day.

Drying off with a towel, he remembered something in their conversation last night. As he was holding her tight and nibbling on her neck, he asked if she wore perfume. *No, I don't believe in it, I think I smell good enough if I may say so myself,* she replied. Then she held him with a fury as if wanting him to take her in; she in her virginal white dress and loose blonde hair; he, in a freshly- pressed muslin shirt bought at the market earlier that day. She wore pearls about her neck, he was shoeless.

In a nervousness engulfing his low self-esteem, he lit a cigarette, and like a movie star in a bad movie, leaned against the ornate bed and smiled. She stared back. Her hands knew what to do, where to go. She'd learned to please her men. *I feel this...love-like thing for you,* he muttered. Yes, she said, she too felt love, like driven, like weighed by his anchor. *Yes,* replied, *I will go with you to the ends of the earth,* no matter what. It was the real thing, this connection, this tugging at her strings. She would not fight it; she would give in.

Grunt, she said, *hold me tight.*

But that was last night.

*   *   *

Dressed in hiking boots and khakis, he was ready for the trek up the mountain. He looked at the hotel sign: *El Fin del Mundo* and smiled.

I'll be back, he said to the four walls as he placed a short note on the dresser.

> *Love of mine:*
> *As I told you, I have been many places but never to the place you took me last night, or even, at this very moment. I have to go, but I'll be back. Leave your address with the Concierge and I'll find you. I will find you no matter where you go. You are the one for me. Grunt.*

There are so many more things to say; he could have been more syrupy, he thought, *take away some of that pain.*

The headache was killing him, and so was leaving her. He went to the *mercado* down the street and ordered a huge bowl of fish soup with a dozen fresh tortillas. The fiery hot sauce in front of him beckoned: with a cold beer everything would turn out fine. He'd learned the cure for hangover from his good college friend Miguelito Alemán, grandson of a well-remembered Mexican President; at Miguelito's beach house the servants cooked the best food in the coast. Fish stew reinvigorates you, it puts vitamins back into your system, the friend said. The *chile* puts hair on your chest. The beer, in turn, is the hair of the dog.

Addison's friends were children of important people. The Alemán kid was no exception: His grandpa, the Pres, did what every good Mexican President does when leaving office: he took the national treasury, leaving the country on the verge of economic collapse. Next, he boarded a plane to New York where within hours he bought the Waldorf-Astoria in cash - and that is why you see the Mexican flag flying over the famous hotel – Mexican owned, a fact unknown but by those who know of the bilking.

Miguelito's prescription worked. Addison Stonefreund picked-up his red Jeep and drove to see the guys Agustín Eliab and Guillermo who were waiting for him at the front door.

Primero se paga, Guillermo said, without speaking, though laying out his hand for payment.

Addison dug into his pocket and counted five thousand dollars.

Orale, he said, like a Mexican. The brothers smiled.

Vamos, pués, said Agustín Eliab. They took off immediately.

The girl woke up just then and began to cry.

*   *   *

I have to do it alone, he said to himself, *I've always done everything alone,* he recalled wanting to say to her as he revved the engine before the trek. And then, with as much perspective as he could gather, he said: *When I get back we'll do everything together.*

These were Grunt's last words to his concubine.

They never would do everything together, but he never suspected this because all he'd left behind in bed that morning was his fate, his unavoidable destiny, an act unknown in a play with a predictable ending. Had he listened to the two brothers the day before, he might still be alive today; and happy with this voluptuous young girl, Norwegian Helga.

She would wait a month for him before returning home to Europe and the letters she would never receive.

Agustín Eliab and Guillermo did not speak a word the whole way; well, not the way we talk anyway for they too grew up mutes at the desperate mile. For a brief moment, Addison thought he was on magic mushrooms because the two men *never spoke, not once opened their mouth,* yet he heard their every word; he did not see them speak like we speak, nor move their mouth to pronounce words, yet he understood everything they said - why they talked through...telepathy! They did not e-nun-ci-ate like you and me; instead, they spoke with their minds! While in Oaxaca City he'd heard that all desperate milers did that, so for an instant he thought he was losing his mind. The brothers looked at him and smiled. A cold shiver overtook his body and he convinced himself it was the *cruda,* it was the hangover playing tricks on his head and not these two trekkers who were just sitting quietly looking about.

He was getting the shock of his life and *it wasn't funny!* Nervous and desperate to solve the puzzle they were in his mind, he pretended everything was all right. The brothers sensed he was freaking out but, hey, they'd seen this a thousand times before. Gringos get freaked out by other cultures, by "the other," by people unlike themselves. The brothers shrugged like they always did. They weren't the ones wanting to reach the desperate mile, so, what did they care. They had another five thousand dollars in their pocket and fresh thoughts of a new property. Better to think of the future.

Addison's mind ran amok. The poor boy did not realize he was heading north, as far north as it is possible to go in this life - meaning Heaven - because his life was planned and decided in advance a long time ago.

The tour guides laughed. They knew his time was up, yet they could not talk him out of going up there, up there to the mountain, into that dense terrain from where few people returned. *We are people who believe in fate and destiny,* they said from deep within. No one wants to see someone die, no, not really, not even people who wish you dead. Death is a sad thing, no matter how you look at it; but it is a necessary thing, well, a necessary event in your life, if you will. Agustín Eliab and Guillermo would die too someday, they knew it well, but they had an advantage over most mortals: they could pretty much tell when their time was up, when it was time to sell the farm. You see, at the desperate mile people looked you in the eye and told you they saw it coming. This gave you time to prepare, to say goodbye, to make-up with those who'd kept you uptight. *It is imminent,* were the magic words; and you, well, you just sort of packed your bags, if you know what I mean. At the desperate mile we sat around, drank mezcal, ate and told jokes; it was the tradition. Hey, if your time is up, why not party? This was the big kick-off, as Americans like to say. The Spirits then welcomed your friend, and off he was to the next world. Some would shout, *Come back as a bird!* Or, *No, come back as Einstein so you can figure this life out!* Even still, others would shout, *If you come back as a cow, we'll take you to India!*

We desperate milers are self-effacing. What do you expect from people who know no fear and prefer to laugh?

So Addison Stonefreund was on his way north and had no clue about it. He did not even know there was a moment in time when you can change your mind, change your life, and change your destiny. Yes, folks, I hate to break it to you but it's true. *You have to know the signs; you have to believe your time has come, know that you want to stay a bit longer, know it's the right thing to do for a while; and then you jump.* Nobody can help you, because, you must be the Kingmaker. This is a secret we learn as children, but a secret we forget as adults.

Addison did experience that moment when he could have walked away from the inevitable, when he could have stayed on earth just a little longer even if it meant spending the rest of his life with the girl, but he was too busy getting on with the trek to see it.

Now, it was too late. Now, he would not ask to turn around because he had his mind set on getting to the desperate mile; the thought would not occur to him to return to Oaxaca and the lovely girl. She would wake up and smile, thinking he went out for coffee.

Agustín Eliab and Guillermo shrugged again. *Oh well, another day, another dollar,* like the gringos say.

*   *   *

Addison was still hurting from last night when the brothers dropped him off at the base of the jungle. They left him at the foot of the mountain and showed him the way up, a thin little path made by the less fortunate who attempted to reach the mutes by hook or by crook. Adventurers are known to sacrifice everything for the sake of experience, particularly for an experience like few others on earth have had, and as such, Addison Stonefreund was no different. While the brothers liked this guy, he was not like the others: arrogant, thick and dumb. This man was conversant enough; he spoke well, he had interesting ideas. When they said, *Be careful on the way up, the road is dangerous,* he kept silent. When they explained that not everybody comes back down that mountain because the wild animals are vicious as they protect the people up there, he smiled.

Lots of turistas never made it up there either, nor did they make it back; the steep climb left them open to the jaguars and panthers, mountain lions and cheetahs. Why those creatures love white meat, they will leap on you and wolf-you-down in one bite, they teased him, knowing Addison would likely laugh at the thought of it. Addison was different indeed because he thought himself immortal. He had already escaped a narrow death after all, what on earth could happen to him up here?

Yes, you are mortal, my friend. You are dead but you don't know it, said Agustín Eliab, scratching his underarms this time. The itch came from one of the many putas the brothers visited at night as they had much money to do so. Years ago they started the habit of going with whores forgetting that some have lice and others don't. This one must have given him something as he couldn't stop scratching.

Addison Stonefreund was thinking of his future. He would not live to read *One Hundred Years of Solitude*, nor *Tale of a Death Foretold;* had he lived, he would have discovered *The Labyrinth of Solitude*, perhaps *La region más transparente* finding the mere thought of going to the desperate mile pompous. The books he read were more like *1984*, *The Prophet* and, *The Stranger*. *A mask, you are wearing a mask*, wrote Octavio Paz, and right he was, though his words were never directed at the Harvard graduate. The old poet Octavio Paz wrote to the Mexican, depicting him as he is, forcing him to look in the mirror, suggesting he change, that he stop being the brute, that he consider becoming civilized, that the Mexican stop pretending to be something he was not, a mythical figure, a superhero like

Superman; the poet wanted his friends in society to see themselves naked before the smoking mirror to consider starting a new country, doing good for the country instead of taking from it, robbing it blind, stripping it naked of its natural resources for the sake of accumulating hidden European fortunes they would never spend. Old Paz wanted the Mexican to stop showering their children with gold and privileges meant for the everyday man: take off your masks, you Mexicans, he said, see the landscape of your inner-being, become a respectable human being. He strip-searched Mexican society leaving them naked, as nude as The Naked Ape.

What are you looking for, anyway, asked one of the guides. *Death, are you that anxious to die? What do you think you are, some Mexican who does not fear death but welcomes it with open arms?*

No. Addison Stonefreund replied in his head, *Immortal is what I am.* And so it came to be.

The brothers walked into the nearest village to board a bus home, leaving the jeep behind. The trekker drove up the mountain terrain, apologizing to himself for leaving Norwegian Helga, for trespassing into the unknown territory that lay ahead. Somewhere deep inside of him, he thought the wild animals would let him pass without a fuss. He would speak to the trees, to nature, to the sky above; they would grant him leave as if anointed for the trip. For a brief moment, Addison Stonefreund believed the gods of nature favored the white man's voice in the same way they respond to Indians. What he did not understand is that in Mexico the plants and wild animals do not speak English.

The Jeep hit a muddy spot at sundown so he pulled over and fell asleep. His Bowie knife by his side was ready in the event a cat might want to devour him in one, sound bite.

*   *   *

Izquierdo was looking at the fish in the river when he heard a strange sound. Turning to look, a red metal thing was bouncing up-and-down, a red thing he'd never seen before. It was the Jeep with a blond man in it. The man looked frightened, his eyes were big. Momentarily possessed by fear, Addison Stonefreund looked in the direction of Izquierdo, and my father, unable to look away from the strange white man, read his life. They say that your life flashes before your eyes as you lay dying, but my father had the ability to see it in the very moment of death.

Izquierdo walked back to the village leaving the young man to fend for himself.

*   *   *

The anthropologist woke to the sounds of birds singing. The creeping sunrise warmed him as he looked about and saw tall jungle trees, their branches reaching for the sky. The early mist dissolved before his eyes. Addison lay unscathed by the animals around him, feeling a pain in his stomach and legs, a pain he did not recognize, nor did he know its origin until he felt his body parts. The Jeep's crash ripped his flesh and knocked him unconscious, and now, dried blood splattered all about attracted flies like a dead man. He felt a thirst, and when he raised his arm to reach the canteen, he felt a knife stab him and cried out. Several parts of his body were broken, the left leg at the knee, his right forearm, a rib too, then a little finger, leading him to think getting out of the Jeep might prove fatal. He did not know he was close to his destiny – the desperate mile - and there was no way of finding out. All he could do for now was concentrate on getting himself together somehow, on getting through, on marching on. *Miracles do happen*, he muttered. As he looked out into the landscape, he thought he saw a mountain lion stare at him. Though the beasts had let him live for the night, in their heart they knew he was on his last legs. Why, even a wolf will not chew on a dying lamb.

He dragged himself to the water, taking a long drink from the desperate river, brushing back his hair with those long, pygmy-envied fingers. He looked so dead already you'd think he was ready to meet his maker. The khakis were soaked-through with blood, his shirt stripped-off to the waist, his boot laces untied as if by a ghost's hand. He tried to stretch to the sky but he felt a sharp pain strangle him by the neck. The wind whispered: *Go back.*

But Addison did not hear the voice. He laid his body carefully on the largest river rock and fell asleep once more, tired as a lion after a day's hunt.

*   *   *

Puta Madre bathed every morning at the waterfall. She was naked as Eve but with no apple in hand. She rubbed her large breasts to rinse off the soap.

Her long, raven hair reached her buttocks, and her bushy forest protruded in a most alarming way.

It was in this state that Addison Stonefreund first saw her. She in turn, did not hear him grunt about from the sound of the rushing waterfalls; he made every effort to keep the aching pain to himself. Behind a boulder he watched her with fascination as he'd never seen such a beautiful sight. His member tingled at her chocolate skin; her lips were red, her legs quite long. Suddenly Norwegian Helga was but a mere memory. The surprise of seeing a human being after many, many days in the jungle alone, made him forget his surroundings. At this moment, all that existed was woman. Sensing a presence, Puta Madre turned his way but did not see him. Thinking she'd seen him froze his penis. Looking about more carefully and out of the corner of her eye she saw something uncommon to her: a man of white skin and yellow hair protruding from a boulder. If she was scared, she hid it well. In a moment she climbed onto a rock, much like lizards do, and laid down in her splendor as if to show her body to this strange human creature peering at her. Addison understood the gesture as an act of generosity, for only a woman that wants to be seen shows herself. The sun dried her wet body as she covered it with turtle oil, her torso gleaming as if on fire. Addison in hiding was also on fire. *Strangely,* he thought, *we understand each other,* each giving to the other without condition. This, indeed, meant being free.

Nothing stopped her from this daily bath ritual. Men peeked daily and she knew it, so what was the difference. She was the proud mother of a newborn child and the happy wife to a handsome man, and everybody knew it.

She got up quickly and just as quickly disappeared into the jungle. Addison jumped to his feet and followed, his leg reeling in pain, his headache pounding, a broken rib rubbing the interior of his flesh; the pain from his broken body almost made him scream. His soul ached, and once again he was in love. A tormented feeling took over and he sat down. This was the first time in his life that he felt physical, mental and emotional pain all at the same time, and it was a feeling he would never forget. *Normally, just my head hurts*, he said to himself, knowing full well something was wrong.

I must be dying, he admitted.

But, who is that woman? Where did she go? What is her name? Addison tried to reconstruct her face in his mind but her features were fading: he wanted her back but the dried blood on his clothes erased her altogether. Was she a dream in this nightmare?

I needed to see her again.

Closing his to eyes to concentrate he could see her green eyes, vivid and challenging.

She can't be an illusion, I saw her with my own eyes! Was the jungle playing tricks on him?

He felt excited, then shattered and hopeless like men do when they see the woman they've always wanted walking down the street. This is the one woman you will never forget, the beauty of the ages, your soul mate: as she walks away and you shout: *Don't disappear, I beg you!* The next thing you know, you sketch her face in your heart, in your mind but just as soon her image disappears before your eyes, because you only saw her once, because you are not familiar with her face; you are miserable for days, you look to find her, ask about her, pray, curse and finally give up. You heart pounds, you have to have her. In a few days you realize she is really gone, that you will never see her again. It's torture not knowing her name, it eats at you, and finally, after walking Central Park for a week, you break down. Your heart sinks. How could you have let her go?

At this very instant, Addison felt this way.

Dejected but determined to survive, he crawled through the boulders down to the waterfall thinking he could wash it all off. *I'll find her no matter what,* he declared. What he didn't know was that a few days later she would see him in his final minutes, as he expired in his Jeep. He, in turn, would see his life flash before his eyes, this strange creature's glimmering body and green eyes his last memory alive. This is how lives end sometimes: n love one minute, and gone the next.

He bathed in the waterfall to the sounds of silence. The water crashed like it does when falling, but Addison heard nothing.

Everything got real quiet.

*　　　*　　　*

The mango was sweet, the bath revived him. After drying off and jumping in his Jeep, he looked for the place where he thought she might be. As the weeks passed without results, his body healed. One afternoon, the vehicle chugged to a stop as the engine was clogged with mud. Opening the hood, he let the sun in. After an hour he chipped the dry mud with his knife, cleaned the spark plugs and continued on his way. There was nothing going to stop him from finding the woman of his dreams, even if it meant death in the end. He would look for her at the desperate mile.

I wonder if I'm close.

Munching on a papaya, he noticed silence take over. *It's quiet, the birds should be chirping.* Looking about for signs of life, he saw fresh footprints. *It must have rained yesterday,* he said excitedly as he climbed into the Jeep to follow the trail. *Someone must have passed this way, thus the silence.*

He came to a *cenote*, recognizing it as an ancient sight of Aztec sacrifice.

This is where they tossed the virgins.

In the darkness below one could hear French being spoken as if by those who ventured to find the buried gold and riches virgins wore to honor their idols. You had to wear your best and look good on your trip, after all. It is said the French were the first to pillage the sacred *cenotes* and so the voices. What they didn't know is those sacrificial grounds are like the desperate mile: while you may go in, you may not come back out.

This place is creepy, he admitted, brushing off the ancient sounds, letting them be. *This has to be the desperate mile,* he said out loud, *It's everything they said it was.*

The desperate mile was now his nirvana. He believed that once he found it, his life would be different. Stopping on a peak for no reason, he ran to the edge as if called by a voice. In the distance he saw a human shadow. Finding his binoculars he confirmed he was no hallucinating, because a man alone in the jungle for too long is likely to see things, to imagine that which is not, to convince himself things not real actually exist. Though he did not know what he saw, he knew there was life nearby: perhaps it was Father Serra's ghost limping along, carrying the cross, mumbling to himself. Maybe the old priest was being followed by a red dog frothing at the mouth. And then he thought he saw a child playing. *Surely I must be near,* he said again to no one. The binoculars revealed a village in the distance, smoke rising from a hut.

A village!

He saw naked people running to and fro.

This must be the desperate mile, I found it!

He ran to the Jeep and sped in that direction.

*   *   *

The villagers heard a loud cracking sound and looked up. They saw a red Jeep flying their way, to them a flying vessel, to them a strange item for they had never so much as seen an automobile. Having never seen such a thing before and having no idea what it was, they looked and waited as the Jeep flew in their direction. Sure, this bird looks big, but it's falling now.

The world stopped for Addison Stonefreund as the Jeep's steering wheel could do nothing and neither could the brakes. As the Jeep was flying off the cliff, he had no control; as he knew he would soon crash and die, the thought of a soft landing ran through his mind, though in vain now as a thousand pounds in the air do not fall lightly. He thought of jumping off the Jeep while it was in the air but at the moment it was too late. His seatbelt was tightly strapped across his breast, his right hand was holding his prized safari hat, and the time it took to ready oneself for the leap was getting shorter by the minute. This crash would surely take his life. He looked at the people down in the village and saw sadness in their eyes, for they recognized he was human and they knew he was dead meat. What Addison Stonefreund would have liked to know was that was Puta Madre was peeking through her kitchen window, a witness to his fall, to his last moment on earth. He would never know he found his dream woman after all.

Izquierdo, planting corn out in the fields, shook his head.

What goes up must come down, he said.

The only thing that flew at the desperate mile in those days was the bird, and any fool on earth could tell this was not one of them.

*   *   *

Why did I take that hill so fast? Addison was asking himself as the Jeep descended onto the village. Suspended in time, like Nureyev at the Paris Opera, he was at the height of his life but did not know it. *What do you suppose will happen on landing? Do I have my seatbelt on?* Would he bounce out of the Jeep like a rubber ball?

He looked down at the people, and felt peace, the very everlasting peace he was heading to without knowing it.

He held the steering wheel again, this time praying for help.

And then it happened. The Jeep landed with a frightening crash, the wheels flying about in different directions; the windshield shattered in pieces as the headlights flashed on and off. The headlights bolted forward like a cannonball shot, bursting on a palm tree 100 meters afar. A high-pitched emergency alarm rang in his ears and Addison Stonefreund knew he was dead.

Puta Madre ran to the scene though an unconscious Addison would never know this. The poblanos looked at the white man bleeding.

Help me! he cried, but they spoke no English.

Anything you want, I'll give you anything you want... he screamed in his last breath. But the help would not come. Izquierdo came near and looked into his eyes again.

Addison Stonefreund stretched out his hand and coughed, thinking he was Artemio Cruz as he expired.

Father Serra came running from the church, his ghostly, pale body a wreck as he'd been dead for twenty years. He prayed for a moment of silence as he read the last rites. The villagers did not move. And Addison did not have a chance to repent his sins.

What have you done my son, asked the priest in halting Spanish.

But the dead do not speak, they hold their tongue.

The wind blew with a mighty force and Addison Stonefreund went off with the spirits. The only one who didn't see it was the friar as he had his head bent in prayer.

The wind died down and so did the breathing sound of Addison Stonefreund, anthropologist extraordinaire.

*　　*　　*

CELEBRATION

Izquierdo led Puta Madre down a long path of flowers as the villagers greeted them with congratulations, hoots and kisses. Just where they were headed he did not know so he followed the littered carnations, poppies and birds of paradise. It was time for celebration. It wasn't everyday Izquierdo got married, and even less to a Puta, so in the tradition of the poblanos he was going to get drunk on as much *pulque* as his young belly could take. Puta Madre followed like a little girl, smiles and coy gestures of her face; she was used to attention, but this moment seemed different. She knew her role in life: to bare children, raise them, feed her husband and take good care of him as time permits. To do differently at the desperate mile was unthinkable. Tradition is defined as customs that are passed from one generation to the next, and at the desperate mile you do as you are told.

She would do what was expected of her, the same as the earth does in accepting the falling rain. Izquierdo went straight to the cantina, leaving her outside to wait.

She tugged his muslin shirt to try to stop him from going inside at such an important time in life, but he ignored her with a slight hand gesture. *Those days are over,* he said, as she asked to go in to turn a trick. She was his now, and the days of prostitution were no more.

Puta Madre stood outside and thought about her new life. She knew she would ache for him, think of him night and day; how time would be taken up with lovemaking. She thought of climbing up the magic mountain of love, he depositing his gold in her forest, she leaving marks on his shoulders; she would crave him in the middle of the day, want him the moment he got home from the fields, and jump him in the middle of dinner. He was her man, who would devour her night after night.

The capture as the desperate milers called marriage was all she could think of. She'd stopped bleeding one month ago and it was a sign of danger, for she always bled, ever since she could remember, and now she was with child. *You have to marry me,* she said to him, *I am with child.* Izquierdo laughed in joy because he knew it was his destiny to be with her. What fate brings us we cannot argue, he declared. Our lives are written already, believe it or not. Why else would we experience *deja vu?*   Why else would we feel we have lived this life before? Izquierdo and Puta Madre knew that life is meant to bring us certain things and that we are stupid to try live differently.

What these newlyweds believed, every poblano believed too.

Father Serra's success was founded on our belief system, because we believed that what happened one minute was intended to be; if the priest came to our village it was because it was already written, and who were we to defy such a prophecy? If we were meant to be evangelized and turned to Christ, why fight it? But the sad thing is the priest never knew this. His ignorance never allowed him see the gold in front of his eyes. *It is your destiny to believe in God!* he could have told them, and they, poor, unclothed heathens, would have bowed and knelt at his feet like true believers. They would have followed him into the old church and prayed, why they would have spoken like men do; these poblanos would have carried the cross for Father Serra, had he so much as paid attention to their world for one minute.

Outside the cantina people watched as Puta Madre decided to enter. Married women were forbidden entry, and although she had been there many times before as a puta, now it was different. In her mind, not much time had lapsed. Bad habits are hard to break and so without further thought, she pushed open the swingdoors and entered the bar.

Something happened with her action, and soon, the whole village was there. Someone shouted for *pulque*, others for *tequila*; a mother said she would go for chickens *"As soon as someone wets my mouth,"* which someone took it to mean with tequila. There was much laughter as Juan Gabriel took his own bottle and emptied it right down her throat. He was a queer singer, with everyone treating him like a girl. A woman in the cantina, the fattest one there, said she had a fresh crop of corn to make tortillas, enough for the whole pueblo, and that this morning she'd had a funny feeling something beautiful was going to happen. A little girl in pigtails and squeaky voice announced she would bring the most beautiful flowers from her garden. A tall, drunken man in a moustache ordered his wife go home and start a fire so he could roast his biggest pig. *And make your delicious mole,* he added, patting her behind as she walked out. Cantinas no longer excluded women.

The mood got festive, the people happy, the room cluttered. This was the beginning. The celebration was always three days: the first, everyone got together; the second day was spent at the groom's house, the third at the bride's. The fourth day the newlyweds were already at their secret place, forgotten as life returned to normal.

Two men walked in with lutes and started to play soft, reassuring music; the newlyweds touched hands and there was a sigh in the room. Someone stepped out on the floor to dance followed by others. Though it was a swoon dance, the people clapped like gypsies. Soon, feet stomped, the ground shook, and the cantina rattled.

Food waltzed in: onions, fresh tomatoes, avocados, lemons and limes, *chayote*, tortillas, *mole*, frijoles, corn balls, a pig, a goat, red meat seared in garlic, *chiles verdes*, *chiles anchos*, and soup. Tomorrow it would be fish; the second day of celebration always was, as you had to take a rest from the heavy eating the day before. The desperate river would provide the clams and crabs, oysters the size of fists, crawfish, *huachinango*, and whitefish; no one would go without. There was a spot at the river where the fish came to you as if in offering. The fish knew it was feast day; and preferred to be with us instead of in a bird's beak. You just went with your basket and they would jump in. We would watch them wiggle, take one last breath and expire. The final act: a smile on their face. Now that I think of it, the gods provided everything for the desperate mile, but we took it for granted. We didn't know then that other men who roamed the earth would soon come and take it.

Someone mentioned to call on Father Serra, but no one moved. He was like us - in some way - except he smelled. He didn't bother us and we did not bother him, and so we began to think of him as one of ours, although he talked and talked until red in the face. We found him amusing, did not know what he was saying, and so we stopped listening.

Things would change one day at the desperate mile, but we did not know it then.

Now the music penetrated our souls. Love was everywhere like a blanket covering the village with its warmth. We looked forward to the next two days, reestablishing friendships, talking to those we'd ignored, or insulted, hugging the very people we'd turned our backs on the night before. Some would reflect on their lives and the beauty it'd been, for there was no violence at the desperate mile in those days. Every celebration included the village, no one was excluded. These were days to heal old wounds, in fact, a rule: forgive your enemy at a time like this so harmony can have its day. For who knows when you will need your enemy, if only for an instant?

Father Serra could hear the music from his quarters. He resisted joining in, though he knew it was best for his mission. Had they come looking for him he would have resisted because there was something that told him he didn't belong there what with all the drinking and whoring he suspected was to take place. Better stay away from sin, he muttered to the book in his hands. *I still have twenty years ahead of me, though forty five left behind,* he chuckled, the idea of living forever an inspiration and a joy. He'd traveled the jungles, looking in the wrong place, climbed abandoned mountains and isolated farmlands, peeked into caves just to find the people he was looking for. In the end it was his donkey and not he that found the desperate mile as it climbed up a treacherous road the priest would have never taken. The beast led him to his destination.

As the celebration took place in the village Father Serra read his book in near darkness, as his candle flickered low. He was taking notes on his latest idea: *The Conversion of the Mutes,* planning to write a book on his experience here; because the poblanos did not speak like you and me, and because they communicated telepathically, Father Serra thought them mute, incapable of normal, verbal communication. Now, he wanted more than ever to write his life *opus* to be remembered by. What he did not know this night was that the Indians wanted him at the celebration, yet not one of them stepped up to invite him.

Father Serra crouched over the book and frowned. His sight was worse by the day and he had a headache. He would not stop working because he'd taken a vow to convert these pagans, even if it meant losing his sight.

Izquierdo, only thirteen years old, drank all he could hold that day. He ate without knife and fork, his wife by his side; he did not need a napkin today as his wife would suck his fingers dry, as was the tradition at the desperate mile. The poblanos needed to know the newlyweds were in love, and so, this show of affection. If they were not in love, it was noticeable and the lovers did not want each other. On the rare occasions that love did not show, the couple were shunned by the villagers and sent away; surely that way they would learn to love as they would only have each other.

Izquierdo enjoyed himself this day. The men displayed themselves like proud peacocks, their starched shirts and combed hair shining, the best *guaraches,* a show of respect. The women, with their brightly colored skirts and fresh flowers in their hair, sang and smiled, and by evening, fed their husbands papayas and grapes, mangos and melons. Everyone laughed as the poblanos displayed their affection for each other. Love was all around, not in hiding today.

This is life, thought the young man Izquierdo, new bride by his side.

This is destiny.

And then there was the secret place.

It was a spot in the jungle where the newlyweds went, a place forever special and only for them; a refuge for future occasions, nirvana. Every couple had one as the husband would locate it in the days before the wedding. You might call it the honeymoon; we called it *the secret place.*

The sun went down as Puta Madre rocked a drunken Izquierdo in her arms. While villagers danced she brushed his hair and murmured, *"Corazón."* She would let him sleep, going to the secret place later.

She felt a pang of love envelop her breast and a tear came to her eye. The joy was touching as she'd never felt this before.

She would love her man forever and prayed he would do the same.

*   *   *

The Catholic priest had a mandate from heaven, and by God he would carry it out!

When he entered the desperate mile years ago, he found the people friendly and smiling. Yes, they were mutes, but the most interesting thing happened one day. He was turning the earth in his garden and heard someone shout Burro! The priest turned to see who spoke, but the person was gone. *What did they just say,* he asked himself. Getting off his knees, he ran over to one of the children playing nearby to look for answers. After questioning the child in a fit of desperation, the boy said nothing, responded to nothing, gave nothing, in fact, he didn't even shrug his shoulders in response to the old man with the bad breath. Now frustrated with nowhere to turn, Father Serra ran to his quarters and wrote down exactly what he heard.

Dicen los indios una palabra:

1) Burro! De donde aprendieron esa palabra?

The poor clergyman felt so bewildered to hear the mutes speak for the first time that he couldn't think straight. Surely these words threw a monkey wrench into his theory; surely now his book would change, maybe it would end in the trash because the villagers now had a voice, a voice he heard and was witness to. But who spoke it? The years wasted away in front of his eyes. Unable to pinpoint if his chance had come to converse with the mutes, to learn about them, to hear them tell their own stories, he sank into a deep depression that lasted five whole years. During those five years he looked for redemption in his work, seeking a way out of this spiraling, vanishing wasted time, looking for solace in maybe one thought to turn his head around. One afternoon as he turned the soil in the garden he realized, *I am the proud outsider to a forgotten race on earth no one has ever seen!* The thought of being the first man to reach the desperate mile was elating, and though unsuccessful in converting these pagans to Christ, he celebrated with a glass of wine what to him meant a door opening in his ministry. The word uttered by a villager meant the future was there for the taking but that was because he didn't know the story of the teacher with no name.

Father Serra had lived there for years now with many opportunities to befriend and evangelize our people, yet he missed out time and again to do so because his training taught him these people needed help, *To be like the white man! They can be like us! They need to be like us!* The missionary wanted to cover their naked bodies with cloth; he wanted to throw them into the river as in baptismal, teach them the fork and spoon, instruct them in deep prayer, lead them to be saved forever, and the truth is that the pueblo could have been his for the taking, had he just so much as opened his eyes to see what was in front of him. He could have reigned like a king, if not for his infinite ignorance. What was in front of him were people who lived in the infinite innocence, people who lived stress free, a village united and in harmony, a community in which every man had his role in life, accepted it and thrived. The poblanos would have taken in Jesus had Father Serra treated them like equals. But his world was made of ladders, of divisions, the people had somewhere to go, things to do, places to reach – or so they thought, to riches and wealth that in the end meant nothing as you can't take it with you. Unfortunately, the old Spaniard died without knowing he had them in the palm of his hand. They were waiting for him the whole time, expectant he would bring change to their lives. Father Serra had the chance to be immortal in converting them to Christ, why, he even had a chance to have a tribe named after him.

But like Izquierdo often said, *It was his destiny to die ignorant.*

He left his writings, his unfinished *Opus,* his journals stored away for years until I found them. He never imagined I would one day read his works to the whole tribe.

The day Father Serra came to our village he found a black trunk unopened and long ignored as it meant nothing to us. What he never learned inside were messages from someone who preceded him; that another outsider had come here to civilize our tribe. The contents were our long-forgotten teacher's anemic writings bound with faded ribbons and dried flowers, all in the form of a book intended for publication. The teacher's works might have inspired him to write his version of our people, but it took him thirty years of wandering the empty halls of the church to even start that work, for how does one document history without a past? The mutes spoke nothing, told nothing, and revealed nothing of the desperate mile until I grew up. Father Serra's mind began to deteriorate for lack of conversation with another, his aloneness was so; his legendary nightmares woke him in the middle of the night to the sounds of his own screaming. He wept in his sleep, he tossed and turned out of loneliness, he spoke to himself and prayed. The solitude crazed him, for he did not speak or converse with a single soul in all those years, though he kept trying to convert the heathens in any way he could. His seclusion one night erupted in explosive crying he could not control.

Now though, as he walked the dark and empty building blind as a bat, he bumped into the teacher's trunk and hurt his leg. Frazzled from sleep deprivation and marathon prayer sessions, he sat down on the trunk to rest, his feet freezing on the marble floor, his knee bleeding. He felt something cold and gummy run down his white wrinkled skin and knew he needed a bandage. The blood would clot, leaving a red trail down his leg that would later crack and fall by itself the next time he washed.

Suddenly and without notice, he was possessed by a familiar surge of emotion we all experience in life: *I can't go on anymore!*

Am I dying, he asked, head to ceiling. *Where is God now that I need him? How can I continue living like this: alone, without a partner, in a deep silence that disturbs my soul...? Have I been forsaken? Jesus,* he shouted, so loud the villagers opened their eyes from under their blankets; so loud the villagers learned His name as if from above. *Jesus!* The old priest would have wept knowing he reached them in his desperation, but his separateness missed this chance at conversion.

He cried out like this until he fell asleep on the teacher's trunk. The nightmare that was his life turned to dreams of a lovely woman reaching for him as in lust, though weeping at the same time. She was speaking of his children, to the very kids he raised in this village, why, he recognized their faces! She was saying something about being a father, about being bad, that he was wanted and needed but he was not there. He tried to reach out to her in his dream, he wanted to say he was sorry, he wanted to repent for being bad; Father Serra cried in his dream, feeling a failure, wanting to speak to this weeping woman but he could not get through. Now her image was clear: she was a young woman, bags in hand leaving Seville on her journey to the New World; excited, alive, and smiling. His dream was like going home to Spain, what with the clothes, the garlic and the music. A sudden peace engulfed him and he smiled in his sleep, thinking the nightmares were over as the young maiden now a woman disembarked a ship to enter a carriage. She was a teacher she said, on a mission to free the slaves. Now she was in the village, his village, she was gathering the children, ordering them into a line, disciplining them while they laughed; they laughed at her just as they'd laughed at him in his attempts to communicate. They were no different he thought, the teacher faced the same problem as me; she failed too, didn't she? Now she was writing her journals, she alone, sitting at a desk surrounded by the many children watching her every move. She was desperate to get to them but she did not have the Word! Father Serra knew his time would come, because while the teacher offered instruction, offered education, the old priest offered salvation! He felt anguish in his sleep and woke up startled. Unable to differentiate anymore between light and dark due to his near-blindness, he fell asleep again, never thinking the trunk was speaking to him. It was heaven in there, and while God had spoken to him in his dreams, and God had revealed the needed tasks for his mission, Father Serra missed the message yet again as he was not one to understand hidden, veiled messages such as are sent from above.

He woke at noon; the sun shining through the stained glass windows of the church. The Indians outside could be heard laughing. His back felt stiff as he stretched to loosen up. Although rested, he did not recall getting there the night before. *How did I end up here last night? My mind is going*, he muttered. As he rose to stand, a muscle pulled tightly and snapped. His body ached, he was going blind, and his mind was no longer lucid like in the early days. The trunk stood unopened under him, a gift from above he did not consider, another missed opportunity to see his life work succeed, yet he never suspected this might be the answer to all his prayers. Had he so much as opened the trunk and read its contents, he would have found the teacher's greatest contribution to him written in a faded white tablet: *Be patient with the Indians.* Thirsty now and walking down the hall for a glass of water, Father Serra made a mental note to return to the trunk one day, but the day never came. Had he so much as read its contents he would have heard the words, *Here I am.*

For the moment, he said, *I need to empty my bowels.*

Father Serra walked to the back of the church, and squatted like the Indians. *Whoever built this church forgot to put in a toilet,* he shouted to no one in particular, his mind rapidly losing touch with reality;

there was no one to tell him he drew the plans for the church himself. He wiped himself with a dry leaf, squinting in the sunlight. Whatever papers he had in his quarters were for writing, not for wiping.

He thought of his youth, of how he'd desperately wanted to be in the church, to be a priest, to help others the way he'd never helped himself. He remembered that he always relied on God to help him through, that he'd felt helpless from a young age; he recalled his constant misery and self-loathing, for he loved boys. The urge to be with them naked and frolicking in the grass was disturbing; he did not know where this came from but he was not like the others. He did not play soccer or wrestle aggressively; he was a pansy who preferred books and dolls. His mother once came out of the bathroom one morning stark naked sending young Serra into shock. He ran to speak to his friend, because he was frightened by her hairy bush. His friend laughed at him. *That bush is most valued by men, sought after, eaten, craved, played with. Man comes from there, you fool. Just wait until you grow up. You're going to want some of that!* That day never came. Instead, he entered the priesthood spending his time around men; older, middle aged, young and stiff. His joy could not be hidden at the thought of spending a lifetime surrounded by masculine beings with similar desires of the flesh. He remembered being celibate for the forty five years at the desperate mile. It didn't matter, for he'd sinned plenty in his youth. The seminary had been a huge sex orgy: at night you walked the hall much the way queers cruise the streets; a hand would appear from the darkness, and then a mouth. The Spanish Conquest of America was won by men like these as women were forbidden to travel with Cortez and his crew.

He remembered the seminary as an exciting time. He never knew the identity of the conqueror, and they, in turn did not know him. There was no getting intimate and even less relationships. This was a haven for Catholic priests preparing to evangelize the New World. As they believed themselves to be mandated to spread the Word and protected by God Himself, their every sin was forgiven.

Father Serra's piss gurgled on the dirt underneath.

Perhaps sex was the cause of my misery, my sins. What was I thinking? Why, if not for my ex-

communication, I might be standing in front of the Pope himself, as Charge-d'Affairs. The old man had been thrown out of the church for refusing a Cardinal who desired him. It was then he decided to find the pagans, to continue with the Lord's work because as far as he was concerned he was forever a priest. Besides, no one in the jungle could stop him from spreading the gospel. No regrets today, his youth had been exciting: the secret hugs, the smooches, the dark and dank corridors, the veiled meetings, the embraces, the whispers, the silent sin. *Was life about sex? Was that my preoccupation? No wonder I'm in this hell-hole. Lord, forgive me? Would life have been different if I'd loved women? Absolve me, Jesus, I bleed!!!* He remembered his father tried to make him a man, sending him to the shoemaker, *to work, to learn to be responsible.* Boy Serra did not like it, it was too hard for him what with *All the yelling and screaming, and me, only a child, and soft. The shoemaker took advantage of me and sent me on errands to the puterías, where the whores asked I fix their high heels. They grabbed my pants and dragged me screaming to their rooms. They tucked my head into their huge breasts and I suckled. They laughed, and made fun, and asked why I walked funny, why I spoke like kings with a lisp. Father knew what I was, but insisted I be a man.* He wished he was back in Barcelona, or at the Seminary, anywhere but in this poor desolate forgotten place where the air was clear.

It's just the way it turned out, isn't it? Me, Father Serra, knows nothing...I, who serve God above and spread His word know no more than these poor, pagan, mute souls! Look how they readily smile at the world! Miserable as can be, but happy. Perhaps they know something about life that I don't. If that is the case, anyone in this misbegotten world knows more than me! He grunted in his squat. The thoughts made it hard to move his bowels. *I have to stop thinking,* he said.

He grunted once more, this time to better results. He smiled, though his legs were cramping. After getting on his feet, he returned to his quarters firmly convicted to finish *The Conversion of the Mutes.*

MARY MAGDALENE Or, *The Pink Envelope*

Today I received an unsigned letter in the mail. Well, not in the mailbox, as the local letter carrier delivered it straight to me at the café where I hang out in the mornings to have my usual. His name is *Bulmaro* but everyone calls him "Bull." So he walks up and - *right in the middle of my croissant and espresso!* - (and just as I was writing about Rufino the Conqueror, no less), he said he was looking for me for days because this one particular letter smelled "very refreshing," and "lovely, not at all like all the others that come in a white envelope with 'Sr. Jaguar' scribbled on them." This one was addressed to "Dr. Healer Jaguar, son of Izquierdo, Oaxaca, City, Oaxaca, Mexico." It was in a bright pink envelope with beautiful, ornate handwriting, obviously a woman's; and it was decorated with tiny, little flowers all around, and get this: No return address.

I was surprised to receive such correspondence, and rather pleased I must say, because someone had taken the time to write me, to find me in Oaxaca City where I did not live, to draw little doodles on the envelope as if in love, or during a phone conversation filled with arid thoughts of sex and rock n' roll.

Perhaps the sketches meant nothing, maybe they did. I would certainly find out soon enough.

I signaled the waiter to bring me a shot of *Sambucca* as I knew it was Bull's favorite drink. As I watched him swig it down in a hurry I thought of the pink envelope, resisting opening it in front of him. I did not want the gossip to start with fictional stories of my new love far away and such, stories that were passed around town before and stories that never came true. As people will believe anything and hold it against you, I walked on eggshells when it came to my life because it is no one's business what I do or who I do it with. Regardless, the truth does come out in the end, but even so, the idea of living in privacy is still comforting. Bull slammed the shot glass on the café table, rocking the umbrella and surprising me and before I could react, he was on his way. Granting him his favorite drink was my way of thanking him for delivering the envelope without a fuss, it was also in the form of a tip; or rather, it was my tip; if I gave him money someone might report him to the authorities and he'd be out of a job and a great pension. I did not want to get him into trouble. Mexico was now trying desperately to destroy the very corruption it thrived on, the bribery that kept it well-oiled and running, a vice that is the heartbeat of the country - all to no avail, as Mexican politicians are weak, heartless, spineless men whose venom spews and drools on anyone traversing their path. These guys will readily steal from their mothers to get ahead in what they see as a free-for-all, greed-obsessed Mexico available to those willing to slit throats and kill without so much as battering an eyelid. The very President's brother was found to have embezzled millions of dollars in drug money, money he personally seized from the drugrunners, thinking he could safely deposit it in a Houston bank and get away with it. Today he was living in a high-security, white-collar prison in the States while his brother the ex-President was in exile in Ireland. These men are the role models for Mexican politicians. The list goes on and on. Mexico would never rid itself of the corruption because it was a necessary good for all involved. Corruption in Mexico is not considered evil because it is the foundation of the very bureaucracy that condemns it.

I looked about now and noticed the city's plaza was uncharacteristically quiet this morning - the birds sang too gently, the sun was not quite bright, no wind to caress the trees; a siren in the distance rang its tune, an Indian woman walked her barefoot children to school as they followed close behind, a flotilla of army men marched the goosestep as if ready to kill Indians; the Hertz rental office had not yet opened its doors. I decided to skip my second cup of espresso and headed to the local *mercado* down the street where an old, one-armed lady served the best *huevos con chorizo* in all of Mexico. On the way there I smelled the envelope, holding it close to my nose; I heard greetings from business owners as I passed by but did not respond as I was in my own little world thinking of the future. The shop owners shrugged shoulders dismissing me in return; I often spent time talking to them and buying little trinkets to befriend them as I knew one day I would need them; more so, I took my visiting American friends to spend lots of money there. The guys loved me.

The envelope gave me giggles, it made me smile, it made me happy today because even as Bull said: "There is something special about this one Doctor."

People loved to call me Doctor because I had a Ph.D. and because they consider me a Healer.

So it happens that I sat at *Ermenegilda's Luncheonette* - on one of the thousand stools in the mercado - and began to read:

Jaguar

      Jaguar

Jaguar   *Jaguar:*

You don't know me o.k. so I'll be blunt - it doesn't matter, does it? like you would say in your own words.

I   am   in   love love love with YOU.
Now, I am sure that you are probably married or have a beautiful girlfriend (or 2) sooooooooo: why not ONE MORE?
I want not only to meet you, but be with you there at the desperate mile; I want to run around naked and happy. (I have a royal-blue thong, in case I need one.) I want to rebuild the jungle w/ BIG papaya trees and mangoes, I want to place fresh fish in the river; I want to be mute too. And learn to read your mind and never speak. I

want to have your children and smile and be innocent and meet Izquierdo too. It really doesn't concern me if you already have a family because I know the truth: that to be with you is heaven on earth. My mother disagrees and says you are dangerous + I should stay away but I just CANT.

I am not:

- neurotic

- or

- crazy

- I am not:

- demanding!!!

- nor materialistic (???)

- not pushy

- nor ignorant.

I like:

SATIE

Debussy (Fields) --- get it, Jaguar? Do you?

Mozart Piano Concertos (No. 21 & 25)

I can live without U2 or the Stones but not without Bob Dylan!!!!!!! Man, he is the poet of the 20th century, isn't he, huh?

I CAN:

paint real good and cook and sew and use the hammer to build things; I have a good chainsaw my Daddy left me and some screwdrivers too. My favorite book is: 100 years of solitude and also ISHI, the last of his Tribe. Pablo Neruda turns me on, he was an incredible poet, don't you think? Contemporary culture depresses me because it is all about ego and money$$$$, the young people today are so vapid. I am not exactly old myself --- I can bare, 'bear, bore? --- many children if I have to. **J_A_G_U_A_R.** You and me. Me and you. I and you. Ha! Life is so down and depressing here in America. Kids are doing their bodies like, entirely with tattoos. They do drugs + carry guns and have babies at 15! They are lost and Daddy-less, or one-parent family thing, and go crazy w/ hate and self-hate. My Daddy died just a few years ago but he lived here w/ us even though he **hated** Mommy. They fought + then went into the bedroom + made lots and lots of love + screamed dirty things I heard them say to each other, and cried together +got drunk and then, like magic, they hated each other again!

Can you tell me what happened in America? Was it my fault? I was a good, always a good girl, so goooood, I got sick of it. I did everything right. I didn't have hot sex with the guys at school like all the trailer-trash chicks do. I am in college, but bored because my visiting professor, Mr. Gracia, says to "live life" like you, Jaguar, like you in order to write.

(At this point I am finished with the chorizo and eggs. I order a cup of cold *atole*.)

And me, just a young thing, want to go live there with you. I want to write and have courage someday. I don't have much now, in fact, I am shaking as I write this silly letter. I am smoking a cigarrette (sp?) in my underpants and blonde hair.

(Note to the Reader: this excites me: I love smoking.)

I am thinking of Jaguar the medicine man, writer, genius. I am S U R E you are sexy and goodlooking too...Why isn't there a picture of you in your books? Like in other writers books? Are you afraid of being seen? Found out? There are no secrets in life my Daddy used to say. But me, I will take some to my grave when I die! Oh!! **will you read my mind when we meet**? Please don't write about my secrets in your book! It would be so embarrassing!

I like to run, so I am in gooooooooood shape. I run about 8 miles a day and am faster than most guys. I think about a ton of things when I am out there on the road, running, running, running, mostly breathing.

I do not go out with guys here they are too backward, so young and unmotivated. They think I am weird because I love to read. Ugh!!! I want to do things w/ my life and go places and not stay here in this small town w/ no soul. Teresa down at the store is cool 'cuz she was in the theatre in New York ---do you know her? - and she likes to direct plays here at the wharf. They call it the wharf though there is no water for hundreds of miles! I dream of the ocean and whales and sea loins-oh, sorry, wrong spelling---and I dream of the desperate river where the fish used to come to you in offering of themselves. I dreampt (sp?) I was on a big kite flying over a lake and the birds were talking and I understood them!

I talked to a plant the other day? and it flowered the next day! I didn't even know the plant had flowers.

My life is boring here but I know that will all change when I meet you at the desperate mile. I think of myself as complete human being. I met a Zen master who said, "Who you are today is who you have always been." I believe that. I live the triangle of life: the physical, the mental, the spirit. Take care of all three + you will be alright!

(Another Note: At this point there is a neat, little row of sunflowers separating the next passage in the letter. I love it so far.)

So when we meet, Jaguar, I am going to scream probably real loud and maybe scare people a little bit but not too much because I'll be excited and all that, maybe I'll jump around 2 like when my team wins on t.v. I like to watch football on t.v. the Miami Dolphins, their outfits are real cool, I mean, their uniforms. My Dad used to sit all Sunday + just watch games till midnight + ALL THE highlites on the sports channel but he wouldn't drink beer like fat men do all over the country on their couches and dirty feet, big bellies + sweating heavily like elephants taking a shit---sorry, got outta hand; I like to get creative when I write and sort of, lose it, you know what I'm talking about? Im kinda trying to imitate you but i'll find my own style +voice someday. Oh I forgot to tell you, Jaguar, you will not Be-liev-e ---IT!

O.K.:

Here I am all alone in town ---it is a way small town here in the middle of america, ugh!--- YUK! actually-----and, the telephone rings. like off the hook and falls to the linoleum floor and I hear a little voice I recognize saying *"hello? hello, are you there?"* and it's my friend, well, not MY friend, a friends-friend who I met a bit of a while ago, maybe three months but I hadn't seen her...AND she goes: *"Mary Magdalene? —that's my name, can you believe it, I mean please! But I like it now that I think of it, huh?"*—Mary Magdalene she goes; *"YOU WILL NOT BELIEVE WHO I MET ARE YOU STANDING OR SITTING?"* And, well, me, I'm layin' down on the kitchen linoleum floor answering the phone, speaking to her and she didn't even let me answer that's how really excited she was to get me, and here I am thinking, maybe Tom Cruise or Johnny Depp but she like says: *"I HEAR YOU LIKE READING AND THE SOLITUDE OF DESTINY CHANGED YOUR LIFE."* And, me, dummy, I utter, *"Yeah?"* or, *"Uhm"* but before a thought comes outta my mouth she says *"she was in New York at this conference and she heard you speak at the Columbia University and she cried and was the only one to speak-up and that you were brilliant and so moving* *but only **she** got it of all those kids there. She won prizes for her writing but nothing like YOU or even like the River Sutra lady with the funny name. She writes boring stuff this girl that people say its like Hemingway, can you imagine how stiff that girl is?"* So I say, "*And what did you two talk about?*" She answers, "*are you sitting down?*" But this time she actually waits for me to answer.

She goes: "*O.K....We did it.*"

And then she pauses.

I ask: "*Did what?*" real stupid-like and she laughs so long her stomach hurts. I don't even know this girl very well at all like, so, her laughing makes me feel sort of defensive. Right?

"*We went and had ourselves some real sex!*" she says.

Oh. Aha! I get it now.

"*He touched me deep inside...at the lecture. I mean, if you listen real well to people you like or even admire or respect, you can learn tremendous things. You can see yourself reflected on them in some ways. And when he spoke, I listened...He made me cry.*"

"*Is he a bastard?*"

"No! Yes! Well, maybe, but not then he wasn't. He spoke with such...conviction, he got through to me and I really cried because I don't want to be vapid and LOST. I don't want my life to consist of laughter and money, money, money!"

And then, Dr. the girl on the other line was quiet, and I was listening to what seemed her heartbeat and she did this little sigh thing and I got JEALOUS because I didn't even know about the lecture-----I couldn't have gone but I would have liked to, even though later this girl told me it was for special writers.

Her name is Brigitte and I am YOURS,

MARY MAGDALENE

That was her signature, and that was the letter. Just like that.

As I said before, there was no return address.

I sat at the Luncheonette staring at the one-armed lady and not surprisingly, at her very stump. She looked at me sadly as if to say: *"If you only walked a day in my guaraches."*

I was embarrassed at being caught in the act of looking at her stump and could feel it as my face turned beet-red. I quickly grabbed a glass of water to hide my indiscretion but it didn't help. I wondered how often I'd done that without realizing it, how many other times she'd caught me doing the same, she, Ermenegilda López López Sánchez y López, as she called herself - but I couldn't remember if she'd ever called it to my attention. I realized quickly that Ermenegilda did not so much as blink when I stared at her because she was accustomed to having people gape at her stump and even ask questions.

"The children always stare" she once said.

I had a chance that day to ask her the story of the missing limb, but I dared not speak up. Normally I have balls like a bull, but for some reason I really felt like a chicken just then.

The pink envelope and Mary Magdalene were fresh on my mind and so was Brigitte, sex, and rock and roll. A cluster of German tourists with cameras in hand, wearing dark sunglasses and speaking in loud voices sat next to me at the counter wanting to eat. I'd seen them out of the corner of my eye searching for a place to eat, recognizing reluctance to lunch in what they must have considered a dirty environment. Speaking in German I heard one of them say he wanted to eat "like a dog." I wondered if he was hungry like a dog or if he normally ate the way canines do out of a bowl on the floor.

The pink envelope smelled so good: was it lavender? Citrus? Polo for Girls? Cloves? Mint, oranges, watermelon, roses, fresh rain, fresh-cut alfalfa, wet dirt, wet hair, the smell of diesel, apples?

I couldn't quite cut it: The smell.

I turned to the Germans.

"Could you define the smell of this envelope?"

I could tell by their arched brows they were surprised someone of my Indian looks spoke perfect German. They did not speak a word of greeting.

One of them said it smelled of women's perfume. "Musk, I think."

Was it Chanel No. 5? Opium? Elizabeth Arden?

"It does not interest me, your conversation" one of them said, protecting the others like a warrior. He turned his back to me.

"Have the picadillo" I recommended a lovely blonde in the group, as I tossed a 200 peso bill in front of Ermenegilda López López Sánchez y López.

"Yah, yah" I heard the German mutter, his back stiff like a pit bull.

Ermenegilda was known all over Mexico for cooking the hottest *picadillo* on the planet. Keeping tradition, the Germans would sweat and cry like children after a spoonful of this *picante* continuing to eat so as not to insult the Chef. They had exceptional manners these Germans.

I laughed out loud and wished them well.

* * *

Mary Magdalene writes interestingly, I thought. Not bad for a college girl. At times he writing seemed forced, but as I re-read the letter, I realized that she was doing a Jack Kerouac trip, or maybe, just maybe - what with all those flowers, doodles and punctuation - she may have a bit of the poetess in her. I know, go ahead and laugh at me, but to tell you the truth, I know very few people who have read more than me. Remember: *I can read people's lives, and with that comes all the reading they've ever done.*

You can never really teach someone to write - you can teach them how to write but not the writing itself. You have to have a nose, a smell, a scent for words, you know? You have to read many, many books and authors, people you don't even like, just to get an idea of writing. You have to work at it everyday for years and years, believe me; you must make a million mistakes and trash words, sentences, whole pages, books sometimes, the dearest words, the ones you love, the ones that don't fit into the story. Go ahead and keep them and see what they will do! They'll haunt you for ages, that's what they'll do. You have to be able to laugh at the words you write, laugh at yourself, even at the very writers you admire. But, and this is only a "but", you may already have the talent to write and not even know it. If you like to write, you will write on: paper, toilet paper, napkins, bathroom walls, on boxes, clothes, on your Dad's favorite newspaper or book; writing becomes a form of *graffiti,* you understand? You become a sort of artist without even realizing it. You will wake up in the middle of the night and shout to your girlfriend: *"Baby! I got it! I got the ending"* and run downstairs to find the typewriter, or the pen and pencil, tablet, notebook, computer, whatever; you stay up hours writing down the ending to the story you're working on, the ending that suddenly and surprisingly came to you in the middle of a dream.

The next morning your girlfriend does not make you coffee.

You write, you hear your voice, you read and re-read your words, correct the punctuation, change it, change it back again, and finally one day, you have a voice; a voice, your own voice unlike any other.

You love your punctuation because it speaks to you. You love your grammar because it replicates your thoughts. You love inventing and creating what does not exist.

I thought Mary Magdalene had the talent; it was, however, virginal.

I read the letter one more time at home.

The thought never occurred to me that one day Mary Magdalene might be sitting next to me, even less on my lap, she holding me, she whispering in my ear and laughing along at the silly things that come out of my mouth.

Instead, I thought I would suffer alone in silence for the rest of my days: my loneliness, my aloofness; "your indifference" as someone once astutely pointed out. I was seen as being indifferent, a thought that troubled me because my every effort with women was to feel loved, be loved, be reciprocated in what I gave; I wanted love to fill the void in my heart, a void without a name because I did not know what went in there. I knew it told me something was missing but I had no idea what that was. This was the mystery within.

This morning I carried my 'customary indifference.' Tonight, however, I would go to sleep with the pink envelope.

*

IN THE JUNGLE EVERYONE'S EQUAL

The day came when Jaguar couldn't stop thinking of the betrayal. He sat in his first-class seat on the battered Mexican train to Zacatecas, and remembered how tellingly insincere Mary Magdalene had been from the beginning. From the moment they met in Oaxaca City she had been one, big lie. As he traced back the memories, he found she'd lied about Humberto the Count, saying there was never anything between them. Humberto, in turn, told me everything, and proudly so, I must say; he recounted events and incidents where the two not only embraced, but also made violent love on rooftops, on top of cars, in the yard surrounded by peacocks – *"how delightful!"* he stressed - and even up in the high Sierras where they'd trekked with the Huicholes. They'd been high on cocaine, mezcal, peyote, tequila, and beer. *"It was at once an illusion, and a dream,"* said the Count.

She'd never been the same after being with him. She got the high, the adrenaline rush of hot love-and-sex; indeed, needed the high in life, because there was something urgent missing in her and that was trust. Sex covered up the emptiness that comes with isolation. She didn't trust herself and she couldn't trust others. Every word out of her mouth was a lie, and all at my expense I must say. She'd gone from man to man without so much as understanding the vicious cycle of repeating herself again and again. As it happened, when I met her, or rather, when she sought me out in Oaxaca, she'd just minutes before ended her relationship with Humberto, and, although she did not tell me then, that was the reason we ran into him in Oaxaca City that particular day. As I recall, when he saw her pregnant, there was a tremendous sadness and hurt in his eyes, a pain and longing he attempted to hide. This is what Mary Magdalene did to men. She used and hurt them and regretted nothing.

"There is nothing to regret in my life," she once said.

"I have never lied to you," she once muttered.

"Never question my loyalty," was another statement she made, one of the many discovered to be lies.

I took the lies, because I loved her, because I fell for her trap, thought Jaguar, bitterly recalling the hurt inside, *because she was beautiful and because if the devil is a woman it was Mary Magdalene indeed.* How ironic the devil has such a name.

I am not saying she did me wrong. No, I am saying I hurt. I am saying she hurt me in the end with all her cover-ups and pretenses and the inability to be open and honest and straight with me. I gave her everything I had and then some, and then a settlement most people could live with for three generations and still it was not enough. She had to rip everything out of me by punishing me with her pettiness, her greed for money, her vengeance, her lust for deceit; nothing was ever enough and that included, in the end, leaving with someone, a new man, a gringo traveler she met in the city, insulting me by bringing him home on her way to pick up the last of her things.

"Oh. you're that famous writer!" he exclaimed as I answered the door, she making sure to hold his hand as I watched in horror. She was so good at hurting and attacking and making a point of it even if it meant hurting herself in the process. Yet, it was all a lie, so,

whatever she said, any action she took, was deception. I learned her tricks and doings, and even accepted them in some odd way because I loved her. I knew she would never change, that she would continue hurting me; that she would jump on to the next man without missing a beat because the truth was she was afraid of being alone. She was getting-on in age, although not nearly as old as me, that's for sure, but then, women age faster than men. I don't know what this man did for a living and I do not care; she subsequently ended with yet another man: an emergency room doctor fifty years old who worked the graveyard shift.

"Fifty years old and he doesn't have his own practice? And he works in the emergency room during the graveyard shift? Can you imagine what a medic he must be, someone asked one day I longed to see her?

A friend called from New York City with news. He'd run into her at the pharmacy where she was getting a prescription - from the 50 year-old medic, no less - for her newly-tucked face: her plastic surgeon had pulled the skin too tight and she needed eye drops to keep them from drying out, funny enough like the guy in *A CLOCKWORK ORANGE*. My friend who ran into her, a doctor himself asked her: *What is wrong with your eyes, Mary Magdalene, they're watering?* He knew, of course, well, he could tell right away that she'd been the victim of bad surgery and he sort of tortured her with questions for me.

She looked deep into her eyes before answering his question, wondering who this stranger was questioning her by name.

"We met in Oaxaca recently when I went to see Jaguar" he explained, jarring her memory. She in turn, pretended to forget. She had to burn me out of her memory no matter what, I had to disappear forever, be null and void, and be dead to her because the memory of me was enough to drive her to drink. She tried to kill me in her heart, but this man insisted on bringing me back to life. *"I came for a prescription"* was all she said. My friend the doctor surprised her by swiftly taking the prescription from her hand to get the information he needed. When he saw the medic's signature he called the Medical Association and discovered the charlatan had several complaints against him for molesting teenage girls.

Mary Magdalene lived with him until she discovered his infidelities.

Oh, well, another man, another dollar. The girl just kept on moving; repeating the cycle that enveloped and consumed her until she got tired and old and nobody looked at her anymore.

Now she wrote horoscopes for a magazine.

As Jaguar thought about her for the hundredth time that morning, the Mexican train halted to a stop. There were loud voices shouting about, you could hear complaints, women yelling and screaming, nothing out of the ordinary in Mexico let me tell you. Suddenly the train filled with masked men, their faces covered like in the movies with big guns like in the movies too, they came barreling down the corridor menacingly pointing at everyone who looked their way. Jaguar, more out of courage than logic, stood up and, with a booming voice, announced: (in Spanish)

"Mexican citizens, fear not evil; for above all, God is our Savior!"

And mysteriously, the masked men stopped in their tracks and looked at him, seeming to recognize him.

"Yes," he said identifying himself. *"I am Jaguar."*

There was a brief moment of silence as people looked in wonder. No one on the train had really taken the time to notice him, as at that time in life, there was nothing particularly outstanding about him, except for his strong Indian face; but then in Mexico many people have strong Indian faces. He was, at this point, unrecognizable because he loathed pictures. They looked at him in disbelief indeed.

"La soledad del destino" he claimed, pointing to himself. That was the title of his first book, an international bestseller day after day after day for years and years and years. It'd been turned into a movie starring the latest teenage star and starlet, with music by *Mochado,* the most sensational new music group to hit the international scene since the Beatles. People had seen the movie and read the book and caught the huge ads on buildings, radio and TV. Jaguar was rich for the fifth time in his life and so, he could, by all means and purposes, stand-up to bandits on any train to display his valor. There was an awkward silence in the compartment as these Mexicans did not want to destroy one of their

own, not yet anyway, for Jaguar was as Mexican as they come what with his strong Indian features and Aztec nose, the black hair to his shoulders, the muslin shirt and khaki pants. All he needed was to be sitting against a wall covered by a sombrero to fill the stereotype.

One of the bandits pointed at him and asked:

"If you are who you say you are, then tell me: how did Addison Stonefreund die?"

There crowd murmured, the masked ones listened carefully. This was surely a test, thought Jaguar, but what the poor bandito didn't know, was that anyone who read the book could answer that question. Jaguar looked about at his newfound audience. He'd piqued their interest.

"I'll tell you what', he said. *'I* will tell you a story instead; one that you have not heard, because I have not included it in my books."

The audience sat, calm now, others smiled, yet others looked on with interest.

Jaguar began.

What he was doing was controlling the crowd, buying time from these robbers in order to read their minds, to uncover their identities, to find their weakness, to see where they lived; later turning them in to the police. But he knew that if he did, the *Federales* would lock them up for life.

"*So you remember the story of Addison Stonefreund?*' he asked, receiving nods all around. '*Well, it turns out that he, in real life, like you and me, was a real person; like you and me.*"

Wow, this got the crowd going. The whole world thought his characters were made up, though every bit of print mentioned the book was based on true stories. There was no way anyone could have missed that bit of information unless you lived on the moon. It was a bestseller because people simply did not believe the desperate mile really existed.

"*Addison Stonefreund was the son of a well-known Vice President of the United States; Nelson Stonefreund*" There were some chuckled responses because, for the most part, old Nelson was but a mere memory, even in his own country, let alone in Mexico. His name alone sounded comical.

"*Well, a few years ago, ladies and gentlemen of this beautiful country, I saw Addison Stonefreund with my very own eyes! Yes! I did, and I will now tell you that story.'*

The passengers shifted in their seats and paid attention; you could hear the steam of the train whistling softly as if impressed by the author. One would have thought the audience was dipping into the popcorn like in a good movie.

"I was driving to the village of Yagul, outside of Oaxaca City, in my old '65 Chevrolet that I keep for memories, when in the distance I spotted a family of four walking down the road. They looked nothing like us Mexicans, well, not from the distance anyway. The man wore a round hat, like from Australia, or somewhere. It wasn't a peasant hat, like yours, Señor." He pointed to a man with a sombrero. The man tipped his hat in respect.

"As I drove closer, I noticed the woman was Indian and very, very beautiful. She wore an extravagant huipil, her hair braided with flowers; the children walked barefoot on the road like we do, no huaraches indeed; but they had blond hair!" Here he made a gesture that stopped the little chatting that was

going on. He flailed his arms like a chicken, as if expressing confusion. Oh boy, was this man an actor!

"Then I noticed the man. He wore khaki pants with a safari shirt, just like Addison Stonefreund! Well, I slowed the car when I knew it was he; I decided to speak to him, to see if it was really him or if it was just my imagination, see? So I asked softly and with a voice the children liked: "Excuse me Señor, do you need a ride into town? "And the man with the hat turned to me, and with the brightest smile I had ever seen, said: "No gracias, Señor. Muy amable."

"And his voice was soft and quiet, reflective indeed but most assuredly, a strong one. His was a voice that had never been listened to but by his lovely wife. You see, no one in Addison Stonefreund's life had ever paid attention to him. His family was busy, and because of their famous name, they simply expected he would do well in life because he was a Stonefreund."

Jaguar took out a cigarette and tapped it on his wristwatch. Before he could take out his lighter, the *señor* with the hat struck a match and brought it to his cigarette. Jaguar tipped his hat, thanking him.

"What the Stonefreund family thought all along was that Addison had died ago dead, you see, that he'd been eaten by cannibals in New Guinea, but the truth was that he was living somewhere in Oaxaca, forgotten, disappeared and loving it. He lived the life he'd always wanted, had a small family, bothered no one, and no one bothered him. He was free, you see? Free from the restrictions in life that we, as human beings, place on ourselves." The pause was stifling. The passengers and the thieves thought this over. *What restrictions in life,* they asked themselves? *You mean poverty? Do you mean oppression? Do you mean to say my dead-end life?*

The professor forced them to think for themselves, to look about and maybe take up where the Revolution ended a hundred years ago.

The people sat in deep thought, considering if they had what it takes to change their world.

"Was this really Jaguar telling the story?"

"Could it be true that he came out of hiding just as the robbers took the train?"

"Were the robbers going to change their minds and leave?"

"*Can we revolt against Mexico again? What will we gain by that?*"

Jaguar looked about the compartment looking for the rebel leader. It turned out he was a boy of fifteen. Jaguar could tell by his eyes.

"*Hijo,*" he addressed him the way *chilangos,* or, people from Mexico City do one another.

"*Ven aquí.*" Come here.

The young man looked about and, just as if obeying his own father, walked up to Jaguar.

"*Sí, Don Jaguar. A sus órdenes.*"

"*Don't call me 'Don' Jaguar'. We are among the people, and you are not my servant.*"

Just then, and in a flash, Jaguar took the boy's rifle, placing it on the seat next to him. He looked the boy in the face.

"*How old are you?*"

"*Fifteen.*"

"*Why do you want to do this, rob people?*"

"*I need to eat.*"

"*Why don't you work?*"

"*This is work,*" said the boy, and everyone laughed. Jaguar smiled.

"Do you know that everyone in this train works? But they do not rob people. They sweat."

The boy bent his head in shame. The passengers now seemed less afraid, feeling easy and happy around Jaguar, who had quite powerfully taken over.

"What is your name, son?"

"Emiliano," he responded. *"Emiliano Zapata."*

The train broke into raucous laughter, but it did not last long because Jaguar raised his hand. The laughter stopped.

"Son: do you know you carry a burden, a heavy burden indeed."

They waited for the sage to speak again. They wanted to hear his definition of "burden." These peasants were getting an education, however brief.

The train was at a full stop, and now even the Conductor stood looking at the action, he quiet too, just like the others.

The boy did not answer Jaguar.

"You have a name of great reputation. And you have a responsibility to live up to it. That name brings tears of joy to people's eyes, don't you know that? Did

you see how everyone wanted to ridicule you because you take that name so in vain?"

The boy began to weep. Jaguar looked about. He walked to the window and pointed out.

"Go out there and continue the Revolution," he said, pointing to the fields planted with corn.

"This country needs you! The people in this car need you! We are all cheering for you. But make no mistake: instead of taking from the people, give back to them! That is the way to live up to a great name!"

And then Jaguar turned him around so quickly the boy did not have time to react; he shoved him through the crowd and right out of the train. Everyone stood in awe as the rest of the thieves followed. The conductor walked away to the front of the train. People looked out the windows, at the side show, the clown show, the circus this supposed Emiliano Zapata had just put on for the people.

As the train emptied of robbers, the train started to roll.

"Go!" he shouted to the bandits, *"go and get the Revolution going again! Mexico needs you!"* And with

this, the train left the station, once again on its way to the heart of the country where it is said God resides.

The rest of the ride was one big party, what with everyone buying Jaguar beers and the peasants popping their prized Tequilas and *mosquito* drinks, the *tehuino*; one old man even lit-up a marihuana cigarette that got the crowd laughing.

"Its good for my rheumatism," he said, pointing to his knees.

"It helps me with happiness!" a young man from the University cried out.

That day there was much happiness indeed. Jaguar felt like part of the people again.

It has been since forever, he thought, *that I felt part of the Indios.*

Where have I been, and what have I been doing? he asked himself as a tear came to his eyes.

It sure felt good to be home.

*   *   *

At that very moment in time, Izquierdo, his father, looked out the window of his *palapa* in the desperate mile and knew his son was coming to see him. Years had passed since they'd shared laughter or a cigarette, a drink, or even a meal of corn tortillas with turtle soup. The two men had parted ways long ago, though in mutual agreement, each going his own way, each in a different direction, each with a load of regret in his heart knowing very well they may never look into each other's eyes again.

Jaguar had long ago decided he was in love with a woman Izquierdo did not like. The three had spent a few days together in Santa Fé, New Mexico, chatting, drinking wine and discussing the latest indigenous news in the country. A renown Native American leader Leonard Peltier, it was whispered, might just be pardoned by the President who was about to leave office; Peltier was involved in defending Indian rights, was said to have led a band of renegades in the killing of a Federal Officer on the reservation. He was doing life without parole behind bars, safe from the *status quo* he so rightfully attacked as murderers of the Indian population. Casinos were bringing in lots of money but nothing was improving on the reservations. Native American languages were being lost and nobody was doing a thing to preserve them. The conqueror's *motto,*

"Kill the culture and you kill the Indian" was alive and well in America.

Now, the woman in this mess between father and son will from hereon be named the *Bitch*. It turns out one afternoon at lunch the bitch got drunk on some fine wine, and as was her habit when in that state of mind, she began cajoling, then pushing and finally insulting Jaguar in public such that he stomped out of the restaurant before the main course was served. Izquierdo, poor old man that he was, didn't move or say a word; he let his son run off as he ate finished his lunch next to the Bitch, speaking a Spanish she did not understand, and she, in turn speaking the English he fully ignored.

Somehow, they got along just fine, both pretending nothing ever happened.

When they returned to the house later, Jaguar was nowhere to be found. His traveling suitcase was gone along with his car, his best suit, and the gold Rolex a Swedish girlfriend gave him long ago. He loved the Rolex, because the girl had loved him regardless of his infidelities. He wasn't going anywhere without it.

The Bitch found a note taped to the door.

"*I am so glad to be rid of you! Hasta la vista, baby!*"

It was signed 'jaguar'. The writer always signed his name with a small 'j' mostly as an ode to his favorite poet, e.e. cummings. The signature was authentic, the ink still damp. The housekey was on the kitchen counter.

The Bitch knew Jaguar was gone.

As she looked at the note, Izquierdo read her mind: she'd never said she loved him, she'd never said she cared. She'd used him and abused him, not once mentioned "I need you" or, "I don't need you."

He sure is gone, thought the Bitch.

Izquierdo stood next to the abandoned woman who wept like a child; he took her chin in his hands. He looked her smack in the eyes and she, poor thing, looked into his, giving her life away. Izquierdo saw her entire life, and knew that she was a cold and calculating bitch, controlling, and fearful too. Her entire life had been a sham: she'd married Ronald Mess, a Swiss millionaire years and years ago knowing fully well that she did not love him. Mess, in turn, had a sexual problem that she would resent forever: he suffered from premature ejaculations.

She'd held this against him for years, ridiculing him at parties and in public until Mess finally erupted. His face red with anger, he vowed to make her pay. He would divorce her and leave her penniless. For him the last straw was the morning she called him limp dick. He never forgave her.

Their daughter Sandra was the product not of love, but of the Bitch's desire to have company, because Mr. Mess was busy running his European empire and had no time for her. She, in turn, could not be alone. Sandra was born from a premature ejaculation that landed in just the right egg.

Now the Bitch was alone again after insulting yet another man in public, alone like she would be for the rest of her insufferable, pitiful life.

Izquierdo saw the deep insincerity in her being and asked himself: *"So this is the woman my son wants to marry?"*

She'd been living in fear all her life: fear that her man would leave, abandon her the way her very own daddy abandoned her in Boston when she was eight years old. What she didn't realize, and what Jaguar couldn't get out of her head, was that her daddy did not abandon her; he left her mother, a bitch herself with whom he could not get along. The bitch-thing ran in the family.

She wept now, not because Jaguar was gone but because she'd have to be alone for a while, or, until she found another man to replace him. Izquierdo took note, forgiving his son for stomping out of the restaurant and leaving him in this mess because it was the best thing Jaguar could do, leave the woman altogether, and Izquierdo knew it. Jaguar needed to get rid of this cut-throat of a woman, get her out of his life, and move on to a young beauty who would appreciate him for what he was.

The bitch had money by the truckloads, houses, cars, servants believing that was her *raison d'être, when in truth she was an opportunist who took from anyone even taking back anything she might give of good will. An "Indian Giver," Jaguar called her because many a time she would gift him only to take it back the next day in retribution for something said.

"This woman is insincere," Izquierdo said, looking into her soul.

At the moment, though, the bitch sat crying on the sofa, trying to muster up some pity from the old man.

It did not work.

"I am going to sleep" he announced and started towards the bedroom. There was the semblance of a voice from behind him, but he ignored it with a slam of the door. The door reverberating was a much sweeter sound to his ears than her cries of pity.

But let me be clear: this little episode was not what created the wedge between father and son. What soon followed did.

A few days later when Izquierdo landed safely at the Oaxaca airport he was picked up by a big fella, a chauffeur sent by none other than his son Jaguar.

"Señor Izquierdo?"

"Si?"

"I am your chauffeur. I will drive you home."

Once on board, the chauffeur read Izquierdo a telegram.

"Izquierdo. I drank too much the other night and got angry. It wasn't you. I hate that woman but for some crazy reason,

I cannot do without her. I'll be with her
if you need me. Getting married today.
jaguar."

Izquierdo blew a fuse, though not because he did not know how to read, nor because he'd never learned to do so; no, Jaguar had learned to read and write with Father Serra at the desperate mile. Izquierdo on the other hand, was from another time, from a time capsule when nobody for hundreds of years even knew that language could be written. The Indians communicated through the telepathy but their rich, oral tradition was now vanishing right before the old man's eyes.

Instead, the note spoke volumes.

The more Izquierdo thought about it, the more insulted he was by his son's behavior:

Why didn't his son call on the telephone to tell him the news?

Why didn't he deliver the news himself?

Why did Jaguar rob him of the joy of attending the vows, even if he was marrying the Bitch?

Why did Jaguar insist on ruining his own life by marrying this insincere person??

He would try to figure out his son and thought it might take time.

He never suspected it would take 28 years.

*   *   *

In those twenty eight years Jaguar married, divorced, argued, fought, got in bar fights, ran marathons, played trumpet in bands, dealt with women, called them names, was put in jail, taught school, tutored students, mentored students, made lots of money, spent all of his money, wrote books, cried on doorsteps, nearly committed suicide, returned to school, got a doctorate, practiced yoga, meditation, Tai Chi, Karate, studied Jazz dance, the Tango and even ballet; he went to church, even the Vatican, he painted churches, saw plays, befriended the actor Richard Harris, betrayed himself, betrayed others, masturbated, drove fast cars, lived in Italy, laughed in German, dined in Paris, and let a cheap girl break his heart.

What he didn't do in all those years was see his father.

Jaguar decided that Izquierdo abhorred the long-gone and now forgotten bitch. He, the son, had so desperately wanted to marry that he betrayed his father Izquierdo. Jaguar lived in shame, in a guilt that consumed him day and night during those three short years of marriage. He carried the hurt, hiding in drink. He drank like a fish trying to drown in the ocean. He went to pot, his health began to rot, but soon realized he could both drink and take care of his body so he began training again for the grueling marathons in Manhattan and Boston, Big Sur, Mexico City and Addis Ababa. The Ethiopian run was comprised of the fiercest runners ever to take the field and Jaguar, being Indian, knew he looked out of place. There was only one white man in the race that day, a sickly-looking Brit who insisted on being considered an elite runner. His time was in the low 2:50's. Jaguar ran a 2:09.

His father's image was always present, always bothering him, always speaking to him, instructing and criticizing him such that Jaguar would wake in the middle of the night soaked in a toxic sweat, a sweat he knew was implanted during his brutal apprenticeship with Izquierdo who never let a thing slide.

Jaguar moved to Barcelona, home of his old mentor at the desperate mile, Father Serra. He didn't like it there and so after three months he moved to France, then to Belgium - where he took-up with a pretty, 18 year-old girl, then is was off to Rome, next Zurich, then Boston; he returned tired and weary to New York, but got assaulted by a gang of drunken Puerto Ricans who nearly took his prized Rolex; he left for Phoenix the next morning where he desperately looked to rise from the ashes. Tucson, San Francisco and LA; Santa Fé and New York again, only to end up in Dallas with Candy, a redheaded who'd once slept with Truman Capote.

Jaguar was running away from something, he didn't know what; not only was he running marathons but he was running from life. He acknowledged it, but deep inside he did not know what ate at him.

He thought it had to do with the bitch, that it was maybe a kind of divine punishment for having married her without his father's consent. Tired of running, he took a brief trip to Santa Fé to look her up, to maybe figure out the past; to see if she was the last piece of the puzzle in making his life work. Maybe being there and seeing her again would help, maybe apologize for leaving her would help solve the mystery of his shitty life. She had been untrue, yes, an insincere bitch indeed, a liar, a phony of the worst kind, yet, she deserved an apology; she spoke ill of all of her friends, her closest friends calling them names. A bigger hypocrite did not exist in this world, thought Jaguar. Still.

At his old coffee shop hangout he ran into a longtime friend. Jaguar hinted about and finally asked if there was any word on the bitch.

"Oh, that bitch!' exclaimed the friend. *"I'm sorry,"* he said immediately, thinking Jaguar still loved her. The writer shrugged his shoulders, encouraging his old friend to continue, assuring his buddy that it was all right to talk openly.

"That woman is the worst," he opened up. *"She promised people money and security, talked up her millions and just bought people right and left. Men fell for her talk. She got old and tired, and I think she's in a home now. They say she's paralyzed."*

A lot of good the money did her.

Jaguar felt a twang of joy, then guilt, for it is not good to wish others ill.

"To see her in a home, an old people's home, just like her mother, and alone, abandoned by her selfish daughter indeed, and paralyzed!"

Jaguar wondered if it was true.

"What did she do to you," he asked his friend. "You sound bitter."

Buddy shifted in his seat. In a moment, he waved his hand as if to say, "Forget it."

Jaguar kept on, never letting up. It was his way. He would get the truth from this guy no matter what. He was so relentless in his pursuits, that he'd once finished a marathon with a broken ankle after the 25th mile.

Buddy relented. He'd kept the resentment inside for years, now it was time to let it out. He smirked as if to want to hurt Jaguar, to pierce his heart like white men love to do.

"She made promises that she couldn't keep. I got involved in one of those promises and she didn't keep her word."

"Did you sleep with her?"

"Who didn't," the white friend replied.

Ouch. That hurt.

The bitch had gone through many men since Jaguar deceiving each and every one of them, and now, she lay paralyzed in a home, unable to hurt anyone, unable even to scream out the hate that possessed her, that ate her alive. Jaguar imagined her sitting there pondering how this happened, how to get her life back.

"What did she promise you?"

"She told me she'd put away 100 grand for my future. I believed it. And when we ended, she laughed in my face when I brought it up."

"I never put anything away for you" she said. *"She used me for sex, Jaguar, for company, like a toy. We slept together for a year or so, until I got tired of her lies and deceptions."* Buddy was not a happy camper either.

"She'd been seeing another guy the whole time."

"Why did the money matter so much to you?"

"I am not rich like you, Jaguar. I am not getting any younger, and my paintings are not selling."

There was a silence Jaguar understood well. He'd *been* this guy way back when. He'd been broke for years, thought his life would never change, that it would never change without money. He'd had to borrow money to finish his first book. You need money to get along in this world. So when the book was published the money made a big difference. He was free to do as he wanted, he could toss fear to the wind, live anywhere in the world and take up with that special beauty he had his eyes on, because he knew she needed heavy maintenance. He could feast without famine, that's the type of money came rushing in. The bitch, in turn, was always scared he would leave her, because now that he had money he didn't need her; her bickering and attacks escalated, her assaults on his manhood, all the time thinking that money protected her from evil, and paralysis.

Sitting in her wheelchair, the bitch recalled how it ended. Buddy left her after the money argument, and she felt abandoned yet again. She could not keep a man that was clear enough; without warning as thoughts tend to take over by surprise, her life's abandonment issue came to a head. Wanting the nurse to take her to her room but unable to shout or speak, she was forced to look at the truth: the truth was it was she who abandoned her father's wishes. It was she who had betrayed her father back in Boston by never revealing to him that Guido beat her. Her Italian father had clearly instructed her the day of her marriage that if this boy ever beat her, she should go to him right away. Instead of reporting the abuse, she left Guido, house and all. The result was that Dad got so pissed at her for leaving the boy he considered a son he promptly disinherited the bitch leaving Guido his every penny on his dying day. And a pretty penny it was.

"I am sorry to hear your work is not selling, buddy" said Jaguar. *"I wish I could help you in some way."*

Buddy stared at Jaguar and grinned.

"You can help me by buying one of my paintings," he said, not knowing Jaguar was ready with an answer, to counter this insulting white boy for offending him earlier.

Jaguar smiled like a cat ready to pounce. *I can see what happened between these two: Buddy and the Bitch. Why they are no different from one another!*

Jaguar did not want to hurt his Buddy's feelings, but the truth really mattered to him. He remembered how the Bitch nicknamed him "the seeker of truth."

"Why does the truth matter so much to you?" she screamed at him at the top of her voice, indicting

him, assaulting him for wanting to get to the truth of things.

She lived in such a world of lies that truth to her was like leprosy.

Jaguar looked at Buddy, ready for revenge.

"I would buy your paintings but I've don't like your work."

Ooh that hurt. Buddy got so pissed he yelled at Jaguar.

"Who the hell do you think you are," and things like that. But Jaguar ignored him as he climbed into his new Range Rover and drove away.

He asked about her around town but nobody knew or cared what had become of her. That was her worth now. Jaguar on the other hand was alive, and well, and strong, with still another forty years to live.

"What color were her eyes, anyway?" he asked himself driving down Paseo de Peralta, past yet another row of his old haunts, past the many ghosts of his long life. As he did not get the chance to apologize, he felt the familiar pang of resentment in his still existing, inner void.

After another day or so of inquiries, she was gone from the radar.

*   *   *

At the moment, Jaguar the accomplished writer, poet, and professor of anthropology thought of the old man; of his frail health, of how he might look bent over in the shame of old age, walking carefully down the dirt streets of the village, his eyes smiling when told of his grandson Izquierdito, the grandson he did not yet know because the years had passed without a word between father and son.

Little Izquierdo was now a young boy living with his mother in New York, a living replica of the old man if ever two people looked alike. His face resembled old Izquierdo, the boy spoke in the same slow manner as his grandfather, why the child even walked with the gait that distinguished Izquierdo from other men. Jaguar marveled at the likelihood of two persons from two different generations being so identical in almost their every way. The day would come when the two would meet and laugh at the sight of each other. *"He looks just like me,*" they joke, looking into the mirror without wanting to do so.

Each lived in different parts of the world though young Izquierdo knew only that his grandfather had the same name and lived in the jungle because his mother Mary Magdalene made sure to keep as much from him as possible. She did not want the boy to favor his father in the end turning his back on her. This way she controlled the boy, keeping him from learning of his past and unique origins. He could travel to the desperate mile when he grew up if the urge came, but for now, all he knew was his paternal side was from a place named Oaxaca.

As the old man had not heard from Jaguar in 28 years he suspected no grandson, remembering him as the last time he saw him, young and in love with a woman he disliked, rich and living in the world outside his place of birth. Izquierdo projected nothing, invented nothing, and expected nothing from his son. The old man would be surprised to learn he had a grandson, yes, but then time would rush at him and forgetting the 28 years that passed so quickly, he would get present to time, to his age and to his fragility. Izquierdo would look in the mirror and see a man older by 28 years and a son, gray-haired and happy.

Because the last time he saw Jaguar he was miserable.

The young boy, Izquierdito, asked repeatedly about the origins of his name. He wanted to know why he had only one name and not two, like all the other kids at school. Mother gave no answers. As she learned to hate the elder Izquierdo for brutalizing Jaguar during his apprenticeship, she never let that go even after the divorce, and so in some strange way time had never lapsed for her, her hate was as fresh in her as the day Jaguar told her of the brutal way the old man treated his son growing up. Jaguar the pagan had unabashedly spoken ill of his father through the years. He told anyone who listened that his dad was abusive and hurtful, controlling and manipulative, mean and evil. Naturally, Mary Magdalene felt her husband's pain and took sides against the old man.

He told a story that made his father look like a monster, and everyone believed it. But Jaguar told this to cover up his shame for having discarded Izquierdo from his life, because after all, the old man at the desperate mile was his only bloodline. His mother had been dead for years.

And so now, as he took in the fresh air of the Copper Canyon, he thought that, yes, the old man would indeed be very happy when told of his grandson Izquierdito.

"I can't imagine a world without Indians," the young boy once said to his daddy. The kid was working on a class project, painting a nativity scene with the characters as Indians. Daddy laughed.

"Why do you laugh, Dad?'

"Because it makes me happy to hear you say that."

They embraced.

They bonded that evening, in a way that nearly embarrassed the two. Their relationship was different from that day on; it was loose and happy instead of dark and strained from the pressure at home, the pressure of keeping a sour-faced, miserable Mary Magdalene happy. They laughed, and played, and rough-housed anywhere in the house, Jaguar turning into the child he never got to be at the desperate mile, the child he would have liked to be. The two playfully wrestled so often that one afternoon mother came home from the store to find the usually tidy house in shambles.

"What is going on here?" she screamed.

The house filled with laughter.

"We've been rough-housing, dear," replied Izquierdito imitating the way Jaguar spoke to her.

Mother was not amused, but the boys ate it up. They giggled and laughed, pointed fingers at Mother who was now visibly steaming in anger and soon the two were laughing at her and her ridiculous and useless seriousness under the present circumstances. Mary Magdalene was upset the two were having their way, and for being made fun of; soon the boys were rolling on the rug holding their bellies from so much laughter, asking the other to *"Stop laughing,"* as they found mother a sight to see. The laughter grew more when Izquierdito cried out, *"I'm going to pee my pants!"*

"Clean this mess, now," shouted Mother, but the boys did not pay her any mind. Well, the only thing *that* caused was more laughter. Soon, Mom herself couldn't take it anymore and joined the laughter, was pulled to the floor by Jaguar and onto the pile. Soon, the family

was laughing together, kicking and screaming every which way to *"Stop it!"*

They laughed until no more tears rolled from their eyes.

They lay hugging each other, breathing heavily, in loving delight.

"We haven't been this happy in forever," said she, never stopping to think she might be the problem.

A deep, penetrating sadness overcame them, and the house was back to normal.

Only the tidying-up remained.

*   *   *

Izquierdo would smile in his deathbed, and wish his namesake well.

"You named him after me, then?" he would ask. *"I thought you forgot me for good."* Jaguar would weep; he would bow his head in shame, and finally, cry like the child he really was, for he'd never grown up, in his heart he had always been a *niño*.

*   *   *

The journey home was grueling. Jaguar wondered why at the last minute he'd decided to cancel the plane reservation taking the train instead. He had to cross the whole country of Mexico on rails, continue south for several days, climb a mule, and traverse the thick jungle he once called home. This meant people, time, waiting, stops, the smokers on the train with their heavy-smelling tobacco; he did not mind the peasants like Gringos do, no, for he himself was once a peasant, and he did not like to distinguish his people that way.

All in all, the traveling took its toll. A quick jet would have done the trick.

Anxiety was eating away at him as he walked through the train. He arrived at the *Café* section without spotting a single interesting, or entertaining thing.

Well, none that looked it on the surface anyway.

Except for Norwegian Helga, who sat quietly in a booth by herself reading a book and sipping tea.

She was alone, and that was all that mattered.

"Avanti," Jaguar said to himself, the conqueror within ordering the attack. He marched to the table his pride glowing.

Jaguar was a man of many flaws. Although he'd worked and overworked his weaknesses to a point of boredom, he still found himself as imperfect as they come. What he had was courage, the very thing that got him through life. His most obvious flaw was a weakness for women. Though he knew they were trouble, he was looking for love and perfection, the two most elusive elements in life, he admitted. Yet, this woman was a now martini, *that* one a Merlot; yet another, a Grand Marnier. Women to him were to drink in, her variations endless, and for that he was grateful, for he never liked repeating himself for anyone.

"This Helga must be a shot of Schnapps," he said and smiled.

The black stewardess he'd conquered years ago was not even a memory. The actor Harvey Keitel's girlfriend, who Jaguar so often and successfully cornered in New York City, was fresh in his mind. She'd fallen for him right in front of the actor and hidden nothing. Jaguar waved her over and together they entered the unisex bathroom and did the nasty in a stall. The actor was so busy talking about his latest movie that he didn't notice his girlfriend disappeared. The writer waltzed around town with her for months until the next girl appeared.

Now, as this Norwegian beauty was about to be surrender, Jaguar felt the pangs to come, salivating at the thought of her milky, white breasts in his mouth.

So as life would have it, it just happened that Norwegian Helga was young, beautiful, entertaining and willing to go along for the ride. Few women ever resisted Jaguar's charm; he could count the women who'd spurned him in one hand. Whether married, divorced, single, young, old, mature: they went for him and his sexual presence. He purred like a cat and they loved it. Sure, he was a famous writer and rich, but most girls never knew this as he kept it to himself. The conquest always tasted better by one's own efforts. All he had to do was show up.

Norwegian Helga looked up from her book as the writer sat at her table.

"Do you mind if I sit here?"

"Please say something interesting, I'm bored to tears."

Instead of letting him say another word, she went on with a lengthy greeting in her accented English.

"I didn't know anyone on this train spoke English; I thought I'd have to wait 'til Mexico City or whatever, but I'm glad you do. I sure am glad. My name is Helga. And I am ---"

She stopped herself.

"--- How is it you speak English? You look like a peasant."

Jaguar chortled and laughed.

"I am a simple peasant."

And then he stood, and with his usual reluctance for handshakes, he extended his hand.

"I am your humble servant."

Helga smiled, and took his hand.

"Does my humble servant have a name?"

"Give me one, I beg you. I am dying to reinvent myself. It's been years."

Helga laughed. She found him amusing, amusing indeed.

"Sit down," she ordered, pounding her fist on the table, making it sound like a Nazi command.

"Do you want a Spanish name, necessarily?"

Jaguar shrugged.

"French, maybe?"

"*No, no. Please not French,*" he pleaded, remembering the reverence high-collared Mexicans have for everything French, forgetting Maximilian was shot dead by a firing squad by orders of Benito Juarez. Jaguar did not resent the French, but he could certainly live without them.

"*German, perhaps. No, no, you don't look German.*"

"*Did Frida Khalo look German?*"

"*What*" she asked.

"*Did Frida Khalo look German?*"

"*Touché. You have a point.*" She took a deep breath.

"*Seattle,*" she exhaled. "*I will call you Seattle, like the Indian Chief. I've been reading the history of Native Americans and so Seattle it is.*"

Jaguar laughed.

"*I like this, Seattle and Helga.*"

They called the waiter and ordered food, Seattle picked the wine, a French Bordeaux, a wine that would melt this girl down to putty he thought. As life has it in Mexico, he opened the bottle because the waiter didn't know to use a corkscrew, you see, he was from somewhere in the countryside where they milked cows, from where they had never seen a bottle opener. What did he know of corks and fine wines?

The new friends enjoyed the company finding many things to talk about. They laughed at the snobbery of Parisian waiters and tasteless British food, ordered a second bottle, and soon began giggling and teasing each other about their respective countries, playing footsies under the table until Helga got so pleasantly like putty that she reached under the table to feel his excitement.

They paid the bill quickly, and what followed next I will leave to your imagination. But they did not play chess I assure you of that.

"I am looking for an adventure," she said. The morning sun entered the compartment; Jaguar lay in bed smoking, with Helga naked on top of him.

"I've been traveling the States and have had little to no excitement there. Mexico suits me."

She smiled that gorgeous smile. The blue eyes sparkled, the chin rose in pride, the cheeks turned pink. She kissed Seattle's forehead and asked, *"Will you take me with you?"*

Seattle cupped her breast in his hand licking it over and again. Her nipples were a shade of pink he'd never seen, and so the merrier. Helga moaned, then laughed, then shook her head in delight. Her hair flew around like a butterfly in heat.

Jaguar did not come up for air until his lungs nearly burst.

The girl smiled.

"Seattle, I want to know if you'll take me with you."

"But you don't know where I'm going."

"It doesn't matter."

"It does to me."

"But, why does it matter?"

"Take my word."

"We can have each other. Maybe fall in love."

"I need love like a leper needs leprosy."

"I need love and excitement, Seattle. An adventure. Are you up for an adventure?"

"I've been everywhere...What do you want... with a peasant?"

It went on and on like this for hours, the more he tried to avoid answering her, the more she asked. The girl would not give up. After a third bottle of red, they fell asleep in each other's arms, warmly, sweetly, unguarded. The sound of the train on the tracks became the sound of pounding rain, then a dream of strangers holding hands; soon, a flower blooming, finally, a kite flying loosely away from its owner. It was Helga's dream, a dream Jaguar saw in her eyes when they woke.

"I'll take you to Oaxaca," said Seattle.

"Oaxaca *and that's it.*"

*　　　*　　　*

The betrayal came quickly, swiftly, painfully; unmitigated by truth. The bitch had planned and acquired an accomplice in the love overthrow. She'd decided to take a lover to counter her fear of living alone, because Jaguar told her he was leaving. He was tired of her complaints, of her controlling ways, of her drunkenness, her bitching. There was nothing he could do to tame the rage in her, and he'd had enough.

But Jaguar did not know the betrayal was coming.

The accomplice was an ordinary man.

And Jaguar was anything but that.

The bitch handcuffed her lover, using him for the *Coup de Coeur.* Together they gave it to the writer. She couldn't do it alone.

"We have not gotten along for a year and a half," she said, strangling the ordinary man's throat as he took it. Most couples hold hands, she strangles throats.

"I love this man."

"What do you love about him," asked Jaguar.

"I love his work."

"The work is not the man."

The poor sucker looked more and more like a peasant standing in front of him. He did not react, nor did he take off his hat to look at it. He held on to the Bitch's hand as it moistened and bled of sweat. He was most assuredly being set-up for a fall, a big fall indeed, but he didn't know it. He looked like a vulture waiting for the bitch to die so he could have her money, and so, he ate shit with a smile on his face. It was evident that he would put up with anything the old whore did and so, on with the betrayal.

Jaguar smiled and wished him well.

"She's your problem now," he said. *"You have no idea what you've gotten yourself into."*

"Don't listen to him, he's just bitter," she shouted.

The ordinary man did not blink. He simply obeyed. When orders had to do with money, he obeyed.

Jaguar was miserable for weeks. First, he wanted to kill her. Then, he thought of setting fire to her home. Next, he thought poisoning her two dogs might put a dent in her, and finally, the thought of killing her daughter's two dogs would surely make her think twice, for this was a woman who learned lessons the hard way; later he decided the best revenge was to call her friends and tell them what they already knew: that she was a phony and a betrayer of the worst kind. He would drain the brake fluid from her S.U.V., and watch her slide into the pit of hell where she belonged.

In the end, revenge was just a fantasy to make himself feel better. He did nothing, until he thought of torture. He sent her a postcard that read:
"You always said you have a casita in the barrio.
Now you have your barrio boy to go with it."

The bitch would rot in hell trying to figure out how Jaguar knew her new lover, but it was evident he was a lowly Hispanic from Santa Fé trying to better himself through deception. The bitch would never show her boyfriend the postcard, she would withhold it from him like she did everything, and he, poor man, would one afternoon discover it tucked under her bed, hidden like she hid everything in her life, as it pained her to reveal herself in any way. The two fought for hours when he confronted her, the resentment of her lies causing him to leave her, his dreams of riches unfulfilled.

Now though, the Hispanic man did not know Jaguar was the love of her life, that he gave her everything in life, every drop of love, every drop from his tired and unappreciated body; this ordinary man would never suspect that she was deceiving him too. There was yet another man she was sleeping with, another lie, another hidden matter in her life, a carousel that never stopped turning.

She had him, but she did not have Jaguar.

Although she knew he was gone for good, the letters stashed under her bed were a reminder of times gone by. Jaguar was alive in her heart, and it killed her to admit it.

The bitch soon disappeared into the great unknown; taking with her what was left of her shattered life and dreams. She went to live in a deep, dark cave called loneliness, the very place she'd avoided her entire life.

Jaguar saw her fall apart, saw her demise, her self-destruction, her isolation; her bitter words eat away at her like a piranha eats a live cow crossing the river. She would never know peace of mind, though she would spend endless nights looking for it.

It was not Jaguar who'd done her wrong. Although it took him a good, long year to figure this out, he realized it was she who undid herself. She betrayed him, thus, she was destined to live out the *karma* of her deception.

Jaguar had an affair with a Yoga teacher and told the bitch about it. He admitted his infidelity, but she never forgave him. Instead, she lived for years arranging vengeance.

And vengeance was betrayal.

Izquierdo, would have asked one question:

"Did you look into her eyes?"

"No, father, I was afraid to."

"Look what your fear has cost you."

This exchange never happened and instead, for 28 years father and son lived separated by a scorn created by woman.

Jaguar wept now at the thought of his weakness. He'd allowed such an insignificant woman to hurt his life, and separate him from his beloved father.

The train Conductor pulled the lever above his head, and the sound of steam blew through the countryside.

*   *   *

Jaguar remembered her as he smoked a cigarette: she'd always looked serious, intense, as if in deep in thought. *She must be planning something,* he once pondered after she gave him one of her "looks," a glance that spoke of irritation, misery and disgust. If it was another man, well, he was not a jealous man because he didn't need to be. The women in his life had been faithful, loving, loyal, only interested in him. They loved being with him, sought him out, searched for him in the city, looked for him in Central Park when riding a cab through the circular asphalt - *he might be running today* or, *"There he is, pounding the pavement, look, girls!"* The women in his life loved him to the core. They ranged from small and short, to fat and tall, blonde, red-haired, brunettes. Russians, Thais, Indian. Canadians and Swedish girls had a thing for him, who knows why, he didn't care. The more he had the merrier. They knew it, because he told each one of them the truth: that he loved women, and that he wanted to be loyal to each one of them. But he couldn't. He couldn't be loyal because no sooner had he met the *blonde,* then a brunette came along, and then the girl from his writing workshop, and then the stewardess would be followed by the teacher and the next one, and so on.

It was difficult being Jaguar in search of himself, a man looking to fill the void within, the emptiness within that hurt so much. He thought women were the answer, yet he didn't want commitment because they just kept on coming. Surely at some point in his life he'd be ready to settle down, but not now.

The cigarette smoke rose above his head, and it tasted good. The story in his head wouldn't stop. Out of that darkness within he saw a glimpse of his father, but soon the vision faded and he continued dreaming.

I remember falling hard, falling so hard for her I could hear the thump. I wrote her daily. I wrote for her. I wrote love poems, love letters, love songs; in Spanish, in Italian, French words, German utterances I'd learned from Heidi. I had the writing fever back then, didn't I?

He looked around, but no one was there to talk to; no one in sight to see his pain.

Why am I feeling this pain? Why the memories? What is this pain? Where is it coming from?

A tear rolled down his cheek. His breath smelled, his fingers, his clothes too. The pain was increasing, escalating like an elevator to the fiftieth floor. What am I feeling in here, he asked, holding his breast, his stomach now where the pain ate at him. It seemed a snake was in there tearing him apart with venomous bites that would not stop the poison speeding through his body like lightning. He concentrated hard on the void, on the pain: was it in his head? He felt the sensations in the body so it was locked in there exactly where he felt it but, was he having a heart attack? As he slowed his breathing he noticed the pain was more like anxiety. It was an anxiety attack he reasoned. I'm too young for a cardiac arrest, and over a woman? No way.

He cried out for mother. He always cried out for mother when in this pain but she was nowhere to be found. Izquierdo had pushed her away.

Now he understood that through the years he'd pretended there was no pain in there - that he could stand it, ignoring it as if it would go away by itself, he was in denial, though the suffering and attacks were like living with a kitchen knife stuck in your back. All his life he'd pretended he didn't care if he hurt or not, he pretended he cared for those women; he pretended that everything was all right, *Just like the goddamn gringos do*, he shouted in his head. The gringos always pretend everything is all right, a big, Texas smile on their face while the pain eats away at them just like me. Jaguar realized just then that he was one, big, living, breathing, walking pretense because he hurt, because of that empty space within that kept him as if on pins and needles, trying anything to fill it, trying to put something in there to ease the pain. But how did he figure this out just now? Though the pain was still there, he took a first step in solving the mystery.

He felt lonely for the first time in many years. But there was no one to comfort him, not mother, not the bitch, not Mary Magdalene, no one.

He saw that the women had been like a sporting event for him. They were distraction, entertainment. I'd been using them!

Agggghhhhhh!

"Aggghhhh" he repeated at the top of his voice.

But I was good to them! They wanted more! I told them! I told them they couldn't own me, they couldn't ever possess me! What did they want, blood?

The wind blew dust in his face and he woke from the dream.

He'd been dreaming, but the tears streaming down his face were real. The memories too were real. The void was more real than ever.

What was I after? What was all that chasing? What was I after?

He needed to be loved. He wanted to be loved. He must have thought that having all the women in the world would do it, would satisfy him, and would fill that void, the void of a child, a child hurt by his own innocence, by his feelings of isolation. He'd grown apart from his blood, from his parents, he'd felt abandoned by Izquierdo, dislodged by Puta Madre, no brother to the twin sisters.

She ran-off to live with that man and with the dead sisters, he said referring to his mother.

He had his reasons for feeling this pain and they all made sense. They made so much sense that he carried them around for 40 years, thinking, "That's it! That's what happened to make me this way!"

He didn't know he'd had a choice in the matter. He didn't have to carry this pain but because no one ever explained it to him, he was blind to it. Some of the answers to this riddle were hidden from his view - that was certain.

He thought love was a way out of the misery. Jaguar couldn't identify the roots of the void, and that was all he was after now. You find the root and you find freedom.

Bitch.

He'd written her a letter saying he wanted to give his total self, how she moved him and made him crazy; she had the power to make him or brake him. He fell in love, he gave himself away, he didn't care how it turned out, he was going for it!

The bitch was a replacement for his mother in some way - that he knew. Although she was older, that was O.K. with him, but he hadn't noticed her unreachable solitude. He hadn't seen it coming. The horror that comes with old age: the solitude of destiny.

Destiny is unavoidable for all of us, isn't it, he once asked his students. They, poor things fresh out of high school, looked at him stupidly; with the same blank faces they'd looked at Daddy the day he announced, "*You are going to have a baby sister.*"

She loved to party like an eighteen year-old, the bitch did; time was running out on her, and she wanted to get-in every bit of fun she'd missed in her twenty-five year marriage to the Swiss Mr. Mess.

She has a thirst for life, he remembers thinking the day he met her. *She lives life on the fast lane. I can keep up with her, yeah!*

But he had more time in life, she didn't.

She raced around town buying needless gifts for friends, trying to buy their love; trying desperately to matter to someone now space and time were in her face:

the space between each other, the divide, and the time she saw running out on her, fading, slowing to a standstill. She ran to the hairdresser, to the shoe shops, to the market, to really any place that had something to sell, something to fill her own void inside.

How similar we were after all, muttered Jaguar as if speaking to her in person, *me with my running, and you with yours.*

And then, again the Agghhhhh! Jaguar saw himself reflected in her; he saw that he was just as deceiving as she, just as false, just as pretentious, and just as phony.

It took forever to see it, though at first sight he didn't. Back then, back at the beginning of their story, in the genesis he wrote her volumes of words, masses of honey. His favorite was the earliest:

Terremoto

An ongoing poem in many parts,
expressly for her.

Part One

Oh, thou knowest not
how
the joy
the pulse
thine perfumed words
assault me,

envelop,
attach
sweeten
spell
upon my
sun:
appreciation.
Plucking along,
woman
has far from seen me---
as a poet
or,
a man of words
whose hands
speak fearlessly
of courage
is but breathing...

Ahhh, to be seen
to be read,
wondered at!

Yes, the river knows
Terremoto,
I speak of thee;
And, no,
the forces not
betray us
but smile upon our worthy
nutrients
of hope,
of foreverness,
inculcating sighs
undulating remembrances
of what we've
wanted---
at finger's reach.

I, a child,
Wonder where you are,
 the storm inside
ravages
tears
and spins

the innocence
seeks the solace
of your
touch.

How this moment
divulges
a surging man
only Nature knows.
That it took you,
a solitary handshake
Terremoto,
emergence,
the giant in me
to become
unexpectedly myself.

In seeing
you are seen.

*

She was his muse all right. *That is the best poem I've ever written, and I am a poet,* he thought as the sun disappeared over the mountains. The air was cold; the chill in the air reminded him of the home they'd shared, the fireplace, the cognac, chocolates, the long, all night hugs and caresses.

In the face of failure we wonder what went wrong. We ask ourselves and others and Mom and Dad and cousins, the therapist, anyone who will listen: "*What the hell happened?*" But we don't look in the mirror.

Jaguar now looked in the mirror. The sky was his mirror: the trees before him, the birds singing, the wind.

Izquierdo knew! He knew all along and never said a word about it.

"*But I'm your son, mister, why didn't you tell me?*"

"*I did tell you, but you didn't listen!*"

And so he had. Jaguar ignored his father's advice not to marry the woman. Izquierdo saw that, yet he let his son live his life, make his own choice. What was the father to do, interfere in love? *Lovers are idiots, if you ask me*, he would add.

I want that love! It feels good! She's great! She loves me! That's how we are, right?

The poem ended being published in a book, though not his book, but a girlfriend of hers. Jaguar gave his permission and there it was pictures and all. He resented giving it away, but she asked.

"*I need it for my book,*" cried the girlfriend.

"*Write your own poems,*" he'd replied.

The bitch laid her hand on his lap and with a sweet intonation said, "*Oh, Jaguar, let her use my wonderful poem.*"

So now it was her poem, and she could do with it as she pleased. Jaguar wrote it, true, but now it belonged to her, and she ruled the day. His name was on it; you couldn't take that away.

The girlfriend's book was a huge success with millions of people reading his poem, but by then, Jaguar had moved on in life.

So in effect, the poem was his once again, and that was that.

*　　　*　　　*

For the longest time, Jaguar ate and drank and caroused his way through life for what to him seemed like an eternity. Leaving such that woman required not only time to heal, but time for insights, time to look into mirrors, many, many days and nights alone, travel, silence, staying strong, forcing the always-erupting pain to stay down there where it belonged; it also required forgetting.

Was he being like her, trying to forget first in order to forgive? He wanted to forgive her. He tried it with drinks and girls.

Paris proved to be boring this time around. In Florence he met a dark-haired woman who took him home, and promptly ate him up until he was but a shell of himself. Her name was Elinda and she loved loud opera to go with volumes of lovemaking, spankings, champagne and caviar. She took him to a famous garden, where they smoked like a kilo of opium and slept on the lawn naked. Their sex was heavenly, his back ached, yet, she all of 28 and already divorced, kept up this furious pace until they, by accident, found their way home. I say, by accident because Jaguar was looking for a one-night stand.

One morning long after this tryst began, Jaguar woke to the sound of licking. A different woman was at him, it was Elinda's best friend. He begged for a shower only to be seduced back to bed for a whole new round of lovemaking that included chocolate drips, honey smears, and sushi madness. Alexa, as the girl was known, ate the rice and fish and soy sauce right off his belly.

Jaguar wondered how he got there, remembering the bitch.

Aaaagghh!

"*A tiger,*" said Alexa.

"Keep going, cabrón," he said to himself, *"fuck so much you get sick of it!"*

"I did want to go to Rome, but now..." he got lost again in pleasure to relieve the pain.

The silent Florentine experience went on for almost a month, until he finally felt like talking. Everything had been silence, sex, opera, eating, more sex, more drink, sleep, opium, sex, sleep, silence, drink, but never conversation. The girl was happy being silent, keeping her life a secret, never having to reveal a detail of her life; she felt free, unencumbered. And then there was Jaguar: there was nothing he could do to forget Santa Fé. The bitch would creep up in the middle of sushi madness and he would lose his erection. Dear Alexa, would ask,

"Que pasó con tu gallo?"

She spoke Spanish, this one, though she was Italian. She's lived in Ibiza during childhood and spent summers there with family.

It wasn't so long ago that you were a little girl! Jaguar would tell her. She'd learned many good tricks from Leonardo, a gypsy boy; he in turn had learned everything he knew from a lonely, distant aunt who lived down the street from him, an aunt who had him visit.

Alexa took a liking to the Professor. She felt strangely attracted to him, perhaps because her father abandoned her at an early age, and she was looking for a replacement. *He can fill what's missing in me.*

No, thought Jaguar, as they conversed between kisses and drinks, he saw inside her: *she is cold hearted; brutally sincere, never vulnerable yet sometimes gentle...Perhaps only because I am her willing slave.*

The scene was reminiscent of *Last Tango in Paris* with the seclusion and silence, the bathing and drinking, the gorging and sexual immersion. Conversation increased as Jaguar spoke of dreams and illusions, disappointments and *batallas,* the battles with those demons within.

"Los demonios no me dejan, chica," he shouted, asphyxiated by the opium, drunk in distress. *"The demons won't leave me!"*

Alexa held him tight.

"Y yo que nomás vine a chingar," she said. *And me, I only came to fuck.*

They slept in each other's arms, coiled tight, warm, desirous, and belonging; attached. They needed to be held, to feel real skin next to them, next to their own emptiness, yet, giving of themselves as if lost puppies in a trashbin.

They were so alike in those moments.

One day the sun came up and Alexa cried. She knew it was over, that this wonderful, funny, tormented man was finally done with her. She knew he'd exhausted himself on her, that she had given herself like never before, that now there were no secrets left to tell after the initial long silences, there was no more anger to reveal, no position they had not tried. Her lips were swollen from licking and sucking, her tongue blue from the acid in her stomach. She needed an energy that would only come in the form of a vacation in the sun, maybe in Ibiza, and far from him.

She cried because she had never, ever before revealed herself to anyone like this, not even in confession, no, not the way she'd done here.

"*Llámame cuando quieras, Jaguar, y dime que me quieres.*" Call me when you want and tell me you love me.

She cried again, this time in the bathroom with the door closed.

What a way to find out you're in love.

"Here I was supposed to just have sex with this man, this stranger and go away! But, I feel like a Puta! Hit me, Jaguar! Spit on me! Slap me! For God's sake, wake me up from this nightmare!

And she cried, and cried, and cried.

Jaguar got dressed after shaving a stubble beard. He too, was exhausted. He too was in love, or so he thought. He looked in the mirror and saw a man unchanged.

"Vamos a México, Chica, donde el aire es transparente. Vamos a la luna otra vez!" Let's go to Mexico, Chica, where the air is clear. Let's revisit to the moon!

But it was beyond hope now, for she was not listening.

"What happened in here anyway?" he asked, in English.

"Elinda wanted me to fuck you and I couldn't. I made love, Jaguar. How'd that happen?"

"I made love too, Alexa. I hurt too, Chiquita, believe me."

"I didn't know I needed you. I didn't know I needed a man."

"Por qué pretender, chica?" Why do we pretend, Chica?

They embraced one last time, and in between tears and confusion, in the moment when there were no obstacles to their love or desire, or lust for each other, in that very moment when they could have decided they were meant for each other for life, they did not speak. The passion that erupted now was not fake, this time it was real, it was from deep within, from loneliness, yes, even from sorrow, yes, that too, from that profound emptiness each felt in their lives at exactly the same moment, a desolation, a longing, a fear; yet, they were so jaded now and in the bad habit of fucking who they wanted, that they couldn't really feel the *now*.

Aaaaggggghhh! he cried out.

Jaguaaaaaaaaaaaaaaaaaar! she cried in return.

They were never the same after that.

He went home to New York City, and she, to Bologna. She married soon after, to a man who'd loved her from childhood. Jaguar, in turn, walked Central Park for months wanting to see her, wanting to call but always resisting.

"Por qué la resistes, hijo?" Why do you resist her, my son?

Izquierdo would have asked.

Jaguar wouldn't know for years that she'd been perfect for him. But like most mortals, he couldn't see it in his blindness. It took years to see this because the void had a hold of him, it dominated his life such that he was blind to what was good for him.

The Bitch.

Now she was gone, light years gone she was, Jaguar didn't know where she went and he cared even less, really, but whether you liked it or not these long train journeys had a way of forcing you to look at your life. Perhaps they captured your very life, he didn't know.

I need to write this down, he said of the nightmare. It would go into his enormous book of notes to himself, largely unnoticed until someday it came into use. Maybe he would place it in his own black trunk and leave it in the church at the desperate mile for someone to find one day.

Jaguar created out of memory. His mind was full of the past, it was like in a movie; Izquierdo as a child would go into a scared frenzy, a fear based on the visuals that entered his young mind. Later, Izquierdo learned those visions were an ability to read lives through seeing, through looking into people's eyes. It was a gift no other human on earth possessed. Perhaps his predecessors, the Aztecs, had done so. Izquierdo believed he was reincarnated from a previous life.

Few, if any people on this earth, believed it though.

It took his son, Jaguar, the Ph.D., to research, write, document, verify and publish controversial articles on his father's life in order for others to believe Izquierdo was indeed a living testament to the Spanish Conquest. Jaguar thought it was somehow poetic that the old man astounded the world with his stories, for here was a man who did not speak as you and I do; here was a little Indian man from a remote village, a place named the desperate mile, who had remarkable memories of history, many forgotten, never documented yet credible because of the details therein because no one who recorded *the truth* of the Spanish Conquest. The known and published writings tell of destruction, of civilizing heathens, natives, brutes in the name of God. *What God did those Spaniards worship,* Izquierdo asked himself time and time again, citing the rape, murder, pillaging and general destruction of the Aztec peoples. Jaguar battled with the same question after reading the complete works of Bernal Diaz del Castillo, Fray Bernardino de Sahagún and others including the gringo W.H. Prescott's *History of the Conquest of Mexico.* While Jaguar was well-read and educated in a way his father was not, he knew the Bible and its commandments, particularly one clearly stating, *Thou shalt not kill,* a divine order time and again defied by the conquerors while they chopped down the native as they saw fit. The conquerors took God's commandments into their own hands, interpreting His word, satisfying their greed and lust for power with arrogant disobedience as if He who gave them life did not matter. *They committed a great sin before the Lord,* old Father Serra would have said, *taking His name in vain.*

Jaguar and Izquierdo both looked to reconcile with hypocrisy.

The train jerked to a stop but continued on until arriving at the station. Jaguar looked out the window, the desolation of the Mexican desert behind as the city came

to view, and feeling redeemed for in his body there was
not a drop of Spanish blood.

*

RUFINO

The Mariachi playing now was not originally scheduled. These second-rate musicians took the gig at the last minute because the band originally scheduled to play on this very important day, was last year insulted by none other than the Patrón Rufino himself. The very rich man got very drunk at his daughter's *quinceñera*, and in that arrogant/macho way of his, he demanded the band play *Amor Perdido*. The Mariachi, drunk themselves from a constant supply of *Hornitos,* played the melancholic tune quite badly. The lead singer hiccupped his way through, and to make matters worse, laughed during the ode. It'd been a joyous evening for all, and the bandleader felt it appropriate to celebrate this way. After all, ranchero bands were known for their liveliness.

What the bandleader didn't know until the insult came was that the request was a heartfelt ode from the Patrón to his irresistible wife, Blanca Cruz.

Blancabella, the evenings celebrated fifteen year-old, had earlier in the day lost her virginity to the village

Lothario, Agustín Eliab. Rufino suspected this, and so his fury tumbled out – on the bandleader, no less.

Rufino squeezed Blanca Cruz under the table, signaling his unease at the performance. He wanted more than anything to please her now, if only to get out of the doghouse, but, the song was going from bad to worse. She knew this, but there was nothing she could do about it, short of crawling under the table to give her man head. That would surely calm him down.

"*Bola de borrachos!*" cried the millionaire, tearing his hand from under her skirt. There was no mistaking his shout, as every person in the room stopped. There might have been five hundred guests, and each one of them shut his trap. When Rufino spoke, everyone listened.

The band went dead. The singer looked out into the audience as if to find the voice, the perpetrator, but he, poor man, fell off the stage, drunk on his ass. The other Mariachis quietly picked him up, and carried him out of the hacienda decorated with flowers, fruits and floating money.

"*Qué insulto,*" muttered the drunk, dragging his trumpet on the ground.

The party was declared over.

The musicians muttered obscenities on their way out and made promises of a ten-year boycott. Rufino would have to hire others less talented at his gigs. And that's why the band now.

Rufino sat sober as a tiger, and seething like a lion. He swore revenge on *Los Borrachos*. He would discredit the drunks, and break them in their old age. A full year had passed and the boss was still pissed.

"Nine years from now they will be old men, hungry, and willing to work for nothing, begging me to let them play at one of my parties, but, no. I will make them kneel in front of me, ask my forgiveness, and maybe even force them to kiss my feet!"

In nine years his daughters Luz Blanca, or her twin Beatríz Blanca would get married. Maybe it would be a double wedding, considering the identical twin sisters rarely spent a moment apart.

"Los Borrachos will be old, and gray-haired, and I will make them play for free!" Rufino loved power, exercising it whenever possible.

Such were the thoughts that ran through this rich man's head.

His wife was presently frowning. He spoiled her to no end, bought her diamonds and pearls, necklaces, wristwatches, homes in exotic places, cars, horses, you name it. But he'd stopped riding her pony. Their life was sexless, and no matter how hard she tried, his interest laid elsewhere.

She was seated at the right hand of the father, Rufino the *hacendado*, like always. Even though Blanca was dressed in a tight, baby-blue dress with slits on both sides, with exposed milky white breasts, he found her unattractive. She wore fine, cotton ribbons in her hair, tied in a *chongo Tehuano,* her finest diamonds, red-hot lipstick and heels; still, not an itch from the old man, not even when she put her hand on his crotch.

Any man in his right mind would have bedded her on the table top, but not this Patrón.

Instead, Rufino had his ears on these upstarts who called themselves musicians, steaming, and disappointed at his own 20th wedding anniversary. This band demanded twice the sum of *Los Borrachos*, and Rufino, whose only alternative was to go without music, reluctantly paid them what they asked. Rancheros are not people you mess with, and somewhere along the line, Rufino forgot this.

Money meant everything to him since he discovered the power in having it and the power in keeping it.

Blanca Cruz turned to him and ran her hand through his hair. Rufino grimaced. She spread her lovely legs and hiked her skirt. Yesterday she'd waxed her legs and today they glimmered as if wet. The Patrón smacked his lips though he was satisfied for the day. Why only this morning he'd taken a horseback ride to see his Cookie, his latest *favorita* who lived just down the road. Although Blanca Cruz looked luscious enough, Rufino had grown tired of her anxious lovemaking that left him for dead. She squeezed him too hard, bit his testicles, cursed him when coming and frequently pounded his back as in anger. Blanca Cruz rattled him like a bell, and he, growing older and less desirous of mad sex, quit sleeping with her altogether.

She took his big, left hand and placed it up her dress. She was moist, and beginning to exude that wondrous smell, but he took no notice. He was satisfied with the gentle Cookie of this morning's tryst.

Blanca Cruz pouted, for she wanted some action. She felt like a bride left at the altar. This was, after all, their 20th wedding anniversary.

Their eldest daughter was presently resisting handsome Jonathan who wanted to conquer her - a boy from a good, respectable family who was said to have a huge member.

Her frustrated mother might suggest, "*Hey, girl, take him out back and give him some! You only live so long.*" Blanca Cruz didn't normally think like this, but at the moment it sounded like a good idea. "*Leave him to me,*" she thought, "*I'll take care of him.*"

Feeling rebuffed by Rufino, she pulled down her skirt and took a long sip of her *Bacardi*. She loved her drink and could hold it, for a woman. In fact, she could out-drink any man except for Rufino, who was a whale of a drinker himself. She could drink, and laugh at the poor souls who tried to outdo her. She would taunt them to slug -it-up, and whoever fell first, paid the bill. They always did. Men loved to drink with her, clearly accepting the humiliation as a gift from heaven, such a beauty she was.

Way back, when Rufino had not yet asked for her hand in marriage, she would drink with any man who so much as whispered her name. For, she was beautiful, with big eyes and light hair; a bright, white smile that matched her creamy, long legs that went on for days and days.

Men would buy her drinks, only to find their heads spinning and gasping for breath as she sat silent, sipping a drink to match theirs. She laughed at the stupid men who thought so little of her. Occasionally, Rufino would come by looking for her, and rant about her license, a familiarity that made her look like a whore.

"We are not engaged. You do not own me," she would say.

As you can imagine, this infuriated Rufino to no end, and he would crawl home like a dog with its tail under its ass. His only consolation was that she was loyal. They were going out then, but she was not the only one. She knew they would marry someday, and so was patient. Back then, he was busy amassing the fortune that by force would take several generations to liquidate. He wanted her at any cost.

Now, though, he thought of Cookie, his *favorita*.

Blanca Cruz could tell he was thinking of her.

Rufino sighed. He peeked at Blanca Cruz and noticed her beauty, the woman he once loved so passionately, he gave her his all, no wonder he felt spent. The woman could not walk down the street without people gawking at her; men stopped and clutched their heart as if wounded. The press loved her and sought her out for photo-ops. The *Bellas Artes* was not an event without her presence. Why the President himself wanted her, if just for one night! She in turn, would laugh and say there was no one like Rufino.

"Rufino Tamayo," Cookie called him, after the great Mexican muralist and painter long dead and buried. Rufino, the hacendado, politician, and banker, only numb when considering his wife.

"What happened to all those beautiful times we shared?"

The music, the songs, the poetry, love letters, and declarations; la desnudéz, the flowers, rumpled beds, snags in her hair, happiness, and the fainting spells?

He decided they should leave town by horse at midnight and ride to Oaxaca for three days and three nights. They would check into the famous hotel *El Camino Real*, once a convent, once a prison; and do the love thing like in the old days.

He knew he was bluffing, that it was every man's fantasy to restore his faltering marriage - to where it once was, to get back the feeling, that love feeling that vanishes and never comes back. He believed in God, and spoke directly to Him.

"Lord, you are cruel! How much do you want? How much more shall I give the church?!"

Just then, he realized that he did not care anymore for his wife Blanca Cruz; no, not enough to do anything about it.

He pondered, in fact, to do anything to end his marriage. Maybe he would find a different *favorita*, maybe a hundred. *It'll be one huge never-ending orgy,* he thought, a smile of satisfaction on his face. His 20th anniversary celebration wasn't going so bad, after all.

"I have to clear out my head!" he shouted over the music. He stood and stretched his back, scratching his balls in accompaniment. Blanca Cruz smiled and stood up.

"What the hell, vieja," he said, grabbing her tight ass.

"Let's go to the bedroom, huh?"

*   *   *

Rufino headed for the door, zipper in hand. His wife lay in bed, smoking marijuana.

"A girl has to do something!" she'd said a moment ago.

Rufino was back to his old self, acting like sex never happened, like he cared more for his favorita than for his own wife.

"Put out that dirty thing!" he commanded and slammed the door. She took a long whiff of the weed and sobbed.

"I have to divorce that man!"

Funny thing, at that moment, Rufino's favorite, Cookie, was in church praying he leave Blanca Cruz to marry her.

"These women all have a lot of balls!" he Rufino on his way down the corridor.

I am tired of both of them; one, because of who she is, and the other, because of who she isn't. If only he could combine the two of them into one. "*Would that be so bad? Would the two in one be a terror unexpected?*"

He stopped at the mirror in the hallway. His hair needed attention, his tie loose, the usual conqueror's grin on his face now a smirk. His life was a mess and he wanted out. He blamed it on the women.

Why would I let a woman - any woman - destroy me, when the most powerful men in this country have failed to do so?

The fear of his imminent demise dated back to when he first started business. Way back then looked out the window of his little, old house in the village, and he saw lots and lots of trees looking beautiful shining in the morning sun. He thought of how those trees stood quiet and tame, surrendered like the workers in his village who toiled for little without a grumble. *Rice and beans was all they wanted,* he thought. They never complained for fear of their very lives, for they could easily be disappeared by the *patrones* into the jungle never to be seen again; these peons would never endanger their work, their livelihoods, the family, their rightful now stolen lands. *They take it where it hurts,* thought young

Rufino, *like the African slaves in the United States.* But this was the 21th century.

Well, the trees were very much like the slaves: you could walk up and strike them, lash them and they wouldn't so much as flinch. Slave: farmer - tree.

A sudden thought came to mind: *I can make lots of money off those trees.*

And he did. It didn't matter that his people loved and protected the trees, he would chop them down and make the best of it, even if his family disowned him.

"What can they give me that I can't earn myself?"

He would need an education. He would apply himself in school, study hard and make it. His father had pushed him, *finish secundaria and go to Prepa,* the old man insisted. He would meet the movers and shakers of this world, their families, show his intelligence and maybe get groomed for high office, a profession, a position in life. The rich and powerful, the well-placed would not refuse him entry into their world because he belonged. And he would make sure of that. If there was anything young Rufino knew at this stage in life was that he was unstoppable, and that he wanted very badly to belong.

His working-class, *campesino* father knew his son would make it. He wanted the best for Rufino, and would move heaven and earth to make sure that his only child did not end up like him.

Dad was a hard worker, but a dedicated drinker. He spent time in the Cantina mostly to get out of the house and away from his wife's bad cooking. He liked to discuss pueblo events and the lives of others. The people loved to talk now, having taken to the practice since the muteness died. Silence was for the sleeping now, it was not a way of life; silence was the past, if a little sentimental. The *fábricas* and *maquiladoras* played loud music all day long, the young people blasted tunes at home and in their cars; the Cantina's jukebox played lively *mariachi* tunes without end.

Rufino's dad encouraged him to study, to make something of his life so he would not be laughed at the way people laughed at him in the city.

"*La suidad*" his father mispronounced the word, "*es bruta.*"

And brutal it was. Shopkeepers laughed at his pronunciation, others at his cadence. Old dad never talked back for fear of ending in jail. He was a tree, after all, just like all the other peons come down the mountain. He was often accused of robbery because of his looks though he never stole; his life in *la suidad* was that of a marked man. The shopkeepers often accused the poor of robbery and cheating as they were vulnerable to the police; what did they know of defending themselves? In the end, they practically gave away their goods for free simply to get back home and avoid jail. It was the shopkeepers who were the crooks and everyone knew it, but corruption is the way of life for these people, so one must take advantage of every opportunity that comes along the way. Those who turn their back on cheating others are called fools. The old man didn't know why he was a target for this, but suspected it was because he was not the brightest star to light the sky. He didn't yet know he was just a lowly Indian to these merchants, that Indians meant nothing to no one.

"*Este indio me insultó!*" the shop vendors would cry out, and he, poor old Indian that he was, a simple *campesino* trying to make a living in his old, khaki pants and huaraches, would be taken to jail just for the color of his skin.

Dad would educate his son at the best schools no matter the cost.

Rufino's childhood was one of hunger, poverty and silence; one day the dark nights, the ignorance and eternal thirst to live life differently would be a thing of the past he concluded; *That memory will belong in someone else's life*, he muttered to himself at the window. Instead of cooking with charcoal Rufino would have stoves of gas or electricity, a maid or two, women to cook and clean his mansion so that he wouldn't have to lift a finger. He would ring a bell and running they'd come. He would have personal slaves; why he could fondle them if he wanted!

It occurred to him that he needed slaves: to chop the trees, to clean his hacienda, to care for his women. He would have lots and lots of women.

"Stop dreaming, child!" he heard his mother cry out from the kitchen where she was standing at the counter making fresh tortillas. *"Go finish milking the cows."*

He felt monumental resentment at the dream perturbed as his face flushed red with shame, for it was possible the dream would never come true. Sticking his hands in his Levy's, he walked to the barn. The sun was shining and the air was clear. A huge hawk flew over and gawked three times.

Rufino looked up, and saw the bird suspended in the air. He remembered his mother once saying birds bring good news. The resentment now magically washed away.

He knew the dream would come true.

At the age of twelve he felt himself a man. He had a feeling he'd lived life before, as if life was familiar in some way, though still young, he thought, *"I wouldn't wish this on anybody,"* meaning the poverty.

He felt wise beyond his years, like an old man in some mysterious way, though his body was far from feeling rickety. No, his was a young boy's body; he was an athlete, he loved to run, to play ball and ride horses. A pride surged in him and he felt that everything would one day work out, that all the things he wanted would be his. One day, he would chop down the trees and make a fortune.

He milked the cow with the force of an Emperor.

His mother looked out the window. She always kept a close eye on him, as he was an only son. She crossed herself in benediction and looked to the sky.

"Thank you Señor, for giving us such a good boy."

In the distance, and in the burning sun, Rufino's father wiped the sweat from his brow as he took a breather from tilling the earth.

Moments later, a flock of birds flew over his head; and each of the feathered-ones dropped a seed from their weary beaks, depositing them in the ground like campesinos do in planting season. The birds came from a higher calling, thought young Rufino, seeing them himself, he on his way to the *milpas,* after milking the cows, sent by his mother to help the old man finish the day, the old man whose hands ached with arthritis and sharp pain. The deposited seeds would take to the earth, sprout and grow, producing enough papaya for the old man to send Rufino to *Prepa*; thus, handing the boy over to a fate and destiny that called out his name.

Years later mom and dad would travel to the city with truckloads of papayas to sell so their son could sit at

Sanborn's drinking Pepsi with pretty girls who never knew the meaning of sweat.

At this moment, however, Rufino's hunger was such that a plate of rice and beans sounded like Oysters Rockefeller.

He didn't even need tortillas.

*   *   *

Rufino sighed when he finished with Blanca Cruz. His sexual power was at its height, and he could go on and on without end. But if his wife no longer turned him on, maybe the fire was dead. She did at least manage a quickie.

He looked at Blanca Cruz in her tight blue dress, and wanted some more. What were these confusing thoughts? First, he didn't want her, and now he did. He had to figure this out. Maybe in the end, it would be best to keep her. Rufino showered and washed himself good. His heart was pounding, he wanted something, but he didn't know what.

He walked a few blocks to the Cantina thinking of the time wasted on women. *I need a grandson*, he muttered as his three children were all girls. His daughter Blanca Beatriz also had three girls as she was unable to produce a boy and this ate at Rufino's heart.

"I have everything in life and it's never enough!"

He found himself on top of Cookie.

"Why are you laughing?" she asked.

"Porque quiero," he answered. Because I can.

Rufino was a prick. He was known for mowing down generals as easily as people eat popcorn. He spoke his mind, and he was nasty.

"You should hire a woman to shine your medals, General," he would say to his face, really to humiliate this army-man-come-from-the-woods. Certainly this heavily-medaled toad was not rich in his own right. *"General, when was the last time you lead your men into battle? How did you earn those medals on your breast? Shooting Indians?"* In Rufino's Mexico, people rarely answered back.

Cookie sure didn't for fear of losing the golden egg.

Rufino was contemplating bigger things.

"It's not enough anymore! This fucking, these girls, the wife, the village, this COUNTRY! It's not big enough for me anymore! I know everybody who is

anybody, and they know me. I own land, and houses, and cars; haciendas, a pied-a-têrre in Paris, Jesus! Why am I so unhappy? Mexico is but a joke to the world, with its corruption and bribery; with it's financial ruin, what with its loans, world loans, US loans, United Nations loans; why the thieves who call themselves President do nothing for the people! I earned my part fair and square, as the Americans say, and NOBODY BUT GOD CAN NEGATE THAT!"

"Qué te pasa, amor?" asked the little tart.

But Rufino was gone. He was pumping away inside her as his thoughts flew in and out of his head. Drilling for oil.

"I have to see the world. I have to do something."

He panted.

The bigness in life lay elsewhere. He could return to Paris and start a new business. His old Mexico City friends living there in exile would cash in, remembering their youth and college days when they had nothing better to do than make money. They would smoke *Galoises* at the bistro, drink red wine, look at the pretty, loose girls and laugh. How generous he was with his ideas back then, when he, a mere Mexican boy studying at *La Sorbonne,* with only one good pair of shoes, gave them business ideas that made them millionaires. Rufino wasn't embarrassed of going without, of being poor, of not having enough for a good croissant or *remoulade, escargot* or *paté.* Today he could feed an entire village in France if he wanted, why the whole of Paris in one huge feast of all saints. But, no, that plan would not do. Rufino could have stayed in France back then and made a bundle, because he was meant to make bundles; he was offered jobs even as a foreigner. He spoke French like the 16th *Arrodisements,* was charming, and handsome, and funny, and sexy, and everyone liked him. But the truth was, he missed his beautiful mother and the raw naked earth, the *milpas* and fields and *campos*, the big, open sky with its many varieties of birds, them, gawking, talking, speaking to mankind below; he missed the fresh air that caught you as if by surprise, the sunsets, the sunrise, the cows - his cows! - but mostly, he missed the papaya trees. The trees that gave great shade on those hot, hot working days when all you wanted to do was drink beer and take shots of tequila; shade that cooled you down and made you stop to think about life. A shade, where you placed a rickety old table and cloth on Sunday afternoons ate and chatted about nothing and laughed like in the old days.

"Like in the old days when I had no worries," he thought.

Back home everywhere you looked you saw rows and rows of corn. But smack in the middle of everything there were rows of papaya whose existence no one on earth could explain. It was a gift from heaven.

On those rows of papaya you would never in a hundred years of solitude so much as see a fallen leaf they were so well taken care of. They produced so much and so well for the family that one day Dad was forced to pick up a dog to protect them. He tied the poor thing to a tree keeping the poachers away. A few days later the dog died of thirst as the old man forgot to leave water.

And France, what did it offer anymore, memories of dead Emperors, memories of a country that came to conquer Mexico only to be abandoned by the Crown?

What is France now? Rufino pondered. Tiny, little apartments where you couldn't take your girl, you had to do it in the park, the parks smelling of urine and shit; the streets full of weak-willed women, and faggy men; Paris with its bad waiters, and close-minded peasants. Today France was unrecognizable as he recalled it, now populated with thousands of immigrants of varying countries and colors. It was no longer white.

France was not the place to be. If he wanted those things, he could find them in L.A.

Rufino longed for the silence of his youth, the bean tacos, candied fruits from the shop down the street, the Mariachis with the loud music, the unpaved streets where he many-a-times stubbed his toe. Back then he rode his horse deep into the mountains where the trees stood silent spending the night alone, happy, asking the gods of nature for permission to cut down the *chicle* trees; he would ask to take their wooden spirits to another place where they could serve mankind, for nature was not for the taking, it was to be respected, it is life after all. You first speak to nature, and then ask permission to offer itself to you: those who do otherwise invite trouble to their life sooner or later.

He would leave Paris and return home.

Rufino decided long ago the *chicle* trees were his, and he could do with them as he pleased, but now he had a problem. At Prepa he met the girl of his dreams,

Blanca the First a girl who read Castañeda, and Bolaño and García Márquez and others; she told him between kisses and squeezes that it was very important to get permission from the tree spirits, from Nature if he wanted to cut them down. *Even a frail little flower like me needs to give permission to be cut down*, she said.

If permission was not asked, one was cursed for life.

Rufino was superstitious.

Trying desperately to impress her, he told her of his dreams thinking he could keep her from the rich kids of her crowd. She might one day consider marrying, he said. He was in love, in puppy love, in that sweaty-palms thing that happens to youth.

Blanca the First smiled and gave him a warning.

"*Don't cut down anything without asking permission.*" Like permission to marry. He never suspected he was just a plaything as Blanca the First used him for his manhood. A classmate ridiculed him for going out with a rich girl.

"*You're just a campesino, hombre!*" said the niño bonito. "*She only wants to rub your cock!*"

Blanca the First became history the day he asked her if it was true.

"*I'll tell you after I taste it,*" she said, unzipping his fly. After that, he never saw her again though the girls at the Prepa smiled at him from that day on.

His heart crushed and feeling betrayed, he vowed to have any woman he wanted, to have as many as he wanted, when he wanted them, and as he wanted. If it took scholarships and full-time work to get through business school, he would do it. He would cook, or sew, or bleed if necessary but he would be rich. *And no one girl would ridicule the giant in him!*

Thinking of what she said, he spoke to the *chicle* trees, asking permission, caressing them, at times telling jokes to befriend them. He asked to be forgiven should he become greedy. He stayed awake all night under the trees inventing his future life, clutching his destiny, assuring he would never be a slave to another, to no one but to himself.

"*I will not be swallowed up by the very earth I walk on!*"

The plan had to be faultless. As he could not afford mistakes, he sketched strategies for unheard-of success. He would go without sleep for a year if need be.

The whole world was his oyster.

"Why, I may even be Mayor of Mexico City someday!"

At the moment, though, he would enter Candy once again, this time from behind. He would make her squeal like a pig in orgasm. Life had to change.

There was something about power that made him hard. If that were the case, he would always be strong as his member was a rod of lighting.

"I will always be electric," he shouted, satisfied for the fifth time this day.

Cookie bit him on the shoulder. He turned and slapped her face.

"You idiot! My wife will see this and kill me!"

*

LAS BRUJAS

Izquierdo heard the footsteps and knew they were coming. The Witches had begun flying every Wednesday night delighting the people with their height, flight and great might. They dressed in the tradition of the dark ones - those who do black magic and hurt others - in dresses of black, shiny silk with big, flowing scarves that undulated in the wind. They flew above us with such ease that any Tibetan monk might be shamed. The women in the sky pointed their feet east to the setting sun, in the direction of those who surf the Himalayas.

The crowd in the village looked up and cheered and applauded the antics as the *brujas* twisted and turned; they applauded not their flight but their curses, for they were evil and black, a sign of what was to come. Darkness enveloped them like a blanket; they, innocent souls they pretended to be, showered us with blasphemy and vulgarities, for we were still innocent back then. We laughed at the sounds of ugly words, thinking they were play.

The witches had practiced their magic for years, learning to fly, to cook potions and recite damnations. How they started nobody knows, but I can tell you this: we all stood silent in wonder of their feats. There were many novelties at the desperate mile as the days passed, but this one topped them all.

As we watched, it was fun.

Many of the witches were true beauties, women any man would lust for, what with their big rumps, exotic silences and solid breasts. It was this distraction that deceived us; they dropped ashes from the sky without us knowing it was poison. Was it the devil's baptismal? We rubbed the substance on our foreheads like we'd learned to do from Father Serra, thus sealing our fate. Children woke to headaches, wives to vomiting; the elders in cold sweats. When we discovered our fate of darkness and impending doom, Izquierdo put together an army to look for the witches, but they were gone. The men carrying wood crosses looked in the caves and in the trees where others said they lived. The warriors waited day and night without sleep for an entire week, but nothing.

We would wait for their return.

We were so innocent then, so void of hurt and encroachment from the outside world that we could not believe evil existed on earth. We wondered if their white skin – like Father Serra's - was the reason for our downfall. When you live in a world of innocence and beauty you don't expect harm to come your way, least of all from your fellow man. The witches were sent by the gods, we said; we had our due coming.

We found it hard to accept this. Year in and year out, we made offerings to heaven, we left food out for the hungry, yet, the punishment was on its way whether we liked it or not. It took, like the fall of the Roman Empire, three hundred years for the white ones to come.

Izquierdo warned us of an invasion.

Though he didn't know what to do about the impending onslaught, he went the mountaintop for forty days and forty nights, praying, asking for answers, for time to be on our side. Whatever was coming was not good, Izquierdo told the others; whatever it is, it will bring us ugliness and pain.

I don't know how it is I know this but I do, he

said; there is something inside that guides me - that
speaks   to   me.

He ate little more than cactus peeled by his
obsidian knife; for thirst he found the *junco de agua,* a
tree only Indians know to find: its hollow branches
holding fresh water for those who know. To this day, I
don't know why but, Izquierdo felt himself the protector
of our people. Everyone respected him, and that was
enough. He'd never misguided us, so his status as warrior
was beyond criticism.

He prayed the black witches would go away, or
be taken by the strong winds; he burned pine and sage,
clove and oil, all to no avail. Not surprisingly the witches
returned as the villagers tried to ignore them. As life
would have it, the next morning excited villagers
reported seeing the witches fly around with parasols and
umbrellas, their piercing and sinister voices filled with
laughter. Ignoring them did not matter anymore. They
were here to stay, and to this day, the white skinned
brujas live among us, torturing our youth and disabling
the elders every chance they get. Our stories are
disappearing too because they take them, our languages
are being lost. The mutes have been silenced with no one

representing us.

One year later, the volcano rumbled. We heard a noise that resembled Don Juan Matos' farting behind the house; when we looked up, the mountain was on fire. Smoke erupted from its mouth, a circle as perfect as the ring around the moon. That circle seemed to look at us, pontificate and chastise us: we sinners below, condemned to a life as decided by others.

We lived in a world of prayers, offerings, pilgrimages and journeys to Ixtlán. Carlos Castañeda came by the pharmacy one day asking for directions, but finding us mute and unable to answer, he bolted and disappeared. Someone said he was scared, others that he needn't be, because *curanderos* have no fear. Still someone said, that if you saw who we were forced to be, you would run too, because we'd been robbed of our power, our beauty, our land. A man without those things is not a man, but a ghost of the past, and if you've ever seen a ghost, you would bolt and disappear too, like the *curandero* from Ixtlán.

I was there the afternoon Carlos came to town and this is what happened. Izquierdo and I were at the shoemaker's when we heard loud footsteps approaching.

Looking out the window we saw the villagers lauding as they followed the writer who was walking on air. I was glad he was not walking on water, as Father Serra had taught me Jesus did, for today we might be different people. Anyway, the writer walked into the pharmacy after looking around for reporters because in those days he was very much a wanted man. Shaking as if cold he stopped at the door and entered. He was looking for Pedro Páramo, he said; receiving no verbal response from us but only stares as we were still mutes, he took-off in a hurry. As Izquierdo was at the entranceway of the shop the writer bumped into him on his way out, and he, Carlos Castañeda, was seen for everything he was as the two briefly locked eyes. I didn't know who Carlos Castañeda was back then, and neither did I care. I just wanted to be like everyone else in town and see the man who walked on air. Standing to his feet after bumping into my father, he made the mistake of looking into Izquierdo's eyes. He gave away his life story in the blink of an eye and didn't even know it. His fear, my father said, showed his future, and this is when I learned that fear lives in every man's eyes.

(Izquierdo looked at me and said: Son, that man writes books, he will write many but one day, he will disappear. He said Carlos would grow tired of being famous faking his own death in order to vanish in silence. He would pretend to die, like Addison Stonefreund and Father Serra. After his "death," his secretary would tell the world Carlos left the earth six months ago, in his solitude of destiny, avoiding interviews, questions and answers. He was no Timothy Leary, she would state; he was a private man who met his maker and now lives in the other world, full of *curanderos*, wanna-be's and anthropologists.)

And so it happened. One early morning, when I lived in New York I walked down to seventy-second street to buy the Times. As I enjoyed the obituaries I saw something about Carlos Castañeda passing away and had a good laugh because Carlos pulled the ultimate disappearing act; I knew that in the six months since his alleged death he'd relocated to Botam, a Yaqui village by the river, where he built his own *palapa* and started a new family. It was said that many women had his children and that in the year 2020, a village will be named after him. He will be old by then, very old, and will laugh at those who believed him, for his stories were not true, but pure fiction. His legacy will bring misery to many: the white women in his life will kill themselves over him as they believed his lies, they will destroy others over the many millions of dollars he left in banks untouched. He will laugh from his grave at those who followed his teachings.

As happens in life I saw him in Botam a year after reading his obituary. My work as anthropologist took me to such places to tell others of the desperate mile. Out of the corner of my eye I saw him talking to the shoemaker, and though he didn't recognize me as I'd been but a child when he walked on air, he did look deep into my eyes but only because his sight had gone bad. Sensing a stranger, he stopped talking to the shopkeeper and slipped away, as if afraid to connect with the real world. The poor shoemaker *Juave* smiled as I shook his hand, saying, *There are people in this world who do not want to be seen.* Just so you know, Carlos, I applaud you in respect of a successful disappearance.

The witches never went away.

The footsteps did get louder after the volcano

eruption. It rained ashes without end, so much that it was sixteen months before we saw the sun again. We walked the village protected by umbrellas, the ashes to our knees, the ashes turning us gray and cold; some villagers looked white-skinned like the witches, others, like aborigines. We boiled water for drinking and strained the food, covering it as it cooked. The people got irritated, some got angry, wanting to leave our rightful land. Where could we go? This was the only place we knew.

One night some angry villagers went to the water well at the Cárdenas Hacienda and discovered it was clean and covered. As we thirsted for its contents, Cuahutémoc welcomed us kindly and asked we stand in line as we each carried buckets. There were fights and arguments to be first, words, curses, and fists flying, until the water was gone. Despite this, Cuahutémoc was elected president, but his election was annulled by others seeking power. Corruption was now the order of the day in our village.

And then, the expected happened: violence took our town the way plagues of locusts covered Egypt.

The morning was quiet, the air of regret hung like a dead man from a tree. I think everyone understood what happened, but now it was too late. Violence was here to stay, for some of the rough ones in the village loved it the way a dog loves his master. Interestingly enough, the water well filled-up the next day and there was plenty for everyone until this day.

Izquierdo was right, the damage was coming, it was done and there was nothing you could do about it.

Funny enough, living in ashes was a pleasure of sorts. As a child you play in the dirt, in the mud, in the rain, in the water, but as an adult, these things bother you. People got edgy at the mess, complained to no avail and lashed out at anyone standing by. The witches laughed louder from the skies as they got their wish. Some people left the village thinking the volcano would destroy us, but when the council gathered to discuss the matter, it was resolved that we destroyed ourselves; it was we who did the damage by believing in evil and all its goods; it was we who lauded the witches, we who applauded Castañeda, we who took on the violence and began to destroy each other, for nature could not be blamed. The blame was placed on the nature of the human being, it was said. An old sage nailed a sign at the entrance of town that read: *What you believe defines you.*

Those of us who stayed in the village were made stronger by the troubles.

What we did not know was we'd surrendered our fate, our destiny, and that we would never be the same again.

MARY MAGDALENE CELEBRATION

On this early spring morning as the sun pounded through the windows of the studio I heard the village dogs bark alarmingly as if a thief in the night approached. Izquierdo was long dead, Mary Magdalene slept in bed, and I had a headache from the night before as all 325 of us in the village celebrated my wife's pregnancy. We'd first gathered to eat and share festive drinks because just that afternoon, Dr. Nicolás Juárez, the village physician, healer, and philosopher king, informed me that new wife was pregnant. Excited to hear the news we danced our way out of his office, me holding her belly, she kissing my neck. Outside we ran into Bull and shared the good news. Being he was the right person to spread the news as postman, I suggested he invite everyone to the *zócalo* for a celebration later. He must have told someone with a bigger mouth than his because every single soul at the desperate mile soon showed up, pets included. My people are that way. We drank my friend Ron's *mezcal* and lots of *Tequila,* and *pulque* from Guadalajara. There was no shortage of beer.

When we got home from the doctor, I sent Apollo the messenger to see if Ermenegilda López López Sánchez y López would cook the feast. I didn't expect he would find her quite as quickly as he did, but the boy knew everything about everyone in the village as his work demanded it; he was the messenger after all, maybe later in life he would become the town's gossip, but now he knew enough about everyone enough to be feared with secrets and news held in his head. Before I was out of the coat and tie I wore to honor Mary Magdalene's visit to the doctor as a formal gesture of gratitude to God for seeing to it Mary Magdalene got good and pregnant, Apollo returned to the front door knocking and out of breath to tell me that, yes, "*She'd be delighted to roast her biggest pig and goat*" for such an occasion. The armless cook steamed a bale of corn, made tamales, paella and delicious tortillas the size of frisbees. Don't ask me how she did things with only one arm but that woman also took the time to make an enormous *flan* that was later lit with rum, a burning spectacle for all to see. And all this with just one arm! Moments later, as if on cue came the local *secundaria* students shooting a mass of fireworks that lit-up the sky. A band of musicians came to our door playing love songs, a girl's choir sang songs from Perú, and someone's little girl gave Mary Magdalene the most beautiful bouquet of flowers ever seen.

I got to pay the bill.

This tribute to Mary Magdalene was an expression of love because the village adored her. They commented daily on her exotic beauty, the dark birthmark below her lower lip, her general good nature, the incessant smile and her memorable laughter like that of a teenage girl. The afternoon was spent with the poblanos hugging and kissing her, accepting her as one of their own, for now she would have a child born to the village.

We were always happy as a couple back then; it was the beginning of our glory days. But the pregnancy was not easy. We'd encountered lots of trouble getting the seed in the right place: it was not me, let me tell you, it was mostly the timing. Dr. Nicolás Juárez saw her twenty times in an attempt to determine if she was barren until finally one day he tapped her on the head and said: *"You are just going to have to go home and try, and try again, until you do it! It will be fun. My wife and I did the same thing."*

He was right. It was a lot of fun. We made excuses all day long to make love: *"I haven't kissed you in hours!"* or, *"Let's take a nap!"* or even, *"We have a duty, love; a mission!"* and, off we'd be, stripping each other naked and throwing the clothes on the floor, grunting, growling and generating. The lovemaking was always unexpected, surprising, and unselfish. We never tired of being together. *"I want to get you pregnant!"*, I shouted, mounting her for the hundredth time.

"I want to have your baby!" she would shout, as she tossed her body about in orgasm. I would clinch my teeth and spurt once more, hold her tight and weep in joy. We would have a child if destiny wanted.

I loved her like no other, always doing as she wanted; I was her slave and I didn't care if anyone knew it.

Once I even risked my manhood by climbing a tree to raid a beehive. (We ran around naked in those days.) On the way down the tree, I spilled honey on me just as the Queen Bee was returning with her army. Out of fright, I let out a piercing yell, *EEEEEEEEEEEh* like my father had taught me to do and the whole swarm of bees retreated, giving me time to flee to safety intact.

Later, the tribe laughed as I repeated the story.

Mary Magdalene told me she wanted a big bed and so I, fool that I am, went into the jungle where the jaguars roam looking for the very wood she wanted. This special tree was only to be found in that part of the world. The black walnut made for the most beautiful furniture.

I fell asleep only to wake to a baby jaguar licking my face, her enormous mother growling at me nearby. I remembered Izquierdo's teachings, and crawled to her slowly to pluck a hair from her mustache. That was the thing to do, he said when I was a boy. *"Pluck a hair from the jaguar and earn its respect."*

The cat let out a squeaking sound and rolled on her back, the baby jaguar jumping on her to play. Sensing the moment to run I took off like a rocket and luckily never saw them again, for animals have memories too and seek retribution when hurt. I still have the jaguar hair; it rests on the mantle along with a tiger tooth necklace given to me by Izquierdo.

The quick getaway guided me where I was going as I cut down the tree and dragged it home to make the bed. Mary Magdalene was mine indeed.

The dogs continued barking in the distance. As my hangover from the night before was getting no better, I dressed quickly and grabbed my walking stick thinking the air would clear my head. My two dogs *Rumple* and *Stilskin* following close behind, I went to the side of the mountain where others stood. Seeing strangers in the distance, I quieted the dogs with one swift stroke of my hand.

From the top of the ridge we could see a band of British *bandoleros* as they traipsed by on their way to nowhere, electric guitars in hand, a dufflebag of drums on one's back; they carried speakers and wires and someone said they were the Beatles looking for strawberry fields. One thing was for sure, they wore psychedelic colors and velvet pants, long hair to the knees, the accents British, and not 'merican. I think they were only passing through on their way to Penny Lane, maybe looking for magic mushrooms but who knows, I didn't really care. The only person who'd found us recently was Addison Stonefreund, and he was said to be long dead - although I suspected otherwise.

We continued on unharmed and untouched, undiscovered in our wild ways.

I stayed atop the ridge all day making sure the band kept their distance. They'd raised a tent for the night, made a fire and sang songs of love. The village kept quiet, in a vigil, so as not to give away our position.

We'd lived in fear of intrusion as the foreigners got closer and closer, almost finding us several times. The only reason we remained isolated was because the gods wanted it that way. The next day the intruders were gone.

Mary Magdalene now fed me tamales from the night before. We made wild love under the cloudy skies continuing the celebration and excitement much to the delight of the chirping birds and buzzing bees flying about.

The celebration was over now and our child was on his way.

"Izquierdito. I'll name him, after my father" I whispered.

"And Mary Junior, if she's a girl" said she, jokingly.

We kissed and fell asleep in the moonlight.

When we woke in the cool of dawn we burned sweet grass and *copal* to thank the gods for protection.

But the protection soon vanished as our destiny was sealed.

*   *   *

Mary Magdalene grew big in the stomach with each passing week, until her walking was like the wobbling of a sea lion. She would come to the garden where I toiled to bring me an apple or a sweet drink of papaya, excited to tell me *"He's kicking!"* or, *"He's going to be a big boy,"* and things like that. I would hold her belly and listen for any sound that might delight us, listen to the future soccer player already kicking the ball in there as if in the game of his life. I sang happy songs on her belly to get him used to my voice. He would soon be born, she said, and would love me the way she loved me. We would be a happy family, and eat, and play, and travel together doing all the things a clan does just as I dreamed since the day my mother left me. Mary Magdalene would teach me the meaning of family.

I remember my mother taking me to the *mercado*, and to the village healer, even once to the old, abandoned church where Father Serra lived; she took me inside and told me the smelly old man would teach me reading, writing, history, and music. *"Things you'll love, my son."*

I believe mother knew she would leave someday and that is why she took me to him, to receive the instruction and guidance in life she would not provide.

She did in fact leave soon after, me with the garlic-breath priest, she with the mighty jungle and two girls to fend for herself. That's what I remembered of family. I wanted mine to be different.

Mary Magdalene and I took long walks together through the jungle as I boasted to the animals of our coming addition. *"It's going to be a boy you'll have to contend with!"* The birds and monkeys, macaws and snakes would applaud and sing in a welcoming gesture sounding like a symphony.

"I will name him Izquierdito, after his grandpa!"

Well that brought down the house as the music came to a crescendo because Izquierdo was loved and protected by this very wildlife, they belonged to him in a way; they would never forget him. Like I said before, animals have memories too.

The music that came from the jungle that day is a thing of legend. What I would give to have a recording of those sounds!

*   *   *

Izquierdito was born under a bright blue sky. The whole village stopped what they were doing to celebrate his arrival. They played music, made food, drank beer; the children made lots of noise with the cookware, pounding pans with sticks, knives and spoons. Many brought the new mother presents: Rivera gave her a painting of mother and child; Frida, a blue chair, Siqueiros sat to drink a cup of mezcal holding my son in his enormous hands. Sánchez, the soldier, said *Nobody Writes to the Colonel*, meaning, I suppose, that since the Army had been stationed near the outskirts of our village, he hadn't received any mail. He laughed saying the girls better watch out because the boy resembled me.

Los Reyes del Este brought incense and a gold medallion with the Aztec calendar imprinted on it. It would someday go to Izquierdito; he would wear it with pride. The Franciscan Nuns from the Convent gave Mary Magdalene beautiful Chinese silks and fabrics to make my son his first clothes. Old man Zapata gave my child a rifle; Hidalgo, a Bible. The brothers Flores Magón came reciting poetry of the *New Reality*.

The house filled with flowers and gifts, chocolates, candy and gum. There were boxes and books and paintings, fruits and leather goods; so much in fact that we lost track of whom gave what. Mary Magdalene was disconcerted with this, considering she loved writing *Thank You* cards to all that gave.

By the end of the night, she retired as a Mariachi played its final tunes. Out of nowhere a Country and Western singer - in honor of the newborn's American side - sang tunes from as far back as Roy Rogers, as the village, now drunk, skipped along and danced like fools. The Clowns appeared, the flute players, balloons, and cats, and dogs, and puppets. The Hernández kid with the big nose walked his giant iguana through the crowd, a big smile on his face.

Everyone enjoyed the celebration that night. One thing is for sure: a person from the desperate mile does not need an excuse to celebrate!

*   *   *

Presently, Mary Magdalene sat next to me, holding the flowers I'd picked. We were at the ridge, on top of the world, deep in love.

"I'll never leave you, Ja-guar. You know that."

"We'll see, love. You never know about life."

"Why do you say that, when I am so in love?" she grumbled.

"Because my mother used to say, You never know what life will bring you."

Mary Magdalene frowned. She knew I spoke the truth. There were times I told her things she didn't want to hear, but that is who I am.

The day we met, well, the day she found me at the Café she said, *"I knew I would find you, and that we would be together, in love. You are soooooooooo handsome, Ja-guar! Take me home."* I did and we made lots and lots of love, drank mint tea, talked and kissed, I served her ripe mangos and *guayabas* freshly picked, and prickly pears. I cooked *huachinango* and lasagna, *pot-a-feu*, *bouillabaisse* and paella. She kissed my hands and shaved my face. We combed each other's hair, picked roses from the garden and tossed petals on the bed. The next day, we smelled each other's skin without *basta*.

It wasn't until days later that we went back to the hotel *Presidio* to pick up her things. I paid her bill, and we took a taxi to the outskirts of town where a bus was waiting to take us home. As the passengers knew me they applauded as we kissed and someone took out a bottle of *mosquito* to celebrate.

We have never seen you so in love, Señor, someone shouted.

We have never seen you in love at all, another voice added.

It was true. I'd been on that bus a million times, day in and day out, mostly with the same passengers, all of us going to the same place – home - to the village, to their respective villages, as the area was populated by Zapotecas of different lineages and tribes. During the ride we talked of the weather, shared the day's events, never discussing personal matters as in our tradition. Never had I revealed myself, and never had anyone asked questions. I didn't ask questions, unless someone initiated the conversation. Writer that I am, I listened and took notes. I knew even less of the poblanos as they generally kept to themselves, whispering such that I could hardly hear a word spoken.

Today on the bus with Mary Magdalene they saw me in a different light. They hadn't seen me with a woman because back in those days I mostly kept to myself. The pain I'd experienced with the bitch lasted for years and I hadn't gotten over her so easily. I was not prepared to give my heart away to another woman in those years these people knew me, keeping myself well-preserved, in my shell, protected and unhurt by others until this very day.

We sang songs of love and commitment. We read poems to each other, held hands under the full moon, listened to Mozart, cried to Leonard Cohen.

Today, I consider that bus ride my wedding vows. We never had a formal wedding, no, not in the way others marry because we didn't have to, maybe we didn't want to, perhaps because we knew destiny had called on us, that we would be inseparable forever more regardless of the future: we accepted fate. Going without though, brought back Izquierdo's wedding day.

Izquierdo and Puta Madre were married by Father Serra without realizing it. You see, their wedding day was like any other day at the desperate mile. So it happened that the evening mom and dad went to their secret place, Father Serra was on his way back from the desperate river where he often sat to pray. His book *The Conversion of the Mutes* was not going well and so he was taking a breather, searching for answers he would never find, mysteries unsolved in a life of desperation and aloneness he never imagined. Something about the river's rushing water calmed his nerves and so, whenever he felt trapped by his memories, to the river he went. On his way home to resume writing, convinced that teaching the natives sign language would bring him results, he saw what he thought were two ghosts in the distance approaching, so protecting himself from the unknown, he quickly knelt in prayer and after the sign of the cross proceeded to recite as many Hail Mary's as he could muster unknowingly giving Izquierdo and Puta Madre the very *bendicón* newlyweds seek to seal marriage. The couple respectfully imitated his every action, crossing themselves too, thus accepting the Lord in the process, thus, the marriage, thus, the union. Back in those early days of the desperate mile the people admired Father Serra, bowed their heads in response to his, though the gesture was more one of respect rather than the submissive faithful gesture of a Catholic believer. Old man Serra nearly died of excitement that night as he welcomed what he thought were two more converts into his imagined, growing congregation.

Mary Magdalene on the other hand, wanted a full wedding. Alive with newfound love and all its pronouncements, she proposed to me on the bus, and, I fool that I am accepted. Excited, holding hands and in a dizzy sweat, we went straight to the village *curandero* who burned herbs and *copal* to clean our pasts of trouble and give us a blessing. I handed him what I had in my pocket completing the ceremony, and that was our wedding.

That was the tradition at the desperate mile, you went to the healer, asked for his blessing then somehow the word got around you just married. A ceremony is what you make it. The marriage soon began to unravel.

I haven't had many lovers, she said.

She was young, and that invigorated me. We listened to Mozart, Boccherini, and Beethoven. We danced and tumbled and laughed.

Now she was pregnant, and me overjoyed.

We have everything we need here, I said, rubbing her belly, meaning, of course, the desperate mile.

But she wanted to go home, be with mom. The pregnancy brought out the longing for home. She was homesick and I would pay for it. Boy, would I ever pay.

Thinking back now, in the pink envelope were the words of a young girl, a girl who was not yet herself, a girl still in search of herself not yet independent. Knowing this I gave her all the security I could muster, making her feel free and secure at home without a worry in sight. It wasn't until our son was born that Mary Magdalene felt a woman.

Presently, we wept of joy in each other's arms as the village celebrated our son's birth. The music was delightful; the joy in the air filled our hearts. The arrival of our child made people happy all around us such that we never forgot the day.

Though we did forget each other because now she lived far away, and I had a new love: writing.

*　　　*　　　*

My knees creak, my feet hurt, I am skinny like a weed, though my lungs are in good shape. I ran one too-many marathons, but it was worth it. My medals hang in the guest house as if welcoming those who run too, those who know the power of the stride; those who are in search of themselves in order to gain the freedom that accompany the discovery.

Running was a drug for me - it was an addiction, a one character play, a monologue, therapy, meditation: a prayer. When I ran back in those days, it was both an exhilarating and a painful experience. I ran to the waterfall, I ran to the sacred *cenote,* I ran up the mountain, around the circumference of the volcano, I ran after my father, eventually after girls, after women, but most importantly, I ran from the void, from the pain eating away inside me. *You always ran from yourself,* Mary Magdalene loved to say. No, I didn't have to do that. I may have run from fear of emotional pain, even from love; I ran from my monsters, from the temptation of self-destruction, to preserve myself, I ran to heal my inner wounds, but I never ran from myself. If anything, my dear Mary Magdalene, I ran towards the shining light within.

Yet in America, in New York, California, Texas, New Mexico, Arizona, in all the places I lived, women would plead I stop running and stay, stay in one place where I could make a life. But my life is on the road, don't you know that? *You're running from life, from love, from yourself, from commitment, Jaguar,* they would say. A man has to know himself, has to know what to believe, has to know his own truth, and I knew mine. I was running because I lived in two worlds, I was between two worlds, each different from the other, and I didn't know how to make amends, how to exist in harmony with who I was brought up to be, and who I became. I was anointed, you see, at the desperate mile, and I even ran from that responsibility. I thought I was running to capture my *being* once and for all, running to find myself. I wasn't lost in the first place. I wasn't even confused. In running, I simply became someone I did not recognize in the mirror.

I thought I had places to go. I didn't feel at home anywhere. I kept on rambling from place to place, knowing that sooner or later I would land on my feet.

The women who wanted me for themselves were selfish. They had the life they wanted, but not the man. But I was not that man, I said to them. I'm just passing through. *I have everything in life except for you*, they said.

Nothing could make me stay, and nothing ever did. I was the runner, and by God, I would keep running.

Women will make any excuse to keep you. They will connive, cry, throw a tantrum, fits of rage, break dishes, they'll hide your possessions, hold things against you, show you love letters from long ago, tell you they're pregnant. Boy, let me tell you, I have seen it all. But they will not ask you to stay.

It must be about pride.

"*Live with your pride,*' I said, '*you don't need a man.*"

They loathe you because they loved you. They'll make you wrong for leaving, they'll hold it against you forever, and hate you in your grave.

A woman I knew once complained because her ex-husband died of a heart attack, "*That fucker died on me and left me with all the responsibility of two houses, two mortgages, the children, a pile of bills! What am I supposed to do?"*

They punish you even in death. Keep you in their heads when you're gone. The heart attack kept him in her heart forever.

I had to keep running. I had to keep running to survive, to stay alive, to feel vital. I had to feel my heartbeat; my feet hit the pavement, the dirt roads, the sand, the water.

Today my knees may creak from running but my heart's strong.

*   *   *

This time there was no pink envelope. A desperate pounding on the door woke me in bed and my heart jumped in surprise because Mary Magdalene used to pound the door the very same way when I locked her out during her crazy episodes. Thinking no one would understand, she yelled and cursed to no avail as the door remained shut until she calmed down like a clam. At the moment, I thought it was she knocking again, asking to be let into the home she no longer belonged.

Screaming and yelling in any language is understood, I would shout back, my heart filled with laughter.

Answering the door I saw it was Apollo, a surprise indeed.

"Emergencia," he said through his thick teeth, handing me a telegram in a yellow envelope. I thought of Mary Magdalene.

"Pásale," I said, inviting him in.

As I sat at the table to read the news I sensed he expected a tip to run off and buy candy. If that's what he wanted he would have to wait. The boy was learning fast and I liked that about him.

"Dear Ja-guar,' she wrote, hyphenating the word like she did in her speech; *"I am leaving you and the desperate mile; desperado that you are. You don't need me anymore. You have your writing. I bore you a child, and he is with me. I love you tremendously - as you like to say - and I always will. You will never run short of women."* It was signed, MARY MAGDALENE in big letters.

She'd been gone for over a month this time.

Now it was she who was running, eh? Now it was she who would breathe heavily, taste the sweat pouring down her face, hear her pounding of her feet leave the road behind, her long, desperate strides pushing the limits of her very being. I must have been in shock as Apollo asked what was wrong. You see, he wanted to read the message, wanted to know the news. As the village messenger, he felt compelled to keep the village informed of the day's news. Looking into his eyes I noticed that the idea of not knowing its contents would kill him. But just then I couldn't speak the truth. I would not give the boy the satisfaction of knowing my pain. The last time she left me I told him she was visiting family in America.

"Tell everyone Mary Magdalene is dead," I said with authority, my heart about to explode.

"But, how can she be dead, Doctor, if she signed the telegram?" he asked. I knew he'd tried to read the message but did not understand as it was written in English.

"She is dead in my heart," I muttered.

I lied to keep from hurting because to me she was very much alive. I lied because she meant everything in the world to me and I did not want that to change. She was my great love, my inspiration, my heart, my soul, my mate. She'd found me the way I'd wanted to find her, the way I'd been looking for her without knowing it was she I longed for. Now, she was breaking my heart the way I broke hearts everywhere I'd been.

Apollo walked out without a tip, scratching his head as if to signal me for money, a gesture I ignored but took note to restore later when the pain lifted.

I thought he was too young to understand heartbreak but I was wrong. It wasn't until years later that I learned he was heartbroken too that day, that he too loved my Mary Magdalene like everyone loved her at the desperate mile, and that I had inflicted pain in his tender heart by declaring her dead. By then, Apollo was a young man on his way to college at Columbia University where I secured him a full scholarship to study indigenous people.

"Does María Magdalena still live there," he asked after a firm handshake, knowing I was the murderer that day, that I burned her figure in effigy like we did at the desperate mile when love was over. He

wanted to see her once more, say hello, clasp her fine hand in his, and kiss her cheek probably as much as I did.

"*No sé, hijo,*" I responded, calling him son, like my son who no longer lived with his mother, no longer talking to me as he too had grown to be a man.

Later that day after the telegram I walked to Father Serra's abandoned church and sat at the altar to pray – and weep. All the people I cared for were now dead, gone, out of touch or missing. My own running wouldn't cut it anymore as there was no final destination.

Where did I go wrong? Did I reveal too much of myself?

It was months before I heard from her again. They'd settled in New York, my old stomping grounds.

*   *   *

She took most of my money, but what did I care? After all, I lived at the desperate mile where everything was provided, what did I need in life but her?

She bought an apartment in the West Village and got a job at a woman's magazine. She started over, she said, her self-esteem shattered but in repair, a little boy by her side. Time alone would do her good.

I left the church and asked for a machete at the Lorca's house. They gave me their biggest and, seeing me in a state of subdued rage they quickly became concerned perhaps thinking I would kill myself. A small group of villagers followed me home. As I was sure everyone in town heard the news by now, I proceeded to chop down our favorite tree in the yard, a tree planted on our wedding day, a tree meant to outlive our love after we were long gone form this earth. Now though, I chopped it at the base and sat at the stub. Suddenly it occurred to me to dig a hole in the ground, and so after tossing my shovel and nearly breaking the handle, I cut the wood in half again fastening a cross with a rope. After standing it to rest, I secured it with a pile of rocks with the inscription: *Mary Magdalene* R.I.P.

Kneeling to the fresh dirt before me I vowed to never see her again. The villagers walked away looking like floating ghosts in plain daylight.

I cried that night until my heart could take it no more.

It was a horror living without her.

In life we think everything will work out, but the day comes when you feel nothing inside, when you don't look each other in the eye, when you walk down the street in silence, passing each other in the hallway without a word to say.

You ask yourself what happened and know it's over.

How do you start over, how do you go on, how do you tell her you're sorry?

You buy her gifts to make up for your mistakes but they mean nothing.

She cries in bed, thinking you don't hear her sobbing.

She slaps your face at dinner, and runs from the table.

You eat in silence together like at a funeral.

She leaves a note, and you know it's over.

You remember it was you this time who didn't ask her to stay.

*　　*　　*

As always after heartbreak we have to go on. My new love was writing.

Our love changed when Izquierito was born. We discovered a rivalry.

I spent time with my son, and she spent time alone. She felt ignored, and I felt different. I didn't want to make love anymore; she was no longer the virgin. Did I really love her? Was I lying to myself? Did I like her to begin with?

One morning I woke up and didn't want her anymore so I started to write again. I wrote to stay alive, like with my marathons: to keep my sanity, my dedication, my passion for life.

"You love writing more than you love me!"

"You don't talk to me anymore."

"Why don't you write about me?"

And on, and, on and on she went.

The world revolved around Mary Magdalene and that was that. But, she was distant herself, and quiet, and accusing. According to her every complaint the desperate mile did not turn out to be what she'd dreamed it would be. It turned out to be too real for her.

The flying witches amused her, the past stories of our village scared her. She didn't believe that Hidalgo broke the chains, or that Zapata died for our lands that the eagle rested on the cactus. The volcanoes erupted and showered us with ashes that lasted a thousand days, the Army was killing Indians in the south, the Mayas were being butchered in their rightful land. For her, the desperate mile was meant to be a party. And now the party was over.

"What are you writing about, Ja-guar, now that Izquierdo is dead," she said in provocation. *You have nothing to write about now*, she'd say, hurting me intentionally the way a cruel person does with a grin on her face.

She hurt me and I let her hurt me. Nobody talked that way about my dad, my hero, my mentor.

"Nothing happens here anymore, Doc-tor. Why stay? It's boring!"

The mangos grew the size of footballs, the birds gathered to sing, swarms of crickets blocked the sun; the fish in the river walked into town. The ghosts of our ancestors took form in the saguaros, standing tall and beautiful, watching over us the way proud parents watch a child take his first steps. The blue *tucanos* sang sweetly at night, the coyotes howled in the day. The bluebirds and crows made music like Mozart violin concertos.

Was the desperate mile dead, or was Mary Magdalene living in a different world that she couldn't see the beauty?

*

MARY MAGDALENE OR, THE LESSON OF CARLOS CASTAÑEDA

It rained and rained the whole day after I got home, and I couldn't help but think it was a sign of draught, that the land would be dry for a very long time to come. Rain has a way of foretelling the future.

The land would dry because man hadn't learned to respect water, the way the Navajo dry farmer does to grow corn without rain for an entire season. Man was meant to survive like that.

The rain banged the rooftop like drums watering the palms outside my window. The mixture of hot air and rain made it almost unbearable to breathe; it was so hot and humid that day, steam rose from the surrounding rocks. The desperate mile for the first time looked like a living hell.

To me it was just life.

The bright, pink envelope sat before me, and I thought of this Mary Magdalene girl who wrote me - was that her real name? I thought of Brigitte and the evening we met. The first time I noticed her she was sitting quietly in her pearls and black skirt, her blonde hair in a bob, her teeth glistening in the darkened room reading the latest novel heralded by The New York Times. When she saw me walking towards her she shrugged her shoulders teasingly, divulging plump, freckle-sprinkled breasts that called out to be caressed. We spent the evening drinking beer at *The Lion's Den* chatting like old friends. Today, I remember little about her as she faded away like all the rest.

I'd given a lecture at Columbia University, where the young faces stared at me in wonder as if I were an extraterrestrial creature. You see, they'd never seen anyone like me before as theirs was a world of MTV, text messages and marijuana parties. Their closest reference to an indigenous face was in *National Geographic*. I was the monkey in the cage.

Standing at the podium, I looked closely at the faces in the seats and saw a blond boy with the blue eyes sitting in the back row: he was Indian I could tell by his strong features, Native American, but it was obvious he had white blood. In this world he was Indian because in the Native culture you claim your mother's blood. The boy lived in two worlds, probably lived his life in search of his identity, a place to fit where he could just be himself, a place free of attacks for being of mixed lineage. Thinking of that night took me away from the pink envelope.

This same student came backstage after my lecture – after my speech – after my indictment of society, my piercing of the blue bloods as I called it. He stood to the side silent as I greeted my friends waiting for his chance to meet me. I felt his presence and decided to greet him, see what there was inside him. The conversation played out like a drama.

Me: Hello.

He: (Doesn't look me in the eyes.) Hi.

(There is a long pause. He knows I can read his mind, so he avoids direct eye contact.)

Me: Do you have a question, maybe answers?

I laugh, which makes him laugh.

He: Can I study with you?

He asks this innocently. I look at him, notice that people are watching and listening, waiting to hear my answer, an answer they can hold against me, words they can quote in the newspapers, magazine articles, gossip about in their circle of friends, words to crucify me by, looking for an answer they can distort to fit their needs.

Me: What do you wish to learn?

He: (doesn't hesitate. I almost see his eyes.) What you know…I have powers, he says. *But why won't he look me in the eyes, if he has powers?* I say to myself. Some people sigh, others 'ooh,' and 'ahh.'

Me: (After careful thought.) "If you have powers as you say, use your powers to disappear right now," I say, rather aggressively.

Just then, I recalled a tale Izquierdo told me long ago. (I have so much to tell you, believe me, and just when you think you are getting to know me.)

This one is about another young man, Janu was his name, who was at UC Irvine, to be precise. The first day of class Janu is waiting for the elevator to the third floor when a man walks up to stand next to him, obviously to be taken upstairs. The man is Carlos Castañeda, the professor where he's going, though he doesn't know it at the time. The two wait quietly for the elevator to arrive and when the door opens, the two enter. Now Janu pushes the button to the Third Floor where his classroom will be for the coming semester. He wonders if the stranger - CC - wants different floor but ignores the thought. *Let him push his own button,* thinks the student slowly riding up to his destination. Not quite in deep thought, he stands in the elevator looking at the wall. So, here they are the two of them in the elevator, both riding up when Janu looks down at his feet checking his shoes but when he raises his head the man is gone from sight, disappeared, vanished not even a ghost. I mean, the man has disappeared from sight right in front of his eyes; elevator door closed shut, O.K.? How is this possible, he asks? And between floors, come on now! No way, he says to himself, alone in the elevator. No way that happened, thinking he imagined the disappearance, that maybe he should have smoked some weed before class to make sense of the whole thing.

Now, Janu didn't exactly freak-out or anything like that, you know, he just sorta got out of the elevator and looked around for the new classroom as he was unfamiliar with the building's layout. So after investigating his whereabouts he finds the classroom and walks in and, guess who's standing there in front of class? His new teacher, the man in the elevator: Carlos Castañeda.

Janu says to himself: *"That's my professor? How'd he get here? How'd he disappear from the elevator?"* he thinks long enough to dismiss it and takes a seat.

CC was his professor for that semester.

CC stood before the class waiting for the students to settle down. Once he saw they were seated and quiet, he looked the room over and exclaimed: *"I'll be right back!"* leaving the classroom never to return, not then, not the next class, not the entire semester.

So the students grumble among themselves that afternoon but return to class the next day ready to work. But you see, what CC did was leave the students to think for themselves, to question, to ponder, to philosophize, to resolve but they had no idea this was the class itself.

"What happened to him?" asked a pretty blonde receiving no answers from dejected students. Someone else questioned his motives, his stature, his integrity, his professionalism. Yet, week in, and week out, the students showed up to class with no professor present.

"What are we supposed to do if he's not here," they asked.

Some dropped-out, those with faith remained. Janu decided to stay.

One day when CC had still not shown he stood up and addressed the class.

"This is the ultimate lesson from him, don't you know," he exclaimed as by then CC had become a legend through his books, though the world had yet not met him. The New York Times Book Review hailed his work as magical.

"He has us here philosophizing and discussing his disappearance; his presence is always here. He is here right now, don't you see?" Janu paused for a moment looking the class over, taking over the room in preparation for the teacher he would later be in life.

"Can anyone here honestly say they haven't discussed this with a friend?"

The students looked at each other. Janu knew they wanted to lie.

"You see? You are all intrigued by professor Castañeda, but refuse to admit it. Instead, you prefer to criticize him and make him wrong. The fact is, he's making you think."

The class fell silent. They were not accustomed to being confronted in life, let alone in the classroom; these students had never been forced to think for themselves, they were spoon fed information that they memorized and readily regurgitated for tests going home to mommy and daddy with a shining report card and a splendid summer vacation. They came to university to regurgitate what was taught them, and heaven forbid they learn to think. Janu spoke again.

"I say we write a story, an essay on this experience; on what he has contributed to our developmental thinking process."

"But who do we turn to if there is no professor?" asked one skeptic.

"That is not important, do you see?" said Janu. *"We have each other."*

After much thought and understanding the value of *carpe diem,* they shook their head in agreement. Surely they would earn an "A."

During the following weeks they arrived to class on time and discussed the disappearance of Carlos Castañeda, professor, philosopher, faker king, the new Houdini. They went over every detail of his disappearance as with a fine comb. What was he wearing? What color shirt, blue, red, white? How long was he actually in the room, three minutes, four? What was his hairstyle, longish, shortish, mod? Did he smirk on his way out?

They went through three thousand questions or more, writing down each one. Near the semester's end they'd scraped the bottom of the barrel and few answers made sense. They couldn't come to conclusions, and no one wrote the essay except for Janu, because he was the only Indian in the class. He was the only one who really got what CC was up to. He understood that Indian culture is not what the white man makes it but what the Indian says it is.

At the end of the semester naturally all the students received a grade. Janu got an "A" and he others? He didn't care.

Now, I, Jaguar looked at the blonde Indian boy standing before me, wondering if he understood my question, my challenge.

He: "Disappear?" he asked.

Me: "Yes" I said. The kid looked stunned. I pointed to a window overlooking the campus as we were on the second floor of this building. As everyone turned to look in the direction I pointed, I disappeared from the room, leaving them to each other's company.

I never saw the blond boy again, but I did read his book years later. It was the story of becoming a Shaman. His book was titled, "*The Ghost's Laughter.*"

I had to laugh at the thought that he learned something.

*   *   *

I thought long and hard about Mary Magdalene's letter and made several attempts to picture her in my mind as all I had was her words in front of me. I imagined her as young, too young for me perhaps but bright and motivated. In her I saw confusion; I envisioned her as a kid with braided hair, maybe braces on her teeth, wearing bellbottoms, a big blouse, flowers in her hair and beaded necklaces, sandals, and smoking a clove cigarette, oh-so-cool.

She did have talent, but was very green. Was she imitating Kerouac, Ginsburg, e. e. cummings?

Maybe she knew of the napkins, the tablecloths, the walls and store receipts, the anguish of being without pen and paper at the moment of inspiration: creation!

Maybe she knows the pain of the writer when he can't write to save his life.

The writer writes. He has no choice, really. What else can he do?

At first you do it because you love to hear yourself talk as you write, you hear your own voice, not knowing that in the end as a writer you need one. You write to keep busy. You write because you hear the words in your head and think yourself crazy. You write because you think you're alone in the world, that you're the only one who thinks out loud, who discusses issues and answers questions to himself. A young writer is like Kostya in Chekhov's stage play *The Seagull*, who writes words only he understands. You long to know love without knowing what it is. Yet, you write about it, sounding hollow in the end, because you have not yet suffered its fury, love's passion and disappointments, its loss, its flowers and pain and dreams. You are so green with desire in your youth you can only write little playthings.

Still, you write.

You hear that only experience will develop you as a writer and try to fix it by writing silly, repetitive, and hollow poems. You don't understand that experience is the writer's fountain, that heartbreak will feed you words, stories, even novels during a lifetime. Experience will make you and break you, and that is when the writer flourishes because now he holds the truth, his truth, his own blood in his own hands one might say.

You want to write the great novel, but have no idea what it takes, or what it means to do so. You start and stop because you don't have the experience to back it up. You keep writing, crumpling page after page, wasting ink, and paper, and your precious time; you become frustrated, you want to learn to write, but fail time and time again.

You think you have something to say, but you don't know how to say it.

I know what I'm telling you, because I was that guy.

*   *   *

I envisioned Mary Magdalene, the writer, as I had been a young writer, a writer who hadn't found his voice. But if she hadn't found her voice, why was I so intrigued, because she desired me, because I liked being desired, because she was young and stood for hope - my hope for starting over after the bitch? Was Mary Magdalene willing to give it her all to learn to write? Was I to be her teacher, her mentor?

People didn't do that anymore, the world didn't work that way.

Truth be told, I was interested in her because she was looking for me without even knowing what I looked like. She trusted me in some strange way, maybe trusted herself enough to settle for the unknown, I don't know, but I was flattered.

As no one was allowed to take my picture, I practically did not exist, you see, and as a result one could say that I had definitely disappeared from plain sight.

My royalty checks were sent to a post office in Oaxaca where I made sure to never show up myself. Instead, I sent a messenger to pick up the dough: my friend Apollo.

I heard there was a village kid who ran about excitedly delivering letters and packages so I asked around finding him at the pharmacy selling newspapers and little candy. I asked him to work for me.

"Sure," he said, *"I'll go over there later. I know where you live."*

On his first errand he ran to Oaxaca City and back in less than an hour. The door sounded, and there he was, a fresh little kid, his left hand on the wall the other hand in his pocket. He looked so relaxed after such a task I thought he was kidding me. He wasn't even breathing heavy from the run.

"Where's the mail?" I asked.

He looked at me and grinned, reaching over his shoulder to pull a bundle from his cloth backpack. When I took the check, he opened his palm for a tip. I gave him a US dollar, thinking after he might get used to my generosity.

A month later he arrived on a bike. Asking where it came from he said he'd saved every penny I gave him. *It's for my new profession,* he said, meaning of course that he was now the village messenger.

Apollo soon dropped out of school to become a full-time messenger. When I heard the news I scolded him for doing so. *You have a bright future my friend, one that only education will reveal to you.* The poor boy looked at me with disappointment and hurt. *Do you want to live in New York, Paris or Rome? Go to school. I will send you to the best in the world. I promise.* And with that, the messenger returned to class happily riding his bike to and from.

No one in the publishing world knew where I lived because I wanted the secrecy. When my editors visited I had them stay at *Casa Panchita* in Oaxaca City because through the years I'd learned that people are a bother as guests at home. That arrangement was easily solved by meeting at the *zócalo,* carousing the day away with me disappearing when the day was done, similar to what Carlos Castañeda did during his years of fame.

My publisher says, *"You could die and no one would know it."* Let me assure you that when I die, someone will show up at the mailbox to collect my royalties, and then, for years to come.

I like not existing. I like being dead.

At the moment, though, I want to exist, because I want Mary Magdalene to find me.

"Be careful what you ask for that might get it," my mother used to say.

And so, the day came to meet her.

Like I said, I go to the plaza every morning for breakfast to sit and write my journal, that's how I start my day now. The shop has the best coffee and croissants one could ever find, so I'm happy from the get-go. I can bet you that no Frenchman makes as good a croissant as Felipe Rodríguez y Risa, a Mexican baker *par excellence* runs the place. I say this because like Rufino the *hacendado*, I have been to every bakery in Paris searching for the ultimate croissant, I like them so. If you ask me, the best is in Mexico.

Sitting for hours some days I like to watch people stroll by and sometimes stumble (the drunks on their way home), I watch the tourists in their khaki shorts and cameras rolling, the modern-day hippies, the girls on their way to work and the many Indians who have taken to spending time in the plaza protesting against a government that ignores them. People-watching is one of my favorite past-times. I am a voyeur, I tell people, no shame in my voice.

And so in this manner I spend my mornings, relaxing, taking in the sun, enjoying my middle age. I can cook, make coffee, espresso, all of those things, but I prefer not to, especially if there are Mexicans willing to do that for you.

So I enjoy life, you see? What the hell, no one is going to do it for you. Besides, I've earned the right. (I have worked as: a gardener, a tree trimmer, weed puller, ditch digger - I once dug several holes the size of a Volkswagen - a waiter, a busboy, a dishwasher, a sweeper, a bartender, a host; I have worked in an office, typing, selling jewelry, as a counselor in a drug-rehab center; I've been a painter - houses, cars, interiors, exteriors, murals, buildings, churches - I was a handy man on an estate, I did plumbing, sanded floors, decks, doors, walls; I built many a coyote fence, I mowed lawns, trimmed edges, weeded fields, built stone walls, adobe walls, plastered, worked for a shoemaker, pumped gasoline at a Shell station, laid new grass lawns, watered gardens, walked dogs, cared for cats - though allergic to felines — I've refurbished houses, done electrical work, carpentry; I cooked and catered movies and so much more you wouldn't believe.) So, I think I have earned my way and have a right to a little "luxury" - as I refer to the pleasures of life. To me, life is a privilege, thus, a luxury.

The coffee and croissant are a real treat for me; I need so little in life anymore.

This day was like any other day. I did everything by rote: woke-up, made a small cup of coffee, showered, splashed on cologne, fed the dogs, got dressed and walked out the door. I arrived at *El Corral* as the café is known, sat at my usual table and had a beer at 11:00 o'clock. A *Negra Modelo*.

So there I am, sitting quietly, reading the morning papers when I hear a woman's voice behind me, dark and deep uttering something undecipherable. More out of habit than curiosity I turn, but cannot see where the voice is coming from. I hear it once again but this time it sounds closer.

A singer sings: (His voice too appears out of nowhere.)

Buscaste, sí

tu destino

buscaste sí

tu querer...

Pero nunca

tuviste

que buscaaaaaaaaaarme.

You sought, yes, your fate

You sought, yes, your love

But misunderstood

You needed not seek me.

Cabrón! I shouted.

The singer sang. The singer knew! And the singer is blind!

I froze at the thought of the lyrics because suddenly as if on cue or as if in a dream I smelled the pink envelope. How could I smell the pink envelope? I don't have the pink envelope, it's at home!

I don't turn around, as I don't want to give myself away.

The woman is speaking English, pleading in English.

"I am looking for Señor, Doc-tor Ja-guar, do you know him?" And by God, I can tell you I love that voice! I cannot tell you how, or why, but I love that voice.

"I am loo-king for Se-ñor, Doc-tor Ja-guar." I freeze, because I know it's her.

Out of the corner of my eye I see my friend Victor Villaseñor gesturing at me to hide, he sees me sitting there, I in turn ignore him, comfortable he knows not to reveal my identity. He owns the bookstore *Rain of Gold*, and we go way back as friends. He respects my privacy, I respect his store.

I hear the voice again. *"Do you speak English?"* But there is no answer. There is no desperation in that voice, no worry, just patience.

The shopkeepers that solemnly stand outside their doors keep quiet, and I know they're trying to protect me. (Do you know that no Indian can be forced to talk, even when burning his feet?)

The voice trails off...

And comes straight at me!

"Excuse me, sir, do you speak English?" she asks. Lord, this voice is sweet, so pure, so innocent, so...heavenly!

I pretend not to hear. I flinch unexpectedly, but it doesn't discourage her. She taps me on the shoulder. Now, I get cold inside. *"She touched me, she found me, I found her, the pink envelope! Her voice matches the smell, can you believe that? It makes sense, see, she was meant to find me!"*

I turned to her, holding my heart, see her sandaled feet and pierced navel staring at me. I wanted to look at her face but couldn't. I knew that if I did, I would see her entire life before my eyes and I didn't want that just yet. I wanted to take my time, to discover her for myself.

My hand is shaking, sweat pours from my forehead, I get a monumental, unexplainable erection. I can't open my mouth to speak.

Before I knew it, she walked away. I wanted to answer, but could not speak. Answer, respond, say, "*Yes! It is me! It is me you're looking for, young beauty! I speak English, and Italian, and French and German, and Russian, and Spanish! Yes, my name is Jaguar, and you are MARY MAGDALENE!*"

Seeing her walk down the aisle I knew she was mine. On her ankles she wore Oriental bracelets with little bells that made the sweetest sound with every step she took. I saw her delicious bottom sway away from me, gone, gone, around the corner, when in a moment she turned and disappeared.

All I heard was the tinkling of her bells from afar.

MARY MAGDALENE PART III

It was several days before I returned to the Plaza for my breakfast of espresso, croissant, and *cacahuates*. The rain had not stopped and my heart had not stopped pounding for her. I took a six-mile run that morning, worked the garden, fixed the roof of my adobe casita, all in the pouring rain. Why, once, years ago, I walked all the way to Yagul just for my friend Fernanda's enchiladas, all this in the pouring rain, the wind blowing, the thunder calling, lightning striking the road ahead of me. I never got a cold that day; nature was with me then, as it is now, in this humid, constant July drizzle.

I didn't have my espresso and croissant at *El Corral* for four days because, the day I met Mary Magdalene, I got home and found Apollo waiting for me at my doorstep. He'd fallen asleep waiting and when he heard me, woke up and straightened his clothes. I knew something was wrong when he didn't speak. He had the saddest look on his face. I didn't think twice when he handed me an envelope. I ripped it open and read.

Jaguar: Your good friend, Jim Mallette died last night. It was signed, **Juan**. I must have dropped the paper and fainted, because the next thing I knew, I was getting up from the ground. My best friend in life had died and I couldn't believe it. I lost my steel.

Apollo rode off on his bike, brooding as if responsible for my friend's passing.

He wasn't responsible for his death, Jim was.

Jim was gay but you never would have guessed it. He was tall and handsome, always dressed in clothes that defined his masculinity. He'd taught theatre at Columbia and was a very good director. I saw his staging of *Danny and the Deep Blue Sea,* his version of *Hello Goodbye* by Athol Fugard, and countless productions, always top rate. He was Black, as black as the bottom of the ocean, the very ocean that he loved so much; and I think that because he was a Black man, we clicked.

We had lots in common.

We were at the Regent's office one morning waiting for an appointment when Jim, seated next to me, asked for a cigarette. I was lighting one of my beloved *Camel* non-filters, my favorites back then, and, way back when one could still smoke cigarettes indoors.

I handed him the pack and lighter, and we started chatting.

"You're that famous writer, aren't you?" he asked, the words sounding more like a statement than a question.

I coughed the smoke. I always thought people who approached me with that kind of line were a bit star crazy. He inhaled and dismissed my sneer.

"I like your books. They're quite imaginative."

I laughed now to counter the remark.

He laughed along with me adding, *"You say your stories are true. But I think they're all fiction."*

I took this as a compliment and shrugged. We had another drag of cigarette.

I muttered something as if to speak. He looked me in the eye.

"How come you never write about black people, he asked pointedly, a tone of judgment in his voice. Man, he was straight forward. I took another drag of the cigarette.

"I ain't black," I said matter-of-fact.

He roared with laughter.

"I can see that! You're cool. I'm only giving you a hard time."

He laughed again.

His face lit up and his big, white teeth gleamed; his whole body shook in laughter the way I have seen other Black people rattle when laughing.

"See, that's the world we live in. Everybody wants to be included... Including me!" he said, laughing still more, this time sounding like a child.

The Regent's secretary glared over at him, ice steaming from her cold, blue eyes. Her hair seemed to turn white at their exchange.

We both noticed her unease as Jim read my thoughts.

"Shit! Don't mind her none. She's just hired help," he said in a voice loud enough for her to hear. There was a brief silence as the secretary shifted in her seat. Jim was a fully tenured professor who felt he could speak his mind. I understood what he was doing and laughed along. He was putting the white man down – in this case a white woman, and relishing the thought of it. Two hundred years of slavery were daily fresh in his mind, and he would never let her forget it. His sardonic

tone was meant to penetrate her, and it worked as she now grunted, got out of her seat, and walked in the direction of the ladies room.

"She's goin' in there to cry! he shouted, making sure she heard from afar.

He laughed some more as I thought him crazy. The truth was, he was very smart but hated white people. He never let an opportunity go by without stabbing them in the gut. I thought I had balls but this guy was a runaway train.

"She always give me a hard time, I come lookin' for the Regent. She's 'a prejudiced bitch, that one. She don't like people who don't look like her." He was from the ghetto, and although he had great diction from years as an actor in the theatre, he reverted to the 'hood slang when feeling good, or attacking whitey. It was like hearing him at the street corner hangin' with the boys. I never asked him this, but I wondered if he talked this way with the regent. "Probably so," I said to myself, why not after all? Culture is culture any way you cut it, and you are a product of your environment like it or not. I liked his social consciousness, thinking maybe he'd been a Black Panther. I thought of the secretary. I recalled

her as polite and cute with me, always wearing short, tight skirts to show off her great legs. Once, she rolled out from behind her desk and stood up to pull down the little skirt that had crawled right up her ass. I saw her gorgeous thighs and did my best to keep from being distracted. I didn't take her out then, because I wasn't interested in her. After numerous visits and after considering the conquest I realized there was something about her smile that was phony. Was she bitchy, unhappy, white trash? I couldn't tell. All I knew is that she looked like trouble.

Jim laughed.

"Just hired help," he repeated with a grin, much like a plantation owner might have said a hundred years ago.

"She has freckles all the way up her thighs," I said, trying to interest him in her looks, trying to dissuade him from further attacks.

Jim kept quiet.

The secretary returned and took her seat. She blew her nose.

"See?" Jim asked, tilting his head toward her. I found him quite amusing and chuckled. Whatever was going on between them was their story.

"You just like me," he whispered; *"nobody fuck with you!"*

Which that was true, nobody messed with me. I didn't let anyone close, so most people just figured to stay away from me, considering me a man they found hard to understand.

That morning, I didn't understand that Jim didn't like women.

What I found out later, was that he liked men.

After mourning his death for three days, I returned to *El Corral* for my usual morning ritual.

Mary Magdalene had come by asking for me until the Balloon Lady across the street gave way.

"He drinks beer at El Corral everyday at eleven," she told the young beauty. Mary Magdalene gave her a dollar and ran off to find me.

"She's mine," I thought, as I settled for espresso.

She was irresistible from first sight. She walked up in her royal blue *huipil* wrapped around her shoulders as if cold from an imagined breeze; the glow on her saintly face, a poem. Mary Magdalene, barefoot, a deep copper-colored peasant skirt slit at the side, her long dark hair now in a braid, loaded with turquoise necklaces on her neck, large silver earrings and noisy bangles completing a look that resembled Frida Khalo. She took a seat next to me without being invited, giving me the killer smile, her tiny ankle bells singing of damnation.

"So you're Ja-guar!" she said indicting me, adding *"And I am Mary Magdalene,"* pointing to herself in pride for she'd succeeded where others failed. She extended her hand, soft and moist, the handshake firm, (she was brought up on a farm, I later discovered) her smile, infectious. *The pink envelope,* I say to myself. *She is the pink envelope.*

"Lord, I know you were looking out for me!" I heard me shout inside. It reminded me of Jim, for I sounded like a Baptist Minister. I wanted to shout to Jim up above, "She's not like the Regent's secretary, O.K.?" Knowing him he would have answered, Doctor: - he always called me 'Doctor,' *"If your ass is happy - so is mine."*

Jim knew my taste in women. But this Mary Magdalene, now she was a gift from Heaven!

"I thought I would never be with you," she once said as I held her tight and kissed her cheek.

Like most famous people, I like being famous. But, you know, not for the same reasons most famous people like being famous. I like being famous because I can be a fly on the wall when I want, if that makes sense. Fame gets in the way of life you see, people act strange when they see you, you begin to lose focus after much attention, others want something you can't give; mostly though, fame makes you look in the mirror to find *you* gone, the inner child in you gone, the creator vanished, the juice disappeared because you realize you want to be someone you're not to others who in the end couldn't give a rat's ass about you. As there is no published picture of me to be found anywhere in the world, I am able to enter worlds most people do not know exist. I find people to be openly cruel, like my friend Jim, you might say. I find people who speak the truth willingly because that is who they are. I hear long confessions of sins and betrayals, partake of parties, events, fiestas, celebrations, talks, and conversations most famous people never experience because they wear a veil. Instead, I climb mountains, travel to exotic places as a voyeur, as one deeply interested in what life has to offer. People hear my name, Jaguar, and they think nothing because that is what I want them to do. Do not think when it regards me, especially if you're a stranger. My fame could rival that of any Mafia Boss. And, like them, I can get the best table at the restaurant, and wine and women. It's great to be famous, and even greater to walk the earth unscathed by the press.

I like to spend time with my friends.

Ermenegilda down at the luncheonette is my friend. Not only does she feed me, she makes me laugh, and jokes about old times and characters I've brought to her counter. I invite her to my celebrations, and she sings with the Mariachis. She doesn't have much of a voice, but she's a hoot, and she knows it, missing teeth and all. I know all her troubles and I know all her fears. The only thing I don't know about her is the story of the stump, as I've never asked, and because she has never offered to talk about it.

When I go to the *guarache* maker, he tells me stories. He doesn't know who I am. Neither does the waiter at *El Corral* know, and neither does Bull. Fernanda in Yagul. Humberto, Roberto, Alberto,

Rigoberto, Roberto Carlos, Carlos Roberto, Gilberto. All of them tell me their sorrows, and all of them call me friend, but none suspect I am a writer, that I can read the mind, that I can write their story if need be. I walk among them a man just like any other.

Mary Magdalene became my friend. Did she see the future in my eyes?

I think she did.

And as you know now, the future didn't last long.

*   *   *

She sat next to me that afternoon and held my hand as if in silent prayer. With that infectious smile, she tilted her head and said: *We have so much to talk about. You can look into my eyes and read my life, Jaguar. I give you permission. I have no secrets.*

I didn't dare. I didn't want to. I wanted to lie in bed and feel her body, her firm breasts, her stomach, her forest; I wanted to smoke a cigarette, hear her tell me stories, of her childhood, her wishes and dreams fresh in her own words.

I kept from looking into her eyes.

"*Otra cerveza, Doctor?*" she asked getting up from the table to fetch beer. The waiter had disappeared, probably to give us some privacy as intimacy grew before his very eyes. Although, thinking about it now, the waiter probably stood behind us the whole time trying to understand a conversation in a language he didn't speak.

Mary Magdalene came back with two beers to rejoin me. I'd noticed her Nebraska accent earlier, but ignored it for the moment. Her Spanish was atrocious, but amusing.

"*Yo hablo español, Doc-tor*" she said, and I laughed. I couldn't help it, I was feeling good, and her funny accent sounded sweet.

"*I learned Spanish when I knew I would be with you. I was meant to be with you, you know?*"

Boy, all this and I had yet to say a word.

"*We have a connection, a strong connection,*" she added, though it sounded rehearsed.

I thought it a good thing I grew up 'mute' and silent. We simply listened and the world made sense. Such was the case with her every word.

I shook my head and smiled.

"Why didn't you answer me the other day when I spoke to you in English?"

She was holding my hand, hers was warm and it felt good. I didn't answer, it wasn't time yet.

"Are you're reading my thoughts now," she asked. I sensed my silence made her nervous, but maybe I was wrong. The excitement she felt at the moment overpowered the fear. Gringos can't handle silence, I don't know why; instead they have to yap-off at the mouth, hear their own voice, make sounds, play music on the radio, honk horns in traffic, keep the mouth moving. She wasn't like that, this beauty, not today anyway.

I snorted like a horse.

"Dear Lady" I said. *"You enchant me."* I felt like a little boy again. Like maybe 15 years old, and afraid to touch young Claudia's breasts.

"Rub them" she ordered me. *"I like it."*

I lifted her blouse and kissed her nipples and then her mouth under a moon that seemed to always shine at the desperate mile.

I wanted to do the same now with Mary Magdalene, now in public, now in the light of day and without a care in the world.

Mary Magdalene clunked her beer with mine as if agreeing I lift her blouse.

"I found you, Ja-guar," she muttered. *"I finally found you."*

I didn't know how to take her. Life gave you everything you asked for, if you only waited.

"And now you're mine," she said.

I was hers all right, and she was mine. There were things to work out; the expectations and details of love, discussing the resolution of future arguments, disagreements, agreements, and promises. The customary "talk" women like to have when you get together: *the rules of the game* my friends call it. Women act as if setting boundaries in a relationship is going to make a difference in the end. People do what they do when in love; everyone knows that. No boundary keeps a woman from betraying you; no boundary ever resolved a dispute. No boundary ever helped keep a relationship in place. If a woman doesn't love you anymore, she leaves. What good is this talk of boundaries?

I know she was asking the same question.

Still, she insisted.

As time passed, the boundaries were broken.

"You have to change," she screamed.

"You don't like me for who I am," she declared. I'm not good enough for you, she cried. I should have known, she yelled.

"You sought me out - trespassed, invaded my life," I answered back.

The pink envelope, I reminded her, was mailed from your corn fields of Nebraska, reaching our cornfields of Mexico. I didn't invite you, you came here yourself. You planned it. You're a social climber, but don't want to admit it. She stomped away in a huff, returning with the old, weathered envelope in her hand. I'd re-read the letter a million times, knew it by heart, could recite it like Romeo recited to Juliet. The scent floated to my nose, and I remembered the day.

She lifted my first novel, *The Solitude of Destiny* comparing the two.

I am the best thing that ever happened to you," she stated, like a minister before his congregation. Puta Madre, she hurt my feelings. I went to a corner and wept. My son walked into my arms. I held him tight, and promised never to leave him.

"*Son, we're going to be apart,*" I remember saying. Or was that the voice of Puta Madre from long ago? Was history repeating itself?

He looked me in the eyes, and held me close.

"*I wanna go with you,*" he cried. He knew that day my life history was repeating itself. My boy was only three years old.

"*Sonny*" I said, "*I'll always be near you. I promise.*"

I never kept that promise.

*   *   *

Mary Magdalene didn't let me close. I couldn't see him or talk to him, write, or otherwise visit with my very own child. Not even after I walked an hour one way to the village of Xanga in the pouring rain to call long distance. The phone line went dead when I asked for Izquierdito.

I walked back home after dialing again and again to no answer. I could afford a car, but I simply detested the idea of having one. I didn't have a phone, none of us did at the desperate mile, so why own a car?

Izquierdito grew up without knowing me. I traveled to New York only to have the door slammed in my face. The school told me to stand across the street. She put a restraining order on me, and enforced it.

She could have stayed in Mexico - somewhere near - in Mexico City, San Miguel de Allende where she had friends; Cuernavaca, Vallarta, Colima where she loved - but chose to move away instead. She detested Mexico and everything it stood for, everything it was and couldn't be; the country was never good enough for her, why, even the Royal Palace would not have pleased her in the end. Something made her unhappy in life, it wasn't all me, I knew that much, instead, it was a void in her no one could fill. All the shopping in the world sure couldn't. The bitch inside her was ranting and raging, the loneliness of an only child, tearing her apart, pushing her away from the ones she loved.

I didn't see this the day we met. I didn't look into her eyes with intention. I wanted to experience her as she was, without reading her life and I paid for it.

Izquierdito was ten years old before I knew it, and by then, I'd missed his childhood altogether. His mother was alone, unhappy, bitter, and lost. I wondered how such a beautiful woman could be so alone for so long. I was sure men saw through her like I did, and certainly stayed away. Mary Magdalene was one of those lonely women you see out on the town with the girlfriends, all dressed up, looking charming and attractive but keeping men at arm's length by their very visible misery. Misery radiates, believe me.

I never spoke to her again.

I wonder if she knows what she did.

Do you have a pink envelope in your life?

*   *   *

I can never get enough of her, this Mary Magdalene. She keeps crossing my mind; haven't you been in love? Have you forgotten your great love? Have you stopped thinking about her though you married someone else? How would your life look if she hadn't walked out?

*   *   *

She let me undress her, and in her nakedness she said, *"I have scars."* I was biting her neck; she, in her black bra, necklace and bare feet. I said, *"We all have scars; inside and out."* We entwined, the excitement in volumes, the sweat, and kisses tormenting our lips in the moment. I bit her nipples, her ankles, her pungent thighs. She yanked my long, black hair, pulling me closer. She cursed, and groaned, and kicked, and pounded my back with her fists; scratching my back like a cat, digging her nails into my chest. The ground shook in a frightening *terremoto*, a scary earthquake.

But, there's a part of her I haven't told.

She was very, very rich. Yes, you ask, a little farm girl from the Midwest? Yes, I say. Yes, yes.

Her family made money for years. But, she kept it from me for a long time. *"What do you have to hide,"* I once asked.

She started doing things that made me shiver. The bra and panties on the floor, clothes scattered all around the house, a dirty toothbrush in the sink, dirty dishes, you name it. At first I didn't notice – well, better said, I ignored it, you know how that goes? When it came time to pay for something, she didn't have her purse or she was broke. I didn't mind paying, but to never offer to pick up the tab? Take me for granted? Expect me to pay for everything? I complained once, and she said I'd agreed to take care of her forever in our talk the night we met. Expectations, arguments, resolutions, remember?

She invited her friends from college, friends from back home, friends from Mexico City; all of them to stay with us.

"*No, no,*" I said. "*You don't get to do that. Not here, not at all.*"

"*We're married,*" she said.

"*I don't like people knowing where I live, you know that. I like my privacy. Why don't you ask your friends to stay at Panchita's?*"

That did it. She had to have her way. That was no way to live life, she said.

Her friends never came, and things were never the same. I mean, she couldn't get over that? She preferred to let other people get in the way.

And then a miracle happened. She got pregnant, and for a while I let her get away with everything.

I put up with her antics: like using the cell phone for hours to call mother, and Suzy and Tiffany, and Annie; keeping them up on her goings-on. Life with the successful writer, she snarled; snatching the prize, life incognito, a baby on the way. I only kept the cell phone for emergencies, not even my publisher had the number. Now it rang day and night.

She stopped bathing and stank up the house. She was being the hippie, she said, something I hadn't bargained for. If there is one thing in life that I cannot tolerate is a smelly human being.

I worked hard at fixing this problem. I tried taking her to the hot springs up in the mountains, but that didn't work. I tried walking in the rain, and that didn't work either. I bought her perfumes, lit incense, and still the house smelled. It wasn't until we made love in the shower that I was at ease.

Soon she smelled again.

I cleaned the kitchen and bathroom, the bathtub, dirty laundry, dishes, floor, the room, made the bed, washed the windows until one day I blew up.

"*What is the matter, Ja-guar?*" she asked, knowing well I wasn't her servant.

"*Nothing, my dear,*" I said. "*I love being your slave.*"

"*Oh, lighten up,*" she said, dismissing me the way gringos do when they don't want to bother. Her eyes grew steely.

"*I am not your man-servant. I would appreciate you picking up after yourself.*"

"Are you calling me a pig?" she said, with that look in her eyes.

"You're used to having someone do those things for you, but it won't be me, see?"

"All you do is write all day. What am I supposed to do, clean up after you?"

"At least clean up after yourself," I urged. A pig bitch is annoying to have around let me tell you. The thing didn't go well. She sat at the table reading her magazine. I knew she wouldn't lift a finger, like rich people don't. I tried to find another way.

"I am the writer, you are the housewife. Housewives clean house. If you would like it, I will hire a maid. You will pay her out of your own pocket."

Oh, boy, that was not heavenly.

She screamed and yelled, accusing that I didn't care for her; crying because I didn't love her, and all that jazz. I watched her have a fit, the stomping, and spoiled-little-girl thing. She sure had an issue with money – on top of being spoiled. I knew rich people didn't speak about money, but I was from the desperate mile. Money was new to us, new to me; we didn't know how to use it. We didn't know how to spend it. We actually spent our money on life's pleasures. Paying a maid was not a life pleasure. Not to Mary Magdalene, it wasn't.

"You have money, Mary Magdalene, but use it only on yourself."

Oh, Lord. That was the biggie, because I called her Mary Magdalene instead of "Honey," or, "Baby." She knew that when I used her name I was serious, and now, by the look in her eyes, she was about to crucify me right there and then. Nail me to the cross, as it were.

"You have so much money you don't know what to do with it," she screamed in return, tossing a glass of wine out the window. *"What do you need money for, living in this old, beat-up adobe house, when you could live in a castle?"*

It was true to some degree. We could live anywhere we wanted, like the wealthy do. Palm Beach, though I doubt they'd accept me there – Bel Air, Madison Avenue, maybe Rancho Santa Fé.

"Izquierdo built this adobe 80 years ago, you know that."

It went like this day-in and day-out, except for today when I walked out of the house because she was really getting out of hand. She held resentment, but wouldn't speak of it. I wanted to know what it was.

I took a bus to Yagul and stayed at a hotel. My friend owns it, it has a restaurant and the food is great. It's usually empty, and I wondered if Addison Stonefreund took his family there every so often. When you grow up with great food, with *cuisine*, I should say, you get used to it, you crave it.

My friend owned the place but he wasn't around. I sat down to write and before I knew it, a bottle of mezcal was in my system. A seething frustration in me took over as I wanted to rush back to Mary Magdalene; when the jukebox played a song by Javier Solís I settled down. He was an up-and-coming singer then, and I thought he would make a great operatic tenor. I imagined him in *La Traviata,* singing his way through, hat in hand like a ranchero, but when thoughts of *Il Trovatore* came to mind, I let the idea go because that work is more demanding for a singer. Though sophisticated, talented and bright, the world was not ready for an insufferable Mexican drunk like him.

I ate tacos, and tostadas, a plate of shrimp, *huachinango al mojo de ajo*, chile, tortillas and frijoles.

The waiter looked at me like he was feeding an army platoon. I finished it off with innumerable beers, and before you knew it, the day was gone and I didn't have a word of writing to prove for it. I remembered Tennessee Williams telling me there were days he sat at the typewriter for eight hours straight without a written word to show to the world.

Hilario the owner finally showed up after a long day, a bottle of aspirin in hand.

"The waiter said you drank a brewery, my friend, so here," he said without greeting me first, like gringos do. People were losing their manners, and it was sad to see it happening in Mexico. But then, Hilario was Italian – A Count – someone said, or a Prince. His home was in Padova, where he had a castle with 24 rooms. He ran away from Italy after being kidnapped by the Red Brigade, settling as far from the pasta as possible. His family had paid like two million dollars in ransom, and he didn't mind talking about it. Money always impresses people, he once said, his accent thick and Padovian. I took four aspirin with the last of my beer as he frowned. In a minute, he sat across the table to investigate the matter.

"Que pasó con Maria Magdalena?" he asked. I was surprised by his question because he rarely asked anything but mostly because he sounded accusatory. We had an understanding that if you asked personal questions, the field was wide open for both sides to inquire secrets or none, all holds barred. He didn't know I wanted to ask about his isolation while captured, being blindfolded and hungry, the lousy food, the deprivation, the darkness, the anger and fear, the subsequent trauma that ate at his Italian stomach the way an African hyena devours a fresh kill while held hostage by the Red Brigade. Did they serve you wine, I wanted to ask? Were you tortured? Were you sodomized? Is that why you stay away from women now? I held back for maybe another time.

I wondered if his question referred to our fight that morning, me walking out on Mary Magdalene, or if he meant something happened to her at the desperate mile. Maybe the guy at the telegraphs said something, maybe Apollo.

I felt woozy.

"Nada," I said, *"No paso nada."* Nothing happened, I lied but he wouldn't let me off the hook. He

wanted to tell me something, but wouldn't come right out and say it. Why was I surrounding myself with people like him, people that have something to say but won't speak a word of it but want you to read their mind? I could easily do that with Hilario but had decided years ago to let people be who they are, and leave it at that. Anyway, the writer in me enjoyed hearing people tell it in their own words.

It turned out that *"Maria Magdalena"* had been to an *herbalista*, he said, a woman who cures with plants.

"La Cu-Cu" he said.

La Cu-Cu is called that not because she is crazy or anything like that, no; her real name is Paloma, and because as a little girl people sang her the tune *"Cu-cu-rrru, Paloma"* and the name stuck.

She was the herbalist.

"Si," said my friend Hilario, Chef, Maitre D', mezcalero, and dishwasher. He did everything at the restaurant as if he could handle it all without help. Except today there was a waiter, a guy I'd never seen. Who knows, maybe they were a couple, what did I care? There are people like that, you know, who have to do everything themselves, or it won't get done their way. He

had the waiter today, who might be gone tomorrow, but that was of no interest to me.

"*Si?*" I asked in return, wondering if I asked a question, or was answering one. I was drunk, drunk, pooping drunk.

I realized I sounded stupid. You mean, the whole village knows she went to an *herbalista* and I don't? Me, her husband? *Por qué no?*

"*Listen,*" I said, pouring another shot, "*Why don't you tell me qué pasó con Maria Magdalena?*"

I tried to listen with disinterest, distant, indifferent without a trace of anger in my voice. I'd been gone from home the best part of the day and something might have happened to her without me knowing. *Did she fall? Break a leg?*

Hilario laughed.

"*Mira, Jaguar,*" he said seriously, moving his hands this way and that like Italians do when explaining something simple. "*Yo no se nada.*" I don't know, he meant.

"*Yo no se nada? What do you mean, yo no se nada?*" I heard myself say, rather irritated. All the sudden you want to hide this from me? So much for my indifference; so much for my attempt to stay cool; I got heated.

He took off his hat, I grabbed his collar.

"Qué pasó con Maria Magdalena" I said forcefully. It could have been anything. She was, after all, achy, troubled, and resentful this morning. It was the first time I worried about her today.

"You ask her," he said, running off to the kitchen as if to grab a knife.

I tried to get up, but found I was too drunk; my legs gave way under me. I sat back down and thought to call home. I wondered why Maria Magdalena's trip to the *herbalista* would cause such a racket in town.

"Hilario!" I called out. *"Get her on the phone."*

I heard him pick up the phone in the kitchen and dial. He knew my number, everyone knew my new number: 15-46-42; I'd waited five months for a line and here it was public information. Mary Magdalene needed her own line, she said, so the cell phone could remain unused.

"Honey, I miss youuuuuuuuu!" she cried out on the phone after hearing my voice. *"Are you alright, I'm worried?"* She cried on the phone and ripped my heart

out. Go ahead, Girl, rip my heart out, I thought. Yell at me, scream at me, be irrational, but tell me you love me!

I listened to her whimpering, my body rocking back and forth to stay calm as I held onto the desk, Hilario's work desk in the tiled kitchen entrance. She was about to tell me for the first time ever that she was sorry for what transpired this morning, but I interrupted her. Instead, I said it.

"I'm sorry, lovebug. I'll be home soon."

It was two a.m. and I would call a taxi. I wouldn't spend the night at the hotel after all.

"Hurry home," is all she said, her voice now back to normal as if nothing happened. The phone clicked dead.

"Hilario, call me a taxi!" I blurted like a drunk.

"He is already waiting outside," said my faithful friend, yelling at me from afar the way Italians so freely do at home.

The bum, he knew. He knew he'd chase me home tonight, that he would play his cards just right. He wouldn't let me stay at the hotel, no, not one single night away from my loved one, Mary Magdalene.

"Dame la cuenta" I ordered. Hand me the bill.

"No cuenta nada." He said, like a Mexican. Mexicans play with words. It's a past time. "Nothing counts," he meant, no bill.

"Yanqui Go home!" he shouted exactly as I'd taught him. We laughed at the expression. He'd liked the phrase and used it viciously against gringos who displeased him. Gringos who got out of hand at the bar, saying stupid things about his adopted country, Mexico. Gringos who wanted something he didn't offer. You could count the many ways gringos weren't wanted in Mexico, but you couldn't miscount their money. Some people put up with the gringos for money, others didn't. Hilario certainly didn't. He didn't need to.

"Nos vemos," I garbled, and tried to climb into the taxicab. In a moment, a dizziness took over, and I tossed my cookies. The driver shrugged.

I woke up the next morning in the back seat of the taxi, Maria Magdalena asleep on my shoulder; the driver, snoring in front.

The two of them tried to get me out of the taxi last night but in my drunken stupor I said I was afraid of the monster that I wanted to stay home, safe inside.

To this day I have no idea what I meant, but it took three weeks of silence before Mary Magdalene got over it. She told me later she thought I meant her.

Today I know I meant Izquierdo.

*   *   *

Three weeks later when she spoke to me, it was to go to Dr. Juárez. On the way she told me she'd been to the *herbalista* and discovered she was pregnant.

*   *   *

I suppose the upside of her tight-fisted ways was that she took care of herself. While always 'broke,' Mary Magdalene came home loaded with bags of clothing, woven bags, shawls, masks, old records, musical instruments, chairs - old and new - necklaces, rings, earrings, thermometers, medicines, herbs, copal; she once showed up with a sewing machine. We had flowers in the garden, but she preferred to buy them by the acres. Every Tuesday, while she was at the market, I spent half a day cleaning up all the dead petals that fell to the floor; I washed the vases and arranged the house, only to see her come home minutes later with a local boy by her side carrying bundles of fresh cut roses, violets, bougainvillea, lilacs, sunflowers, elephant ears, birds of paradise, poinsettias and tiger lilies.

And because we had an agreement that I cooked lunch on Tuesdays, I was busy all day long. I missed out on my writing, and I was pissed.

"I'm ready for lunch" she ordered, as if I were the waiter down at Hilario's place.

On one particular day I couldn't hold back my resentment. I was working on my trilogy, reaching the end, when Tuesday came around. Izquierdo and Puta Madre were put on hold. I let her have it in one, quick question.

"How'd you manage the flowers, I thought you were broke."

I tried to sing this, like Mexicans do when they speak. It didn't go off too well.

I got the stare. She slammed her spoon on the plate.

Her clear, blue eyes went right through me, and I felt a shiver in the back of my neck. If the devil is a woman, her name is Mary Magdalene.

"I sold my gold earrings" she said, knowing she lied because just moments ago I'd seen them sitting on top of her dresser as I was cleaning the room.

You're bullshit, I thought. I couldn't believe it, but she heard me. She knew me. She would not take her eyes off me until I was well enough intimidated, which was no easy task with me, considering the power in my eyes. But she was pregnant, and I did not want to make her unhappy.

I finished my *sopa de fideo* and chewed on a fresh tortilla.

Poor Mary Magdalene had to lie to cover up the truth.

That very night, I decided to do the same.

It didn't work.

A pregnant woman needs to eat as much as a capricious woman needs to vent.

There are no secrets in life the saying goes, and so it is. Everything that you are and have been is eventually revealed. Even if you think you take it with you, in the end, you don't. Because, someone, somewhere knows the truth! Somewhere back in the past, a trace of your action is left hanging in the air, incomplete; a circumstance presents itself, an accident unfolds fate, and you're revealed. The secret is revealed and is a secret no more. A secret is only a secret if you have never talked to anyone about it, see? If you have a secret, keep it to yourself, and as time goes by the secret disappears because you never shared it with someone in the first place; it does not exist in the conversation anymore, and you forget it altogether. Do you see?

In our youth secrets are very important: we need them desperately as a way of possessing something. We need them for the rush, for the tingle, for the self-described glow of pride that marks our clandestine joy. Or shame as it were. You know shame, depending on the secret?

On weekends we played. I still ran every morning, sometimes taking the dogs along. On Sunday afternoons, the guys would take me to play soccer, Mary Magdalene brought her magazines. The game over, we hit the Cantina.

This particular Sunday, we were on our way to *El Disparo,* a quiet cantinita where the lame accordion player made the habit of borrowing cigarettes from the customers all day long. Mary Magdalene and I walked slowly to the bar she now quite pregnant, we hand in hand, in love. Turning the corner, we ran smack into Humberto from Mexico City. Mary Magdalene knew him, I didn't.

An exchange of "looks" occurred, and his is how it played out:

When Humberto and I bumped into each other, Mary Magdalene was startled. He, Humberto, carried a folded newspaper under his right arm. He was wearing a clean-pressed white *guayabera* with black pants. I don't remember his shoes. Mary Magdalene goes, "Woops!" the way Americans do when an accident happens. Just then, Humberto - who I immediately recognized as a nuisance - said, *"Disculpe."* In a flash, he recognized Mary Magdalene but, she quickly turned her head and walked away from me. Humberto having recognized her, shouted: "María!" She turned and whispered: "Humberto?" I had never in my life seen Mary Magdalene squint, but now she did as if she needed seeing-eye glasses. I had no idea she was pretending to hide.

Who is this guy? How do these two know each other? What's the connection, I asked myself on that suddenly lonely street.

She was holding my arm but now let go. They spoke together, simultaneously, like people do when nervous, each asking the same question.

"What are you doing here?"

Laughter broke the ice. We let down our guards, including me, to a long silence. They stared at each other, emotions hidden quickly, the past, catching up, the secret revealed, see? The silence between them told a bundle. I watched their every move and tick.

"You first," said Humberto to Mary Magdalene, sounding much like the gentleman I later discovered he was brought up to be.

"I live here," she responded after fidgeting with her long hair.

"Seriously?" he replied.

He seemed simple enough, direct. He was a light-skinned Mexican; a Count, as I would later learn, full of Spanish blood from the old country.

He turned to me now.

"I am Humberto," he said softly, extending his hand to shake mine. If you know me you know I don't like handshakes; they feel uncomfortable and besides, we don't do that at the desperate mile. We bow to one another, something like the Japanese do when greeting. I leaned my head instead of taking his hand.

"And I am..." I started, but he cut me off.

"I know who you are," he said arrogantly.

Mary Magdalene closed her eyes. I'd never seen her do that either.

"I love your books. They are the truth. It does not worry me how you feel about the Spaniard. I feel the same way."

This was interesting. Was this acceptance of me, stroking, and flattery? But, how did he know me without a picture? I didn't know what to say to this Humberto person. How do you respond to something like that?

Mary Magdalene helped break the silence by now holding tight to my arm.

"Congratulations," said the stranger.

"Say again?" I mumbled.

Mary Magdalene looked about.

"You are pregnant," he said, pointing to her belly. *"How far along are you?"*

"Six months," she muttered. The exchange between them was now very clear. They knew each other, I could see, and I wanted to know how, their story, the secret. *We talk about everything,* she once said, *I hide nothing.* She'd never mentioned this guy, the Count. Why not?

We stood on that street corner for what seemed like an eternity. Here I was in my soccer uniform, a pregnant wife by my side, me thirsty, ready to join my team mates, and this guy is keeping us with small talk I didn't care for. I realized just how much I dislike nosy people, with him asking silly questions and such. I like my privacy, and answer to no one. If my publisher asks, I answer, but to hell with everyone else. Humberto was asking questions, and I didn't like it.

I thought I was being generous with my silence, and saw that Humberto got the point. He fiddled with the newspaper. If he sensed my discomfort, he wasn't such a bad actor after all.

"I have to go. It was a pleasure meeting you, Jaguar. Maria."

They shook hands, and he kissed Mary Magdalene on the cheek. He kisses her in front of me? Mary Magdalene walked me down the street in total silence with each of us deciding it was better not to say a word about the encounter until we got home later that afternoon. When we got to the bar, she kissed me as if nothing had happened just a minute ago on that lonely and now dark street.

"I'll take a taxi and wait at home for you."

Women weren't allowed in the bar, I was dying for a beer, and we both knew there was much explaining to do. How did he know me? Who is this guy? Was she trying to avoid me by leaving? Was she running home to think up an excuse? One thing was for sure, after a few *Negra Modelo's*, Tequila and songs, I would find out for sure.

But if you ask me today, I don't remember a thing about that afternoon at *El Disparo*, though the guys say I had a good time.

*   *   *

Wanting to avoid a discussion with Mary Magdalene, I stayed at *El Disparo* the whole day drinking and laughing it up with the gang. Consequently I woke up with a colossal headache or, *"Con un ratón,"* as my Dominican friends used to say. I had a mouse in my head; a hangover.

Mary Magdalene was nowhere in sight or so I thought as I couldn't hear a sound, so I made myself a cup of coffee and took a shower. Izquierdo built the house years ago, with this unconventional shower, a contraption on the roof: a cone collects rainwater, the stopper opens when you turn the valve downstairs, a coil heats the H2O on its way down, you receive a shock of freezing water. Sometimes, like this morning, you pull the lever and the coldest water on earth just about gives you a heart attack. The coil must be disconnected again. It seems the birds on the roof have something to do with it because I have found them several times picking at the cardboard cone as if it was birdseed.

Awake and with a cup of coffee in hand, I went to meet the day.

I found Mary Magdalene sitting in the garden, knitting. I thought of Puta Madre and how she spent countless hours with her embroidery, making flowers like Renoir, stars like Van Gough, thunder and lightning.

"Good morning," I said, standing naked before her.

"Put some clothes on," she said, without looking up. *You'll catch a cold.*

"Are we going somewhere?" I asked sheepishly, knowing full well I had to engage her in conversation now, or forever keep my peace. When she kept her eyes from me, I knew she was hiding, and when she hid from me, I felt like a dentist pulling teeth.

When she didn't respond, I knew I was in for something. OK, I thought, here it comes.

"You never told me about this worm Humberto."

"He is not a worm. He is a Count. And you never asked."

"Asked what? I'm asking now."

She looked up with the Clint Eastwood *stare* thing.

"What? What are you asking, Ja-guar?" The annoyance in her voice was clear. I felt like a two-year old bothering his busy mama.

"Humberto. What's the story?" is all I could muster.

She clenched her jaws like a pit bull and didn't answer, she didn't want to, and I knew it.

"You are standing there stark naked, freezing," she pointed out, as if I didn't know it. I wasn't about to walk away for a towel, not in the middle of this for she would win the first points and maybe declare victory. Her answers were important and my rising jealousy couldn't wait. It was my turn to throw a glass of wine out the window.

Pause. There was always a pause when she was either lost in thought, or forced to think. She was plotting an escape, she knew I had her in a trap, but she wouldn't budge.

"So?" I asked, challenging her. She would not intimidate me with her stare, or by the fact that she wanted to keep her mouth shut. Silence meant defeat, and I'd obviously won the verbal battle but was about to lose the information war. The less she said, or the longer the silence, the more I knew the exchange between us was over.

She would not answer. I would only get what I wanted from her one way; I had to go to the heart of the matter and that would take time.

I walked away pretending to sneeze. With the eyes I have behind my head, I saw her sneer at me in dismissal as if the whole issue was declared settled.

*   *   *

I didn't write a word that morning but instead I took a bus to Oaxaca enjoying a pleasant ride. I didn't like being run-out of my own house, not by Mary Magdalene, not by anybody. I thought her rather pushy lately, distant and quiet. Though I didn't mind the silence, the pushy part concerned me. I was the conqueror, I was the man. The way I knew things to be, the man didn't get pushed around. Her distant manner hurt me because it got in the way of our love. I'd waited a long, long time to find love again, and I wasn't about to waste the opportunity to be happy.

I'd been like a young Rufino poor and broke, struggling to stay in the game; I had friends in high places and wealthy beyond measure. Having dinner with them was embarrassing because I didn't own a suit. Back then, I still wore the muslin shirts from the desperate mile, huaraches and a red belt. In the big cities that didn't go off very well, but after my first professor's paycheck I managed a good pair of shoes and pants from a second-hand store. I was, after all, celebrated; an artist, a writer, a Professor. None of my friends came close to my accomplishments and they knew it. They had money, I had scholarships, literary prizes, athletic medals, certificates, diplomas, acknowledgments in books both historical and scientific; I'd rubbed elbows with Presidents and Kings, Counts and Princes. None of my friends could debate history or literature with any sort of credulity like me, so they mostly let me rule when discussing Napoleon or MacArthur, Maximilian, Juárez and even Simón Bolívar. Even though I'd been hounded by the press and repeatedly asked to make paid speeches about the desperate mile and its wonders, I turned it down because the money didn't matter. At that point I could have left school to make money by the truckloads, but then, what of my accomplishments? I'd grown up with no idea of money and its uses, why would I change now? Choosing wisely, I continued my studies and research to live life as I saw fit. Soon enough as fate would have it, the "Indian look" came into trend as the rich and well-known dressed like Frida Khalo and Juan Diego. I kept my *campesino* look for a while, but as the years went by, I moved to New York, taking on more of a

Wall Street look. Certainly I had earned my keep. Now though on the bus, my khakis, white shirt and *guaraches* made me out as a local.

I arrived at the *El Corral* and ordered my usual; the croissant flying off in flakes as I bit into it. The espresso lit me up like a Christmas tree. This was, after all, what I needed after a difficult morning with Mary Magdalene.

I took out my notebook and started to write. A new ending to my new novel was coming into place, and I was excited. It would be a matter of weeks before I finished the manuscript which meant time for a vacation.

Just then a voice from behind greeted me, *"Doctor,"* I jumped in surprise as I was in deep concentration. Before I could turn to see who it was, he was sitting next to me. I felt violated.

"Tragos!" he said to the waiter. Drinks! *"You were about to have your Negra Modelo, weren't you?"* It was Humberto, the Count.

What did I do to deserve this? How did he find me? What did he want? Who gave me away this time?

For years the poblanos kept strangers away from me. Now, someone was talking, and I didn't like it. Were the times changing? Had I betrayed someone without realizing it? Were people once silent now selling their words for money?

"I won't be back," I once told the owner.

"But why, Doctor? You are our honored client!"

"People find me all the time now. Someone's talking." I took myself a bit too seriously then, implicating the staff, blaming anyone within sight.

"Most assuredly not!" said the owner, walking to the curb, taking a spot in the middle of the plaza and shouting, *"Whatever son of a bitch is talking, better shut up!"* Cual hijo de la chingada esté hablando, que se caye la boca!

The crowd looked at him knowing very well what he meant. This man was known to have a bad temper so the gossip would stop right quick. Someone said long ago that you didn't mess with him which made me think of Jim Mallette. *"Nobody fuck with you!"*

The plaza fell silent. Someone gave away my locale because the Count found me.

"Tengo un ratón" I said without explaining.

"What?" he asked. I purposely did not explain. Let the worm figure it out, if he's anything. The beers

came and we chugged them, me because I already wanted another after seeing him sit at the table. I thought he looked nervous. I was right as he ordered another round immediately. He broke the silence after burping like a peasant in front of me, thinking I would not be insulted. Maybe he was a man of the people after all because royalty does not act this way.

"So a little Jaguar is on the way, huh?"

"Uh-hum," I grunted. The beer took effect, rattling the *ratón* in my head.

"I suppose you wonder how it is I know Mary Magdalene," he gloated.

"Let's speak English, huh? Business," I forced the issue.

"French, Italian, English, as you wish," he said, the urge to spar obvious. We were fencing now, two Mexicans, he with his mask, me without mine.

"German" I countered. A point for me! He didn't speak it.

"O.K.' he said, acknowledging defeat. *"English it is."*

And so a conversation took place. We sparred, attacked, countered, scored, and injured one another like

Romeo defending the Montagues. We drank beers and tequila as appetizers preparing for a lunch we both knew had to take place as there was so much to talk about. We walked around the corner for local enchiladas with *mole negro*. We spoke of food and Paris, DF, the East Village, Trastevere in Rome; French bistros, the Swiss restaurants at Real de Catorce in the Huichol mountains. He'd travelled everywhere like me, so I began to feel at ease in his presence. Maybe he mentioned those places to open me up for conversation, I don't know, but whatever it was, it worked. Was he on a similar journey as me? Was I on a similar journey as his?

We hadn't spoken a word of Mary Magdalene though we knew the subject was a must.

After lunch we walked a bit, stopping for Cohibas across the street from a temple; we passed by the Cathedral, smoking and puffing along the way. At the Tamayo Museum we looked at the fabulous pre-Hispanic collection and talked. The guard let us in after I placed a small wad of bills in his hand to keep a lid on the tourists so we could chat in privacy. I had, years ago, written a book on the famous artist and befriended him having spent lots of time together laughing and recounting old

Indian stories few people knew. The guard remembered me from those days and insisted on closing the door to tourists. We had the whole museum to ourselves.

The famous fountain in the courtyard sang gently as we talked about nothing.

"You know that I am not Indian, like Tamayo himself prided," he said, in bad English.

His mistake was glaring, and one that made me laugh. Humberto turned red, relighting his cigar. The guard let us smoke in the fresh air.

"Like Tamayo prided himself on being" he corrected himself. Aha! I could use language against him to shame him if need be. Why, I could probably tie him up and hang him in French. Maybe in Spanish too - his own native tongue!

"You pride yourself in your speech, I admire that. You are at once aware and learned, educated and intelligent enough to correct yourself immediately." What horse did I ride in on? But if you know men, you shouldn't be surprised as we talk to each other this way. We press each other into mistakes, back each other against the wall. Only sissies don't do that. Humberto might be a Count, but a sissy he is not.

"The ancient civilizations - and I specifically refer to those people who built with stone - prided themselves on their communication skills; verbal, artistic, architectural, spiritual, mental, in public speaking, through their pyramids, also through human sacrifice, through prayer, and through achievement. Those who spoke best were anointed priests, royalty, even were believed to be sacred. The best speakers were made professors, teachers, priests - which brings me to the question: What do you do for a living?"

Humberto flinched.

I have to tell you that it is neither polite, nor a habit among people of this region to ask such questions – particularly, what they do for a living. In fact, it is considered plain rude. Often, you know people for years before you discover they dig graves, or water gardens, for example, but he didn't know this, and I was not about to tell him. I was, however, a Professor, and we were, decidedly, sparring.

"I have a Foundation. I am a humanitarian," he said with finality.

I wondered what he meant by the term 'humanitarian.' Was he like a gringo who is out to save the world, or like Father Serra the Catholic priest, out to evangelize the savage? Or better yet, is he like the anthropologist who enters a village of naked people and immediately wants to cover them up with clothes? Is the humanitarian a person who enters people's lives to change them? Why not let people be who they are? Why do people need the restrictions of civilization, the money, the cars, the debts?

The cigar smoke thickened the air. There was no wind today, so the Cohiba clouds remained close, sticking to the skin like leprosy. I thought of anthropology and the damage it's done to civilization. It all started out with a group of learned men who wanted to change people - the Indian for example, but as the field investigator with white skin soon discovered, his work was not a science. Disillusioned and wanting attention, rogue anthropologists invented the American Anthropological Association, declaring their work a social science, in this way legitimizing the destruction of the natives as we know it. They invented the art of intentionally changing people's lives – with a scientific justification.

"And that brings me to Mary Magdalene" he blurted out of nowhere, like a smart-aleck.

I imagined he would have a million questions about our wedded bliss, but I was mistaken. He proceeded instead to tell me everything about their friendship, saying he should have left Oaxaca this very morning but felt obliged to find me to talk. Perhaps, his own inner turmoil needed settling.

"I am man in turmoil," he'd said this morning. I did not dig into that but let it fester to see where it went.

I suspected he needed money, though he paid for drinks and lunch. I didn't read his mind, preferring to listen instead. I let him take command, because he was on a roll.

I met Mary Magdalene at a friend's gathering in Zacatecas, he told me, starting the story from the beginning. As both spoke English and French they found things in common. Humberto seeing a chance to rein her in, mentioned he was soon going on "a very exciting trek with the Huichol Indians," intending to catch her attention, which he did. Exhilarated at the opportunity to spend time with Indians, she tagged along uninvited. Many things happened, he said; she was made an honorary member of the tribe, she learned to "sense" danger approaching, she learned to be with a group of rough men as the Huichol. He told of the annual tribal walk, *wirikuta*, a *peregrine walk* through their sacred mountains; how the experience was productive, instructive, and a success according to all. Many things happened, he repeated, preparing me for what I foresaw as an intimate relationship between them. I closed my eyes, envisioning Mary Magdalene interacting with strangers in mountainous Mexico, talking the truth into the fire as the Huichol is known to do. I imagined her as happy, serious, sad, intentional and pensive. She brought joy where ever she went, the Count exclaimed, the Indians loved her, in the end inviting her to stay for good.

Flattered by the offer, she opted to leave the tribe to continue searching for me. She told him she came to Mexico to find me, but apparently Humberto forgot; now he was heartbroken to see her pregnant and by my side.

"We shared our heart, Jaguar, I want you to know, and I am disappointed."

Why is he telling me this?

She kept this secret from me. I wondered what she was doing at the moment, certainly not cleaning the house.

"*She never told you about me, did she?*" he asked, knowing the answer.   I guess my face must have fallen because he saw my disappointment.

He was sitting in front of me, waiting, watching for a reaction, trying to penetrate me with the same hurt he now felt because I had the woman and he had only the memories. The sun was going down and we were both tired of talking.

I shook his hand - reluctantly - and wished him well.

"*Gracias, Humberto.*"

"*We'll see each other again!*" he responded. "*Give her a kiss for me, will you?*"

I walked to the bus stop, information in hand, and: straight from the horse's mouth!

But, would she be forthcoming?

*   *   *

The next morning, I asked about the guy we ran into on the street knowing very well I meant Humberto. She had no idea we spent the day chatting, that Humberto searched for me very much the way she did just a year ago.

"*Look, Ja-guar: that's my past. I didn't tell you before, and I don't feel like telling you now.*"

It didn't matter. I knew the story. Humberto was generous in telling me everything.

"*Besides,*" she said, "*you might get jealous.*" She laughed.

I stood my ground and said something to the effect of, *You'll tell me in your own time.* She arched an eyebrow in challenge, but I didn't engage. The raising of eyebrows was another one of her famous defenses. I'd found out about it the hard way, months ago, when talking of the future, of children. I'd said she would be a great mother and that she would take good care of the babies, you know, changing diapers and dressing them nice. She raised an eyebrow – the left one to be exact – and looked at me like I was insane. "*You are just as able to do that as me,*" she said, keeping the eyebrow raised to great effect. The sixties were booming, women were feeling liberated. A man was just a mouse.

Humberto's story flashed by my very eyes.

They went on a Huichol trek together, mapping the sacred sites of the tribe, she, the photographer, he, writing data and taking notes. They intended to get a definitive reading of the tribal property to be used for historical documentation. Many a Mexican rancher and Spanish settler had long ago invaded the Huichol Mountains in search of gold, taking the land by force, kicking the Huicholes out of their sacred space; you know, in the customary conqueror's way of doing things. Now the Huicholes demanded their rightful land back, insisting on the government's full support, and while the world was changing, with democracy replacing military regimes, Mexico was not about to move a muscle. The 'good-old-boy' Mexican network was growing richer and stronger, taking from the population all it could; the corruption machine was at its best.

The Huicholes kept quiet about this issue through the years for fear of local reprisal. They couldn't officially complain to the government because the neighboring ranchers would hunt them down the way

Italian *cacciatori* shoot down wild boar on Sunday afternoons for fun. As the tribe lived within distance of these proprietors, the tribe decided it was better to live than die.

The Huicholes consider themselves keepers of the universe, and that is why Humberto was there to help them. The humanitarian changes the world.

They met in Zacatecas, immediately hitting it off, though mostly because she spoke little Spanish and he, lots of English and French; he took her to see a friend, John Steinback, a world-renown anthropologist living in exile there; he was no longer an American citizen having abandoned his country 40 years ago, never to return. He'd been ex-communicated from the Huichol community years ago because of his greed for money; his thirst for notoriety drove him to publish a story of the Huicholes revealing sacred secrets; they of course felt the betrayal of confidence primarily because he knew to first ask permission to divulge this information, which he didn't. The white anthropologist assumed it was OK to betray these people - that they needed him more than he needed them, and in the end paid for it as he was no longer welcomed among them. John Steinback needed the money, he said, the publication would make them all famous as at the time there were no published works on the tribe. Few countrymen knew the Huicholes for in Mexican society they were mostly a nuisance. To make matters worse, Steinback underestimated the Huicholes thinking they did not read or write, driving him deeper into the hole that was now his life as a recluse and *persona non grata*. But the Huicholes exercised their power to "see" man, in the end catching John Steinback at his own game.

Like in civilization the Huichol lives by easy-to-follow rules: if they say you need permission for something, you ask for permission, if not, do not attend the butchering of the cow because the ceremony will destroy you. It's that simple.

So the anthropologist fucked-up big time and he knew it. Properly ousted from the Indian world he went to live in a decaying, dark hacienda filled with scorpions, books and cases of whiskey. Feeling betrayed after publishing the article, he nearly drank himself to death as punishment for his sins, though more pointedly for having lost the golden egg, for the Huicholes are a tribe undocumented in anthropology, a private, secretive clan difficult to penetrate, impossible to study. John was now belligerent and unhappy, dissatisfied with life, resentful of the very people he betrayed.

John Steinback was the namesake son of a famous anthropologist from long ago, a man said to discover a lost tribe in Japan at the turn of the 20th century. What Steinback the Younger did not know was that he hid and lost himself in drink, a dark, desolate corner of the world, unnoticed forever by mankind.

One morning, Mary Magdalene accompanied Humberto to visit the betrayer, only to soon find herself assaulted by the anthropologist.

Why do you wish to see the Huicholes, he asked, drunk at ten in the morning, as if in control of her destiny. *They will eat you alive, little girl - do you want a drink?* He poured a glass of vodka all around without so much as waiting for an answer. She refused the drink.

"*It's ten in the morning,*" she muttered.

"*Drink it,*' he said, '*where you're going they have mezcal,*" he insisted, pushing the glass to her bosom, she taking it in hand only to push his away. His slimy hand retreated. Humberto didn't say a word. Mexicans are like that.

"John Steinback?" she asked, *"You were at Stanford,"* she stated.

She looked at the bloated anthropologist.

"I don't drink when I'm told to and I don't take orders from anyone," she said asserting herself, slamming the glass of vodka on a rickety, old table. Steinback leapt from his chair, going for her throat. Mary Magdalene evaded the attack with a swift move as the anthropologist tumbled to the floor knocking his head on the wall. Now Humberto laughed as life was getting interesting. He was getting to know this girl, her every word and action a description to remember for future reference; evidence to throw in her face should the occasion call for it.

"I'll drink it, then" he said pompously with a British accent, after getting to his feet and straightening out his rumpled clothes. Humberto knew Steinback well, knew him as a drunk, and knew he was unruly except in front of Mexicans who didn't take his crap. They would just as soon slap his face silly than let him ridicule a woman in their presence. Humberto didn't interfere, he reasoned, because this Mexican didn't need to defend a woman who did pretty well for herself.

The rest of the day was pretty much the same as the drunk threw verbal lashings Mary Magdalene's way every chance possible. Humberto laughed to ease the discomfort concentrating instead on the Vodka buzz as she ignored his every insult. She ran her hand through Humberto's hair as a distraction, getting warm and fuzzy herself down there, softening him up for the hotel. They could have made love in front of this drunk the electricity between them was such, instead waiting until he passed out.

"Why are you going to Huichol country girl, to help the Indians?" he asked, a snide tone to his pigheaded voice.

"Leave your camera. You can't take pictures there!" he added.

Yes, I can take pictures, she thought, so you can sell them, buy booze with the proceeds and drink yourself to death. She knew his story.

He was dead broke, living in Zacatecas on his daddy's book royalties.

Stay the night, he finally said, alluding to the eight bedrooms in his decrepit hacienda.

"I have to go," she said, looking Humberto's way.

"The loo is there," he said, pointing to the bathroom. His laugh was demon-like, he was in stitches laughing like a fool at his own feeble joke.

Humberto smiled, but Mary Magdalene left in a huff.

She went straight to the hotel and slept like a baby. She dreamt of the enormous green cornfields of Nebraska, of Johnny Rogers the neighbor who kissed her in the fifth grade, of the fire she started in the high school science lab in tenth grade.

Humberto knocked on the door.

"How do you like my friend?" he asked innocently after entering without permission.

"He's great!" she cried, telling a lie that was so bad they both laughed.

The night was uneventful.

They travelled to Real de Catorce the next morning, checking into a Swiss *pensione*, the only hotel in those days. Gunther let them in.

"Welcome," he said, handing Humberto a key.

They slept together that night though not in each other's arms but in two beds, 250 pesos altogether. Neither mentioned the arrangement as they were hot for each other, yet neither wanted to make the first move for fear of rejection. They were like two teenagers afraid of the first kiss. Though Mary Magdalene wanted to sneak into his bed, she kept to herself, lonely for company, longing for the touch that left her feeling complete if only for a quick minute.

The next morning she took a bath as he watched in delight. Her breasts were firm, her bush round. Staring in wonder at the naked girl before him, he kept from jumping into the tub to join her.

He sat at the edge of the bed and said they had to wait for the Huicholes, that it might be today, or tomorrow, or even the day after, *I don't know when they'll arrive,* they were unpredictable these Indians, all the while pretending he wasn't watching her bathe. They were unpredictable, these Indians, he repeated without realizing it, unruly in their ways. *They live in a concept of time we don't understand.*

Mary Magdalene wanted time to herself; she told him to fetch breakfast downstairs. The silence would do her good; she would read Carlos Castañeda in preparation for the journey.

Humberto, ever so obedient like a faithful puppy, went downstairs to babble with Gunther, who gushed of freedom away from home.

When the Huicholes arrived a few days later in Real de Catorce, Mary Magdalene and Humberto were rested and ready to roll because they would need every ounce of energy for this peregrine walk, not an easy chore for anyone as the days were long and the road longer. Humberto decided it was good they'd let the sexual energy cool instead of burning it to a crisp leaving them drained for the arduous trip. The thing would happen in time.

Gunther gave them a dozen loaves of bread, salt and pepper and a can of olive oil for comfort as he knew things could turn brutal; he also knew that comfort food will bring you back to reality. After two days of walking the mountain, they reached the Indian village.

*   *   *

"This will help you," he said to Mary Magdalene in broken Spanish. It was Vito, the Huichol guide handing her a snort of cocaine. She'd seen Humberto take it earlier, but pretended she didn't see.

Swoooosh; it went up her nose, the sting momentarily numbing her brain.

The Huicholes also carried cocaine leaves but the powder was preferred at the moment.

The best was yet to come: *peyote.*

"We have to reach the tribe first," said the Count. They would trek up the mountain and through the peregrine path until they met another branch of the tribe. The Huicholes had separated into different families during the Spanish Conquest as a way to keep the culture intact; if the Spaniard butchered a family, there was another hiding away somewhere prepared to keep their traditions alive. Their blood would not die out, no, not by another man's hand it wouldn't.

The sound of Humberto's voice echoed in Mary Magdalene's cocaine brain as they marched up the mountain into the thick forest of green trees smiling.

*   *   *

This village was not like the desperate mile. It was a dark and barren place, desert-like, quiet, almost dirty, but mostly, just old. The shacks these Indians inhabited were not of ancient or rustic adobe, they were thatched huts only used as a stop for travelers. This was a nomadic tribe indeed, moving about constantly, ditching the killer ranchers, the poachers, and the greedy white man. I mean, when the man is after you, you run, don't you? In these high sierras the ranchers were after the Indian as if he were a cougar or mountain lion after his precious cattle: these ranchers, they shot to kill.

In spite of the constant danger of extermination, the Huichol language and culture survived. Their costumes were a bright red Mary Magdalene had never seen. The hats with tassels, guaraches like skin, the muslin pants and shirts to match. Their thick black hair made them look like Apaches; later in history and through DNA studies they would be linked to the Hopi tribe of Arizona.

Arriving at the village, no one turned to greet them. They were expected, and so there was no need to salute the incoming comrades. Their reasoning went like this: when expecting a child you are not surprised at his birth. If you are expected to be shaman of the tribe one day, there is no surprise either, but when attacked by ranchers with bullets, this is considered surprise.

"The unexpected is surprise," explained Vito after Mary Magdalene asked if Huicholes greet each other.

Later, as fate would have it she received a surprise. She was ordered to carry a forty pound *mochila,* a back pack up the mountain. Being tall with an athlete's build, they reasoned, she could handle the weight of assorted foods, mezcal and blankets to be used on the trip. She realized this is what Steinback was talking about in Zacatecas; that each person on the journey had a responsibility, and now this was hers like it or not. Mary Magdalene would not have gone on the trek had she known the Indians would use her this way because as we now know, she hated responsibility. Humberto got the doghouse, if only briefly.

"You'll get over it," he said, using the familiar American saying.

She followed behind in single file like a good woman. When Vito and Humberto entered a small shack and sat on the dirt floor, she was right behind. The place smelled of heavy smoke, and she coughed. No comforts here, she thought, missing the plush sofa of her childhood, the designer pillows for her head.

"Vito says there is firewood outside and a ravine to bathe in." The men walked out of the hut leaving Mary Magdalene alone. She looked around finding her own place to sit. She smoothed out a handkerchief to keep the butt of her skirt clean. The trek, she didn't know yet, would challenge every clean part of her body, with dirt ending up in orifices you didn't know existed.

"What is this place? What did I do? I should'a just kept going, looking for Ja-guar," she mumbled to no one, irritation beginning to take root.

She was on a journey, yes, that much she knew. But how did she end up here, with the Huicholes, in the mountains, in the sierras? *Might as well keep going now, go with the flow.* Humberto was a pleasant man; he wasn't bad looking so maybe there was no turning back now.

"Tomorrow we leave on our journey," said a voice outside the hut, and though Mary Magdalene was napping, she heard it loud and clear.

Now she was in her underwear covering up as Humberto entered.

"Excuse me," he said, turning his back like a gentleman.

"No, that's alright" she said, thinking, *He's already seen me naked.*

Humberto was excited. He'd been drinking mezcal with the Indians, with old friends for many years and now he was in front of a beautiful woman he very much desired. What more could you ask for in life?

"Come have a drink with us," he motioned. He reached to take her hand but she refused.

"I'm not dressed."

Feeling rejected he left the hut.

After scrambling to dress she stepped outside, but Humberto was gone. She noticed the Indians staring at her, gloating at her beauty, for she was very beautiful indeed. They knew she didn't speak their tongue; several of them muttered compliments, one pointed in the direction of the sea, and she took it to mean that Humberto went that way. The Indians were resting, drinking mezcal, squatting with cigarette in hand, taking in the fresh air, smiling, laughing.

She caught him pissing by a *maguey*.

"Hey!" she shouted as he turned to reveal a worm. Shaking the piss he muttered, *"The guys are over there,"* pointing with his chin like Indians do.

Mary Magdalene laughed. She thought it funny he paid her attention while pissing.

"Vamos," she said like a man, waiting for him to zip up. The executive order sounded like her father long ago. He shouted at the workers, he shouted at the animals on the farm, he shouted at the TV, at Mom and even at her every once in a while when she got out of hand. Daddy taught her well that shouting gets results.

Humberto ran up to her wiping his hands as if to clean them.

"Why do I get the feeling that nothing shocks you?" He meant to say she caught him in a private moment.

"I'm not what you think I am - whatever that is."

Oh, she sounded so brave, so self-assured, so sure of herself.

"Let's meet the Shaman," he announced. What he really meant was, *Let's see what you're made of, little girl!*

He guided her down a quiet path to a group of men sitting, heads bowed as if in prayer. In reality, or, in their world, they were napping, as most were old and needed the rest. Humberto the nobleman sat next to the elders without saying a word, she following his lead. He took a swig from a mezcal bottle nearby and passed it to her. She refused by pushing it back. The men kept their heads down.

"It is an insult to refuse an offering in this culture," he whispered very matter-of-fact.

Though no one was watching or directly looking at her she felt undressed down to the last string of clothing, like she was naked in front of them indeed.

He could just be saying that, she thought, *to have his way with me.*

An eagle squawked above them and the wind blew in her ear. The grass waved at her from the distance. Considering his words she took the bottle and poured a drop on her palm, sucking it up, slurping.

The guys woke up like after an electrical shock: BOOM!

"No woman is allowed on the trek, you know?" muffled the Count, handing the bottle to another.

"I'm part Indian" she said, in defense, intimating that her bloodline gave her permission to be on this rugged trip.

"What do you think those women are?" Humberto retorted, indicating the Huichol women back at the village.

"They are not me," she urged in Spanish; the Indians understood. They were looking at her now; studying her - for it had been years that a young white beauty like she was in their presence.

The men shifted and grinned. One of them started the fire by snapping his finger and mysteriously the sun began to lower in the horizon. It turned dark quickly up there in the mountain.

With the fire started all except Mary Magdalene tossed an offering of twig or branch to light up the night. Seeing she was out of synch with what appeared to be the start of a ceremony, the girl walked into the nearby darkness returning with an armful of wood. The men grinned. She laughed aloud breaking the silence when Humberto nodded his approval like a father to a daughter. The Huicholes spoke softly to one another.

Their language sounds beau-ti-ful, murmured the girl.

Someone tossed an empty bottle into the distance, disregarding nature. *Not too respectful of nature these Indians,* she mumbled, though no one heard.

A fresh bottle made the rounds inciting Mary Magdalene to consider why so much drinking. Was this to be an alcohol-induced ceremony? Searching for her cigarettes she lit up a *Faros* as the Indian men watched, a one muttering to Humberto, who turned to her.

"He wants to know about your Indian blood."

The girl smiled. Though she didn't look Indian, her blood ran thick.

"I am the descendant of a famous man who led his people to freedom," she said. Her great-great-grandfather belonged to a group of men who led the Cherokees out of the Carolinas and into the vast wastelands of the Oklahomas during their great relocation, but she didn't share this, keeping it to herself.

The men stared, wanting to hear more. Though they spoke no English, they understood her every word.

Humberto didn't translate to Spanish as he'd learned to never to do so unless asked.

Do not assume anything, the shaman once told him. *People understand, you see, language is not necessary!* This was like something like out of the desperate mile, why these guys could read your thoughts, your mind. But, no, that is not true; the Huicholes do not read minds; instead, they hear your heart speak.

The men took another swig of mezcal and returned their attention to Mary Magdalene. They stared at her beautiful breasts as her blouse was unbuttoned to the navel, her pink nipples protruding. She was not aware of it but she looked arresting. Her lips shone in the moonlight, and her dark eyes glowed along with fire.

"*I am afraid of nothing. I carry my own weight,*" she blurted, perhaps wanting to impress, more likely to assert herself.

The Indians looked at each other.

Mary Magdalene did not yet know the power of her beauty, the radiance that turned heads and made men weep. She'd always seen herself as normal and nothing much to look at, but mostly, because the boys back home were too uptight to talk to her, too serious to tell her that she was beautiful, unbelievable, strangely exotic, sweet, tender, unapproachable - because they were scared. Boys love girls but are intimidated by true beauties fearing rejection. Mary Magdalene intimidated them, and that is why she saw herself as just normal. She liked men as far as she could remember, but, where she grew up, she thought there weren't many around. When a man fears woman he is considered a boy.

Now she was among men, Huichol sages who chanted prayers the way men back home picked corn; these were men who scared evil away, men who walked barefoot for forty days and forty nights on a Holy Pilgrimage, sometimes in *guaraches*, the whole journey with little food and no complaints. *I'd love to see one of your Nebraska boys make this trek*, said one of them who read her heart. The others laughed in agreement.

The men in this circle were not to be confused with children. Their very carriage reflected the seriousness of their mission in life, their erect walk determined; their eyes reflected purity. Why these men could eat cactus off the stem to survive!

These were the men with Mary Magdalene and this is part of Humberto's story the day of *El Corral*.

*   *   *

"You will learn many things on this journey," Humberto said in Spanish for the elders to understand.

"Yes," she said in return, confident the experience would help her grow, make her wiser on her way to me, Jaguar, in Oaxaca.

She tossed the butt of her cigarette into the fire.

It was a beautiful night, she thought, *another white woman might be scared, but not me.* This is probably the reason the white man killed-off the Indian; they saw the dark-skinned people doing what they do, doing the things they do, and because the white man does not understand ceremony, they shot them down like dogs. Why, their very color must have scared them, let alone the painted faces and spears in hand!

In contrast, imagine the Indian first seeing the white man. *How very frightening it must have been!* There are stories told by the Aztecs of first seeing the white man: you see, the Spaniard arrived in armor top 'a horse; as the natives had never seen neither horse nor armor they raised spears in defense. More alarmingly, when they saw the "spirit" jump off his horse they believed this creature separated as it came in two. Imagine the fright when the armor came off to reveal a white, bearded face with the devil's blue eyes!

You see, we know our stories of the past as ours is an oral tradition, we speak to each other, we pass stories from one generation to the next, thus keeping them alive like the African tribe in the desert apprentices their young, teaching to repeat word-for-word the history of the tribe, the central characters, the names, the places, the events that took place. It takes years to memorize village history, three days straight to tell it.

Mary Magdalene would dream well tonight.

Yes, she whispered inside, *in this sweet corner of the universe, I will sleep with the Keepers of the Earth.*

*

RUFINO SEES

As Mayor of Mexico City, Rufino thought he ruled the world. There was no place he could not enter, get into, break into, steal, rob, detain, hold hostage, bribe, blackmail or otherwise destroy like a terrorist given the opportunity. If he wanted American Whiskey someone would fetch it. A puta? *Bring two!* The President? At your service. In short, Rufino Tamayo, as Cookie the Coke-Whore called him, had everything he wanted, any time he wanted it, wherever he wanted it, and no one, no, not even his lovely wife Blanca had a thing to say about it. He had little, or next to no idea how he came to be so corrupted after leading the clean, hardworking life of a businessman; his hardworking father broke his back harvesting and selling papayas for the kid to go to school in Mexico City, dying of heatstroke in the field while whispering his son's name. Theirs was a humble life. Mom now a hunchback was a woman who boasted of her son's success in Mexico City, "el DF." What the poor old lady did not know and others would not tell was that dear old "Finito" as she called him, was about to be busted for running what was basically a Frat House in the heart of her ancestor's country, Mexico. Little was getting done during his tenure as Mayor, few personal appearances were kept, interviews were at a standstill, the budget was a mess - So what's new, right, in Mexico?- trash was left on the streets to rot and stink; the Media wanted to see him, talk to him, ask questions, get answers, quotes, promises, threats, *"Anything for God's sake,"* but he had vanished for unknown reasons. *Solovisión*, Mexico's only television station and money-making machine for its Lebanese owner – a fat old man believed to be the richest man on earth - was broadcasting nonsense 24 hours a day, indoctrinating citizens to buy cellphones, newspapers and the many goods of its sister company, UnaVisión. The TV station wanted to help in the Mayor's downfall to place their puppet in office for better results, yet he was nowhere to be found.

What few people knew was that Rufino the Mayor was hidden away with his latest romance The Queen of Samba, a Brazilian transsexual who sang at the local Discoteca for pennies and drinks; the Mayor's assistant, a money-grabbing brute if there ever was one had taken over the day-to-day office decisions so it was to his benefit Rufino stay the hell away. Now though, he too was nowhere to be found. *Solovisión* could only whimper.

The present managerial style was on its sixth month of operation.

Lo único que me da placer en la vida es el amor, said the Mayor when he absconded power. The only thing that gives me pleasure in life is love. The Samba Queen inhaled deeply. She was smoking the best damn weed found on earth, compliments of the Mayor himself, the two of them playing naked in bed like children, laughing at one another over nothing, snarling at politics, at the idealistic bureaucrat buffoons out there who believed in justice. He thought of his wife, and laughed even louder.

"*Do you know what she does, mi Reina?*" he asked the Queen between puffs. "*She goes on shopping sprees to Houston and Miami for days on end. She can never get enough shoes, dresses, hats, or cars. She changes cars like I change my underwear! That woman, I tell you, could spend a million dollars in five minutes and still be unhappy! Me? Me, look at me,*

Reina: I am fit and strong, and can fuck like a rabbit, drink like a fish and piss like a horse!"

He laughed at the thought of it all, though he wanted to cry. Reina did not find him entertaining anymore, but she loved his money. She would pretend to be happy until she figured out how to get a good settlement out of him, for her plans were to go to the magazines with their clandestine story of sexual bliss, drugs and rock and roll. She would move on to the next man or *woman* who would have her and that was the plan. She was a tart, a hooker, a bad dancer who worked because she had a luscious body; boy did she have a sculpted body. She looked like something out of a Pedro Almodóvar film, blackmailing any man for plastic surgery. Presently, she needed a butt-tuck.

The Mayor picked up the phone.

"*Vengan a recogerme,*" he ordered. *Come get me.*

Rufino read the Queen's mind. The tart would not get her wish, she would not take him for his money, instead, she would disappear, beauty that she was, great fuck that she was too, it didn't matter, the bitch would vanish for thinking like that, for thinking she could take advantage of this very rich man who came from nothing. *"Girls like her come and go,"* he considered, taking a deep breath in preparation for her demise. Tomorrow her face would be disfigured or burned, her body cut to pieces, beaten to a pulp, *anything to keep her from working again,* he mumbled.

The bitch, how dare she think Rufino would pay a ransom, or leave his wife, or be blackmailed by a Brazilian puto; *"better off dead,"* like the song says.

Vales más muerta

que viva,

vale más al panteón

Lejos,

Muy lejos

De mi corazón.

She will be gone and the Mayor will sleep soundly after a few glasses of Glenlivet; he will wake up in the morning and read the papers, see the story of the Queen of Samba dead, or at the hospital, her head wrapped in tape like a mummy in a cheap Hollywood movie. He would hold his aching head from the night before, from the Scotch that didn't mix well with Tequila, the Tequila the Queen loved so much she bathed in it. A quick coffee would wake him, and then perhaps the office. *"Ah, to be Mayor of DF,"* he cried longing to return to that thankless job, a job that only demanded of you what you couldn't give. *Certainly I will not be a suspect in her murder,* he asserted. Sure he slept with her the night before; sure he'd been photographed with her in the Zona Rosa arm in arm, the Mayor visits many places, qué no? Sure, everyone knew he was upstairs when she was taken away, *"So what?! I am untouchable!"* he cried out. *"Nobody fucks with Rufino!"*

What the Mayor didn't know was that a certain young man from Guadalajara was looking at her body this very moment. He was bent over her plump, naked breasts and exposed penis, deciding in whose hands to put this crime as he didn't want anything to do with it. As Investigator with the DF police unit he may not be the right man for the job. On the other hand, if he "sensed" the criminal, or that he could find him within hours, he would take the job to earn another brownie button that really meant nothing. He could sense one plain truth: that he/she was gang-raped, sodomized, beaten, sliced and stabbed repeatedly while still conscious. He would have to report this to his superiors - or say nothing at all until the investigation was over. Little facts in a case often break it wide open, so keeping a lid would only be to his advantage. After considering the circumstances he decided the Mayor was responsible or, at least, that the Mayor gave the final order. As Chief Forensic Investigator for the Distrito Federal of Mexico, the young man from Guadalajara was mandated to point fingers at criminals regardless of their position in life. But in Mexico City, life does not work that way. One does not live life according to mandates. In fact, life works the other way: mandates actually mandate *your* life, especially in a position such as his. A drug trafficker kills a boy for example, and the young man from Guadalajara whose name is Margarito knows the murderer. He knows who killed the child but cannot say a word about it nor reveal his name because the next thing he knows, the drug trafficker has sent an army after him. The police department is infiltrated with rats —officers seeking higher pay though settling for the well-known *mordida*: the graft. A man's gotta feed his family, they say.

"*You pointed a finger at me?*" the criminal will

ask the Investigator, shooting him dead before hearing the answer. Margarito in effect, invites his own death by virtue of doing his work. *"And that,'* as they say down South, *'explains it all. "*

Margarito, Chief Forensic Investigator who everyone in Mexico comes to in times of trouble, found a pubic hair under the Queen's fingernail, her middle finger, to be precise. It was black and short, nothing out of the ordinary for most Mexicans have short, black pubic hair.

"They had her/him by the short hairs," he mumbled, referring to the transsexual. Who did this hair belong to? He would find out if it took a year.

The following morning Rufino appeared in public for the first time in more than six months. Looking well-rested and handsome in a blue suit with matching tie he gave an impromptu speech to the graduating class of The Law School, detailing a future of hard work, money, success, power and freedom. His was a world of self-made men he declared; why these green graduates needed divine motivation indeed and by God, he would beat it into them such that they would walk on air from this rite. He had to beat future success into them because after all, these very kids would one day run the country.

"*Mexico waits for your justice. In the future, you will walk down these halls proud to be corruption breakers. Open your eyes and follow your heart.*"

What a crock of shit, he thought; *these sons of bitches will just as soon kill their children than be killed themselves over laundered money or corrupt practices. In twenty years this country will be unrecognizable.*

He got a standing ovation after leaving the podium, a joke without knowing it after revealing his very hypocrisy. To top it off, his tie was on crooked.

The newspapers loved to spill ink on the Mayor. While they liked his easy rapport, his big, toothy grin and good looks, they despised his arrogance.

So you speak French, Mr. Mayor?

Oui.

And your blood is Indian?

Just like Benito Juárez.

How did you make your fortune?

I inherited it.

What's your net worth?

I'll show you mine if you show me yours!

50,000 pesos, Mr. Mayor!

Can I borrow a peso, I'll pay you tomorrow?

His interviews went on like this, the press loving every minute, Mexicans laughing at the buffoon who saw himself as a sophisticate. What they didn't know was that Rufino could spin and distract, make others laugh at him while avoiding serious questions. He didn't mind the laughter as he was self-effacing and because, he knew to stay the hell out of trouble. Until now.

Margarito thought long and hard about this crime. He knew the Queen of Samba had spent his/her last hours drinking and fucking the Mayor, listening to loud Soul music and snorting cocaine as the neighbors loved to detail the Mayor's every move: wanting to complain, they knocked on his door only to hear his familiar insult: "*Váyanse muy a la chingada!*" They scrambled for protection. Margarito interviewed two neighbors from across the street who told him a big, black limousine picked up the girl last night, but that the mayor wasn't with him/her. Instead, Rufino left early in the morning, "*at about 6:15,*" said the local shoemaker who for fifty years left his house every morning at that hour to walk to work. He congratulated the mayor on work well-done, he told, but the político did not pay him any mind. *"He was probably thinking of important things,"* the old man added. Margarito shook his head. The Chief Forensic Investigator thought, a) his own life was at stake, b) he could turn-in the Mayor (and be killed); c), he could keep quiet and say nothing, d) he could tell his superiors he was stuck in the investigation with no leads (play dumb), e) achieve very short-lived notoriety by pointing a finger at the mayor, or, f) resign immediately, which at the moment looked like the best thing to do based on suspicion. His conscience disturbed him. Sitting in his office he took a long drink of Tequila and Squirt, a favored drink in his hometown of Guadalajara, Jalisco. It was the last of the bottle, he saw - not to worry. The Chief Forensic Investigator was a hell of a drinker, and as we all know, heavy drinkers always stash a bottle somewhere. Feeling a buzz, he slurred something unrecognizable to no one in particular, opening the new bottle of tequila to sip throughout the day.

"*Uno de estos días me la van a pagar*," he said. *One of these days I'll make you pay,* he slurred, meaning his department, a unit that existed more to appease politicians than to uncover the truth of things. His drinking got heavy a few years ago after becoming forensic specialist. Today his work was to visit the crime scene, look about, add, subtract, smell, discover, and take notes and interview witnesses, often the criminal himself, as a good cop knows, returns to the scene of the crime. If you as investigator keep this in mind during your work you will often discover him in the crowd – listening to the officials as they uncover clues, watching the body as it's carried away, things like that. *Why does the criminal love to show up at the scene of the crime?* Margarito didn't know, yet given this fact he would play the bystander in plain clothes showing no badge, milling about the crowd asking simple questions, in this way, finding his way to the killer. Margarito would intentionally repeat stupid things to push his buttons, like "*She was raped,*" when he knew she was not. Almost always the perp would give himself away by correcting the cop. "*She was stabbed, not raped.*" The handcuffs surprised him as Margarito took him into custody. Margarito got so good at finding the killer within hours of a crime that wherever he went, plainclothesmen followed close behind for they too wanted glory and so, behind him they went. Crimes were committed by association. A cousin, a jilted lover, jealousy, money, step-Dad, it was always someone close to the victim who committed the crime. His theory rarely failed. He was known to always find the *cabrón* as he called the criminal of the moment, it was his job, and he did it well, but with time and success the heavy hitters, the drug traffickers, the assassins came his way with graft; why Margarito knew, he literally knew the assassin who killed the next president of the republic; it was in Tijuana, but the government blamed it on a drug cartel. The assassination of the popular political candidate was considered a smart move by the opposition. With strict instructions of *"Avoid doing it in Mexico City,"* the killers followed the candidate to Tijuana where he would give a speech shooting him dead point-blank. It surprised no one. Margarito now could not reveal the assassin for fear of his life. As fate would have it, he had personally shaken hands with the assassin in a bar. Standing alone by his tequila and Squirt Margarito, after a long day at work, was approached by a complete stranger, a smile in one hand and a drink in the other. After giving Margarito a third-degree look, he whispered, "*Yo se quien eres, cabrón,*" and calmly walked away. I know who you are, said the assassin. The criminal revealed himself that day to Margarito Chief Forensic Investigator; the next day as Margarito was studying the candidate's assassination on tape, he saw the guy's face moving toward the podium, gun in hand. A shot was fired and the candidate was dead. The assassin disappeared from the screen in a flash. Now though, how could Margarito pin down the assassin? How could he tell his superiors he shook hands with him? Who would believe him?

"Just look at the videotape of the assassination, the man who shook my hand is there," he would state firmly. Margarito would never tell his superiors, he would never step up to the plate to hit a home run with the information. Instead, he would drink his liver away.

The next morning after his hot *Nescafé* mixed with hot water, he was inspired to tell. Life was not getting any better; on the contrary, it was getting to be a daily bitch. His biweekly check disappeared quickly, his drinking got heavier, his weight ballooned, the women in his life got to be fewer and fewer, he felt alone and unappreciated. Turning-in the Mayor of Mexico City would make his farewell sweet, a final act of bravery. He could die a fallen hero. The papers would write a brief obituary, run a picture, applaud him; the department would bury him the same day the way Jews do. In this way, the Chief Forensic Investigator of the Distrito Federal of Mexico would be properly disremembered.

But something happened before he could divulge his suspicions to his superiors: Rufino came to see him in his office. Followed by bored bureaucrats, top brass, federal police, television cameras and newspapers his office filled with interested parties, with even the lowly secretaries downstairs who had never been to the second floor now crowding Margarito's space.

"Yes, Mr. Mayor," he asked, standing to greet the man.

"Call me Rufino, the ruffian," he responded.

A giggle quieted the crowd. The two looked at each other as silence deepened. The hour of truth was here, a dual of titans, and Margarito knew it.

Are you looking for me? The mayor asked in a simple voice. In life, if you listen really well you can hear the sound of regret, you know? It's a smattering of sadness, pain, and arrogance. How would Rufino's wife and family take it? Surely they would recognize his soft voice, the question; its intonation and implication of guilt broadcast live on *Solovisión* throughout Mexico. Margarito answered quickly and without thinking.

"Yes, I am looking for you. Please accept my condolences." Now, you know he really wanted to say, *Yes, Mr. Mayor, you are culpable and under arrest,* but couldn't muster the nerve to say so.

Still, the crowd reacted with gasps and whispers because Margarito's words were expected: they knew Rufino was involved in the murder, they knew him to be cruel and ruthless, and certainly not above suspicion. Margarito admittedly gave strong meaning to his carefully chosen words, wanting to frighten the mayor while appeasing him at the same time. He was the mayor after all, and he was deserving of respect whether he liked it or not. The crowd of sharks obviously wanted to see him go down, go to jail, then prison, then to death row. Instead, they got politeness.

So, you are looking for me, repeated the Mayor, wanting to turn himself in, knowing full well this Investigator knew the truth, had arrived at the truth. How he'd figured it out was not important, the fact was, *Rufino was had.*

Yes, Mr. Mayor, I am looking for the killer, thus, I am looking for you, because we all know you were close to the victim, the Queen of Samba.

But I am here, responded Rufino. Here I am.

I see that, sir. We all see you, sir. He turned to the others: Do we see him?

A chorus of cheers filled the room. "Yes,' they all say. 'Yes, we see the Mayor, Rufino standing before our very eyes," they exclaimed.

Yo soy el cabrón, Rufino repeated himself, now frustrated, now impatient using the lingo of the law, *Cabrón*. Another chorus of voices affirms that, Yes, Mr. Mayor you are a cabrón! *Eres bien cabrón!*

Rufino was used to getting respect wherever he went, but this was stupidity itself. I am the *cabrón* you are looking for, he said, and these half-wits didn't get it. They thought he was boasting like a good Mexican, saying he was a *cabrón* you don't mess with, a *cabrón* who does not walk away from a fight; a *cabrón* who does what he wants and nobody has a say about it. But since Margarito did not understand this as a confession, Rufino faced another dilemma: Never in a hundred years had a político admitted guilt! No, no such thing had ever happened in this country, and it wasn't about to start, he said to himself. Corruption was the order of the centuries, beginning with Cortéz the killer. Why Cortéz himself deceivingly took the Aztec king to a room and locked the door ordering him to fill a warehouse this high with gold to earn his release. After pleasing the conqueror the Aztec king was properly beheaded, Cortéz keeping the loot. I don't know if that is a good example of corruption for you but it sure stinks of betrayal.

Váyanse muy a la chingada, Rufino exclaimed with finality, dismissing everyone from the room. He wasn't getting through, and lashing out always left him in a good mood. Insulting others was a way of life.

Those are the exact words the neighbor heard the Mayor shout through the door last night, Margarito recalled, shivers running through his body. Now Rufino was walking away from this circus atmosphere, laughing, cursing, thinking he got away with bloody murder, that these people are idiots, that he would never be arrested for the crime. *Why, here I am turning myself in for murder, and these idiots laugh at me!* He continued walking.

So it was the Mayor, after all, I was right! Margarito had to act fast as the crowd was dissipating.

Mr. Mayor? He called out in a loud voice, loud enough to stop the crowd in its tracks, and the politico too. He did not move from his power spot.

Dígame, responded the Mayor, tell me, he said without turning around.

I am looking for you, said Margarito, in almost a whisper.

Jesus, we just went through this, responded the Mayor. The crowd laughed. But Margarito, Chief Forensic Investigator for the Distrito Federal in Mexico asked from afar:

Is there something you would like to tell me?

Damn he was good, this Margarito. He pounded on the Mayor in front of everyone, for everyone to hear, creating a climate of mystery and tension, perhaps a climate of confession. Rufino was tired. Last night's romp was catching up to him, the booze, the drugs, the long hours of sex. He turned to leave, ignoring the Federal Agent. His limo was waiting.

Váyanse muy a la chingada, he said once more, walking away from it all.

Now, as the Chief Forensic Investigator was a man of integrity, he had to find a way to *beat around the bush,* a way to implicate the Mayor without really doing so by placing him at the scene of the crime, or through corroborating evidence; he had to do this right now before the suspect vanished, in front of all these people, witnesses really, for they would hear the Mayor implicate himself in the crime in his own words. Imagine that, Margarito arresting the Mayor of Mexico City in front of all of these city officials. Just as he was getting the nerve, doubts came rushing in: The Mayor could lock him up for ridiculing him in front of others! Why the cells are just a few steps away! How dare you accuse the Mayor of murder? In Mexico we do not elect criminals to political office; we elect hard-working patriotic men to lead the country. His fears were real, not imagined.

Rufino sighed and left the building, followed by his assistant, a grinning fool if there ever was one. They rode back to City Hall in silence.

Margarito climbed the marble steps of City Hall passing photographs, paintings, and portraits of past Mexico City luminaries. He was shaking in his boots that was for sure, for he'd never handcuffed a Mexico City official before. He was not really a cop, *per se*; he did not have the authority to drag someone in; that, he left to others. But in this case, this *big* case, he wanted to be the *chingón*. Margarito wanted to take political corruption and strangle it with his own hands, because, after all, if he was already just about dead after this action, he might as well go in style.

"CHIEF   FORENSIC   INVESTIGATOR
FOUND DEAD"

Not bad headlines, he muttered. Margarito wanted the Mayor jailed, so when he was told to wait outside his office, he paced the hallway dreaming of a quick and swift death, maybe while in the shower as he washed his sins away.

Rufino stomped out of his office and straight to the Investigator, who he now saw as a nuisance.

Te dije que yo soy el cabrón, pinche pendejo, he whispered to the Chief Forensic Investigator so the secretary would not hear.

Margarito whispered back: *Come with me, Mr. Mayor, right now.*

There was no Mexican stand-off. Rufino returned to his office and grabbed his coat. He knew he was had, that he must follow orders, that the public would not witness his arrest. Good for him.

The jail cell stunk of urine. There were drunks, a transvestite with nice legs, a whore, a queer, a criminal – who looked like a murderer - with Rufino Tamayo, Mayor of Mexico City, Distrito Federal all sitting together like one happy family. Someone was smoking a cigarette and Rufino took it from his hand. They all recognized him but said nothing. The queer laughed and whispered to the whore: *Give him head, make him feel better*!

A police officer came to the rails. *Mr. Mayor please follow me*, he ordered. They walked down the hall arm in arm like old chums. The Chief of Police greeted him with a firm handshake.

Thanks for turning yoursef in, Mr. Mayor. *We'll make this as brief as possible. What made you do it?*

Just get me the fuck outta here, said Rufino, in his most eloquent Spanish.

The Chief shook his head, "*Cien mil dólares,*" he said. I need a house in the country, see, gotta get out of the city every once in a while, you know with my sweetheart? I have my own Queen to look after. The whole police department listened to the circus act. The Chief of Police could do as he pleased, his power was such. Besides, who would stand against him?

Rufino spit in the Chief's face. *Te voy a chingar,* he hissed. I am going to fuck you. He turned to the crowd. I came here to turn myself in, ladies and gentlemen of this beautiful city. And, here I am taking responsibility for my actions, and this pig demands a *mordida*! You all heard it. He wants a hundred thousand dollars to release me. Now, I am a man of integrity, and that is why I am here. For your information, I shit 100 thousand dollars a day, this is not a question of money; it is a question of integrity. Now, somebody bail me out immediately, I demand it! I promise you will be generously compensated for your efforts. And don't forget for one minute that I am still Mayor of this beautiful city. And I promise every one of you fools standing here like vultures, the minute I am released, you will all be fired!

A silence baffled the staff. The Mayor was right. He could be bailed out, and promptly walk in here to dismiss everyone right there and then. Now, that was power! The Chief of Police, once the Mayor's friend, was now dead meat. Rufino would not kill him, no, he would do worse. He would call a Press Conference, confess to the murder, and charge him with bribing an official. How's that for revenge?

Not a soul in the house moved as questions swirled. How do we resolve this matter? Do we lock him up? What'll happen when his attorney arrives? Rufino, who could read minds, for he was from the desperate mile, began to sing.

La-la-la; la-ra-ra-la-di-da...

He had them by the balls and they knew it.

Margarito walked in.

Mr. Mayor?

I want bail. What was your name? I want to remember you.

Oh, shit, I'm dead, thought Margarito. Damn. He looked at the Chief of Police who nodded his head as if to say: Go ahead, take him, collapsing all form of protocol with one swift gesture. Was the Chief Forensic Investigator to arrest the Mayor?

Come with me, sir, said Margarito in a trembling voice leading the politician down the hall to a place where no one could hear.

I found the murderers, he affirmed.

Cómo? Pero yo soy el cabrónl! Rufino screamed. His high position protected a true confession. Did he have to *convince* the police department he committed the crime, did he have to beg them to charge him with murder? This could only happen in Mexico.

They tried to rob a bank minutes ago and we caught them, said Margarito. *The hairs match the ones found this morning at the crime scene. After a little, coercion, you might say, they confessed,* said the Chief

Forensic Investigator, really meaning they were tortured.

Did they implicate me, say I gave the order?

No, they stabbed and raped her of their own accord. Nothing was said about you.

But I told them to kill her!

If this thing was already out of hand it was getting worse by the minute. While the Chief of Police wanted Rufino locked-up, Margarito had evidence to do otherwise.

Rufino shouted: *Let's get to the bottom of this*!

But we have a confession, Mr. Mayor. You are free to go.

But I...

Imbéciles, he shouted. These idiots can't get their head straight. I am asking to be charged with the crime of murder and they ignore me.

Just another day in the Distrito Federal.

Everyone is scared of you, Mr. Mayor. That is why we did not want to press charges; that is why we tip-toed through the tulips with you. We all know, well I know - you killed that woman, but other people confessed. We have done our duty.

Rufino was exploding inside. He wanted to be

charged, he wanted to fess-up to the crime, he wanted a clear conscience.

Como chingados le hago para que me culpen? How do I do this?

Se puede ir, said Margarito. You may go.

The Mayor exhaled deeply and walked down the street towards his office only blocks around the corner. He thought long and hard. I failed, he said. I failed myself, my city, my country. I could not get arrested. What have I come to? How did this happen? I kill and they fear reprisal? I got away with murder.

The next morning he called a Press Conference on the steps of City Hall to announce his resignation, but the people would not allow it. The papers called him Mexico City's most influential politician since the days of Lázaro Cardenas. They begged him to stay, staged rallies, protested; masses marched down Paseo de la Reforma with banners proclaiming Rufino, the Mayor of Mexico City a national treasure. The streets were cleaned like never before, the parks groomed, crime was at its lowest ever, taxi drivers made money, finances and revenues were at an all-time high, traffic decongested as if by magic, something unseen in forty years. The city was unrecognizable in a matter of days, all because Mayor Rufino Tamayo confessed to the murder of his transsexual lover, the Queen of Samba but was found to be innocent of all charges. The man had balls.

The killers were promptly sentenced to three consecutive life terms, their news disappearing from the press soon after. Rufino ran the city until his term ended. Finished but not defeated, he went home to the desperate mile where he lives today three houses from Izquierdo's old thatched hut. His daughters have numerous children from rich, powerful, and corrupt men who run the country from Chihuahua to the border with Guatemala.

Not one grandchild is named after him.

*

Rufino went home.

Coming home captured me, my mind, my spirit in a way I have yet to understand, he said, speaking to himself out of habit now as few could stand his presence. Returning home I did not know how to reconcile myself to my old self - how do you do that, anyway? I am speaking of my old self, the person who lived here as a boy, and as a young man before going off to conquer the world. The boy who was happy, alive, in peace, in one piece – well-put together - if you know what I mean. This is my rightful home, I grew up here, I learned to read and write, where I did my apprenticeship with old man Izquierdo. Old Dad is buried over there in the papaya field, and my dear old mom recently gone to heaven, she is buried in her beloved rose garden where she said Young Finito used to play. Mother called me 'Finito.'

Now, I must reconcile my new needs, my new dreams, my wishes in this present life. It was not easy leaving Mexico City, Paris, and New York. Here, there is no hustle-and-bustle. Here, I am alone, you see, for there is a wedge between my wife and family. They got used to the money and cars, the luxuries most Mexicans dream of; here there is no Sanborn's, no Saks Fifth Avenue, no Bloomingdales to shop 'til you drop. Here there is peace and quiet, no electricity, no taxis, no phones, no banks. Today I live in a world of resentful lovemaking, her vulgar screams a nuisance as she yells and bites me, at times slapping me awake; oh, she is angry with me. Mostly though, there is silence. To silence the mind, an old Zen Master would tell me, is to attain nirvana. Here I plow the fields, I stucco the palapa, I plant the corn and vegetables, water them; my hands are caked with dirt when I get home, my fingernails filthy. They say the grass is greener and I agree, because there is nothing in life like coming home.

But there is a man that haunts me: I look in the mirror and see his face. It's me, looking at me; me Rufino the madman, me, Rufino the Mayor, me, Rufino the social climber. And what did it get me? I feel as if my life caught up with me, leaving me empty inside; I see the same people around me every day, recognizable faces from childhood, kids I grew up with, but don't know what to say. These "patriots," as Izquierdo proudly named them, stood ground and were not moved when the worst came. Some died in skirmish; many lost limbs and loved ones, some their land, and children too, for the forces of evil are strong indeed. But let me tell you that these vanished souls are here; they visit us as ghosts on Sunday evenings when we gather in the plazita. Our ancestors do not abandon us, no, they are all around us, like the saguaros up north where the Yaqui Indians believe they are the spirit of the ancestors. We Indians think alike. What most disturbs me in life is that I don't know whether I want to stay here for the long run or not. I have seen the world and lived in many places, met Kings and Queens - I had a few of those I guess - movie stars, heroes, dealmakers, deal breakers, party crashers, drunks, athletes and whores. Do I stay and live out my life here in silence, listening to the chirping birds in the morning, watching the flowers grow and the mountains glisten? While I don't feel connected to the stars, I may, I just may rush to be with them again. Life here is such that the constellations I see form spoons and forks, knives, kitchen utensils as if to tell me to lead a home life; these star constellations are not the bull, nor the unicorn, even less the Orion of my childhood. Do I want to wake up every morning to a field of flowers, or to a field of tall buildings?

Now that I am home again, this hits me in the face. This is how I grew up, yet, it's not easy accepting it, or getting accustomed to it again. I feel like I fell from the sky and came crashing down here, the least expected place for me.

I suddenly remember a friend from the city, one I often visited in Manzanillo. He lived well, very well indeed, he was happy, successful, with cars and 100 dollar American made shirts, with country homes, modern TV's, friends, drinks, you name it. One day though, this friend got fired from an important, faltering bank during Mexico's last economic crisis. As he lost his job and could find no other, he noticed he was getting on in age. In the ever-predictable effort to stay on top of the game - like many in life do after being on top of the mountain - the attempt to keep up with the Jones' drained his bank account - the money began to quickly disappear as he was no longer depositing his customary large salaries: one morning the private school called; the following morning he placed his children in public schools. The credit cards bugged him with phone calls as the various mortgages went unpaid. He quickly sold the new Mercedes Benz for a profit, replacing it the same day with an old Ford station wagon that would do until he got back in the game. The wifey got pissed, they fought in front of the children, vowing to commit suicide if the situation did not return to normal, meaning, to the plush comfort they were accustomed. In that the two agreed.

Then it was *basta* for the wife when he sold her pearls without asking.

I don't know what to do for money anymore, he shouted.

She cried; he bought a gun.

I have two choices, he said to me the day I flew down to see him, not knowing he was near financial ruin. *I can either kill myself, or I can disappear.* What disturbed me most about that day is that he held the gun next to his temple as he spoke those words. He reeked of cheap tequila and cigarettes.

I tried to reason with him but he wouldn't listen. I didn't want him to pull the trigger of course, because one, I would eventually feel guilty for not saving his life, and two; I would surely lose a good friend. Given the circumstances, I could also be blamed for his death –

surely this time I would not get away with murder.

But he was no Ernest Hemingway. In the end, he was chicken.

My cousin came to visit me the other day, he slurred through his misery. *Do you know what he did in a similar situation,* he asked me without waiting for a response. *Well, he left a long time ago, he disappeared, well, he found an ejido way out in the country, a plot of land outside of Mexico City, even farther than Toluca, in fact. And he's happy there.*

He said this in a way that surprised me, because it was unthinkable that a former member of society in Mexico City would sell everything and move to a pueblo or rancho mostly populated with cows and dung and chickens running back and forth. I admit, though I knew his cousin, he was a fine man, he was powerful in his day, accomplished, learned, spoke well, but the rancho life was not his cup of tea. Or so I thought.

He is happy, my fallen friend repeated, a drop of jealousy in his voice.

That night, my friend wept in front of me the way Mexican men weep when drunk and suffering. He fell asleep under the stars, looking less than angelic due to the smirk on his face. His wife covered him with a blanket much to my relief. There would be no death in front of me tonight.

I continued with my life after that, doing what busy people do, forgetting my friend for some reason or the other, probably because I thought less of him for losing everything: and probably because I judged him as feeling sorry for himself. He, in turn, was probably embarrassed about the evening, as he did not call or look for me again. But three years later, in a moment of deep nostalgia and after downing a bottle of *Genlivet*, I called around town, locating the gringo who bought his Manzanillo home, who said my friend went to live near his cousin in Toluca. Remembering the pueblito, I found him out in the field, hoe in hand, which spurned me to recall the Mexican Revolution, Izquierdo and Los Rebeldes, hoes, machetes and picks in hand challenging the powerful.

He gave me a big, broad smile.

You look happy, I said

How did you find me? He asked quite surprised, because as he explained later, not even the Federal Government has been able to find him, let alone the credit card companies.

I have friends in high places, I joked, and that's how I found you. People love to talk, you know. "Don't ever say anything you don't want repeated" my mentor Izquierdo used to say.

His wife made us a dinner of *moronga con papas* with lots of chile *picante* and garlic. There was much mezcal and cerveza, laughter, discussion, and intrigue. She looked at the floor the whole evening, embarrassed I guess at her stage in life, her place, after having led a life of privilege and freedom in the big stage. Her eyes looked sad, with little trace of joy left in them. Looking inside her I saw a disillusioned human being who found it hard to live with herself now, for she was materialistic and uneducated, now only able to work at home and in the fields, the last place she ever expected to end up in life. She came from a humble people, from a *vecindario* where theft and murder were the order of the day, and where one was expected to spend a lifetime. Ending up here was like a shark ending up in a pond. She'd married my friend for money.

After dinner we sat in the night air, on broken old chairs, looking at the magnificent bright sky above.

You see those stars up there, he asked, after a long silence. We were smoking the *Cohibas* I brought as a gift accompanied by a fine French cognac. Suddenly inspired, he stood and pointed to the sky. *That is my television,* he proclaimed with pride. He was invigorated by the land, he said, by the darkness surrounding his home; the quiet, the fresh air. *My children play out there in the fields, at night we read poems, literature: García Lorca, García Marquez, Cervantes, Neruda, Juan Rulfo; we sing songs, laugh, and tumble like children. I make a bonfire and we stare into it like the Huicholes do in the mountains. I have never been so... at peace in life, do you know?*

But how did you do it? I asked, knowing the answer but wanting to hear him tell. You ran out of money, had nowhere to go, no one to lend you or give you the money needed to keep your old lifestyle. I wanted to hear him say it, damn it! I guess I wanted to feel superior.

Like I told you years ago, Rufino, I only had two choices: to either kill myself, or disappear. He smiled again, triumphantly this time. It was then I knew he was truly happy.

What do you do about dinero my friend?

Oh, I do jobs for people in exchange for a goat or a cow. I plant a garden that yields enough for the season. And we don't need much water! He pointed to the well nearby. The gods had indeed blessed him.

I don't need anything, see? I have everything I need right here. Anything I could ever want, he continued.

As the scene played itself out, I understood what he meant. He'd found nirvana, though at the height of success he would have laughed at the idea of living this way. *I have a lot of time to think now,* he boasted, trailing off somewhere inside his head, thinking of making a dime perhaps, maybe of survival.

Looking at the sky, there were many stars, many brothers and sisters up there having a good time. I had to laugh at the thought of it all because, while to him this new life seemed like heaven on earth; I'd grown up this way; what was evident to me now was that in my desperate need for attention, greed and money, I'd forgotten the beauty of this lifestyle. I forgot Mom and Dad breaking their backs picking papayas; I forgot the big forest that I cut down making me rich.   I forgot my horse *Relámpago,* the long rides through the mountains, the jungle calling out to me, the stories of love, the silence of the mutes.

I waived hello to my old friend the sky.

My friend the *paisano* smiled and puffed his cigar, probably the last cigar he would ever smoke out here in his solitude of destiny.

I pulled the ultimate disappearing act in life, don't you know, he exclaimed the next morning as I was leaving bag in hand. *You see, to Mexico, I do not exist.* What he meant was that he was hiding away in the *ejido,* that he was not a member of society anymore, not a club member, not rich, nor powerful even less, elite. I didn't tell him of my own life, what had transpired, where I lived, what I was doing at the desperate mile, a place, in many ways, similar to his, mostly because he didn't once ask, he was so self-absorbed, and also because I saw that he was working hard to prove to me that "everything was alright." Take off the Mexican mask, I wanted to say.

I did not envy him, for at the desperate mile, to this day we lived as if we didn't exist. It was a given, it was our history, our inheritance. We were like ghosts, the forgotten Indian, invisible but to ourselves. In

Mexico, Indians are like that, they are the misbegotten.

One last hug sealed our friendship for life. I pointed to a large cloud behind him, and as he turned to look at it, I disappeared in clear daylight.

I never saw my friend again, but I am sure that wherever he is, he is happy.

Now, it's my turn to be happy.

*

OAXACA AND THAT'S IT!

It turns out that Jaguar had one more girl, one more woman to add to his ever-increasing list of conquests. The train ride ended in DF, Norwegian Helga tagging along to visit Jaguar's *chilango* friend, Eje. After the long train trip, a day in the city would do.

Eje, ("Axis," in Spanish) was a man of few words. Those he used were solely for the purpose of advancing humanity, he said. "Too many words go out into the world," he wrote, in his *Journals to the Unenlightened World*. He was a healer, a writer, and philosopher king in every sense of the word. His spiritual affiliation to the world was as member of the *Orden Tezcatlipoca*, a group of direct descendants from a seldom-mentioned Aztec deity. I say 'seldom mentioned' because it is important the Aztecs keep the deity's name a secret. This deity lives in and through the Aztec Empire, the members of this credence being descendants of her blood. The members of this clan today number less than 2,000 altogether, living in Aztec strongholds no Mexican in his right mind would dare visit, for Mexicans fear the Indian ways, the Indian culture – the Indian belief system – witness the Huicholes and the desperate mile.

Axis was a great listener. Part of his responsibility as leader was to master *the art of listening*, and as a result becoming extraordinary at hearing what others had to say. His *modus operandi* was to listen carefully, acknowledge the speaker by nodding his head in agreement, disagreement or disinterest, he would light a cigarette, and take his time to consider before responding. It was a well-known fact that he had never interrupted a single person in his 19 years as master 'listener.'

Norwegian Helga knew this as I'd shared the fact with her, and now, she got the impression that Eje was a man of deep thought. Jaguar, on the other hand, knew better: while not reading his mind, or therefore his life, he concluded that Eje used his mind to sort out the single, clearest response to the matter at hand. In other words, Eje could ponder a question and have perhaps 35 answers - if not more - to the same question within a minute. And not just one answer to a single question, Jaguar reasoned, but many answers indeed.

Eje lived in the outskirts of his hometown DF. After a life fulfilled through education, professional success and accomplishments large and small, he returned to his ancestral roots and the *Orden*. Today, he was the *Keeper of the Energy,* a position not unequal to a demi-god in his cult, and the logical next step upward after mastering the art of listening. His post carried enormous responsibility for it was through his efforts, work, and communication with the Aztec bloodline that he maintained the aforementioned Aztec energy within the field and radius of Mexico City. How he did this was a mystery you need ask him – it is not for me to divulge such information, and my name is not Steinback, nor am I a betrayer like he. One thing I will say: that in keeping the energy within its boundaries, the Aztec lives. Should the energy end for some reason, the end of culture as we know it – you call it civilization – will arrive, and we all know what that means. Personally, I saw the similarities in keeping the Aztec energy alive to keeping *faith* alive in Christianity, but that is another book altogether.

His Aztec bloodline ran thick, going back to pre-conquest times, to Moctezuma indeed, and it showed in his handsome face. He had some 15 children from many wives, all living with or near him, all participating in the daily life of the *Orden* each with an assigned daily chore.

Presently, they ate lunch, drank tequila, and smoked cigarettes (like Europeans do while eating.) Kids of varying ages, heights and shades of skin color came and went with Eje the proud dad looking on, occasionally whispering something in *Náhuatl,* the language of their gods, proof that their culture was alive and thriving.

"When will you come to apprentice with us?" he asked Jaguar, a question posed many times before, a question that would not go away, a question that would only satisfy Eje with compliance, for he believed Jaguar could be of great benefit to the *Orden,* and to the world.

"When the desperate mile dissolves," Jaguar answered expectedly, meaning, never. It was a joke between the two; Eje knew well the desperate mile would never cease to exist as it will never be conquered or killed, for you cannot destroy it, you see, because we Indians were placed on this earth to take care of it. Like

the Huicholes, we are the keepers of the earth. We have always been here, and will always be.

Still, Eje could use a man like Jaguar on his team, for his money, for his many contacts, for his serious approach to life.

Norwegian Helga squeezed her breasts, using that familiar Marylyn Monroe tactic: biceps to tits, squish, pop. The milky white plumpness of her rack excited Jaguar. He wondered if she was doing this for him or for Eje. The act did not go unnoticed by the High Priest of the *Orden Tezcatlipoca*.

"Pueden usar el cuarto si quieren," he said in Spanish, pointing his chin to a back bedroom, knowing well the beauty did not understand. Jaguar salivated at the thought, Eje laughed.

"Ay, hombre! Que gusto me dá verte!" he said, with joy. So happy to see you.

Jaguar liked having Helga with him though time was running out for both. He would cut her loose soon; she'd be alone, or in need of finding another man. That was not his concern, as she would be quickly accommodated.

"Si gustas es tuya. Un regalito." She is yours for the asking, muttered Seattle.

Eje slurped. She looked delightful, this young beauty, edible, manageable, a feast. He'd had as many women as Jaguar, he thought, perhaps as many, though probably not. Was it possible to have a voracious appetite for women like Jaguar? It's possible, but unlikely you would ever find a man to compare.

"Eso no lo tienes que pensar" said Seattle, now Jaguar, once the professor. Eje did not think long. You need not think about it, is what the traveler meant.

"Sí, verdad?" said the healer, roaring with laughter.

Helga looked on and smiled. Not understanding the exchange between the two, she sensed it was something about her, *but I don't know what.* Cigarette smoke rose to the ceiling, disappearing from sight, leaving the dining room crisp with fresh air blowing through the window.

They ate and drank beer. It was good being together. Spending time with friends is a very Mexican thing, and these two men were friends. A silence took over the table. Each person was in his own world: Eje delighted, Helga excited, Jaguar united.

"Could you do a healing on me, Eje?" asked the delicious young woman.

Boy, things just do work out in life, don't they, thought Eje in broken English, without giving away his infectious smile telling of the pleasure to come. He'd spent many months in the U. S. working his magic and was sufficiently proficient in the lingo to understand and be understood in English, especially with women.

He would take the opportunity to heal her, to see her in her nakedness, in her regal beauty. The healing required you enter the room naked, because, the healer needs to see your body as it is, see your every scar, your shape, your fat; the way you are, you as you take care of yourself. Nakedness is very telling in a person, and that is the reason most people do not like to be seen naked in either private or public, because you're seen, you have nowhere to hide.

"Do you have something specific in mind?" asked the Aztec, meaning, what do you want me to heal?

"Yes." she said, just like that, shooting a quick 'look' at Jaguar though not willing to share the issue with

him. Jaguar wondered what it could be. *She's kept things from me,* he thought as they'd shared everything those few days on the train. He kept back some things too, so, in the end all is fair.

"*Mañana muy temprano,*" responded the Aztec woman-eater. Helga smiled. I will work on you tomorrow early morning.

They drank more beer, more tequila, smoked more cigarettes, Jaguar told stories, and Helga laughed, holding his crotch under the table for one last time insinuating the fling was nearly over.

Eje smiled. The Aztecs sacrificed virgins, but he welcomed a popped cherry any day of the week.

*   *   *

"*Power is a beautiful thing,*" said Jaguar. "*I love it.*"

Eje was in the bedroom with Helga. The healing was in process, and you could hear ferocious yelling emitting from the girl. She had a loud voice; she could project, as they say in the theatre. Jaguar knew she would transform, never be the same after this healing as he'd been treated by Eje in New Mexico, way back when Jaguar was still living with the bitch. That healing, Jaguar stripped his clothes and entered the room. What happened next was like nothing he'd ever experienced. Eje pounded his body with strong fists like a Japanese masseur, for the way to release the devil pain inside is through beating it out of the body. Most mortals don't know this, but we humans hold our bad energies, our emotional pain in our bodies the way a rich woman clutches her purse in the supermarket when shopping. The pain gets stuck in your neck, in the shoulders, in your legs and it takes someone like Eje to get rid of it, to bring you back to life. No chiropractor can do this, I assure you because the pain I'm talking about is stuff that goes back to childhood, to your first heartache, to divorce, separation and loss. It is no cracking of the bones I speak of. What Eje attends to, no shrink can shrink.

Helga was with him for one and a half hours, and the pain kept coming out. Jaguar remembered spending two hours with Eje, at first growling like a bear the pain was such, then purring like a jaguar, now like a coyote, finally whimpering like a dying dog. At the moment, Helga was far from feeling the coyote.

The experience cleaned out some lasting emotional disturbances in Jaguar; giving him a new view of life. He went home exhausted and slept for three days. When he woke up, the past had vanished, the pain, the hurt, the anger was gone. Eje expunged these feelings from him masterfully, in a manner that Freud himself would have envied. The Izquierdo hurt was gone, the bitch was suddenly lovable again, and life seemed great. Not many people experience a healing of such power. If you mismanage your life after this treatment, the pain and suffering returns. But when the shit leaves you, it does so forever let me tell you.

Now Eje used his power on Helga. Jaguar would leave her with his friend knowing the Aztec would take very good care of her; everyone would end up happy. Helga had no say in the matter, for on the train she'd confessed, *"Without a man I am nothing."* Jaguar leaves, Eje takes over.

Women are like that: they are left by one man and they run to the next. Not all of them are this way, mind you, but many, many more than care to admit it.

Helga most certainly fit the category. I am sure you know a Helga in your life.

"You'll need to rest for a few days," said Jaguar, after watching her exit the room. The poor thing carried so much pain. As she'd experienced most animals in the zoo, she resembled a wet tortilla.

"Orale," she responded, imitating the Mexicans. OK.

This was Jaguar's goodbye though she didn't know it. He would leave in the early morning as she slept, go to Oaxaca, get on a bus, find the tour guides Agustín Eliab and Guillermo, and get on into the desperate mile by donkey or mule, whatever manner it took to get there this time. Donkeys were alright because they were just plain stupid, but mules bugged him because he always saw in them the hard-headedness in himself.

Helga lay in bed as Jaguar held her one last time. She looked peaceful and beautiful in her blanched skin and blonde hair; her eyes clear now from the healing. He wanted to kiss those lips one last time but held back. She would ask for one last tumble.

"Will I see you in Oaxaca, Seattle?" she moaned, reading his mind.

"Try finding me," he chuckled. *"And call me Jaguar from now on."*

He gave her a name on the plazita.

"Ask for me there." He wasn't afraid to give her his personal address, she was a foreigner, after all, who didn't know his books, she would come to the village and disappear sooner or later - that was certain. Foreigners always return home.

She fell asleep, and he left. He'd had his fill of her last night, and they'd done everything imaginable with much, much passion.

Eje promised to help her in any way necessary.

"No te apures. Ella tiene plata."

Don't worry about her, she has dough.

Eje sure didn't. He lived for the *Orden,* did his work without pay, most often accepting whatever donation came his way. People regularly exchanged food, clothing, or some electrical item in return for his treatments. He didn't see money very often.

Jaguar reached into his wallet and gave him a hundred dollar bill. That would last the healer a while. Maybe he would spend it on Helga, maybe not.

The two men shook hands. They admired each other, like accomplished men do. The world looked different because of them; better, you might say.

"More enlightened," as Izquerdo would say.

Deciding to stroll through his old haunts in college, Jaguar walked all the way to the airport.

* * *

Eje's power was not only in his hands, but in his mind and spirit. He was not a conventional man in any way; instead he was a man who knew humility was necessary in one's life. His power was over mankind, you might say, because it was mankind that came to him, needed him, and sought him out where he went. He'd traveled the world many times teaching the word of the *Orden,* informing the world the Aztec universe was opening its door to all. There were no exceptions now, no reason to hold back the Aztec prophecies as the world needed healing. Terrorist attacks all over the world pointed this out. Ireland, Israel, Palestine; Mexico itself was in turmoil.

"It is possible to live in peace," he often stated to his followers. He lived unimpeded by the restrictions in life: time, space, and money.

Could you personally create peace in the world? If so, how would it look? What would you do differently? Eje posed those questions repeatedly, living as an example for others to follow.

The average human being does not think this way. We Indians, on the other hand, have always lived in a world where respect for others, for nature is imperative. Sure there were the warriors, the corrupt Indian nations, but they were the result of wayward, selfish men who forgot community and the importance of taking care of one another. I suspect that we will continue to live this way for eternity.

When Helga woke from her long sleep, Eje came to life. As she wanted to see Mexico City, off they went. He took her to historical places downtown, to the pyramids, to the great Anthropology Museum, to hear the mariachis, and to eat the city's best tacos on *Paseo de la Reforma*. That night when they found themselves in bed she was not surprised. Jaguar had been right all along. Helga needed this, she knew she was finished with him, with Seattle, and now, it was time to move on to the next man. She devoured the Aztec in no time. She'd needed a change and it appeared for her like magic.

They stayed together four months, she learning Spanish including bits of rituals in the *Orden;* he, feeding her anything that fit in her mouth. He saw the similarities between himself and Jaguar, and this made him laugh. They each had voracious appetites for women, and they both liked her, shared Helga.

She left one morning *"just because."* Eje bid her well, no hard feelings, in a way relieved to be rid of her.

"This trip has served me well," she said. *"I've had no fights at all,"* meaning of course that in her love life she lived fighting with whomever. She too was fighting her demons, she too was fighting *something inside,* probably resisting what was good for her as most of us do, and maybe she was fighting to stay in touch with the Helga she lost along the way. She wanted to go home, back to Norway where the little girl in her would wake in the morning, happy at last.

Let me tell you that more people could take trips
like this.

*

THE DEAD SISTERS

There are many things I haven't told you.

I have kept you from other parts of my life, I suppose because, in everyone's life, as I know it to be, there are those events we find difficult to reveal; but a time comes for everything, and so, here it is.

I have become much Americanized as a result I am selfish, self-centered, and ethnocentric. Much of my Indianess has been lost to the white ways, to the way I live since leaving the desperate mile. I have lived longer as a white person in fact, than I have as Indian. There is no solace in that believe me, and certainly there is no going back to change it. Admittedly I lost a big part of my identity along my life's journey, by taking in the white world and making it mine. I am not proud to say this, and as a matter of fact, I suspect many of my friends will now dismiss me because of it, but modernity influences identity as my friend Anthony Giddens writes, "The maintaining of habits and routines is a crucial bulwark against threatening anxieties." (1991.) I did not maintain the habits and routines of my Indian ways, instead, I appropriated new customs as defined by my environment, habits that in the end were self-destructive, ultimately the deconstruction of self - as I knew myself to be. You might ask just what I mean, and I will tell you openly that, in wearing a suit and a tie, in lusting after babes, in immersing myself in sexual abundance and rituals with innumerable women throughout my travels; in permitting my greater self, my higher self to abandon all thought of the desperate mile, Izquierdo and Puta Madre until now, I gave credence to the death of my legacy, or, shall I say, to the annihilation of the Indian and everything he stands for. I did not set out to kill the Indian nor myself. I set out to educate myself as mentored and recommended by Father Serra, who I must say, saw greatness in me, a force of intellect capable of contributing much to this world. My irresponsibility in that area is glaring such that I have sought to find forgiveness of myself daily, by prayer, by meditation, by surrendering to higher power. It is only through this confessional that I have discovered my errant ways. And it is only at this moment that I see who I have been: the arrogant womanizer, the little, hurt boy seeking love and acceptance, an adult who trampled over our fellow human beings fulfilling his own pursuit of lust, greed, and avarice.

God knows I would give anything to have Father Serra before me now to confess to, to help me back to myself, to help me understand the complexities of self-forgiveness.

There is nothing wrong with being white, even less, with living the life of a white man. What has gotten in the way - in my way – is forgetting my roots, my heritage, my "habits and routines," as Anthony says. The silence, the extraordinary listening abilities, the empty and meaningless way of seeing life that was our way at the desperate mile, the trust in others were lost in my transition to the dominant culture. I do not enjoy being white, the truth is, I would not wish it on anyone, because to be from a legacy such as the desperate mile is to be born of the gods, and to reject the gods is to ruin one's life. In essence it is tantamount to betraying the biblical commandment, "Honor thy father and thy mother."

I betrayed that commandment, as the following story will demonstrate.

We knew the end of the desperate mile was near. (When the Indian says the world is coming to an end, he means the outside world, or, better put, the white world.) As our village was being affected by greed and violence, destruction, and the maladies white people brought with them, we began to take on different forms as human beings. The old tales of our upbringing could not keep us from stealing wood from the Alemán Lumber Co.; none of us were dissuaded from killing raping, maiming, or strangling each other, or from committing the sins of the Bible: "Thou shalt not covet thy neighbor's wife."

This is where I get to tell you how I lost my family, how I decided to change my life, what made me run away, run for my life, stray from what I knew was good for me.

Way back in the early years of marriage bliss, Izquierdo – while I was an embryo - had a long and fruitful fling with a woman by the name of Violent Violet. (Oh, her smell, her neck, her forest!) Puta Madre knew of her but back in those days adultery was common and tolerated. She not being the jealous type said nothing. If Izquierdo wanted to be with Violent Violet so be it. But, what Puta Madre did not know, was that her man and the woman smelling of perfume started a family. No one in the pueblo knew. How is that possible no one in town even suspected such a thing? Well you see, when Violent Violet got pregnant she went crazy because Izquierdo decided to return to his family. The poblanos in turn saw her craziness as the wrath of God and nothing more. The flying witches were said to be crazy, and Violent Violet, being a woman, was considered of their kind. There were no *locos* in our world then, only *locas*.

When word of her pregnancy got around, my mother gave Izquierdo an ultimatum: he would be my father; he had an obligation to me, as I was the chosen one, and he must keep to that responsibility. There would be no running back and forth between two families.

Izquierdo reluctantly accepted, promising he would leave the girl, though he did not stop seeing her immediately - because his hunger for her needed to be satisfied. He returned to Puta Madre for good the day Violent Violet gave birth in the jungle to twin girls. If the new mother chose to bring up the newborn girls in the darkness of the jungle, so be it. Izquierdo washed his hands of the burden, living his life as if Violent Violet had never existed. She, poor young beauty, did the best she could to bring up the girls until she got tired of being broke, alone, and without a man. The solitude of destiny was not for her.

One early morning she showed up at the door demanding to see mother. When Puta Madre answered, two smiling little girls in pigtails appeared from behind their tattered mother's skirt. Violent Violet shouted resentments at Izquierdo that woke the entire village. "You are the father," she screamed, you have done little to help. Living isolated deep in the jungle the twins had never seen a man thinking the world was populated only by women. They would grow up to be monkeys, or macaws, she screamed, beasts roaming the land without solace. Izquierdo must do something, she added, pushing the girls forward. The rage was such that she salivated at the mouth, making all a believer of her madness. Izquierdo came to the door. Violent Violet did not hold back.

"These girls are proof of our love, now, you take care of them! If you want to be with this Puta, then stay; but take care of our girls. They are more important than the love we had between us." And with

this, she walked away leaving the twins at the doorstep, only to return a second later, tears in her eyes to give them one last farewell kiss.

That is how I met my half-sisters, Euridice and Eros. They were inch by inch identical to their mother, only with my father's facial features. Their beautiful Indian noses were not noticeable then, they were just dots on a face. Their milky, white skin and violet eyes were a shock for all to see. No one in the village had skin like that, and, to further confuse the issue, no one had an idea how they got such pale skin. In our world we were dark-skinned. It didn't make sense.

Puta Madre was upset at having to take care of the two girls so unexpectedly. As a strong woman from a fierce clan, she dismissed the violet-eyed mother with translucent skin continuing her journey to please Izquierdo.

But resentment was in the making.

When Izquierdo went back to work leaving them alone, Puta Madre took one good look at the girls and slapped their faces.

How can you two be so astonishingly...ugly, she screamed, knowing full well they weren't.

The sisters became house slaves Puta Madre pushing them to work all day scrubbing and cleaning and sewing and cooking, gathering herbs and fruits, wood from the forest, gardening, fetching the eggs, feeding the chickens, you name it. Puta Madre spent days on end thinking up new tasks just to keep them busy, and they, poor souls, happy as could be. The silent, strong smirks on their faces could not be crushed. They had dad's blood in them, after all, so little could move them: they were rocks those two. If they missed their milky mother in any way, they hid it well. If the work got heavier and the days longer, the only sound from them was a murmur: like the purring of a cat. At the beginning, they slacked-off without noticing mother was right behind watching their every step. She pelted them with peanuts on the rear to get them going. Once, she soaked them with freezing water to wake them from a dream, they, shocked but laughing in stitches. I found myself laughing along but mother shushed me with a quick snap of her fingers. The girls picked-up the slack, later making a big batch of fat tortillas to appease mother.

"Get me a pinch of salt!" she ordered. This is how you eat tortillas, she said; roll them up with a pinch of salt, hm, hm!

One morning, Izquierdo witnessed Puta Madre's cruelty, seeing the girls cry for the first time.

"Look me in the eyes, girls," he ordered. He never spoke this way, and I remember thinking the moment memorable. Maybe the sisters shook in fear of being revealed, I don't know, but they kept their eyes to the ground.

They'd been told by Violent Violet that to look Izquierdo in the eyes would be a fatal sin, which they would never be the same after. He would read their minds, she said in warning, their lives and dreams and hopes and wishes. Better not look the tiger in the eye. Until today they had avoided doing so. Sure, at night they would cuddle up to him, he was their daddy after all; but they did this in a quiet way, like the way a *geisha* does in the presence of her tormentor.

"Are you girls all right," he asked, after eating breakfast. The egg yolk ran down his face and he wiped it with the sleeve of his shirt. When they did not answer he looked at me and asked, Jaguar, do you have anything to

say about this? He knew something was not right at home.

I didn't want trouble, nor did I wish to get in the middle of things, I was happy in my world, there was nothing to say. I loved my sisters, though I never said so to anyone. I didn't want to take sides. I didn't want to start now. "I think my sisters are beautiful, but they are shy," I muttered. The boys from across the way are always sneaking by to take a peek at them. Which was true, the young boys, a bit older than me, were always hanging from the mango tree in front of our house, doing tongue things and waving at the pretty sisters who ran my house. They wanted to touch them, they said. *"I want to touch your skin!"* they cried out in agony. *"I would like to taste it,"* said another. I heard everything they said thinking they were right, because, as they grew older, the twin girls got more and more beautiful. Although we rarely spoke to one another other as mother ordered me to keep away, I wanted to be around them and watch their moves; I wanted to see the way they bent to clean the floor, the way they walked so tenderly across a freshly mopped floor. On their tiptoes, I marveled. They walk on tiptoes. I was in love with them and, being the obedient boy that I was,   I kept the distance. But I wanted so badly to be their brother too.

Those were the days when the desperate mile started to change!

That is when we began to hate!

That was a sign I didn't see!

Those were the days when the rebellion started and my father fought and killed men!

Dad sat there staring at me and the girls. If he'd read my mind, he knew what I was thinking, and if he knew I was in love with these strange beauties, he said nothing; I guess because he loved women himself and knew this love was part of my training: as a boy I had to learn to love girls. A boy needs socializing with girls. Besides, I'd done nothing wrong and if loving your sisters was wrong, well then I would pay dearly.

If something was out of loop Izquierdo could tell. He'd welcomed the sisters into our home, they never complained; now though, *el aire no era transparente.* The situation was not transparent at the moment.

Izquierdo ignored my silence. He turned to Puta Madre instead.

"Have you been good to my girls?" he asked in a quiet, unassuming way. Puta Madre blew her stack.

"What do you mean, 'have I been good to the girls? Don't you see me after them every day, teaching them, guiding them, helping them understand their role in life? How dare you ask me such a question?"

She stormed out of the house.

"I only asked a question," my father retorted. But it was too late. Puta Madre returned, and without a word, picked up her rebozo and left again. The hidden resentment that accumulated through the years now burst like a balloon. If only she'd told dad she was jealous of the girls, that he gave them too much attention, that he forgot her along the way, that she felt ignored and useless as a wife. Instead of complaining she took it out on the girls, punishing them beyond acceptance but only when Izquierdo was at work.

We stood silent as Puta Madre disappeared out the door. As nothing like this had ever happened in our family, we did not know how to react. Yes, we were shocked and scared because this feeling was new to us. But where did her behavior come from? Where was it learned? I wanted to run after her but for some strange reason I didn't even move. Today, I think Izquierdo was too stunned by her departure to chase after. Nobody acted like that back then. People were quiet, and patient, and loving.

Was this a sign of impending doom?

The girls ran-off the next morning to find Puta Madre in the jungle. They swore true allegiance to her, begging her to take them in, promising to do as she said, as they only wanted to be happy in life. She could not read their minds, which meant she had to go by instinct; Did *Izquierdo send them to fetch me?* She knew she could not control them or keep them down. She also knew she did not want to be alone, live alone in the jungle now that she left home. As the girls had grown to believe Izquierdo was evil because he read minds, she had new allies. What Violent Violet had instilled in them was now a gift.

The girls got their wish. Puta Madre took them in, and together they spent their years living deep in the jungle just as they did with Violent Violet, happy together until the day she died. But what the girls didn't know until much later in life was that Puta Madre died of sorrow, the heartbreak of knowing she betrayed herself, her husband, and me, all because a thing called pride kept her from exercising the great act that is known as forgiveness. Forgiving herself would have killed the resentment in her. Forgiving Izquierdo would have opened her heart to be a mother again. She never thought about me.

In the end, Izquierdo understood her leaving, but I didn't. It took me years to handle the impact of her desertion. After decades of seeking mother's love in other women and living with a void nothing could fill, I understood fear of abandonment. Though women declared to love me I did not believe them, because I suspected that sooner or later they would leave me. Like with Mary Magdalene, I ruined our love because I was not living in the present; instead, I was waiting for our love to die. That is why I left women before they could leave me, like the bitch in Santa Fé; Elinda in Italy, and many others. I never gave them a chance to break my heart like my mother did, and so, *hasta la vista* I would say, and be gone.

Well, look at it from my point of view: I was a child of twelve, the chosen one when my mother leaves me. Adding insult to injury: she takes the girls, and not me, her rightful son. Were they aligning themselves as women?

Izquierdo had to bring me up. I had my destiny, and he had his.

At night I wondered how Puta Madre lived with those two girls she so abhorred. Perhaps she didn't want to be alone - none of us wants to be alone - but maybe it was to spite Izquierdo, to hurt him by leaving, to show her independence, betray him by taking the girls, curse him, defy him, erase him from her memory, erase me from her life, (she never spoke to me again); maybe she wanted to start a new life, to find a new man, to punish Izquierdo for Violent Violet, maybe even to punish me for something I'd done. She broke village traditions, all because Izquierdo asked her if she'd been good to the girls after suspecting mistreatment.

So now you have it. The sweet pretense that everything at the desperate mile was perfect is hereby broken. The fantasy is shattered. My truth of my life lands on the runway like an errant plane.

The way I've described it, the desperate mile seems unbelievable doesn't it? Well, it was. Though I was chosen to lead the people out of future misery and pain, I had to experience it myself, didn't I? I had to know it well. Was it Izquierdo who brought misery to the village, or was it the intruders who found us? Come to think of it, did Izquierdo intentionally allow it into our lives? How was I to learn the important lessons in life like love, family, village, pain, disillusion, respect and betrayal? Was Father Serra intended to lead me to worldly things? Were the signs and murals of protest telling Izquierdo of the change to come? Did I become white because of this? Could we have stayed isolated until this day? Would I be the same? How would I reconcile my life without my mother?

*   *   *

I never saw my mother again. Not in person anyway. I didn't see her at the mercado, or at the plazita, nor at the fabric store where she loved to shop and where she spent hours looking for yarns to make the *tejidos* she loved; her hand-crafted, colored patterns seen on shirts, blouses, tablecloths and napkins. My mother's *tejidos* were the most beautiful I have ever seen. She designed them herself, carefully drawing each jaguar, tiger, snake, bear or scorpion to perfection. She sculpted with needles, sewing such beauty that any artist worth his salt would weep at the sight of them. Flowers would appear out of nowhere, trees as green as money, snakes, fruits, birds, bees, leaves, worms. Once she drew a family of Asians sitting at a table as if at *The Last Supper,* their tiny eyes, lines across their faces, the hair in buns; all were dressed in kimonos. If you looked real close, their diminutive hands held more diminutive sake cups. A Japanese Jesus in kimono.

I asked her how she did it.

"Your father said there is an artist in all of us... that there is no right or wrong in art."

That was back when we were a family, before the dead sisters.

The first year she was gone I asked about her to no avail. I would enter a store, but no one knew a thing. If they did, they didn't tell me. I didn't know I could read minds then as the apprenticeship hadn't started. It would be years before Izquierdo trained me in the discipline. I was just being a boy, learning to read and write from Father Serra. Izquierdo later told me the apprenticeship, the art of reading minds was going on the whole time, I just didn't know it. Everything we learn is meant to serve us in life, he said.

One day outside the *pulquería*, I heard a man say something about Puta Madre. "She took up with _____, didn't you know," he said. The man was conversing with someone as I walked by and her name jumped out at me like a fish out of a tank. Neither knew I was her son, or that she was my mother, so I guess that's why he spoke freely. He walked away never noticing I heard his every word, never looking at me, and I remember thinking he gossiped like women do, saying things to punish others, venomous, mean and nasty. One day when I was running long distance in Oaxaca, training for an upcoming marathon I remembered that particular man and suddenly had the idea that Izquierdo put him up to it. Izquierdo didn't want to tell me, so he asked a drunk at the pulquería to make sure I heard him within distance, so to experience life the way men do; as if by accident. The master teaches the lesson the way he sees fit.

I never knew the man's name. I sit down in the plazita to consider who mother had taken up with, who my mother was with now. With time, I heard things about her, though never directly, I guess because people wanted to protect my feelings. It was always through someone else's conversations that I learned bits and pieces of her. She reappeared in my life through others.

"*Oh, the man loves her desperately,*" said a woman in a pink *huipil.*

"*And he adores the girls!*" said another. I overheard a plump woman with a batch of tortillas in hand say they lived together in solitude and silence, like in the old days, that they ate well, never having problems with another.

This made me very sad as I cried myself to sleep night after night.

After years of searching for mother I found a hut that looked like a home. I'd looked for her day and night for months on end, determined to at least get a glimpse of her. I needed to see her; I wanted to visit her, chase her, to get a glimpse of her new life. Had she been in or about the village, I would have followed her around like a puppy. I think she knew this, and that is why she sent the girls into town on errands.

I sneaked up to the hut as close as I could. Through the window I could see my sister Euridice saying something to someone. She was running around half-naked, her breasts were growing plump. She quickly disappeared after laughing. I waited behind the mango tree for what seemed like hours, but saw nothing more: not the man, not her twin Eros, least of all my mother. She must have been sitting somewhere, embroidering.

I fell asleep and woke to the sound of slithering. A serpent was staring at me, and I spoke to her.

"I want to see my mother," I whispered.

The serpent replied, *"Some things in life are useless."*

I ran home crying. I never said a word to my father about the experience, but I suspected he knew. I was twelve years old now, and had to control my pain. A man must control his pain.

"Little man," he would call out to me, *"bring me a goat, I feel like a feast!'*

And, off I would go, do my duty and return. Then I fetched the wood for the fire, we sharpened knives, light the fire, roasted the beast and cleaned up. Father had me so busy that I didn't have time to think about mother. I think he knew this, and so, the chores all day long. At night when in bed I would imagine long conversations with her, though she wasn't there; I would tell her of the events of the day, what I did, who I played with, who said what. I told her I missed her every day, and that I loved her, that I'd forgive her for anything if she only came back. I said she didn't need to feel bad for ignoring me, and that she hadn't done anything wrong.

I wept like a baby in a world where my mother took part of my daily life.

I never understood why she didn't speak to me again, why she didn't seek me out, why she wouldn't visit, or ask for me, or even have me over to the new house, after all, she knew where to find me, she could find me if she wanted. It was years later and only after Izquierdo's death that I learned the truth, but by then it was too late for reconciliation. My mother had been dead for decades, and there was no seeing her again.

When I was fifteen I sent her little messages through my neighbor who was friends with the girls. The three slept under the stars together, and I wished that someday he would let them know little Jaguar was not a bad guy. He might tell them that I ached to see them, that I didn't hate them, not then; that I needed to touch and hold my mother's hand, to look her in the eyes and say I love you.

But no word ever came back as Bradley, my neighbor, swore he relayed every poem and letter to my mother but that the sisters got jealous, thinking they would lose her, so they probably tore up my every composition. The girls feared she might come back to me, her rightful, full-blooded son. I learned to write to communicate with mother; Father Serra knew it, encouraged it without ever saying so directly, but his instruction was clear: *Write from your heart,* he commanded. *Be courageous.*

It went on like this for months until Bradley stopped seeing the sisters. Someone said he moved on to a sweet-smelling virgin who lived across the street, others said he was tired of being the middleman in family affairs, still some said I was too young to understand my mother did not want to see me. My heart was crushed as I had no one else to help me get to mother. On rare occasions, I saw the twins in town, but they never even looked my way.

Feeling disowned and misbegotten, I threw big, fat, juicy blackberries on their pretty white dress, their behinds a splotch of dark purple stains, but they never even blinked. I showered them with water from rooftops, but they kept on walking. Once, the kids on the street got together, and we pelted them with salted peanuts like my mother did long ago. Why, even a crow would have squawked at such mistreatment! These girls were so numb, so soulless a hungry tiger would have walked away. I prayed when they got home mother would scold them for the berry stains: "You've been sleeping with men under the bush!" But the prayers were never answered.

I did these things more out of amusement than anything, because I didn't know how to hate then. The hate we know today was on the way; it would take Izquierdo to teach it to me. Bullying the sisters was my only way of staying close to mother.

The girls dressed well for their lifestyle, with jewelry and ribbons in their hair, always looking as if ready for fiesta or celebration. I wondered how they managed because their new father, I learned, was a *macehuali,* a mere laborer who traded his work for animals or food. Perhaps the girls traded goats or chickens for beautiful jade, turquoise, silver, gold or diamonds. (Yet, diamonds? That's a lot of chickens!) Perhaps the girls acted like agents procuring work for him around town. They did *something* to keep up that nice lifestyle, I didn't know what.

One day I went to the *curandero* because my skin was getting red rashes for some unknown reason and surprise, the twins were in the office waiting, sitting pretty, eyes to the ground. I sighed heavily to get their attention but nothing came of it. I don't know if they noticed me or not, but as I was not yet strong and handsome I went ignored. I cried that night, feeling disowned yet one more time.

I felt like I didn't exist.

I decided to forget mother. I would make them all go away: Puta Madre, Euridice and Eros. They're dead, I declared. Dead as Shakespeare and no longer in my heart like a poem.

*   *   *

Don't get me wrong, the dead sisters are alive and well, though I gave you the impression they are dead and buried. They're fat and ugly like pigs, snort like pigs and even eat shit from a plate. They married big monstrous men, the kind you see tumbling down the street stuffing their mouths with food. I am told the sisters spend all their time in the kitchen cooking meals to fatten up even more. If I never see them again, I wish them well.

I suspect they don't know the truth behind my abandonment.

Well, years after mother died I felt her presence again. In a dream, she came to me, looking exactly like the day she left, her hair in a bun, a big turquoise necklace around her neck with earrings to match. She wore a long, embroidered tunic with roses up and down the sides. She was barefoot.

I cried in my sleep, and woke to a squirrel sitting on my window. It was staring at me, chewing on a nut, looking me in the eye. The tears spilled onto my chest. Just then, a man came to the door, and said he needed to speak to me.

I thought he was from another country trying to employ Izquierdo in carpentry, as that was his profession. I was mistaken, he was a local.

It turns out he was my mother's widower, who I'd never seen or met, a father to my dead sisters. After identifying himself at the door and after me getting over the shock of it all, I asked him in. I offered him a cornleaf tea, but he declined. I was a bit older then, seventeen, and ready to go to college. In that early arrogance of mine, I snickered that he came to see me. Barely awake, with a fresh dream of mother, she appears in the form of a man.

My heart pounded as I looked him over. His eyes, the nose, the facial wrinkles that adorned his mug; his hair was white; he slouched his shoulders in defeat as his enormous teeth glistened when speaking of her. He resembled the late Mexican president Díaz Ordáz.

He said it had taken years to speak to me because it was necessary to plot an escape from my jealous sisters. Funny, he called them my sisters. This guy had balls. He had to get away from them, he said, in order to talk to me, and today was the time. He didn't want them knowing he came to visit.

"They have always been maddeningly jealous of you, don't you know?" he asked, expecting me to understand. How could I know this?

The twins were in Chiapas for a fiesta, he said, and wouldn't return until Tuesday. He took the time to see me, and it proved to be fruitful. My life would never be the same after today, he thought in his head, "You're heart will grow, and you will be a man." I don't know if he was told I could read minds but if he knew this, he didn't hide a thing. The day had come to meet me, and he was here with a gift.

My mother, he said, whispered my name daily, frequently in fact, making sure everyone heard. Though she took up with the girls and later with this man, she made certain they knew I mattered. She spoke to me when doing the garden, he said, in her sleep even, and while in the kitchen. *"My rightful son, Jaguar,"* she would cry, said the stranger, imitating her voice and intonation. She wept in her sleep, he added, asking your forgiveness. She missed me, he said, and died regretting the day she left.

Like Violent Violet, she roamed the house in her sleep, walking and talking and looking for answers she would never find.

"I want to see him," she said one day, meaning me Jaguar.

"I'll go with you," he answered. But she never got the nerve to do so.

She was weak, he said, weak in the heart.

My mother was weak? No, no, no. You have it wrong!

She held me close at night and told me you were everything to her, he added. He was seated leaning toward me, making sure I got his message. He would be patient in getting through to me if that's what it took. He knew I didn't believe him; that he was making up a story to appease me. I declared my mother didn't love me that day. I said, *She did not love me.*

Did she whisper my name in the dark? I asked.

He stared at me with hurt in his eyes.

He bent his head to cry. I panicked, as the thought of hurting this stranger cut through me. I was hurting myself after hearing his story, this fictional account of my mother, yet, this generous, gentle man moved me to join him in weeping.

I apologize, *Señor*, I didn't mean to hurt you. Please, take my handkerchief.

He blew his nose and straightened his shirt. I saw that my mother loved him. I knew he'd given his all – that he held her, that they discussed things without rancor. I saw that he granted all her wishes; perhaps this was one of them, coming to see me. I knew at that moment there was darkness between them, that in keeping her secrets to herself, she kept him at arm's length; they were separated by the very love mother had for me, as if she was unable to fully love him after betraying me.

She whispered your name, he said, on her deathbed. It was her last word.

I felt the urge to run.

My heart was pounding, it was hurting, crying inside like this man was crying in front of me with no shame at all. We were crying together and somehow it felt normal, almost like family. The birds sang a beautiful tune outside the window and I wept some more. I wept because mother loved birds; she loved animals, she treated them with the tenderness I needed now in my arms. The tenderness only a mother can give a son. The tenderness I would later seek in women with a vengeance never imagined even in books of fiction.

The widower took a deep breath.

She loved you and only you, Jaguar, he said, pronouncing my name like the petal of a rose.

And my father Izquierdo, did she love him? I asked myself, in my head.

I accepted that she didn't love me, he muttered, but I loved her to no end. I was a devoted husband and father.

This was a kind man indeed, sacrificing his chance at love to give everything to a woman who probably disliked him, because a man who doesn't stand up for himself loses respect with woman. Mother might have used him. The girls need a father after all, and he would do. This man sitting before me lived with unrequited love, and apparently accepted it just to be with the woman he loved. It was a one-way love such as I'd lived to this day, as I loved mother but she didn't love me.

Now you know, Jaguar, he said with finality, standing to shake my hand.

When I looked in his eyes I knew he'd spoken the truth.

He left and I wept more in my father's chair.

When I stood up to go, I saw long-forgotten embroidery of mother's on the wall: it was titled, *Christ on the Cross*.

What I remember most:

My mother sitting in her chair at night on the front porch that Izquierdo built with his own hands, staring at the stars in the sky. She would hold me tight in her milky arms and rock back and forth as if singing. I knew she was in deep thought: sometimes about love, sometimes about mankind.

One night she looked up to the sky and asked me, do you see that star up there, son? I nodded, though I didn't know what to answer, I didn't know where she was going with that.

That star up there is you, she said, and there is a star up there for every person on earth.

I didn't quite get what she meant then as I was just a child but every time I see a star I get the urge to cry.

Amen.

THE FIRE THIS TIME

"We turned out to be, not what we wanted, but what Fate did."

Old Man at the desperate mile

I got sick and tired of the phone ringing, getting calls at my NY home asking for interviews with newspapers and magazines, journals, and foreign publications wanting to hear me talk, to lecture on my youth, my home, the desperate mile.

There was a gathering of the brightest young writers in America and the agents wanted me to be Guest Speaker. They wanted me there come rain or come shine, and the powers-that-be would move heaven and earth to get their wish. How much are you willing to pay me, I asked?

"Mucho dinero," said the agent in his Brooklyn accent. Limousine, hotel, expenses, you name it. I didn't need any of these things because I literally lived down the block from where the event was to take place. I didn't need a limo, I didn't even need a taxi because the place was within walking distance. As for

dinner, *Le Cirque* would do, but it was too far uptown from me and I did not feel like seeing Sirio the owner as we'd had a falling out over a table he refused me one important evening. I declined dinner for I was feeling a sense of completion in life, a calm and serenity becoming of success. Some call it laziness; I call it peace of mind. I went to *I Tre Merli* instead, where I knew the Italian waiters and where I dined when in the mood to laugh at others. Giovanni, Marco and Carlo were long-time friends. In Italy they might have been comedians. At work they were entertainers, telling jokes in Italian few understood, putting down the ridiculous gay clientele in their bleached hair, pierced noses and tight pants. What did I care for the limos, the material life America lusts for? Hell, I grew up in the jungle, running naked and happy. Limos were for the disenfranchised, I thought, the poor people who needed be recognized by impressing others, superficial people needing attention, a little stroking of the ego. What these sycophants don't know is that the ego gets stroked, one day the people disappear, and in the end you're back to taking a taxi and standing alone with your old, insecure self.

I took the money.

"*Good evening,*" I started, looking out into the audience and straight into the eyes of America; the future, the present. Who are you? I asked myself as they settled in their seats;

citizens, taxpayers, artists, writers, the Intelligentsia? Were they subversives, creators, destroyers, perverts, sharks, vultures? Surely, I would find out soon.

Apparently, my arrogance was still intact.

The young, well-groomed faces stared at me: the boys in suits and ties, the girls in skirts and stockings; pearls around soft necks. Where the hell am I? These are people from *one* walk of life: they are all *white* people! (Unbeknownst to me, there was a Native American kid sitting in the back row, but I did not notice him in his blond hair and blue eyes.)

I felt anger rise in me. Who put this lecture together? Why is America being represented by only white people, when the truth is very little of the US is White anymore? Why my son tells me all his friends at college speak Spanish!

You do not want to see me angry, believe me. But, it was too late; I had to go on.

I started with my lecture, going straight for the jugular. This would be my form of protest during an event I saw as politically incorrect. I was the only person of color in the hall.

I was asked here tonight, persuaded to conduct a lecture on writing. Now, make no mistake: I am neither Tennessee Williams, Pablo Neruda, nor Carlos Castañeda - all friends of mine, all, admired and respected; all, very different one from the other. All are writers to who I am deeply connected as a human being, as a creator, even as entertainer, because, as I stand here before you, I indeed consider myself an entertainer because you are members of America's entertainment society, a people who must be entertained at all times for fear of boredom. But let me add that I would not wish this on my worst enemy.

The students chuckled, they are nervous, being they are the great (White) minds of the future, and so, understandably they fear more than I do.

Now, I will not speak to you like Peter Matthiessen, nor like N. Scott Momaday. I intend to speak to you more like a hero of mine, James Baldwin.

I pause for effect. Do these children know him? Have they read his works?

You see, I have heard each of these writers speak, I have sat with them, I have shared stages with them, and do you know that not one of them was like the other? No. Each had his own way, his language, his comportment, as I have mine. But the reason I want to emulate Mr. Baldwin is that he came out of a time, he lived in a time when, to be Black was not to be beautiful. He lived in a time when a Black man was not free, and this during our 20th century! He lived in a time when a Black man was forced to sit at the back of a bus.

I pause again for effect: because black is beautiful, baby, let me tell you! Jim, you Black Nationalist up there in heaven are you listening? The crowd stirred. White folks do not like to be reminded of the social injustice they create daily in this, their America.

Out of the corner of my eye I see a very attractive, soft, young beauty, looking me in the eye as if I were Jesus. I'll have her later, I say to myself. I have always helped myself to pretty, little blondes, why stop now?

What I want you to see is that you all are a product of your time. Mr. Baldwin, by sheer force, developed his own voice. Do you have yours? I asked this in a rather harsh, aggressive manner, because I know that I am in America, land of the free, land of immediate gratification. I want the answer right now, they scream, taking more time to tantrum than to think. Think for yourself.

I feel a stir. Gee, it's only two minutes into the lecture and they are already restless, these natives. Just you wait. I haven't even started.

You see, I continue, *you are writers*. I smile, I look, try to calm that fear I sense creeping into their young hearts. They, in turn, chuckle once more. They are Americans, after all; Americans are always smiling and laughing like children, chuckling. In their fear and ignorance these kids feel they have to respond to what I say, and a chuckle will do.

I shake my head.

Yours is the voice of the future, I stress. How often they have heard this, I wonder. But this time I do not give them time to think, I go for the throat.

And that is what disturbs me, I punch. I punch this line like Muhammad Ali punched George Foreman in their second match. A jab here, a fake there, a right cross to the chin and down goes the rival.

Well, now I have their full attention. Now they prick-up those ears. Do they understand that I am baiting?

I would like to see courage raise its hand, I state, instead of asking. Asking young, white people to be courageous is like asking a pig to move out of the mud. They look at me in silence and fear, but not a single one of these puppies raises a hand. I was right. I baited and got the expected answer. I think of why white people are so very afraid of everything and come up with a short answer. They live in fear these people do, probably because they were terrorized as children, bound and beaten, as a result they felt unprotected. They live in fear of losing everything and being left with nothing. They live fearing failure, as if success is achieved without it. Personally I know Mary Magdalene lived in fear, and that's why she left me. The bitch lived in fear of being abandoned, and so, just like I had done so many times with others, she struck first.

Am I speaking English? I ask because no one answers. The stirring starts again. A preppy boy looks me in the eye, as if insulted. He's moved, it appears, why, maybe even anger shows in his face, and that counts for the moment. The indignation in his eyes is enough to make me cringe though I resist, because any emotion from these numb "intellectuals" is evidence they are alive. The boy does not like being talked-down to. I love it. What he doesn't know to do is to dust it off and continue like I did for many years in Mexico as a poor underprivileged Indian boy from the country. What he does not know is this makes you strong, this is muscle for the soul, this talk is intended to put some spunk in your tank so you can go into the world with the sense of a conqueror, because the conqueror blazes his path, he mows down the forest, confronts lions and witches, is forced to kill, is forced to subdue those who resist his every order. The conqueror does all this until he wins, until he claims the land, until he is crowned for his achievements. The boy may never learn, I mutter under my breath unaware the microphone broadcasts this over the room.

So, not a hand in the whole place, I challenge with a short laugh. I laugh in their faces. I look about, contented, happy, and triumphant. A sense of restlessness takes over the room.

Do   they   not   get   it?

I cannot help but wonder what happened to this tattoo generation.

I'll tell you a short story, I say, to calm them down. My voice is soft, surrendering to their needs. I'll keep them captive; lead them to the slaughterhouse without their knowing.

I was at a party one night, a very snobbish bunch, you know, like... most of your parents are, by what I can see. They laugh, recognizing the truth in their lives, but not seeing it in themselves; they think themselves different from their parents, and this, in turn, makes me chuckle. For a moment they think we are laughing together. Little do they know that in 20 years they will become just like their parents.

I continue.

So at this party, we are drinking champagne and talking nicely-nicely. The patroness of the gig is an anemic-

looking middle age woman; in the group there is a rabid bitch known by all; a well-known architect with his partner wife. A morbidly rich woman sits with her daughter, next to them, rests a millionaire - said to be impotent - with his trophy wife: they want to adopt a Korean boy for $250,000! An indistinguishable gentleman sits alone, sipping champagne. And then, there is my gorgeous girlfriend clutching me, the Indian guy.

I point to myself. The students giggle again. The air is different now. I have them in the palm of my hand, and I can do as I wish. I can stab them if I want, for I am the Matador! No, wait: the bull's legs are not parallel. The bulls' legs must be parallel for the Matador to plunge the sword right between its shoulder blades.

I decide to wait. The Matador always waits for the bull.

And so this assortment of guests is making small talk. Someone asks a question as all turn to me for the answer. They talk in this chalky way, you know, assuming and setting you up for ridicule, expecting a stupid answer from you to make them laugh: in other words, you are their entertainment for the evening; you are in their Coliseum, you are the Christian being fed to the lions. Now, the question posed was related to success

and money and none other than 'How did you make it in life?'
In other words what they mean to say is, You are but a mere
*Indian, not white like us, how did **you** become successful in life?*
How did you get smart? Were you bred intelligent? Sure,
Neruda, Márquez, Páz; but you, an Indian with similar literary
recognition?

The students need to hear this, and I have been dying to say it. They read my books, these young ones, they seek me out in my desolate empire, they hound me, find me, but they do not understand me. They live in a world where they make sure you feel that if you are not *white*, you are not good enough. But I do not feel this way. No one can make me feel this way. I do not buy into this. You see, this is their way of thinking, not mine. They believe white people are superior. They believe, and have been brought up to believe that the lighter color of skin you have the more privilege you deserve. They believe being white is automatic entitlement in our society. They believe they are destined to run the world because of the color of their skin. The believer believes! (You see, Father Serra, I am no pagan after all!) But the world has changed.

I can tell the kids don't get it. They do not stir, they do not move. Even their breathing is now untraceable. Is it because they believe this very thing, like their parents and their parents before them? Are they disappointed to hear America is fast changing, leaving the white man to scurry around for help? Do they see their white-only generation crumbling before their eyes? Do they know our youth today is largely of color and ethnicity and preparing themselves to take over this country? Are they scared of this?

I continue. *And so, at this party we talk about the Indian, because the white man always wants to talk about the Indian. We talk about the ways we survived, how we're still here - in spite of it all. How we are the keepers of the earth; we discuss the seventh generation. We procreate with always the seventh generation in mind, you see, future life, we live for the future so that we will always be here. We are here on earth now, have always been, and will always be - here. You see, the white man thinks he got rid of us - that he killed us off, but he is mistaken. There is no getting rid of the keepers of the earth. Why, we knew what the white man was doing and we created what is today known in anthropology as compartmentalization. We hid in the caves, sent the shaman, the holy ones, the women and children away, to keep the blood flowing in our tribe. We hid for hundreds of years like the Aztecs to make sure we would not be erased forever.*

I see they are thinking, considering, wondering where I am going with this story that appears to bother them. What they don't know yet, these young ones, is that in every conversation there is a lesson to be learned.

I keep on. *We sat at the party, they looking at me, and me, looking at them. I talked of the ways Indians found to survive. We survived in the desert, on the Plains in winter, on reservations throughout the land, in the jungle. We have survived; I nearly shouted at them, we are still here. You didn't kill us off like you wanted to. You did not destroy our pyramids, can you see?*

Well, the rich and famous at the party got very serious; exactly like all of you here, all of you rich kids staring at me now.

Boy, that got their attention!

It sounded like an attack against the brightest and so, I made it one.

Now they do not chuckle. Now they do not smile. Now they listen intently.

So, I put down my drink, I continue, pausing for effect. *I ask the partygoers: Do you know what it is to be destroyed as a culture? But they say nothing, they are silent. So I continue by ranting about the American Holocaust, yes, the massacres*

and near total annihilation of the Indian race - the very issues
you do not read about in your high school history books because
in America, this did not happen! The party turns quiet, still as a
Van Gough painting; some appear to be mad or angry, others,
irritated. Still, they say nothing these fortunate ones, these rich
people; still, they do not defend themselves, even less their own
country. What American here has the courage to stand up for
their country, I shout at the partygoers, baiting them, insulting
them, laughing in their faces. No one responds, no one stands to
their feet. The undistinguished gentleman sitting alone, winces,
but does not speak up; his face is ashen white, blanched, and
drained of life. And, I, Jaguar, in my very own intrusive
manner, finish with a bigger laugh. These champagne drinkers
are no longer sipping, nor are they thirsty. No one says a word
for a long, long time. You can hear the sound of a train in the
distance, that's how quiet it got in that room. All are staring at
the floor, in shame. And so the evening ends. I leave
triumphant.

Here, I pause again as I do out of habit when I know
people need to process.   I give the children time to straighten
their ties, to wipe the sweat off their furry brows. The girls bite
their nails.

What are you driving at, you might be asking

yourselves now; am I correct?

I look into the audience. Several kids squirm in their seats, crossing and re-crossing legs. I am looking straight into their eyes. They do not want to make eye contact; except for the blond kid seating way in the back, not the girl with pearls, no. It is a blond kid, a boy who makes eye contact.

I continue with the story.

The following week, my girlfriend and I are arguing about something or the other when, out of nowhere, she calls me 'insensitive.' Well, I have to admit, I am human, and have been insensitive a few times in life. They like this and snicker appropriately. *I ask my girlfriend to explain what she means by that. It turns out the night of the champagne party you insulted the man sitting next to you, she says with contempt in her voice. That was insensitive, she says with finality. I get that she's talking about the undistinguished gentleman who sat alone all night. He was a sole survivor of the Holocaust, she adds, he lost his entire family; apparently she has more to say about my insensitivity than I expected. His entire family died, she repeats with an exclamation. I am insensitive, I replied, I apologize for that. But tell me, how was I to know this? You didn't say a word.*

"I didn't know until the other day," she responded.

And this, boys and girls, is what I'm talking about. They look puzzled.

I feel a sense of condemnation coming on; I am willing to condemn these kids at the risk of a good lesson. What am I risking after all, my reputation? But this is what I am known for, condemning the white man for his atrocities. I do not apologize for it. After all, he has never apologized for his actions.

No one spoke up at the party. Why didn't anorexic Wendy the hostess say something to me on the way out? Why didn't she stop me mid-speech? The architect, he knew, and the millionaire too, they knew to stop me from insulting the guest in question. More importantly, the undistinguished gentleman himself did not say a word.

I am looking at the students now, remembering the undistinguished gentleman, the party, the silence. I'm on a roll; this thing is moving right along. My timing is perfect; Al Pacino could not have done better.

It was politeness, I say. *Every one of those partygoers wanted to be polite. Or, was it that deep inside, they wanted the Indian - the celebrated Indian - to belittle himself at the cost of a*

Holocaust survivor?

I pause again, letting the question settle in. This is going well. I am a storyteller, after all. They are learning to be.

Personally, kids, I say with a grin on my face, *I think it was the absence of courage that stopped them from speaking a word of caution. No one at the party had the courage to tell me I was out of line, that I was hurting someone's feelings, that I was being an idiot, mind you, being insensitive. Why didn't anyone tell me to shut my trap?*

With that inaction on their part, my dear children, I felt insulted.

Well the audience is quiet. They have been quiet since my last chuckle a while back. I can tell they still don't understand where I'm going with this.

Politeness kills, do you see? But, what I am pointing at is courage. Where has all the courage gone? Why is it so very absent from our society? Has politeness taken its place? I pause one more time, giving time for the question to sink in. I let these kids look in the mirror, think of the last courageous act in their young lives. But they do not expect the next words to come out of my mouth.

Do you kids, would you have had the courage to shut me up?   I am indicting them now, though they do not know it. I am penetrating their minds the way I will soon penetrate the lovely, young, brave blonde girl with the pearls sitting in the front row.

I move from the podium. In the millionth of a second it takes me to move a step, I hear, in the intense silence of the auditorium, a great, big sob.

My God, I affected somebody, I say with joy. Hallelujah! I got through! I turn to find the voice and see it is the blonde girl with the pearls. I feel sorry for her. She looks so soft, and round and beautiful; virginal. I will comfort her later with kisses and caresses.

What sort of writers do you all want to be? I demand, returning to the podium pointing my index finger at them as Pearl Necklace sobs. The rich rids squirm again. They look at me with that very familiar fear the white man carries on his face when seeing me stare them down. My body feels hot, I am getting hot, could it be the blonde girl is turning-me on? Does her crying excite me? I realize that I'm nearly shouting, yelling at them, and waking them to life, accusing them and their parents, and their mother's mother of cowardice. I am raging mad inside. Yet, this is what I meant to do. I planned it in my head the moment I saw there were no people of color in the crowd. In a moment I quiet my heart, feeling compassion for those I've tortured.

Do you have the courage to write what you really feel? I ask the young people holding their seats like they held daddy's hand when crossing the street. *Do you have the courage to confront society with your words, your thoughts, your questions? Do you have the courage to do so at the expense of failure? Because I am here doing that with you; I have been paid an embarrassing amount of money to be here, and I have the courage to get you up!*

This last bit came blasting out of my mouth as I was not one of them, a polite cookie sitting pretty. Just then, an important thought crystallized in my mind: *This generation is all about money.* These kids will never speak unless there is a payoff involved. You can forget about thinking, progress, courage, these kids are all about money. I have not gotten through to them.

Something unexpected happens next: the pretty blonde creature with pearls stands up to confess.

I will write with courage! I will stand up for my beliefs, she cries, a declaration of hope, of love, of courage for the future.

I turn to her. Did I hear you right? Is this a dream?

I gloat the moment. I knew there was hope in the world. *"If you inspire one individual during your lifetime, you have contributed to the world,"* Izquierdo used to say.

Well, it seems I finally contributed something to the world, my beloved Izquierdo.

The blonde with milky breasts stands sobbing, wiping her tears and runny nose; she unconsciously cleans off the mucous on her tight black skirt, much like a child of three does without thinking while soiling his pants.

Thank You, I say, not knowing her name, but knowing for sure that I will soon.

Thank you for your courage; for your heart. I

see that you are alone in this, that you alone have courage in this room. Always treasure that. Now all of you go home and read The Fire Next Time.

With those words I walked out of the auditorium and to my green room, where I knew the blonde would seek me out in about 30 seconds.

I ignored the applause, not because I did not deserve it, but because it sounded too polite. The blonde girl was named Brigitte. And she gave me hope.

*　　*　　*

Jim Mallette and I would meet for coffee on Friday afternoons at *El Péz Dorado,* a chino/cubano restaurant on upper Broadway. The food was excellent; cheap at this hour of the day. The place was deserted. We were usually the only customers there and so, we could talk openly and laugh and make all the noise we wanted; they had cerveza and vino, lobster, noodles and salads. Usually, we got good and buzzed on Chinese beer. The waiters spoke little English so we were frank and courageous in our conversation. He told me of his loves, and me, I spoke of interests, writing and travel. I was reading African-American writers back then because I wanted to know the origins of their culture, their thoughts, protests, recriminations, anger, and love. James Baldwin was a literary giant living in Paris, and the two of us would meet at the Charcuterie to discuss ways to open the white man's mind; to free him of the misery he imposed on others. James always said that if the white man accepted homosexuals, he would understand the Black man. I often thought about the ramifications of his statement understanding how much time he'd philosophized on such a social issue. I think James Baldwin and Jim Mallette were thinkers many years ahead of their time; I believe they knew the complexity of being black and homosexual, the difficulties in life for such a man. Being black is one thing, but being both is a brand of its own, it's like being an outcast twice over. Malcolm X was on the scene too. There was fire in the streets; Black people were taking charge of their own lives. President Johnson, a Southerner himself, took great steps in the Civil Rights movement - much to the displeasure of his bigot peers – by pushing the white majority to accept the changing times. People were out in the streets protesting against racial discrimination, women were burning bras, the Klu Klux Klan insisted "negroes" remained in their place – meaning of course, in the back of the bus. I read *Narrative of the life of Frederick Douglas* in one night, astounded to find that slavery was still practiced in America, though not necessarily with *the Negro*. That Mr. Douglas achieved so much against such great odds is admirable and enviable; his was a time when to speak up for justice was to be lynched. I thought of my lecture and the themes of time, money and courage. The time we live in must be a time of action. We cannot wait for others to reach an agreement on social issues; like Malcolm X and Martin Luther King, we must step into the streets and demand equality. *Same old shit, different day*, Jim Mallette would say as nothing changed around him. But the times were looking different, and they were indeed changing.

Ossie Davis and Ruby Dee, now those two are unbelievable, shouted the Black Nationalist across from me, slurping up the *asopao* at *El Péz Dorado*. He would pound the table in exclamation. *You ever see them act?*

I hadn't.

*Man...*he would trail off, his eyes glassy with joy,

his smile the ocean. Successful Black people meant the world to him. It meant progress, it meant change. He'd grown up on the streets of Chicago's South Side, attending the early speeches of Reverend King who moved there to mobilize Black America – and to get respite from the South.

I was friends with a Black man in New York, sought to understand his country, and through him I discovered the need to look at my own heritage, my own past, my own people. I had to find a way to explain to myself why I had become white and didn't know it.

Remember back in the Regents office how that lady looked at me when I laughed? Well, that's how my whole life is, every day. People look at me and laugh. Jim was self-effacing, but I found this hard to believe. Get out of my face, I would say. You're successful, you're intelligent, and you dress well and have all the material things others live for. Why would anyone laugh at you?

I'd experienced life the same way and he knew it. I'd been ridiculed at college in a polarizing Mexico society where I was told I did not belong. I had withstood the pain of rejection by a girl I thought of marrying someday. I had been laughed at for wearing my *guaraches* to parties, for dressing in muslin shirts as I had nothing more to wear. As Jim looked out the window at the passersby on their way home from work and on to their busy New York City lives, I remembered an interview I did that year. The interviewer was from a literary magazine in England. He asked me who I liked, but did not specify the field of interest. I jumped on the chance to ridicule him in his own language.

Paul Robeson, I answered.

Paul Robeson wasn't a writer, he said accusingly.

But he was a communist, see? I replied, *and Black. Your question was nebulous.*

I did not like explaining myself too much back then, I preferred writing. I preferred to tell my story in the written word, not in person.

The interviewer raised his eyebrows.

You see, I added, *Paul Robeson stood up for his beliefs. Few people in America do that, you know? I assume it's the same in England.*

The interview slammed his notebook on the desk. I let him fume.

I have a dream! I shouted at him. The poor guy

wanted to get up and leave but the best he could do was shake his head.

Why. . .you admire... Blacks, he whispered in a very English way.

And Salvador Allende, I shouted; *Dalí, Caruso, Picasso, James Baldwin, Dostoyevsky, Lorca. . . Mozart, Ghandi; what difference does it make who rattles your chain?* I asked the Brit, rather arrogantly. I saw he was trying to catch his breath.

You see, you are an interviewer for a magazine. You write what you think you hear. Federico García Lorca wrote what he felt..and died for it. I went on and on for a bit too long. The interviewer didn't understand that courageous, thinking men pay a price in life. Galileo, and on and on the list goes.

This Brit would never pay. He lived a safe and sheltered life in Brighton. Pretty in pink.

Let me ask you one final question, Dr. Jaguar: If you had to pinpoint one event in history that changed your life, or rather, affected your life, what would that be?

Why the assassination of Mohandas Gandhi, I replied, without hesitation.

Boy, did that get his goat. He was English, after all, therefore, responsible for his death. I meant it.

The possibility of world peace was killed that day. Had he lived, Gandhi would have traveled the world to bring people together. I wanted the magazine readers to understand and see the value of peace and innocence; I did not need to promote peace, others at the moment were doing that quite effectively, John Lennon among them. I'd grown up with true peace and an infectious innocence at the desperate mile; we knew nothing of war and destruction, so of course Gandhi would be my hero.

Thank You, Doctor, he said and stood. *A most interesting interview indeed,* he claimed, putting on his coat. He looked hurt, or pissed, but I didn't care. I did not carry the English legacy of terror, and he knew nothing of my legacy of innocence, of unity, community, of giving your last piece of bread to the hungry. He might have learned something from me had he been a less indignant and ethnocentric Brit.

I knew I let him down, and I knew he wanted to hear something different.

Months later he called to thank me. His Editor

said it was the best interview he'd read in a long, long time. I asked why. *It is what our readers want to hear,* he said, as if his magazine talked.

Jim looked me in the eye. We were buzzed and it was time to go.

Miles is playing at Carnegie tonight, wannago?

Shit, yes, I exclaimed. I cancelled my plans for the evening.

Years later I would get the telegram at the desperate mile with the news of Jim's death. He died of AIDS, in his own bed, looked after by his buddy Juan, a Puerto Rican thug from Queens.

We were friends like you don't find these days. Jim Mallette was the kindest, most authentic person I ever met in America. *Hypocrites,* he called white people. *They'll stab you in the back while looking you in the eye,* he added. Admittedly, there were numerous occasions to agree with him but, how could I say that when my son was born of a white woman?

Today, Jim would be happy to see the progress made in Black America, for blacks have their own economy now in sports, music, entertainment - much success, but most of all they have a unity in freedom that nobody will ever take away from them. What they have earned is theirs, and their success cannot be denied. They don't need the white man anymore, and that is a fact of life.

Que en paz descanses, amigo mío. May you rest in peace.

*

VIOLENT VIOLET PART II OR, A LESSON TO MY FIRST YEAR CLASS

Addison Stonefreund was but a legend in the village by this time as the ghost of Violent Violet roamed the streets at night singing songs of loss and virginity. She was a ghost to whom no one paid attention. Her beautiful blanched body with its pointy breasts called out for a love that she would never have again; she could be seen running through the streets of the desperate mile screaming like a lunatic, looking like a Frenchman without wine.

She was desirable even as a ghost, her fragile flower exposed, her purple eyes luminous, her hair long and dragging on the ground. I was growing older - how do you grow younger? - feeling a strong force pull at me when I saw her at night. She never looked me in the eye, she never looked anyone in the eye; yet, she stood before me in all her radiance, glimmering and gabbing away, perhaps at Izquierdo who left her, perhaps at me, her new admirer. Her voice made no sound, remember, none of our voices made sounds for we were still mutes;

we spoke from the mind.

I was a young boy, excited at her beauty, I did not know better than to ignore her. But in me, she stirred feelings of lust. Hers would be the ideal look.

In retrospect, I think of her as a sign of our downfall, for no one before her turned crazy, and we'd never heard of the word either; Izquierdo once recounted he'd seen a conquistador in Aztec times act that way after losing his beautiful Indian woman to torture. The desperate mile was on its way to change, but we did not know it. These strange, never-before seen occurrences, such as Violent Violet's insanity and Puta Madre's indignation were unexplainable to us. Yet in some strange way Violent Violet helped us see the future. I know she was the first sign we would come to an end. No, I don't mean to say the world would end, but that the innocence, the beauty of the desperate mile would soon be just a memory. Some neighbors thought we would end up like Violent Violet: we, the naked humans, the innocents, the keepers of the earth, the silent ones as Father Serra referred to us, would one day be mad and crazy, homeless with nowhere to turn. We'd come here to our rightful land many years ago, perhaps 3000; some spoke of a people called the Anasazi who lived in silence too, in caves deep in the Arizona desert. They lived far away from everyone, away from anyone who could hurt them, or conquer them, or destroy and pillage their way of life. The Anasazi had seen destruction first hand, but it was a deserved one as their gods took revenge on them by sending a plague, followed by famine, ending with a drought lasting seven years that drove them from their dwellings southward to where we lived. Would experience the same fate? They'd disappeared, the Anasazi, with no trace left behind. Would we follow suit? We did not know the white man, or the yellow even less the Black; we knew only of ourselves and of our past.

We had a designated speaker in the tribe, his name Dos Passos; keeper of the history responsible for memorizing, teaching, and passing on our legend. Every twelve moons we would gather together by the fire and he would spend three days and three nights telling us our past. Every name and every child was mentioned; the families and what they did; the activities and stories of the past three thousand years, bit by bit. Dos Passos would apprentice a young man for a year. The boy would learn the history line by line, memorizing until he caught up on three thousand years of tribal history. It was a grueling apprenticeship, one that kept one busy thinking and absorbing, repeating and finally memorizing the story of just who we were as a people.

At the campfire we sat with ears open and our hearts beating fast, listening to the wonderful journey we'd been on for years and years. This is how we learned of our ties to the Anasazi, the Aztecs and the Mayas. Some of us looked like Moctezuma, others like Maya deities; still some like Apaches and even some like Navajos. Regardless of our differences, ours was a life of harmony.

When I went into the real world, as Father Serra referred to the world-at-large, I decided to leave my origins behind. People were curious about me as I looked rather different from most human beings, what with my white pajama pants and cotton shirts, *huaraches* and long hair.

"Are you Lacandón, Huichol, Hopi, Kogi?"

"I am from heaven," I would answer, an angelic look on my face.

It was years before I told anyone my past partly because I wanted those questions to disappear; too much emphasis was placed on my origin. I wanted to be seen for who I was, for what I contributed to a conversation, to disputes, discourses, discussions. There was also the old sense of doom hovering over me, thinking that should I give away our location at the desperate mile, numbers of gringos would go down there and spoil what we had left of life. They might want to build resorts by the waterfall, homes by the river, huts in the jungle. They would come and rape and take the animals, the birds, our village dogs that were of a deep purple color. I'd heard too many stories of deceit from Father Serra; the white man comes and takes what he wants, or thinks he owns by virtue of vision: if the eyes see it, it belongs to him, he would tell me. There are people like that everywhere, he said. I was told the story of a man named Doug in Santa Fé who worked as Director of the School for American Research, an institution partly responsible for guarding sacred indigenous objects; well, this man took the liberty of appropriating these ancient, valuable art objects, personally taking them to decorate his home. I found this difficult to believe, but possible enough given his ancient heritage. He, the protector of the objects! I would love to find this Doug guy and take a dozen Mohawk Warriors to his home to reclaim what rightfully belongs to Native America.

But what this Doug person doesn't know is that the urn on his mantle is ceremoniously cursed for thievery, such that the thief dies suddenly from an unexplained illness. I am sure he thinks he can get away with the pillaging.

In New York I had many Indian friends, though none from the desperate mile. I felt lonely and alone, to tell you the truth; but being 'lonely' is one thing and, being 'alone' is another, they are two very different things indeed. What often saved me was keeping the ceremony, the daily rituals I learned from Izquierdo. I performed them in my home daily, and the Spirit of the Creator would speak to me and answer; life did not seem so hard then. But if I skipped a day I felt the world coming to an end. I needed something to keep me strong, and faith was it. Yet, at some point in time I stopped the rituals altogether.

I befriended many Indians because after all, they too were curious about me. We spent time with each other preparing feasts in celebration of life as music blared from the stereo and beer ruled the day. I went to

Pow-wows and 49's, dances, ceremonies and rituals; sweats were a common occurrence. A Healer friend of mine from the Lakotas asked me one day to apprentice with him.

"My apprenticeship is over," I said, cursing under my breath as Izquierdo put me through the ringer doing things few mortals ever do, ordering me around like there was no tomorrow, testing my physical, mental and spiritual abilities time and again until I grew strong.

The Medicine Man looked me in the eye.

"We need to heal the earth," he said.

"I agree, but that is not my mission in life," I replied.

I had plenty to say to the world in my own way. I'd sacrificed for my people by coming to the city; I'd sacrificed for the desperate mile, for our voice to be heard. We had our own mission to stop the killings, the rapes, the plundering of the earth. The way I saw the earth being healed was not through individuals but through a bigger voice. Who was that voice? I did not know.

Still, I became a healer in the end. It was inevitable in many ways I suppose. I was called to that, you could say, as Luther put it so well, and so I went and became the healer I was born to be. The poor look for help, the diseased need curing, children need laughter. The illiterate, among others, need education.

In any event, the healing I do is at night, so in the day I can tell you stories.

*

EL GOLPE

We were living happy and free, quiet and innocent, enjoying the desperate mile and the jungle in all its glory: the macaws clucked for attention, the spider ants bunched-up into great big black balls only scattering when the anteaters approached; scurrying by the bunch to hide in trees and *palapas*. The mighty jaguar still roamed the land, the black panther chased the white-tailed deer that love to eat salt; we ran naked, carrying lances like pygmies do. We covered our bodies in mud much like the Watusi of Africa, and like the Hopi of Arizona. We were a peaceful bunch who'd never had to defend against anyone.

We never argued among ourselves, fought, or told lies; we spent our lives in joy, in silence, looking at the world, at nature, at the sky above; we ate mangos and papayas, *tamarindos*, watermelon, oranges, peaches, and fig. Everything was available at the desperate mile, anything you wanted was there. We didn't know hate or greed, violence, luck, the sound of shotguns, or the spoken word. We played music with flutes, guitars, and trumpets made of palm leaves.

We spent our days and nights this way. Every twelfth moon we heard the story of our people and the pilgrimage to the sea where we originate. Upon sunrise, it was our turn to pilgrim to the sea.

Our peregrine walk was through the jungle, up the sloping mountains to a designated spot where we spent the night, joining others who waited to accompany us on the trek. It took three days and three nights to reach the top. The nightly ceremonies were for cleansing, for restoring the harmony among us being lost daily. Harmony is energy, and when it's gone, one need charge up again.

Those were joyous days full of ceremony, chants and prayers. We asked the Creator to heal those who harm the earth. We'd seen things on our travels, things that Izquierdo explained: black liquid being sucked from the earth, fires that burned our trees; big, ugly buildings with smoke rising, *fábricas,* they called them; big, fat silver birds flew over our heads screaming.

We knew then we were not the only humans on earth; we considered ourselves keepers of the earth; we were not responsible for other men's actions, or, were we? Long nights were spent discussing if we should walk down the mountain and speak to the strangers, that they might hear our message. Once you take from the earth and strip it naked, she cannot be clothed again. Mother earth is not like a woman you bed at night.

We were living alongside modern man who thrives on progress – would seclusion bring us joy? Was it time to walk down and greet them?

The stories of Addison Stonefreund were enough to tell us of a world where man lived with no conscience as to one another, no feel for the earth, no respect for the only living organism we absolutely need. Without Mother Earth, what do we have? What do we do? What happens when the empire takes over?

When we heard man was out to destroy mankind - the Black people of the South, the yellow man in Viet Nam, the Indian, the Arab, the Jew, we prayed for forty days and forty nights, abstained from food and cleansed our souls. How else was man to survive if we did not pray for earthly harmony?

We talked of the possibilities of joining forces with the destroyers, of the chances of reaching mankind in our way, we discussed alarming them of the inevitable doom of civilization should they continue raping the earth. It was then that Izquierdo gave us the warning. He heard the footsteps, he said, he'd seen the future. We would have to defend our land, like the time we watched the Beatles from afar knowing they brought a drug culture we did not want to be part of; Izquierdo said that although we were not yet encroached, the white man would one day come to destroy us, for they were all around, getting closer every day, salivating at the mouth like hungry lions in greed at the thought of possessing our land.

I was just a boy then, a learner already chosen to lead the desperate mile out of the predicament. At that time, I didn't know what it would take to save our people, or what it meant to do so. I was only ten years old, so I listened.

"We will organize ourselves, paint our faces and go to the nearest settlement to see what they are doing. We must prepare for this event."

Izquierdo saw the future, he said, and it didn't look good.

El Golpe would come, the thrashing. Prepare, all ye soldiers!

The pilgrimage was ultimately halted as the elders of the village understood how we would be affected by change. Izquierdo in the end was right.

We finished this trek in silence – was this the silencing of the mutes? - returning to the desperate mile sullen, and quiet, thoughtful and sad but courageous. We knew it was the end of the infinite innocence, there was no turning back. Some cried openly while others knelt in prayer, brought to our knees by something so out of our reach. Some went in their *palapas* and stayed for days without eating or mingling between us.

There was silence for days, the birds quieted down; the dogs lay on their bellies until Izquierdo called the pueblo into action. We gathered at the plazita one evening to hear him speak. It was time to carry out the measures for our continued survival.

*

MARY MAGDALENE PART IV

When Mary Magdalene left me, I decided to clean out her closets. She'd taken up three full bedrooms: one for her clothes, another for 'trinkets,' and the third, "to hang out in, read and write and do stuff."

I cleaned her mess for the last time. The woman was a waste of money, lots and lots of money; she wasted money on unnecessary objects of beauty and on things of no use to anyone. It wasn't her money, so why not?

In one of her many shoe boxes I found a letter in what looked like a biography or a journal, I couldn't tell at first. She might have attempted to write a novel, I didn't care. Although it was not autobiographical in nature, it smelled of it. It may have been about someone else, of her alter ego, but anyway I recognized her style: discovering many things she never revealed to me. This work was so much like her that I felt like a dentist pulling teeth trying to figure out what the hell she was saying. If it was about her life, I could not tell, and if she were revealing her past, it was far from delicious reading.

You will find a sample page below. Tell me what you think of it. Write me. (Address your mail to *El Corral, Oaxaca City, Oaxaca*. What the hell, everyone knows where to find me anyhow.)

There is no title to her work and I don't know why. She knew better though.

By Mary Magdalene, briefly a wife to Jaguar

(Author's Notes.)

Well, I come from a big family even though I am really an only child. How is that, you ask? See, I don't have the same mother as the rest of my 14 brothers and sisters. All the other kids are - belong to Dad; they're from another woman, a Catholic woman who is of no blood to me. The not-so-funny thing is that MY mom is a Mormon, and I am her only child! Weird, I know, it's, like, backwards, right? But.

So I have 1/2 brothers and sisters yet we don't really talk or get along 'cuz Daddy hurt his first wife real bad by leaving her for Mom, so everyone is uptight. I can't remember all of their names they are too many but I do know they are all biblical names, like mine. The tragedy is that I have a Catholic name --- Mary

Magdalene --- while my mother seethes. See, Daddy is Catholic, so that explains my name.

It hasn't been easy for me. Mom dislikes me 'cuz I do what I want instead of doing what she says, example: she doesn't drink, I do. She won't ever smoke, but I LOVE my *Faros*. I cuss like a truck driver, she faints on the floor.

I guess I'm more Catholic in a way than Mormon. And she hates that. I don't know.

Yet Daddy is Catholic but acts like a Mormon. Won't drink - now, but he used to! Won't smoke, even if you chain him to a fence and force him to take a puff.

He likes the BYU Cougars, not Notre Dame, see?

Anyway, I wanted to tell you about the family.

Grandpa was Irish.

Grandma was Scottish. She was tight with her money - did I inherit that trait? Ja-guar says I did - but that I didn't inherit her love for people. (Love is free, I figure.)

Her Daddy, in turn, made money selling maple syrup in the early days, and when he died he left her every penny. With the inheritance she bought land, lots of land indeed.

Grandpa, on the other hand, was sort of a rogue. He ran off with the Confederates during the War, but that only lasted a few weeks because before he knew it, the War was over. Then he met up with another rogue, a man with a red beard who offered to line him-up with gold mining. There was a cave, he said, a mine, a fortune. This man had fourteen gold bricks with him and he made Grandpa his right hand man. Grandpa boasted that he could kill and have no guilt, making them the perfect pair. They gathered up another dozen, fourteen men in all, made their way to the mine, see, when they were suddenly ambushed by a Jesse James type a' gang, killing Redbeard and ten of the men. The James Gang in the end was defeated by grandpa's group, with a lone survivor riding off at daylight. The four men still breathing in Grandpa's gang looked at him and said: "It's your call. Where you go, we'll follow."

It was in this way that Grandpa became the leader and the inheritor of those gold bricks.

They looked and looked for an entire month but never found the promised mine, because only Redbeard knew its location.

Tired and hungry, Grandpa gave each man 100 dollars and they split-up, he keeping the gold. With that gold he went on to buy a building, where he made a business - a Brewery for the local gold-diggers. The business went from good to better and, just as everything was running smoothly, old Grandpa runs off again, rogue that he was. But this time he ran to Indian country where he bought lots and lots of rugs and silver jewelry. The silver was a step down from gold, but he would make it work.

In the end it was the rugs that made him richer than he ever imagined.

He bought Navajo, Pueblo, Plains and even some Pacific Northwest weavings so beautiful most ended up in museums, in the White House and even, in England!

His collection grew until he had people actually weaving for him as far away as Persia. (Now Iraq-Iran for those of you weak in geography.)

His Brewery did enormous business because he promoted it with stories and pictures of his heroics as a Confederate. But also, it was good beer at a cheap price. He sold volumes of quality beer and as a result, he made a fortune.

But as an adventurer he ended up getting tired of it all, and by then, his son was grown up and needed a job, so he gave him the brewery . The son ran it for years, he became an alcoholic, and my Daddy one day took it back right under his eyes. Few years later, he lost it. Well, he sold it, didn't keep it, he sold it because he'd stopped drinking. See, he fell in love with a Catholic girl whose Dad was an alcoholic; so she gave him an ultimatum: it's either the brewery or me, right now, you decide, she said. People say she made him sell it, so now our family has the beer name but not the beer. The new owner was no fool: he kept the famous name to make all the profit he could.

Anyhow, Grandma was real good to me. She was the first person there at my birth and since my mother was in lots of pain at my birth and almost died, she, Grandma, held me first the day I was born.

And we were real close all of my life, closer than even the other thirteen grandchildren. We used to play together and laugh and she did lots of things for me that she never would consider doing for the others like bake me cupcakes and decorate them with little paper American flags she made herself in her spare time.

Course, the others got real jealous and that is why I think they don't like me to this day. I ain't heard as much as a split word in two from them.

Anyways, Grandma one day got real sick with the flu and was about to die and would not let *anyone* near her at all. She called only for me. I was sixteen years old then. I came running to her deathbed all dirty and sweaty from milking the cows but she didn't care and we spent the last three days of her life together in that room. We held hands and I fed her and told her stories and she told me family secrets and on the third day she finally said: I see angels up there, Mary. She always called me Mary. She was the only person I EVER let call me that. I just wanted her to be the only one in the world with that privilege.

Then she died, right smack in my arms.

And the cycle was complete, see?

I was born in her arms, and she died in mine.

I have never been the same since. I miss her soooooooo much.

That part of the journal ends there. As you can see, this is quite the story. I have no idea how true, or how close this is to her life. I do know that she never shared anything like this with me. I know there was money in the family, but I always, well, once, heard that it was from farming. I mean, anyway, how much money can a real farmer make? O.k. a rancher, yes, but that's not what she said. She said farming. There is a difference, you know.

Mary Magdalene had aspirations of being a writer. I mean, the pink envelope was proof of it. This journal version/story/fantasy of her life was pretty good, and the truth is, whether it's fiction or not, it doesn't matter. Had she continued to write seriously there might have been something, and we might have stayed together, who knows? I might have writing in common. And she could of had something significant to do, meaning, something more important than spending money all the time.

Lesser writers get published, after all.

Mary Magdalene was fond of leaving the desperate mile. She had to go to Oaxaca, San Cristóbal de las Casas, Veracrúz, San Miguel de Allende, Cuernavaca, to Puerto Escondido where Agustín Eliab and Guillermo lived. She needed her life back, she said; the people, the crowds, the ceaseless noise of modern man. We had an age difference after all.

I was writing everyday now and so didn't miss her like I did when she left the first time. Back then, I had to have her near me every minute. I would make her sit next to me at the desk as I wrote one story after another. She would read her fashion magazines and the New York Post, hold my arm, place her leg on my lap, she would bring coffee, anything to be near. She too wanted it that way.

At times I thought she was some sort of appendage, a curse of creation. Concentration and dedication are most important in writing, and, as I locked myself in the guest house, only her love could replenish my energy.

But now we were apart.

She began to feel abandoned, she said, something she knew little of, since she'd grown up with a family, unlike me. It was me who'd been abandoned, I said, my mother left me.

Still, she felt alone, lost, exiled.

I wasn't much help because I was busy writing, and that's why the trips.

I knew she didn't have a lover because she always looked me in the eye when returning. Not only did she know I could read her mind if I wanted, she knew that the minute I heard the door open, I would rush into her arms and tell her I missed her. She would start by taking off my clothes. We always made lots of love, so in a way, it was refreshing to have her go away.

But I'd stopped reading her mind a few years back.

Because the love was gone, and I knew it, though I wouldn't admit it.

I killed her slowly, with time and with patience, never quite willingly, or intentionally, mind you. It happened before you could say your name, and by then, there was no turning back. I got upset several times when she got jealous for no reason at all. Mary Magdalene thought women were after me, that everywhere we went there was a former lover, a woman more beautiful than she – not possible! – she thought that I was getting tired of her, that I would one day leave without so much as a goodbye the way John Lennon left

Yoko after saying he was going to the corner for a pack of cigarettes.

This is how it ended: after dinner and a few bottles of wine, and after hearing her complain and scream at me for ignoring her because I worked too much, she stood in front of me and pushed me while in my chair. My automatic reaction was to slap her smack in the face. Our love was never the same again.

"You're a whore!" she screamed at me as I followed her down the street.

"And you are Mary Magdalene, remember?" I said in return, meaning, of course, the Immaculate Virgin, Humberto the worm, her lies, the hiding, the deceit, the seven demons eating at her. Standing in front of me and expecting an apology that was not forthcoming in my raging anger, she pounded me with her tiny fists, kicking me in the groin for a good ending.

Whack, she went. It was too late for both of us. Her cheek was still red from the blow; her head now was bent in shame, tears streamed from her eyes. She looked angelic in her white tunic and turquoise necklace, *just like Mother looked the day she left*, I recalled in my own, burning shame.

The light from the lamppost cast a halo above her head but soon disappeared.

"You can't kick me in the balls and expect no reaction from me!"

"You deserved it," she whimpered, as I tried to take her hand to kiss it.

We walked for miles in silence, passing young lovers holding hands, a grey-haired couple sitting silently on a park bench, and daddies with little girls playing on the curb. I hurt so much inside I wanted to die right there and then. I wanted to take it back, to make life joyous again. I offered her a night at the Presidio, the famous hotel she loved.

"No," she shook her head.

"Would you like to go to Florence? You love Florence" Nope. It seemed irreparable.

But who did what?

We were both wrong.

She provoked the blow.

I didn't blame her.

But she blamed me.

It was weeks before she let me touch her again.

*　　*　　*

"Your silence kills me," she said one night as Izquierdito slept on the floor. (He loved to sleep on my father's mat, his *petate,* the woven, straw bed of the centuries.)

"You go weeks without saying a word."

I realized I was just like Izquierdo.

She was right. I was reverting to my childhood days at the desperate mile when we were mutes. Was I punishing her for the intrusions on my writing? Was I paying her back for making me feel betrayed by her love?

I felt betrayed. She didn't love the desperate mile anymore.

I resented her because it was she who chased me, she who found me, she who married me, she who gave me a son and then she discovered she missed society.

I felt betrayed that she no longer wrote, nor painted - oh, what a painter she was - nor cared for the very thing she sought to experience fully: life.

Her addiction to spending money and buying material things was incurable. There was a void in her that nothing could fill but I didn't know about it until it was too late, and there was nothing I could do about it either.

"You are so materialistic" I would say.

"I can't live with nothing!" was her reply.

"But you knew who I was! How I live. You knew."

But it was all to no avail.

I was wrong, and there was no making it right.

*

THE CONQUEROR'S FINALE

Jaguar woke up and went outside to piss against the adobe wall. The house was quiet and the dogs asleep, the hummingbirds buzzed from flower to flower, feasting in the field of blooming buds. Izquierdo was long ago dead, Puta Madre, but a dream. The ghost of Violent Violet vanished along with the passing of the infinite innocence; Father Serra's old, weathered cross inside the church leaned to the side like The Tower of Pisa; it was leaning closer and closer to the ground without anyone so much as rectifying it. There was much excitement in the desperate mile as it was full of tourists eager for a glimpse of the author, a quick autograph or maybe a cup of coffee.

At the moment, though, only the sound of his trickling urine could be heard hitting the river rocks that once held a levy in place, keeping the water from rising to flood the village. A gust of wind blew as Jaguar released his first leak of the day. He sighed and looked at the heavens.

"I'm tired of being alone," he said. He sighed again and shook his head. Was there another woman out there, waiting for him? Would he live to see another conquest?

"I don't know what happened to my life," he said to no one, walking back into the house after zipping his pants.

He'd been alone for many years now, so long that the last woman whose breasts he felt was but a mere memory. She'd had no face that woman, she was only a body. She bore no personality, only a distant smile. He recalled a hearty laughter like that of a prostitute, but then he wasn't sure if it belonged to her or to another woman he'd also forgotten along the way.

Where did I meet her?

He squinted in the bright sun like Father Serra, his memory, echoes in a cave.

She had no name, she had no country. She could have been from here, he thought, for all I know. When the memory starts to falter, we stop caring; caring for others, caring for ourselves. He shook it off and washed his hands.

Coffee started the day.

Mozart no longer moved him, not even when played by the great Murray Perahia. What moved him in the past no longer did today. The music player was shut-off, the Mozart Piano Concertos rested.

He sat staring at the coffee. His bladder was weak now from all those years of drinking, from endless celebration; his face wrinkled, his liver ached, his mind was beginning to fade. Is it possible to age so quickly? He talked to himself like Father Serra did in his quarters long ago. He saw his reflection in a spoon.

I aged so quickly, I was so handsome.

His hair had turned white overnight. The mirror was not a liar that morning; instead, it was a terrorist. Jaguar had been terrified at the old man in the mirror.

The bombing in New York was terrifying too. Jaguar had been in bed when a neighbor crashed through the door to tell him the news: "*Come to my house to see the 'tele,'* meaning the television. Jaguar was so startled he went to the neighbor's in his underwear. The bombings struck New York, where his son lived with Mary Magdalene. Though in Oaxaca it was near noon, to him it was morning as he was wrestled from bed. The neighbors watched the news in Spanish, ignoring Jaguar in his underwear, waiting to hear something about Mary Magdalene but he could not speak. He was clearly in shock; certainly in a state no one had ever seen him. Sure, they'd seen him drunk, and in love, in a playful mood, even angry at Apollo the messenger boy but they'd never seen him afraid, certainly they'd never expected to see him in shock. He looked like he wanted to tear his hair out in clumps, he moved about so, rocking back and forth like a baby, scratching his arms in desperation, entwining his arms like a lunatic. He asked for a cigarette, someone handed him a bottle. He drank, he smoked, the sweat pouring from his forehead, he at once stood then sat, only to stand up again and repeat the action again and again, blurting *Oh, my God, Oh my God, Oh my God help them.* His now prayer became a trance, the neighbors praying along to his every word; he asked Jesus to keep his family safe and alive. After what seemed like a lifetime of prayer Jaguar realized he was in shock. Coming-to, he ran to the local store and without asking permission to use the phone, he dialed home, New York City, his old stomping grounds, home to his lost family. The attendant let him craze as the news had reached him too. As the phone rang time and again,

Jaguar thought Mary Magdalene wouldn't answer the phone out of spite, keeping him in his present state, sending him into a rage the village would not soon forget. *Damnit, he's my son, Izquierdito, I need to speak to him,* he shouted into the phone, the same phone that unexpectedly went dead. Damn Mexico and its mediocrity! Damn phones that don't work here! Damn electrical company! The list went on and on until he nearly broke the phone after slamming it against the wall. After calming himself by grunting and groaning, he dialed anew only to hear a recording say that all the lines were busy. The phone lines in New York were jammed with calls from all over the world, people were trying to get through, and his one attempt ended in endless ringing with not even the message machine picking up. He freaked for the first time in years, really losing it right there in the store. He took the nearest object – an old wood chair on its last legs and broke it. Next, it was a bottle of vanilla extract, and the air smelled of fresh-baked cookies. The attendant kept quiet as there was nothing to do for a writer was fighting his demons. Jaguar, now slouched against the wall, would surely calm down - given time. Insisting on getting through, he stayed in the store for hours still unaware of being in his underwear, his bare feet now cold on the chilly marble floor. He kept trying to get through on the phone, hanging up time and again, looking like a runaway from a mental hospital doing the same thing over and over again, never with a new result. The villagers now crowded into the store pretending to buy merchandise. They looked at him like a monkey in a cage, and so did the tourists who got wind the famous author was going nuts in the store, they unaware of the deadly attack in New York, they tourists out for a good laugh what with the tequila, mezcal and beers flowing from the bar next door. You could hear the jukebox playing, it was something about a brother and a sister, and how they had to stop fighting for their mother's sake. Jaguar didn't eat, or drink or piss that day, he went from worried to desperate, to despondent, to terrified, to horrified, to plain fried. The phone finally went through and Mary Magdalene answered.

Finally, she said, in a husky voice, as if Jaguar would never call or didn't care one bit for what happened. He let it slide. Now was not the time for reproach.

How are you, he asked.

How do you think, she replied rhetorically, like she always did when upset.

Can I speak to my son?

The phone went dead again but it was more like a *plunk!* She must have put the phone on the table. The young man picked up the line.

I'm fine, he said. I'll take care of mom.

How had the young man come to this? To a brief "I'm fine" instead of a "Dad, we were afraid the explosion wouldn't stop" or something like that? How did the communication between us die? Jaguar called once a week for years, the two talked about school and sports, his preppy friends and the latest music – Jaguar wanted to be part of his son's life but now it seemed Izquierdito had only a few words for his father. Maybe he didn't want to be part of his father life.

"We're fine," the young man repeated.

"What are you doing, son?" Jaguar asked with a tone of resentment in his voice. Nothing, I'm not doing anything, answered the boy, not letting his father in on what must have been a horrific experience for him earlier in the day waiting to hear his mother's voice on the phone, know she was alive, not letting his father know he was into Rock n' Roll now, the latest R&B, and Wyclef Jean. He was reading Fuentes and Márquez, Neruda and Allende, the boy, wanting to know his dad through books; he was on the track team, running the mile. He liked archery and soccer, girls, writing and carpentry. He wore his tie loose at school, drove a 911, smoked reefer. His guitar needed strings, the drum, polishing. The girls loved him; they chased him, goosed him, called him on the phone. He was tall and handsome, and always smelled good. He liked Brando and De Niro, thought of Frida Khalo and Selma Hayek, Paulina Rubio, Javier Solís, Marco Antonio Solís. He yearned for the mangoes his daddy loved; on Saturdays he stopped at the Korean's to buy a few when in season. He would walk Central Park looking for traces of his father. Jaguar walked these streets, he'd mutter like Izquierdo his namesake. Jaguar ran this loop, he would say, walking around the reservoir. I remember he told me, he thought, that he beat the best, the fastest in his marathons. The boy traipsed through Bleecker Street where Jaguar lived as a young man at "156 Bleecker Street," he recalled, dad's old address. He looked up the apartment windows trying to figure out dad's old place. Will I live in Italy, and Mexico, France and Switzerland, Tucson or Santa Fé, like my dad did, he asked himself. Will I marry a girl like my mother, or will I find a woman of my own, one who'll take care of me and never leave me? All this he kept from dad.

The explosions that day scared Izquierdito, but only because everywhere he turned people were crying. The world was not going to end, he kept repeating to himself, no, not today it won't. First I have to find mom and then I have to hug my dad before I die. The boy loved and missed his dad more than he cared to admit, but his pride got in the way of saying so over the phone. The best he could muster was a sloppy *"We're fine, dad."* The resentment he felt for dad would not eat at him just yet; he would let it build until one day it would all come rushing out of his mouth in one fell swoop. Jaguar would not be surprised on that fateful day, as he'd prepared for it for years; Jaguar knew one day he would hear it all, every bit of resentment that piled up in this young man and he knew too that his son would burn a hole through his heart but hey, I did the same to my old man, Jaguar said to himself, I deserve just the same. The boy's hurt, his pain would hurt both of them with only Jaguar knowing how to respond, for in his old age he'd learned to let others speak their truth. The world would not come to an end that day either; it would only be different for each of them. The two would be friends from that day on, Jaguar respecting his son for speaking his mind, admiring him for showing his always hidden emotions, loving him more because the confrontation would only bring out the man in him, for it took a man to speak his mind, a man to confront the father in what life calls a "coming of age ritual" that Jaguar knew every man on earth needs to experience. The boy would feel empowered, but the boy first had to grow up.

Jaguar exhaled after hanging the phone. He was freezing in the chill of the early evening as the sun was setting, and for the first time that day he realized he was standing in his briefs, with only a pajama top to cover his torso. He walked home without even a thank you to the store owner who knew tomorrow the writer would come to apologize. Watching him stray home, the villagers knew Jaguar's family was safe in New York. He had spoken to two different persons; he was calm now, drained of energy with his every step. Tomorrow Jaguar would pay the phone bill, for the broken chair too, and tomorrow all would be settled with the villagers and life would return to normal. Tonight though, it would be back to bed.

On the 12th of September Jaguar woke up and it was while brushing his teeth that he noticed the gray hair. The next day, he noticed a new patch of grey here, and the next day more until two weeks later all the black hair was gone. His face creased and the tightness now fell into wrinkles; his famous, recognizable smile was now a frown. His bones began to ache, his bowels moved like with Father Serra.

He was only 48.

The conqueror ended up alone, grey haired, his fame and fortune no longer attractive to women. When at *El Corral*, the girls paid no attention. He was, after all, 30 years older than the college girls he liked, nearly a granddad to them. He once offered a college girl a drink and she snorted like a horse, making him feel like a fool. It finally sank-in his days were numbered.

His days of savoring the blonde were over.

He was overcome by a deep sense of loss. He asked the waiter for a bottle of Scotch. As it was an unusual request from the Doctor, the waiter asked to repeat the order and hearing it again, he ran to fetch it for it meant a generous tip. Jaguar decided to sip until he could sip no more; if his life had just changed, if he saw himself as old now, well this was certainly cause for celebration because he always celebrated change; if he were to be young no more it meant he would always be old now – older and older as the days went by. When the Scotch clicked in, his heart pounded with desperation, because his youth was now officially gone. A crazy fog took hold of every part of his being. He would have to confront his demons tonight needing to win the battle once and for all. The alcohol didn't help; though it provoked his will to win.

To clear his head, he walked to the waterfalls. Stripping naked he jumped into the water. The memory of Puta Madre came rushing at him as she stared at him from behind a boulder. As she watched her son bathe, Jaguar remembered Addison Stonefreund's first sight of mother at the waterfall. Wasn't this her place of refuge? Wasn't this her sacred place? Is she appearing now in my hour of need?

Jaguar knew something big was about to happen in his life, he knew that if his mother was appearing before him, that if his life was now different forever, it meant a significant closure lay ahead. What that closure was he did not know, but he knew he welcomed it.

What was my life about, the women, the conquests, the success?

How did I end like this?

He considered the answer as the appearance of his mother faded into the night. The rushing water calmed his spirit for the first time ever giving him a lucidity gone missing for years. Perhaps I can tackle the question, he muttered. Normally, he stared at his drink for answers. Once, a long time ago, he recalled, the drink had all the answers, but not today. He would have to change his life, make it different somehow, give-up the past, the memories eating away at him, the disappointments and faded dreams. How this was done he did not know, but surely with time he would find the answer. The excitement of starting a new life lifted him out of the water; he rushed home like a child after discovering a secret. The loneliness would soon be gone, the resentment too, as would the anger and the dents of self-esteem, the impatience, the longing: *I can live in clarity once again,* he shouted, the sound bouncing off the jungle trees like the day Izquierdo summoned the rebels. These emotions had conquered him, they had run his life without him ever knowing it; he'd been living on automatic pilot for too many years but now, he would live moment to moment in his newfound independence.

A shrink in New York once told him Puta Madre made him this way. His mother left him at an early age, and he'd spent a lifetime looking for a love to replace hers. He looked to fill the void, the space left by her absence. It occurred to him how similar he was to Mary Magdalene after all, how the two shared empty spaces within, something that he could never again criticize in her. The difference between them was that her void was unidentifiable as she never talked about it, but his void was filled with writing. In the end, we fill the void the best we can.

"At some point you declared, Mr. Jaguar, that you would have all the women in the world. We do that. We declare things, and then we live them out. You lived out your declaration."

The shrink was right, but he never got to the void in me, he whispered, finding tenderness in the words, pronouncing them quietly as if to not scare them away.

When we discover an answer to life, we act on it, said the shrink on a different occasion, meaning of course, that when we 'get' that we have been monsters in a person's life, for example, we change. Did Izquierdo ever get that? *You will act on it the day you understand it,* was the last bit of counseling Jaguar remembered hearing. That day was today.

What was the declaration I made, and when did I make it?

The hummingbirds were off someplace, but the big black crow that rested on the fence cried out. It was like a signal, a revelation.

As the crow spoke he remembered Katarina. Katarina did it! Katarina of my childhood.

The memory came rushing back to when he was thirteen and living at the desperate mile. There was this beauty, he remembered, who ran around with the dead sisters. She was a stunning beauty with full lips, lavender skin, and curves to her body in those tight clothes she wore adorned by her long, black hair crowned with flowers. He liked her the first time he saw her, and she was just his age. As a girl in pigtails, he remembered, she was a little idiot: beautiful, gorgeous, a little idiot.

Her laughter excited him, her spirit, the smile, the soft hands; perfection.

It was difficult getting close to her because she ran around with the dead sisters, *persone non grate.* He didn't chat, or smile, laugh or flirt with her as he'd wanted, keeping his distance instead, watching her every move, always ready to pounce on her the minute the sisters disappeared for a Coke.

To his surprise one day, the moment came. Young Jaguar standing solemn by a fig tree quickly took a seat next to her at the plazita bench as she sipped a Pepsi. She smelled of lilacs.

"*Lilacs!*" he shouted now. It was all coming back, the declaration made sense: Puta Madre loved lilacs.

Hello Katarina, he'd muttered. She didn't move, didn't look, not a word. She drank her Pepsi as Jaguar shivered in anticipation of things to come.

You're alone today, came out of his throat.

Uh-hum, she muttered back. Katarina swung her feet fastening them to one another. If she was interested in him, if she was nervous to see him no one could tell. Not even Jaguar, who at the time was learning to read minds.

You're not with those girls, he added, meaning the dead sisters.

Hmmm, she snorted, twitching her shiny nose. She had a beautiful nose: aquiline, pointy, and shiny.

Not with those girls, he'd said as a way to avoid mentioning their death, as blood, as sisters. He hadn't said their names in ages and couldn't gather himself to pronounce them again.

Now what, he asked himself. She won't say a word.

Will you go to the dance with me?

There was a dance that night at the plazita. As the band played in the *zócalo* the boys walked in a circle in one direction, the girls in the opposite direction. The enamored would meet and brush hands like old lovers. The cheeks would call for a kiss. The boys would pray for a touch of the girls' tender waist; the girls in turn, prayed their daddies sitting on the kiosk bench didn't see them giving themselves away.

It was all coming back to Jaguar - Katarina.

The girl never responded to his proposition. Jaguar being stumped, cried out for Izquierdo to help him. As he was only an apprentice at the time, Dad would only speak to him with instructions, to teach him a lesson. Izquierdo did not give answers, he gave instructions. The girl was his personal lesson in manhood. He would have to learn this all by himself.

I am the chosen one, he said to her, more out of desperation than to impress Katarina.

The girl laughed.

Not for me you're not, she said abruptly and walked off, leaving Jaguar to sit by himself in rejection and pain.

The young man was crushed. Lovely Katarina pounded in his heart; he wanted her, he needed her, he would have her, he told himself; he would marry her too, have her hand in marriage, her arms, her legs, kisses, warmth, and tenderness.

This would never come to be though, for it was not his fate in life.

Young Jaguar wanted to run just then, much like Izquierdo ran all those years in the jungle, up and down the trails until about to burst his lungs; instead he sat still, holding-in the humiliation, the put-down, the let down in Katarina's five simple words. He sat boiling in the hot sun, getting hotter and hotter inside and about to burst himself like a *piñata* on his birthday. Katarina crushed his heart.

I will show her, he declared in a hushed voice while still seated in the plaza, Katarina's half-empty Pepsi bottle beside him, his eyes bloodshot red, holding back the tears he wished would rush out of him quickly.

That was my declaration, he said now. That was the moment when I declared myself a conqueror!

So that's what happened.

Why didn't Katarina like him? He was the chosen one after all, the would-be-King of the desperate mile. She could be his queen, hold the throne and have his children. Have it all. Instead, Jaguar's life was totally changed by this one, little rejection that he interpreted as the end of the world.

I see, he said, remembering the shrink.

What satisfaction did you get from conquering all those women, Jaguar, the analyst once asked.

He walked the rest of the way home, wet to the bone from the river, his clothes in hand, naked as the ape. If anyone saw him, so be it. He was at the desperate mile, after all. We used to run naked at the desperate mile, he muttered.

At noon he sipped his coffee. It was very cold now, but he would have it anyway.

He got what made him tick all those years: the arrogance, his good looks, his intelligence, Father Serra's teachings; the constant conquests in hotels, bars, restaurants, the streets were his way of losing himself, it was his way of filling the void. With women came the loss of identity, the collapse of habits and rituals. Instead of praying every morning, he conquered a young girl. Instead of practicing discipline, he'd have another.

God help me, he muttered to the Heavens. And, lo and behold, the Lord appeared, coming right down from Heaven seating next to him, Jaguar, the chosen one, he, Doc-tor, as Mary Magdalene used to call him.

Jaguar felt His presence. He realized this was his only chance to talk to Him, as He was a very busy man.

This moment will never happen again, he urged himself, gathering his thoughts.

Just then, as if on cue Father Serra's ghost appeared, desperate for attention.

Jaguar, my son, take heed! Why the Lord never appeared for me, the old man shouted. Father Serra wept of joy and watched the action. For one brief moment in life Jaguar was standing with his long-dead mentor and God by his side. The triumvirate stood together.

Dear God, I need your forgiveness. I need redemption. Please forgive me, please accept me back into your fold, and please make of me as you will. Give me the strength to carry on, to change this arrogant way that ruined my life. Cleanse my soul. Give me the chance to apologize to those I have hurt and taken advantage of, dear Lord. Let me live a clean, healthy life, that I shall never again trespass another human being.

God stared down at his poor soul.

Your sins are forgiven, said the Mighty One, disappearing into the darkness that now enveloped the desperate mile. God disappeared in front of Jaguar but not from his life as the professor promised to return to the ways of the Lord, to what he knew worked in life, to prayer, to songs, to reading His holy words. Sensing that his life's work had not been a waste after all, Father Serra cried like a baby in memory of his own redemption, for he'd died of sorrow, believing his life had come to nothing because he had never been able to convert a single soul to Christianity outside of Jaguar, his best and only convert.

Jaguarcito, he said before departing to the other world, *you gave me the greatest gift of my life. The Creator came down from the heavens to hear you, to confess you! Think of it, Jaguar. It's never happened. It's a miracle!*

Father Serra sobbed for his dream came true. Even as a ghost he cried, even as a ghost, he felt the misery, the joy, the triumph of giving his life to his ministry. The old priest was finally complete. They say a ghost will live until his task is complete. This would not be the case with Father Serra anymore.

Jaguar looked into the distance where the old man was disappearing, into the thin air like a raindrop disappears from a ledge. Into the thin, Mexican air, the priest shouted, *donde el aire es transparente*!

Jaguar wept. His mentor now gone, his many loves too; his beloved Mary Magdalene lived in another country, his daddy Izquierdo, Puta Madre, Violent Violet, friends, acquaintances, all gone and lost forever. What came next, he did not know. But what crossed his mind was that he could start over, for he was clean now, absolved, as the Lord said in His own Voice. The numerous women were a thing of the past, his amorous encounters but a lesson in life. One single woman would do. One girl was perfection, one woman would do; *any girl would do*, as Eje once said, *Pick any girl. Any girl will love you, adore you, will want have your children.* It was up to Jaguar to settle down. He had the responsibility to create his own paradise, to make a new declaration! He would see to it the new woman understood him; that he explained himself properly, correctly, with clarity. Little could go wrong that way and he would have an ever-lasting happiness only found in books and movies.

He would erase his past - the arrogance now humility, the conquered now friends, his manhood in its rightful place. She would only know what information he shared. He would socialize always with her by his side, assuring his new love of his loyalty. She would never see any part of his past, his old self the lion. He would be the lion tamed.

Jaguar thought of the old days, the days of Cortéz, the Conqueror. He'd become a conqueror himself, he considered. But, why, when he held so much scorn for destruction? How had he become the very thing he despised in man?

The sun left the horizon and he shook his head. He spent the entire day sitting at the table without so much as moving, determined to be still until he figured out the whole thing. The Scotch from the day before evaporated with the heat of the sun. All that accompanied him now was the empty cup of coffee he drank to start the day.

How did I allow myself to live such a life, he laughed. *How could I've hurt so many people?* Were these the words Cortez asked on his deathbed?

The Conqueror sinned and God Himself forgave him.

There was only one thing left to do, and that was to be fully Indian again.

The End

Agustín Eliab Juárez attended Stanford University earning two degrees, the latter a Master's in Cultural and Social Anthropology. He studied and researched the Evangelization of the Native at the prestigious El Colegio de México in Distrito Federal. Among his mentors stand the late poet and novelist Fernando Alegría, trailblazer Jean Franco and the writer and professor James de Jongh. An advocate for Hispanic and undocumented youth, Agustín supports completion in higher education. His daughter Sofia Paloma lives and works in New York City.

The Solitude of Destiny is his first book.

www.ingramcontent.com/pod-product-compliance
Lightning Source LLC
Chambersburg PA
CBHW020821030726
47496CB00001B/32